The Minerva
Book of Short Stories 5

Giles Gordon was born in Edinburgh in 1940.
He has published ten novels and collections of
stories. He has also edited a dozen collections
of short stories and recently compiled for the
British Council a bibliography of *The British
Twentieth-Century Short Story*. Like David
Hughes, he is a Fellow of the Royal Society of
Literature.

David Hughes was born in Hampshire in
1930. He was educated at KCS, Wimbledon,
and Christ Church, Oxford, where he read
English. He is currently the fiction reviewer
for the *Mail on Sunday*. His better known
novels include *The Pork Butcher*, for which he
won the W.H. Smith Award, and *But for
Bunter*.

The Minerva
Book of Short Stories 5

EDITED BY
GILES GORDON
and DAVID HUGHES

Minerva

A Minerva Paperback

THE MINERVA BOOK OF SHORT STORIES 5

First published in Great Britain 1992
as *Best Short Stories 1992*
by William Heinemann Ltd
This Minerva edition published 1993
by Mandarin Paperbacks
an imprint of Reed Consumer Books Ltd
Michelin House, 81 Fulham Road, London SW3 6RB
and Auckland, Melbourne, Singapore and Toronto

A CIP catalogue record for this title
is available from the British Library
ISBN 0 7493 9968 6

Printed and bound in Great Britain
by Cox & Wyman Ltd, Reading, Berks

Contents

CONTENTS

Introduction

Anyone might assume that our task of selecting the 'best' short stories published in magazines or broadcast during the previous twelve months becomes easier as time goes by. This after all is the seventh consecutive year our anthology has appeared. But in fact the responsibility grows more challenging as the years pass, and this time, more even than before, we first argued vociferously in favour of one story or another, then mourned two or three of those that failed to make the final twenty-five. Among the 'runners-up' – it would be invidious to mention the household names – was a talent really to watch for: Mary Gentle, with a tale in *Interzone* that was sadly too long for us.

We trust we are the opposite of schematic (and certainly of didactic) in our search and in the opinions and prejudices that accompany it. If we set out each year with an ambition, other than to present to you between covers the variety and scope of the short at its best, it is that we may pick our blooms from as many different beds as possible. We scour an annually increasing number of periodicals that publish stories in English written other than by Americans: these latter are excluded if only because they have their own indigenous collections. But this year, for the first time and against our instincts of fair play, we bring together more than three or four stories which first appeared in one publication: paradoxically the *New Yorker*. In truth that veteran remains – indeed has become again under the catholic editorship of Robert Gottlieb – the premier display case for stories. Writers of ambition and achievement who have the distinction of sharing its pages with cartoons and poems can write either succinctly (Jonathan Treitel's story here establishes a glittering world in two magazine pages) or at dangerous length (Alice Munro's masterpiece here, five stories in one, must be over sixteen thousand words) and be paid properly.

British magazines and national newspapers seemed in 1991 less interested in artistically achieved stories than for some years – which is odd; the quality of work offered is high, readers relish such stories, journals these days have innumerable pages to fill. Yet if you had bought only the Christmas issues of various publications you might have surmised that the short-story writer was an influence in the land. The sad fact is that although editors manically commission tales from well-known authors a few weeks before Christmas, the results usually do little more than pay as much lip service to the form as to the festive season.

Thus the undercapitalised literary magazines of every colour and provenance play a crucial part, and we are delighted to be printing three stories from *Stand* (including the 4th and 5th in that magazine's latest short-story competition, which we preferred to the winners), two from *Critical Quarterly*, and one apiece from *London Magazine* and *New Edinburgh Review*. After our strictures on *Granta*'s over-transatlanticised stance a year or two back it is satisfying to reproduce three stories from its pages.

Two of our stories were originally bought by the UK edition of *Esquire* but only one appeared in the monthly's pages, a further hazard of the writer dependent on the vagaries of press politics: the editor who acquired Ken Smith's evocative piece departed before the story came up in proof and his successor failed to favour it.

Although Salman Rushdie's celebration (in a wry manner of

speaking) of Christopher Columbus – may 1992, his 500th anniversary, also prove the year that releases Salman Rushdie from his outrageous sentence of death – first appeared in the *New Yorker*, it was subsequently brought out here in the third annual edition of Bloomsbury's *Soho Square*. Every go-ahead publishing house seems currently to be developing its own literary magazine, and we are gratified to note that Gollancz has revived the once influential SF *New Worlds*, which first published Brian Aldiss's confident state-of-the-universe story we select (though professing some bafflement as to the appearance of Sir Kingsley Amis as a wine waiter).

Not the least of our pleasures in selecting these stories each year is to spot newcomers of style and originality, with something to say that is unique in manner or content or both. This year we recommend the baroque imagination of Don Rodgers, the measured way in which Seamus Deane (hardly a novice, if new to these pages) despairs of the state of Ireland, Mary Morrissy's glimpse of Dubliners post-Joyce, Steven Heighton's elegant assessment of the new Japan, and no less impressive the precision of Matthew Kramer's menacing beachscape. Above all we congratulate Nicholas Royle, himself a prolific short-story writer, for editing and publishing the first of what he intends as a regular visitor to the scene, based on his belief that good writers of horror were missing out. We might easily, had space allowed, have fallen for more of his choices than Steven Gallagher's restrained treat of a ghost story.

It would be a jaundiced or uninspired reader who did not find much to his or her taste, profit or delight in the pages that follow.

Giles Gordon and David Hughes

Foam

BRIAN W. ALDISS

'There's nothing for it when you reach the Point
of No Return – except to come back.'
E. James Carvell

MANY CENTRAL AND Eastern European churches had been
dismantled. The deconstruction of Chartres Cathedral was
proceeding smartly, unhindered by Operation Total Tartary.

On the previous day, a guide had taken me around Budapest
Anthropological Museum. I had wanted to see the *danse
macabre* preserved there, once part of the stonework of the
cathedral at Nagykanizsa. Although the panel was in poor
condition, it showed clearly the dead driving the living to the
grave.

The dead were represented by skeletons, frisky and
grinning. The line of the living began with prelates in grand
clothes, the Pope leading. Merchants came next, men and
women, then a prostitute; a beggar brought up the rear, these
allegorical figures representing the inescapable gradations of
decay.

As I was making notes, measuring, and sketching in my
black notebook, the guide was shuffling about behind me,
impatient to leave. I had special permission to be in the gallery.
Jangling her keys more like a gaoler than an attendant, she

1

went to gaze out of a narrow window at what could be seen of the prosperous modern city, returning to peer over my shoulder and sniff.

'A disgusting object,' she remarked, gesticulating with an open hand towards the frieze, which stood severed and out of context on a display bench in front of me.

' "What is beauty, saith my sufferings then?" ' I quoted abstractedly. To me the *danse macabre* was a work of art, skilfully executed; nothing more than that. I admired the way in which the leading Death gestured gallantly towards an open grave, his head bizarrely decked with flags. The unknown artist, I felt sure, had been to Lübeck, where similar postures were depicted. The helpful guidebook, in Hungarian and German, told me that this sportive Death was saying, 'In this doleful jeste of Life, I shew the state of Manne, and how he is called at uncertayne tymes by Me to forget all that he hath and lose All.'

For a while, silence prevailed, except for the footsteps of the guide, walking to the end of the gallery and back, sighing in her progress, jingling her keys. We were alone in the gallery. I was sketching the Death playing on a stickado or wooden psalter and goading along a high-bosomed duchess, when the guide again shuffled close.

'Much here is owed to Holbein engraving,' said the guide, to show off her knowledge. She was a small, bent woman whose nose was disfigured by a permanent cold. She regarded the work with a contempt perhaps habitual to her. 'Theme of *danse macabre* is much popular in Middle Ages. In Nagykanizsa, half population is wipe out by plague only one years after building the cathedral. Now we know much better, praise be.'

I was fed up with her misery and her disapproval. I wanted only to study the frieze. It would buttress a line of thought I was pursuing.

'In what way do we know better?'

It is unwise ever to argue with a guide. She gave me a long discourse regarding the horrors of the Middle Ages, concluding by saying, 'Then was much misery in Budapest. Now everyone many money. Now we finish with Christianity and Communism, world much better place. People more enlightenment, eh?'

'You believe that?' I asked her. 'You really think people are more enlightened? On what grounds, may I ask? What about the war?'

She shot me a demonic look, emphasised by a smile of outrageous malice. 'We kill off all Russians. Then world better place. Forget all about bad thing.'

The grand steam baths under the Gellert Hotel were full of naked bodies, male and female. Many of the bathers had not merely the posture but the bulk of wallowing hippopotami. Fortunately the steam clothed us in a little decency.

Tiring of the crowd, I climbed from the reeking water. It was time I got to work. Churches long sealed with all their histories in them were to be opened to me this day. By a better guide.

Everyone was taking it easy. Headlines in the English language paper that morning: STAVROPOL AIRPORT BATTLE: First Use Tactical Nukes: Crimea Blazes. The war had escalated. Everyone agreed you had to bring in the nukes eventually. Hungary was neutral. It supplied Swedish-made arms to all sides, impartially.

The Soviet War marked the recovery of Hungary as a Central European power. It was a godsend. Little I cared. I was researching churches and, in my early forties, too old for conscription.

Wrapped in a white towelling robe I was making my way back towards my room when I encountered a tall bearded man clad only in a towel. He was heading towards the baths I had just left. We looked at each other. I recognised those haggard lineaments, those eroded temples. They belonged to a distant acquaintance, one Montague Clements.

He recognised me immediately. As we shook hands I felt some embarrassment; he had been sacked from his post in the English Literature and Language Department of the University of East Anglia the previous year. I had not heard of him since.

'What are you doing in Budapest?' I asked.

'Private matter, old chum.' I remembered the dated way he had of addressing people – though he had been sacked for more serious matters. 'I'm here consulting a clever chap called Mircea Antonescu. Something rather strange has happened to me. Do you mind if I tell you? Perhaps you'd like to buy us a drink . . .'

We went up to my room, from the windows of which was a fine view of the Danube with Pest on the other side. I slipped into my jogging gear and handed him a sweater to wear.

'Fits me like a T. I suppose I couldn't keep it, could I?'

I did not like to say no. As I poured two generous Smirnoffs on the rocks from the mini-bar, he started on his problems. ' "Music, when soft voices die, Vibrates in the memory . . ." So says the poet Shelley. But supposing there's no memory in which the soft voices can vibrate . . .'

He paused to raise his glass and take a deep slug of the vodka. 'I'm forty-one, old chum. So I believe. Last month, I found myself in an unknown place. No idea how I got there. Turned out I was here – in Budapest. Budapest! Never been here before in my natural. No idea how I arrived here from London.'

'You're staying here?' I remembered that Clements was a scrounger. Perhaps he was going to touch me for the air fare home. I gave him a hard look. Knowing something about his past, I was determined not to be caught easily.

'I'm attending the Antonescu Clinic. Mircea Antonescu – very clever chap, as I say. At the cutting edge of psycho-technology. Romanian, of course. I'm not staying in the Gellert. Too expensive for someone like me. I rent a cheaper place in Pest. Bit of a flophouse actually.' He laughed. 'You see, this is it, the crunch, the bottom line, as they say – I've lost ten years of my memory. Just lost them. Wiped. The last ten years, gone.'

He shone a look of absolute innocence on me. At which I uttered some condolences.

'The last thing I remember, I was thirty. Ten, almost eleven years, have passed and I have no notion as to what I was doing in all that time.'

All this he related in an old, accustomed, calm way. Perhaps he concealed his pain. 'How terrible for you,' I said.

'F O A M. That's what they call it. Free of All Memory. A kind of liberty in a way, I suppose. Nothing a chap can't get used to.'

It was fascinating. Other people's sorrows on the whole weigh lightly on our shoulders: a merciful provision. 'What does it feel like?'

I always remember Clements' answer. 'An ocean, old chum. A wide wide ocean with a small island here and there. No continent. The continent has gone.'

I had seen him now and again during those ten years, before his sacking. I suggested that perhaps I could help him fill in gaps in his memory. He appeared moderately grateful. He said there was no one else he knew in Budapest. When I asked him if he had been involved in an accident, he shook his head.

'They don't know. I don't know. A car crash? No bones broken, old boy. Lucky to be alive, you might say. I have no memory of anything that happened to me in the last ten years.'

Unthinkingly, I asked, 'Isn't your wife here with you?'

Whereupon Clements struck his narrow forehead. 'Oh God, don't say I was married!'

He drank the vodka, he kept the sweater. The next day, as suggested, I went round with him to the Antonescu Clinic he had mentioned. The idea was that an expert would question me in order to construct a few more of those small islands in the middle of Clements' ocean of forgetfulness.

The clinic was situated in a little nameless square off Fo Street, wedged in next to the Ministry of Light Industry. Behind its neo-classical façade was a desperate little huddle of rooms partitioned into offices and not at all smart. In one windowless room I was introduced to a Dr Maté Joszef. Speaking in jerky English around a thin cigar, Maté informed me we could get to work immediately. It would be best procedure if I began to answer a series of questions in a room from which Clements was excluded.

'You understand, Dr Burnell. Using proprietary method here. Dealing with brain injury cases. Exclusive . . . Special to us. Produces the good result. Satisfied customers . . .' His thick furry voice precluded the use of finite verbs.

Knowing little about medical practice, I consented to do as he demanded. Maté showed me up two flights of stairs to a windowless room where a uniformed nurse awaited us. I was unfamiliar with the equipment in the room, although I knew an operating table and anaesthetic apparatus when I saw them. It was at that point I began to grow nervous. Nostovision equipment was also in the room; I recognised the neat plastic skull cap.

Coughing, Maté stubbed his cigar out before starting to fiddle with the equipment. The nurse attempted to help. I stood with my back to the partition wall, watching.

'Wartime . . . Many difficulties . . . Many problems . . . For Hungarians is many trouble . . .' He was muttering as he elbowed the nurse away from a malfunctioning VDU. 'Because of great inflation rate . . . High taxes . . . Too many gipsy in town. All time . . . The Germans of course . . . The Poles . . . How we get all work done in the time? . . . Too much busy . . .'

'If you're very busy, I could come another day,' I suggested.

He squinted at me and lit another cigar. 'I am expert in all science, so many people take advantage of me. Even when I am small boy, I must carrying to school my small brother. Three kilometre to the gymnasium . . . Now is shortage of material, I must do all. This damned war . . . Many upheaval . . . Spies and traitor . . . Everywhere same . . . Today toilet blockage and how to get repair? You cannot be nervous?'

'I have an appointment, Dr Maté. If later would be more convenient . . .'

'Is no problem. Don't worry . . . I treat many English. Get this nurse to move, I explain all.'

Maté sought to reassure me. They had developed a method of inserting memories into the brains of amnesiacs, but first those memories had to be recorded with full sensory data on to microchip, and then projected by laser into the brain. That at least was the gist of what I gathered from a long, complex explanation. While I listened, the nurse gave me an injection in the biceps of my left arm. They would need, Maté said, to append electrodes to my cranium in order to obtain full sensory data matching my answers to his questions.

'I don't really know Montague Clements well,' I protested. But of course I could not simply refuse to co-operate, could not walk out, could not leave poor Clements without doing my best for him.

Indeed, my eyelids felt heavy. It was luxury to stretch out, to groan, to relax . . . and to fall into the deepest slumber of my life . . .

The cathedral in which we walked was almost lightless. My extended senses told me that it was vast. I asked Dr Maté what we were doing there. His answer was incoherent. I did not press him. He seemed to be smoking a cigar; a little red glow formed occasionally as he inhaled, but I could smell no smoke.

In order to keep my spirits up – I admit I was apprehensive –I talked to him as we progressed step by step. 'I suppose you read Kafka, you understand the complexities with which he found himself faced at every turn. As a psychologist, you must understand that there are people like Kafka for whom existence is an entanglement, a permanent state of war, while for others – why, at the other extreme they sail through life, seemingly unopposed. These differences are accounted for by minute biochemical changes in the brain. Neither state is more or less truthful than the other. For some truth lies in mystery, for others in clarity. Prayer is a great clarifier – or was. My belief is that old Christian churches served as clarifying machines. They helped you to think straight in "this doleful jeste of life".'

I went on in this fashion for some while. Dr Maté laughed quite heartily, his voice echoing in the darkness.

'You're such good company,' he said. 'Is there anything I can do for you in return?'

'More oxygen,' I said. 'It's so hot in here. As a church architect, I have visited, I believe, all the cathedrals in Europe – Chartres, Burgos, Canterbury, Cologne, Saragossa, Milano, Ely, Zagreb, Gozo, Rheims – ' I continued to name them for some while as we tramped down the nave. 'But this is the first time I have ever entered a hot and stuffy cathedral.'

'There are new ways. Neural pathways. Technology is not solely about ways of conducting war. It brings blessings. Not least the new abilities by which we may see human existence anew – relativistically, that is, each person imprisoned in his own *umwelt*, his own conceptual universe.' He let out a roar of laughter. 'Your friend Kafka – I'd have lobotomised him, speaking personally – he said that it was not only Budapest but the whole world that was tragic. He said, "All protective walls are smashed by the iron fist of technology." Complaining, of course – the fucker always complained. But it's the electronic fist of technology which is smashing the walls between human and human. I exclude the Muslims, of course. Down they go, like the Berlin Wall, if you remember that far back. In the future, we shall all be able to share common memories, understandings. All will be common property. Private thought will be a thing of the past. It's simply a matter of microtechnology.'

I started laughing. I had not realised what good company Hungarians could be.

'In that connection, I might mention that Jesus Christ was evidently pretty *au fait* with micro-technology. All that resurrection of the body stuff. Depends on advanced technology, much of it developed during that lucky little war against Saddam Hussein in the Gulf. Strictly Frankenstein stuff. Robbing body bags. Dead one day, up and running – back into the conflict – the next.'

Maté was genuinely puzzled. We halted under a memorial statue to Frederick the Great. Maté had heard of Frankenstein. It was the other great Christian myth which puzzled him. This was the first time I had ever encountered anyone walking into a cathedral who had never heard of Jesus Christ. Explaining about Jesus proved more difficult than I expected. The heat and darkness confused me. I knew Jesus was related to John the Baptist and the Virgin Mary, but could not quite remember how. Was Christ his surname or his Christian name?

My father had been a Christian. All the same, it was difficult to recall the legend exactly. I was better on 'Frankenstein'. But I ended by clarifying Jesus's role in the scheme of things by quoting, as far as I could remember, from a hymn, 'He came down to earth from Heaven, He died to save us all.'

Although I couldn't actually see Maté's sneer, I felt it in the darkness. 'Where was this Jesus when Belsen and Auschwitz and Dresden and Hiroshima happened? Having a smoke out the back?'

Somehow, I felt it was rather sacrilegious to mention Jesus's name aloud where we were. The cathedral was constructed in the form of a T, the horizontal limb being much longer than the vertical, stretching away into the endless dark. Oh, the weight of masonry! Like fossil vertebrae, great columns reared up on every side, engineered to support vast weight, as if this whole edifice was situated many miles under the earth's crust, the mass of which must somehow be borne.

So I say. So I understand it. Yet those stone vertebrae – in defiance of the dull facts of physics, writhed like the chordata, climbing lizard-tailed into the deeper darknesses of the vaulting. It was the cathedral to end all cathedrals.

Maté and I now stood at the junction of the cathedral's great T. The vertical limb of this overpowering architectural masterpiece sloped downwards. We stopped to stare down that slope, more sensed than seen. Kafka could have felt no more trepidation at that time than I, though I covered my nervousness by giggling at Maté's latest joke. He claimed he had not heard of the Virgin Mary either.

I stood at the top of the slope. With me was another church architect, Sir Kingsley Amis.

'The font is somewhere over there,' he said, gesturing into the darkness. 'But I'd better warn you it's not drinking water. Even if it was, you wouldn't want to drink it, would you?' He gave a throaty laugh.

Both he and I were greatly diminished by Dr Maté, who now made a proclamation, reading from a box. 'We're here now, on the spot you see indicated on your map, adjacent to the *pons asinorum*. Presently a devil will appear and remove one of you. I am not permitted to say where he will remove you to. We have to keep destinations secret in wartime, but I am authorised to say that it will be somewhere fairly unpleasant. As you know, the war between humanity and the rest is still on. But Geneva rules will apply, except in so far as fire and brimstone will be permitted on a strictly controlled basis. All torture will be attended by an authorised member of the International Red Cross.'

'How long do we have to wait? Is there the chance of a drink before we go?' Sir Kingsley Amis asked.

'Devil should be here shortly. ETA 2001,' Maté said.

'Shortly' was just another of the euphemisms such as surface in wartime. It indicated an eternity, just as bombs are described as deterrents, 'This'll spoil his day' means 'We'll kill him', and 'God' means 'A ton of bricks is about to fall on you'. Myself, I prefer euphemisms.

Phew, I was so tired. Time in the building was lethargic, with every minute stretching, stretching out in companion-ship with the night towards infinity. Reality wore thin, bringing in illusion. At one point I almost imagined I was sitting typing while a dreadful, senseless war was waged in the Gulf. But the gulf of time I was in was much greater. Forget reality; it's one of the universe's dead ends . . .

Interest is hard to sustain, but my feeling was as much of interest as terror. Only those who enjoy life feel terror. I admired all the melancholy grandeur round me, the reptilian sense of claustrophobia. It compared favourably with the slum in which I lived.

At the bottom of the slope before us, a stage became illuminated. You must imagine this as an entirely gradual process, not easily represented in words. A. Pause. Stage. Pause. Became. Pause. Ill. Pause. You. Pause. Min. Pause. Ay. Pause. Ted. Trumpets. It was illuminated predominately in bars of intersecting blue and crimson.

Funebrial music began to play, brass and bass predominating.

The music, so kin to the lighting, was familiar to me, yet only just above audibility, as the lighting hovered just above the visible end of the spectrum.

These low levels of activity were in keeping with the enormous silences of the cathedral structure. They were shattered by the sudden incursion of a resounding bass voice which broke into song. That timbre, that mixture of threat and exultation! Unmistakeable even to a layman.

'The devil!' Kingsley Amis and I exclaimed together.

'And in good voice,' said Dr Maté. 'So this is where I have to leave you.'

I was stunned by his indifference. 'What about that sewing machine?' I asked. But he was not to be deflected.

Even while speaking, he was shrinking, either in real terms or because he was being sucked into the distance; darkness made it hard to differentiate. However, I had little time to waste on Maté. Attention turned naturally to the devil. Though he had yet to appear on the dim-lit stage, I knew he was going to come for Kingsley Amis.

'I'd better make myself scarce too,' I said. 'Don't want to get in your way.'

'Hang on,' he said. 'You never know. He might be after you. Depends on whether or not he's a literary critic.'

When the devil arrived on stage, he was out of scale, far too large – ridiculously far too large, I might say, meaning no disrespect. It was hard to discern anything of him in the confused dark. He was black and gleaming, his outline as smooth as a dolphin's even down to the hint of rubber. He stepped forward and advanced slowly up the ramp, still singing in that voice which shook the rafters.

This struck me as being, all told, unlikely. It was that very feeling that all was unlikely, that anything likely was over and done with like last year's cricket match, which was most frightening. I trembled. Trembling didn't help one bit.

I turned to Kingsley Amis. He was no longer there. I was alone. The devil was coming for me.

In terror, I peered along the great wide lateral arms of the cathedral.

'Anyone there?' I called. 'Help! Help! Taxi!'

To the left was only stygian darkness, too syrupy for me to think of penetrating, the black from which ignorance is made.

As I looked towards the right, however, along the other widespread arm of the building, something materialised there like a stain: light towards the dead, dull end of the electromagnetic spectrum.

All this I took in feverishly, for the devil, still singing, was approaching me still. Perhaps I should apologise for my fears. As a rationalist, I had but to snap my rational fingers, it might be argued, and the devil would fade away in a puff of smoke. To which I might say that, rationalist or not, I had spent too many years in my capacity as church architect investigating the fossils of a dead faith not to have imbibed something of the old superstitions. But – this was more germane – I had a belief in the Jungian notion of various traits and twists of the human personality becoming dramatised as persons or personages. This enormous devil could well be an embodiment of the dark side of my character; in which case, I was all the less likely to escape him.

Nor did I.

As I took a pace or two to my right, starting to run towards that faint dull promise of escape, a vision distantly revealed itself. Fading into being came a magnificent palladian façade, lit in a colour like blood, with doric columns and blind doorways. Nothing human was to be seen there – no man to whom I might call. If the burrow to my left represented the squalors of the subconscious, here to my right was the chill of the super-ego.

I ran for it. But was hardly into my stride when the singing devil reached me. I screamed. He snatched me up . . . and bit off my head.

To any of you with decent sensibilities, I must apologise for these horrific images. You may claim they were subjective, private to me, and should remain private, on the grounds that the world has nightmares enough. Perhaps. But what happened to me was that my head was bitten off almost literally.

My memory was wiped.

It's a curious thing suddenly to find oneself walking. Imagine yourself in a cinema. The movie begins. Its opening shot is of some character walking, walking across a featureless landscape. Photography: grainy. The shot immediately holds your interest, perhaps because our ancestors right back to the Ice Age were great walkers. Now imagine that you're not sitting watching in your comfortable stalls seat: you are that character. Only you're not in a movie. You're for real, or what we call real, according to our limited sensory equipment.

Your life has just begun and you're walking across what turns out to be Salisbury Plain. It's cold, there's a hint of rain in the breeze. The place looks ugly. But walking is no trouble. It's everything else that's trouble.

Like how you got where you are. Like what happened. Like what your name is. Like who you are. Even like – where are you going?

Night is closing in. That much you understand.

What do you do? You go on walking.

Over to your right in the distance, half-hidden by a fold of land, is a circle of stone monoliths. You kind of recognise it, although no name comes to you. It's the ruin of a Stone Age cathedral, taken out in the war with the Neanderthals, cobalt against the overpraised English countryside. You continue as dark continues to fall. Your legs keep working, your pace is unvarying. You become slightly afraid of this remorseless body, asking yourself, Is it mine?

Dusk gathers about you like a coat when you climb a fence and reach a road. There is almost no traffic on the road. You try to thumb a lift from the cars as they approach from either direction, sweeping you with their headlights. Past they go, never pausing. Bastards.

The fourteenth car stops. A woman is driving. A man sits beside her. They ask where you want to go, and you say Anywhere. They laugh and say that is where they are going. You climb in. You huddle on the back seat, unable to answer any of their well-meant questions.

They think you are a loony, and drop you in the nearest village. You are inclined to agree with their judgement. You wander hopelessly along the road, then, frightened, back into the village. The village is called Bishops Linctus. By now its streets are deserted. Lights glow inside the pub, The Gun Dog, but, with no money in your pocket, you are afraid to enter. There are countries where you might enter and be looked after in a hospitable way; you do not feel that could happen in England.

A young man in gumboots saunters along the road with a shotgun under his arm. He stares at you hard as he passes. He returns and addresses you. He is guarded but friendly. He seems not to believe you have lost your memory. Nevertheless, he takes you along to his house, which is one of a line of council houses on the edge of the village, just before the plain recommences its reign.

His old mother greets you. She is surprised, saying that Larry never speaks to anyone. He tells her to shut up. You stand there, back to the kitchen wall, while she fries up Larry's favourite meal, which is sausages and mashed fish fingers. You and Larry sit and eat at the table. It is good.

He has a room he calls His Room. It is locked. The old woman interrupts to say it is full of guns. He says to shut up. He tells you he is a farm labourer or sometimes a brickie. At present he is out of work. He lets you doss on the floor of his bedroom. The place is full of gun magazines, and there is a Kalashnikov in Larry's bed. He sleeps with it.

You express your gratitude.

'I like helping people,' Larry replies. He puts out the light.

You lie there on the floor. Despite all your worries, you feel pleasure and comfort in those words of his, 'I like helping people.' Words of Jesus. And so you sleep.

Only you're not in this movie. This is my movie. I'm for real – or what I call real, according to my limited sensory equipment.

Morning. When I woke, Larry was already up and about. I could hear his mother shouting at him. For a few seconds, I was living with this present situation. Then the edge of the abyss reappeared. I could remember nothing further back than the time I was walking over that miserable plain.

When I got up, the old woman gave me a cup of thin, instant

coffee. I stood with her against the sink. She had a canary in a cage.

'It's Kevin. We call it Kevin. I think it's a girl. One of the family, aren't you? Keeps me company. Say hello to Kevin. I wash it every Saturday, under the hot tap. It likes that. Don't you, Kevin? You like a nice wash under the hot tap. It's one of the family. Sing for your mummy then. Who's a good Kevin?'

I was watching through the window, as Larry loaded boxes of ammunition into the back of an old, battered Land Rover.

His mother caught my glance. 'He's going into Swindon to try and get a job. You stay here with me. He's a dangerous driver, is Larry. We'll go down and see Dr Roberts. She's a sympathetic woman – trained in London, she was – and she'll help you.'

Larry was looking preoccupied. His movements were slow, his gaze abstracted, as if he were composing a poem in his head. Without glancing back at the house, he climbed into the cab of the Land Rover. Nothing happened. I went to the window to watch, obscurely thinking something was wrong. The back of his head could be seen. Motionless. Not trying to start the vehicle. Just sitting there in the driver's seat.

The council houses followed the curve of the road, which wound up a slight incline. Beyond the houses was open agricultural land, the plain. The village lay in the opposite direction. From the last house, three hundred yards distant, a woman emerged, wearing an old blue raincoat and pushing a baby's push-chair. She had a scarf tied over her head and was evidently going into the village to shop.

Larry moved as she drew nearer. The window of the vehicle wound down. A rifle muzzle protruded from it. A shot sounded.

The woman in the blue raincoat fell to her knees, still clinging with one hand to the push-chair.

As three more shots rang out, the push-chair blew apart. The woman's face was covered with shreds of baby as she fell on the road.

Larry's mother had seen at least part of this. She was drying a plate on a tea towel. She dropped the plate, ran from the kitchen, and opened the front door.

'No, no, Larry! Stop it, you fool. Whatever do you think you're doing?'

Larry had descended from the Land Rover after firing the four shots. He moved slowly, with a sleep-walker's lethargy. With that same lethargy, he snugged the butt of the rifle into his shoulder and fired at his mother. She was blown from the porch back into the passage. He fired two more shots into the house. I ran to the bedroom and heaved myself under the bed, fighting blindly with the magazines. I was sure he was after me.

There the police discovered me, four hours later, lying in a pool of my own urine.

So it was that eventually I found myself in a hospital in Swindon close to other victims of Larry Foot. After shooting the woman from the council house and her baby, and his mother, Larry had walked into Bishops Linctus and shot dead the first three people he met, wounding several others. BISHOPS BLOODBATH screamed the tabloid headlines. The quiet little affair roused much more excitement than the Soviet War (in which British troops were involved) then reaching one of its many climaxes outside Tbilisi. Why had Larry done it? The explanation given was that he had always been keen on guns. Presumably the same explanation would cover the Soviet War.

Armed police from Bishops Magnum and Salisbury shot Larry down behind the Shell garage. He had liked to help people, poor Larry. At least he gave a little pleasure to the bloodthirsty readers of *The Sun*.

This incident got me swiftly – in an ambulance – into the realm of professional medical scrutiny. Within a few days, I again had an identity. I was Roy Edward Burnell, a university lecturer and specialist in church architecture. I had written a learned book, *Architrave and Archetype*, a thesis linking human aspiration with human-designed structures, cathedrals in particular.

The chief medico in charge of my case, a Dr Rosemary Kepepwe, entered my hospital room smiling, bringing with her a copy of my book. 'We're getting somewhere, Roy,' she said. 'We'll contact your wife next.'

I smote my forehead. 'My God, don't say I'm married.'

She laughed. 'I'm afraid so. At least, you were married. We'll soon have her tracked down – and other people in your past. What is the last thing you remember before the white-out?'

Even to me, her attitude seemed amateurish. When I said something of the sort, Dr Kepepwe explained that most of the original staff of the hospital were serving with British troops in Operation Total Tartary, in Murmansk, Usbekistan, the front in the Caucasus, and the new revolutionary area opening up round Lake Baikal. The disintegration of the Soviet Union had created a tremendous demand for medication.

'My husband was a brain surgeon,' Kepepwe said. 'The best husband a woman could have. David won the Isle of Wight Sea-Fishing Trophy two years in succession. Everyone respected him. We have three children, one of them at Eton and one now working as a waiter in a Little Chef off the M25 at the South Mimms Service Area. But David volunteered to serve with Total Tartary. I had picked up a bit of surgery from him, of course, so here I am. You were quite lucky to get here. Salisbury Plain is all mined these days.'

'Lucky me,' I said. But it appeared I did not know how lucky. I had marvelled that it was such a quiet hospital, and ascribed this to efficiency. Not so, Dr Kepepwe explained. I was the only patient in there. All the other wards were empty. Civilian patients had been turned out three days earlier, as the hospital prepared to receive wounded from the Eastern theatre of war.

'Anyhow, I'd better take your details,' Dr Kepepwe said, reluctantly. 'Then I'll bring you a cup of tea. What did you say was the last thing you remembered?'

I told her. I had gone to South America to view some of the ecclesiastical architecture there. I arrived in Buenos Aires and checked into my hotel. I remembered going up in a gilt elevator. And then – white-out. The fear of standing on the edge of a great abyss overtook me.

Dr Kepepwe saw the expression on my face. 'Don't worry – you're not alone, Roy. How does it feel?'

'An ocean. A wide ocean with a small island here and there. No continent. The continent has gone.'

As I spoke the words, some strange thing struggled in my mind. A name almost came back to me, then died.

So I waited. Waited to be restored. To pass the time I had access to the hospital library on VDU, together with TV and video. Also the new media craze, the NV, or nostovision. Laser projectors could beam whole programmes into the mind where the programmes became like your own lived memories, though they faded in a few days. In view of my deficiencies, I avoided the NV and stuck to the library; but little I read remained in my mind.

What sins, what meannesses, what grave errors I had committed in the previous ten years had been forgiven me. I waited in calm, without apprehension.

Dr Kepepwe assured me active steps were being taken to trace those who had been intimate with me during the ten blank years: my parents, my academic colleagues. The confusions of war, the tight security covering the country, made communication difficult.

When she left in the evening, I wandered through the great empty building. In the dark of the long, antiseptic corridors, green LEDs glowed, accompanied often by hums or growls. It was like being in the entrails of a glacier.

On the desk in Rosemary Kepepwe's office stood a photograph of her husband David, very black, smiling genially with a large fish on a scale by his side. I wondered about their lives; but there was nothing on which to speculate. She was little more to me than an embodiment of kindness.

Only my slippered footsteps on the stairs, the tiles. I was a ghost among the ghosts of multitudinous lives whose c.v.s, like mine, had been lost. Who had lived, died, survived? A phrase came back uncomfortably from the white-out, 'the sorry jeste of Life'.

But, I told myself as I took a service elevator up to the roof, I should not think in the past tense. Any day now and the hospital would be filled again with the living – the military living, harpooned by their wounds, poised on the brink of a final white-out. They would survive or not, to accumulate more memories, happy or sad as the case might be.

On the roof, the habitations of air-conditioning plants painted black by a city's grime lived and breathed. I stood on the parapet, looking out over the town of Swindon, willing myself to feel less disembodied. The stars shone overhead, remote but always with promise of something better than the brief rush of biological existence. As I drank them in, a roar of engines sounded.

Three B-52 Stratofortresses flew overhead, from the west towards the eastern stars.

I went downstairs again, to my ward, my nest in the glacier. I must wait. Waiting did not require too much fortitude. One day soon, Dr Kepepwe would do the trick – with luck before the war-damaged moved in to supplant me in her attentions.

The days would pass. Help would come.

Indeed, the days did pass.

And then Stephanie arrived.

Stephanie was a vision of delight, tall, fine-boned, aesthetic of countenance, walking easy and free inside a fawn linen suit. Hair tawny, neat, almost shoulder-length. I admired the way she strolled into the ward, doing quite determinedly something not to her taste. With a cautious smile on her face. And this lady had been my wife. I could have forgotten that? I could have forgotten all the times we had enjoyed together, where we'd been, what we'd done? So it seemed. My head had been bitten off.

Like most gusts of pleasure, this one brought its pain. She sat facing me: calm, sympathetic, but at a distance I had no way of negotiating, as I listened dismayed to what she revealed of those islands, that lost continent.

Stephanie and I had married eight years ago, only four weeks after meeting in Los Angeles for the first time. We were divorced five years later. Here indeed, I thought, must lie some of those sins, meannesses, and grave errors. She broke this news to me gently, casting her clear gaze towards the window in preference to seeing my hurt. The hospital authorities had traced her down in California, where she was enjoying success as a fabric designer and living with a famous composer of film music.

'You don't owe me anything,' she said. And, after a pause, 'I don't owe you anything.'

'It's good of you to come and see me. The war and everything, and that jumbo blown out of the skies over the Atlantic . . .'

A small laugh. 'I was interested, of course. You're a bit of medical history.'

'We had no children?'

She shook her head. 'That whole business was the reason for our falling out.'

'Shit,' I said. A long silence fell between us. I could have crossed the Sahara in it. 'Did I ever – I mean, since we split up – did I ever – did we communicate at all?'

'It was final,' she said. 'I didn't want to know. I like my new life in the States. What you did was up to you, wasn't it? But you did send me postcards. Generally of draughty old churches here and there – of the kind you used to drag me into when we were together.'

'You can't beat a good old draughty church,' I said, smiling.

She did not return the smile. Perhaps the woman lacked humour.

'I brought a couple of your cards along in my purse,' she said. I noted the Americanism as she dipped into her handbag. She pulled out one card and handed it over, extending it between two outstretched fingers – as if amnesia was catching.

'Huh, just one card. I tore the others up, I'm afraid.' That, I thought, was a little unnecessary pain she had no reason to inflict . . .

The card, crudely coloured, showed a picture of a church labelled as St Stephen's Basilica, although I saw immediately that architecturally it was not a basilica. I turned it over, glanced at the Hungarian stamp, and read the few words I had scribbled to Stephanie, only three weeks earlier.

'Budapest. Brief visit here. Making notes for lectures as usual. Need some florid Hungarian architecture. Trust you're well. Have met strange old friend – just going round to Antonescu's Clinic with him. Love, Roy.'

I went back to the Gellert. There, not entirely surprisingly, was Montague Clements, still wearing my sweater.

He raised his hands in mock-surrender. 'Pax. No offence meant, honest, old chum. Since I lost my job I've worked as a decoy for Antonescu, luring on innocent foreigners who come here to take advantage of low Hungarian prices. Economic necessity and all that.'

'You had your hand in the till – now you've had it in my mind. Stealing a memory is like murder, you miserable slob.'

'Yes, and no doubt it will be legislated against when nostovision becomes something less than a seven-day wonder. Till then, Antonescu earns a modest dollar from his bootleg memory bullets. They're short of hard currency, the Hungarians. Let me buy you a drink.'

I almost threw myself on him. 'You've poisoned my life, you bastard, you'd probably poison my drink.'

He was very cool. 'Let's not fall out. You have a contempt for me. Think how I might feel about you. I've had to edit ten years of your memories, a lot of which weren't edifying. You should be happy to be rid of them.'

'I see, Clements – The F O A M Theory of History . . . Never learn anything. Just bloody forget. Haven't you ever heard that saying about those who forget history being doomed to repeat it? Why do you think the world's in such a fucking mess?'

He remained unmoved. 'I have no idea, old boy. Nor, I suspect, do you, for all your academic posturing. Without wishing to hurt your feelings, your last ten years were full of crap. But there – everyone's last ten years were full of crap . . .'

We were standing in the baroque foyer of the hotel, which had been built in the great European hotel age during the peaceful years preceding the First World War. I gestured through the doors, through the glass of which traffic could be seen crossing the Szabadsag Bridge. Beyond lay the dense

Magyar thoroughfares, the grandiose piles of masonry, where fat profiteers sweated over their calculators.

'I was already on my way to the police, Clements, old boy. Don't pretend we're friends. You had me dumped on Salisbury Plain, don't forget.'

Clements turned on one of his innocent smiles. 'Just think, it could have been the Gobi . . . I interceded on your behalf. Be British, old chap – let's compromise. Let's do a deal.'

'What deal?'

He said, 'We could discuss business better in the bar. You want your memory back, eh? Don't go to the police and I'll bring your memory this afternoon. Agree? Say three-thirty, after I've taken my customary nap. OK?'

So I agreed on it. I agreed, thinking I would go to the police later. Clements turned up at three-fifty-five.

We sat at the upstairs bar with two tall glasses of iced white Eger wine, for which I paid. He produced in the palm of his right hand two slender plastic spools, which I recognised as nostovision bullets, ready to be inserted into the head-laser.

'I had some trouble getting these, old chap. How about fifty dollars each?'

'Maybe you really have lost your memory or you'd know I wouldn't fall for that. Hand them over. Why two bullets?'

He took a reflective sip of his wine. 'Antonescu's at the cutting edge of psycho-technology. We have to know our customers. They're mainly in America and the Arab World. It's a specialised market. We boiled your memory banks down into two categories – the rest we threw away, sorry to say. There's your speciality, church architecture and all that. That spool has a limited but steady sale to academics – a tribute to all the knowledge you had packed away. I suppose you'll be glad to get that back. Surely it's worth fifty dollars to you?'

'Come on, Clements, what's the other bullet?'

'A hundred dollars, old chum? It's all your life and activities with a woman called Stephanie. Very erotic stuff, believe me. Very popular in Saudi Arabia.'

I threw my wine in his face and grabbed the two bullets.

I leave it to you to decide which bullet I played first.

*

The Soviet War continues. Heavy fighting in the Caucasus despite bad weather conditions. Radio reports said that Alliance forces used chemical and bacteriological weapons in the Kutaisi area. Questioned, American General 'Gus' Stalinbrass said, 'What the heck else do we do? These assholes don't give up easy.'

Last night, four Georgian soldiers crossed the Tbilisi lines, found their way through a minefield, and gave themselves up to a British journalist, Dicky Bowden. One of the soldiers was a boy of fourteen.

Bowden said, 'Starved and disaffected troops like these are all that stand between our advance and the Caspian Sea.'

He was confident that the war would be over in a week or two. Say a month. Maximum two months.

Lizzie's Tiger

ANGELA CARTER

WHEN THE CIRCUS came to town and Lizzie saw the tiger, they
were living on Ferry Street in a very poor way. It was the time
of the greatest parsimony in their father's house; everyone
knows the first hundred thousand is the most difficult and the
dollar bills were breeding slowly, slowly, even if he practised a
little touch of usury on the side to prick his cash in the direction
of greater productivity. In another ten years time, the War
between the States would provide rich pickings for the
coffin-makers, but, back then, back in the fifties, well – if he
had been a praying man, he would have gone down on his
knees for a little outbreak of summer cholera or a touch, just a
touch, of typhoid. To his chagrin, there had been nobody to
bill when he had buried his wife.

For, at that time, the girls were just freshly orphaned.
Emma was thirteen, Lizzie four – stern and square, a squat
rectangle of a child. Emma parted Lizzie's hair in the middle,
stretched it back over each side of her bulging forehead and
braided it tight. Emma dressed her, undressed her, scrubbed
her night and morning with a damp flannel, and humped the
great lump of little girl around in her arms whenever Lizzie
would let her, although Lizzie was not a demonstrative child
and did not show affection easily, except to the head of the

house, and then only when she wanted something. She knew where the power was and, intuitively feminine in spite of her gruff appearance, she knew how to court it.

That cottage on Ferry – very well, it was a slum; but the undertaker lived on unconcerned among the stiff furnishings of his defunct marriage. His bits and pieces would be admired today if they turned up freshly beeswaxed in an antique store, but in those days they were plain old-fashioned, and time would only make them more so in that dreary interior, the tiny house he never mended, eroding clapboard and diseased paint, mildew on the dark wallpaper with a brown pattern like brains, the ominous crimson border round the top of the walls, the sisters sleeping in one room in one thrifty bed.

On Ferry, in the worst part of town, among the dark-skinned Portuguese fresh off the boat with their earrings, flashing teeth and incomprehensible speech, come over the ocean to work the mills whose newly-erected chimneys closed in every perspective, every year more chimneys, more smoke, more newcomers, and the peremptory shriek of the whistle that summoned to labour as bells had once summoned to prayer.

The hovel on Ferry stood, or, rather, leaned at a bibulous angle on a narrow street cut across at an oblique angle by another narrow street, all the old wooden homes like an upset cookie jar of broken gingerbread houses lurching this way and that way, and the shutters hanging off their hinges and windows stuffed with old newspapers, and the snagged picket fence and raised voices in unknown tongues and howling of dogs who, since puppyhood, had known of the world only the circumference of their chain. Outside the parlour window were nothing but rows of counterfeit houses that sometimes used to scream.

Such was the anxious architecture of the two girls' early childhood.

A hand came in the night and stuck a poster, showing the head of a tiger, onto a picket fence. As soon as Lizzie saw the poster, she wanted to go to the circus, but Emma had no money, not a cent. The thirteen-year-old was keeping house at that time, the last skivvy just quit with bad words on both sides. Every morning, Father would compute the day's expenses, hand Emma just so much, no more. He was angry when he saw the poster on the fence; he thought the circus should have paid him rental for the use. He came home in the evening, sweet with embalming fluid, saw the poster, purpled with fury, ripped it off, tore it up.

Then it was suppertime. Emma was no great shakes at cookery and Father, dismissing the possibility of another costly skivvy until such time as plague struck, already pondered the cost-efficiency of remarriage; when Emma served up her hunks of cod, translucently uncooked within, her warmed-over coffee and a dank loaf of baker's bread, it almost put him in a courting mood, but that is not to say his meal improved his temper. So that, when his youngest climbed kitten-like upon his knee and, lisping, twining her tiny fingers in his gunmetal watch-chain, begged small change for the circus, he answered her with words of unusual harshness, for he truly loved this last daughter, whose obduracy recalled his own.

Emma unhandily darned a sock.

'Get that child to bed before I lose my temper!'

Emma dropped the sock and scooped up a Lizzie, whose mouth set in dour lines of affront as she was borne off. The square-jawed scrap, deposited on the rustling straw mattress – oat straw, softest and cheapest – sat where she had been dropped and stared at the dust in a sunbeam. She seethed with resentment. It was moist midsummer, only six o'clock and still bright day outside.

She had a whim of iron, this one. She swung her feet onto the stool upon which the girls climbed down out of bed, thence to the floor. The kitchen door stood open for air behind the screen door. From the parlour came the low murmur of Emma's voice as she read *The Providence Journal* aloud to Father.

Next door's lean and famished hound launched itself at the fence in a frenzy of yapping that concealed the creak of Lizzie's boots on the back porch. Unobserved, she was off – off and away! – trotting down Ferry Street, her cheeks pink with self-reliance and intent. She would not be denied. The circus! The word tinkled in her head with a red sound, as if it might signify a profane church.

'That's a tiger,' Emma had told her as, hand in hand, they inspected the poster on their fence.

'A tiger is a big cat,' Emma added instructively.

'How big a cat?'

'A *very* big cat.'

A dumpy, red-striped, regular cat of the small, domestic variety greeted Lizzie with a raucous mew from atop a gate-post as she stumped determinedly along Ferry Street; our cat, Ginger, whom Emma, in a small ecstasy of sentimental whimsy presaging that of her latter protracted spinsterhood, would sometimes call, Miss Ginger, or even, Miss Ginger Cuddles. Lizzie, however, sternly ignored Miss Ginger Cuddles. Miss Ginger Cuddles sneaked. The cat put out a paw as Lizzie brushed past, as if seeking to detain her, as if to suggest she took second thoughts as to her escapade, but, for all the apparent decision with which Lizzie put one firm foot before the other, she had not the least idea where the circus might be and would not have got there at all without the help of a gaggle of ragged Irish children from Corkey Row, who happened by in the company of a lean, black and tan, barking dog of unforeseen breed that had *this* much in common with Miss Ginger Cuddles, it could go whither it pleased.

This free-ranging dog with its easy-going grin took a fancy to Lizzie and, yapping with glee, danced around the little figure in the white pinafore as it marched along. Lizzie reached out to pat its head. She was a fearless girl.

The child-gang saw her pet their dog and took a fancy to her for the same reason as crows settle on one particular tree. Their wild smiles circled round her. 'Going to the circus, are ye? See the clown and the ladies dancing?' Lizzie knew nothing about clowns and dancers, but she nodded, and one boy took hold of one hand, another of the other, so they raced her off between them. They soon saw her little legs could not keep up their pace, so the ten-year-old put her up on his shoulders where she rode like a lord. Soon they came to a field on the edge of town.

'See the big top?' There was a red and white striped tent of scarcely imaginable proportions, into which you could have popped the entire house on Ferry, and the yard too, with enough room to spare inside for another house, and another – a vast red and white striped tent, with ripping naphtha flares outside and, besides this, all manner of other tents, booths and stalls, dotted about the field, but most of all she was impressed by the great number of people, for it seemed to her that the whole town must be out tonight, yet, when you looked closely at the throng, nowhere at all was anyone who looked like she did, or her father did, or Emma; nowhere that old New England lantern jaw, those ice-blue eyes.

She was a stranger among these strangers, for all here were those the mills had brought to town, the ones with different faces. The plump, pink-cheeked Lancashire millhands, with brave red neckerchiefs; the sombre features of the Canucks imbibing fun with characteristic gloom; and the white smiles of the Portuguese, who knew how to enjoy themselves, laughter tripping off their tipsy-sounding tongues.

'Here y'are!' announced her random companions as they dumped her down and, feeling they had amply done their duty by their self-imposed charge, they capered off among the throng, planning, perhaps, to slither under the canvas and so enjoy the shows for free, or even to pick a pocket or two to complete the treat, who knows?

Above the field, the sky now acquired the melting tones of the end of the day, the plush, smoky sunsets unique to these unprecedented industrial cities, sunsets never seen in this world before the Age of Steam that set the mills in motion that made us all modern.

At sunset, the incomparably grave and massive light of New England acquires a monumental, a Roman sensuality; under this sternly voluptuous sky, Lizzie abandoned herself to the unpremeditated smells and never-before-heard noises – hot fat in a vat of frying doughnuts; horsedung; boiling sugar; frying onions; popping corn; freshly-churned earth; vomit;

sweat; cries of vendors; crack of rifles from the range; sing-song of the white-faced clown, who clattered a banjo, while a woman in pink fleshings danced upon a little stage. Too much for Lizzie to take in at once, too much for Lizzie to take in at all – too rich a feast for her senses, so that she was taken a little beyond herself and felt her head spinning, a vertigo, a sense of profound strangeness overcoming her.

All unnoticeably small as she was, she was taken up by the crowd and tossed about among insensitive shoes and petti-coats, too close to the ground to see much else for long; she imbibed the frenetic bustle of the midway through her nose, her ears, her skin that twitched, prickled, heated up with excitement so that she began to colour up in the way she had, her cheeks marked with red, like the marbling on the insides of the family bible. She found herself swept by the tide of the crowd to a long table where hard cider was sold from a barrel.

The white tablecloth was wet and sticky with spillage and gave forth a dizzy, sweet, metallic odour. An old woman filled tin mugs at the barrel spigot, mug after mug, and threw coins onto other coins into a tin box – splash, chink, clang. Lizzie clung on to the edge of the table to prevent herself being carried away again. Splash, chink, clang. Trade was brisk, so the old woman never turned the spigot off and cider cascaded onto the ground on the other side of the table.

The devil got into Lizzie, then. She ducked down and sneaked in under the edge of the tablecloth, to hide in the resonant darkness and crouch on the crushed grass in fresh mud, as she held out her unobserved hands under the discontinuous stream from the spigot until she collected two hollowed palmsful, which she licked up, and smacked her lips. Filled, licked, smacked again. She was so preoccupied with her delicious thievery that she jumped half out of her skin when she felt a living, quivering thing thrust into her neck in that very sensitive spot where her braids divided. Something moist and intimate shoved inquisitively at the nape of her neck.

She craned round and came face to face with a melancholy piglet, decently dressed in a slightly soiled ruff. She courteously filled her palms with cider and offered it to her new acquaintance, who sucked it up eagerly. She squirmed to feel the wet quiver of the pig's curious lips against her hands. It drank, tossed its pink snout, and trotted off out the back way from the table.

Lizzie did not hesitate. She followed the piglet past the dried-cod smell of the cider-seller's skirts. The piglet's tail disappeared beneath a cart piled with fresh barrels that was pulled up behind the stall. Lizzie pursued the engaging piglet to find herself suddenly out in the open again, but this time in an abrupt margin of pitch-black and silence. She had slipped out of the circus grounds through a hole in their periphery and the dark had formed into a huge clot, the night, whilst Lizzie was underneath the table; behind her the lights were, but here only shadowy undergrowth, stirring, and then the call of a night bird.

The pig paused to rootle the earth, but when Lizzie reached out to stroke it, it shook its ears out of its eyes and took off at a great pace into the countryside. However, her attention was immediately diverted from this disappointment by the sight of a man who stood with his back to the lights, leaning slightly forward. The cider-barrel spigot sound repeated itself. Fumbling with the front of his trousers, he turned round and tripped over Lizzie, because he was a little unsteady on his feet and she was scarcely to be seen among the shadows. He bent down and took hold of her shoulders.

'Small child,' he said, and belched a puff of acridity into her face. Lurching a little, he squatted right down in front of her, so they were on the same level. It was so dark that she could see of his face only the hint of a moustache above the pale half-moon of his smile.

'Small girl,' he corrected himself, after a closer look. He did not speak like ordinary folks. He was not from around these parts. He belched again, and again tugged at his trousers. He took firm hold of her right hand and brought it tenderly up between his squatting thighs.

'Small girl, do you know what *this* is for?'

She felt buttons; serge; something hairy; something moist

and moving. She didn't mind it. He kept his hand on hers and made her rub him for a minute or two. He hissed between his teeth: 'Kissy, kissy from missy?'

She *did* mind that and shook an obdurate head; she did not like her father's hard, dry, imperative kisses, and endured them only for the sake of power. Sometimes Emma touched her cheek lightly with unparted lips. Lizzie would allow no more. The man sighed when she shook her head, took her hand away from his crotch, softly folded it up on its fingers and gave her hand ceremoniously back to her.

'Gratuity,' he said, felt in his pocket and flipped her a nickel. Then he straightened up and walked away. Lizzie put the coin in her pinafore pocket and, after a moment's thought, stumped off after the funny man along the still, secret edges of the field, curious as to what he might do next.

But now surprises were going on all round her in the bushes, mewings, squeaks, rustlings, although the funny man paid no attention to them, not even when a stately fat woman rose up under his feet, huge as a moon and stark but for her stays, but for black cotton stockings held up by garters with silk rosettes on them, but for a majestic hat of black leghorn with feathers. The woman addressed the drunken man angrily, in a language with a good many ks in it, but he ploughed on indifferently and Lizzie scuttled unseen after, casting an inquisitive backward glance. She had never seen a woman's naked breasts since she could remember, and this pair of melons jiggled entrancingly as the fat woman shook her fist in the wake of the funny man before she parted her thighs with a wet smack and sank down on her knees again in the grass in which something unseen moaned.

Then a person scarcely as tall as Lizzie herself, dressed up like a little drummer-boy, somersaulted – head over heels – directly across their paths, muttering to himself as he did so. Lizzie had just the time to see that, although he was small, he was not shaped quite right, for his head seemed to have been pressed into his shoulders with some violence, but then he was gone.

Don't think any of this frightened her. She was not the kind of child that frightens easily.

Then they were at the back of a tent, not the big, striped tent, but another, smaller tent, where the funny man fumbled with the flap much as he had fumbled with his trousers. A bright mauve, ammoniac reek pulsed out from this tent; it was lit up inside like a Chinese lantern and glowed. At last he managed to unfasten and went inside. He did not so much as attempt to close up after him; he seemed to be in as great a hurry as the tumbling dwarf, so she slipped through too, but as soon as she was inside, she lost him, because there were so many other people there.

Feet of customers had worn all the grass from the ground and it had been replaced by sawdust, which soon stuck all over the mudpie Lizzie had become. The tent was lined with cages on wheels, but she could not see high enough to see what was inside them, yet, mixed with the everyday chatter around her, she heard strange cries that did not come from human throats, so she knew she was on the right track.

She saw what could be seen: a young couple, arm in arm, he whispering in her ear, she giggling; a group of three grinning, gaping youths, poking sticks within the bars; a family that went down in steps of size, a man, a woman, a boy, a girl, a boy, a girl, a boy, a girl, down to a baby of indeterminate sex in the woman's arms. There were many more present, but these were the people she took account of.

The gagging stench was worse than a summer privy and a savage hullabaloo went on all the time, a roaring as if the sea had teeth.

She eeled her way past skirts and trousers and scratched, bare legs of summer boys until she was standing beside the biggest brother of the staircase family at the front of the crowd, but still she could not see the tiger, even if she stood on tiptoe, she saw only wheels and the red and gold base of the cage, whereon was depicted a woman without any clothes, much like the one in the grass outside only without the hat and stockings, and some foliage, with a gilded moon and stars. The brother of the staircase family was much older than she, perhaps twelve, and clearly of the lower class, but clean and respectable-looking, although the entire family possessed that pale, peculiar look characteristic of the mill operatives. The brother looked down and saw a small child in a filthy pinafore peering and straining upwards.

'*Veux-tu voir le chat grand, ma petite?*'

Lizzie did not understand what he said, but she knew what he was saying and nodded assent. Mother looked over the head of the good baby in the lace bonnet as her son heaved Lizzie up in his arms for a good look.

'*Les poux . . .*' she warned, but her son paid her no heed.

'*Voilà, ma petite!*'

The tiger walked up and down, up and down; it walked up and down like Satan walking about the world and it burned. It burned so brightly, she was scorched. Its tail, thick as her father's forearm, twitched back and forth at the tip. The quick, loping stride of the caged tiger; its eyes like yellow coins of a foreign currency; its round, innocent, toy-like ears; the stiff whiskers sticking out with an artificial look; the red mouth from which the bright noise came. It walked up and down on straw strewn with bloody bones.

The tiger kept its head down, questing hither and thither though in quest of what might not be told. All its motion was slung from the marvellous haunches it held so high you could have rolled a marble down its back, if it would have let you, and the marble would have run down an oblique angle until it rolled over the domed forehead onto the floor. In its hind legs the tense muscles keened and sang. It was a miracle of dynamic suspension. It reached one end of the cage in a few paces and whirled around upon itself in one liquid motion; nothing could be quicker or more beautiful than its walk. It was all raw, vivid, exasperated nerves. Upon its pelt it bore the imprint of the bars behind which it lived.

The young lad who kept hold of her clung tight as she lunged forward towards the beast, but he could not stop her clutching the bars of the cage with her little fingers and he tried but he could not dislodge them. The tiger stopped in its tracks halfway through its mysterious patrol and looked at her. Her pale-blue Calvinist eyes of New England encountered with a shock the flat, mineral eyes of the tiger.

It seemed to Lizzie that they exchanged this cool regard for an endless time, the tiger and herself.

Then something strange happened. The svelte beast fell to its knees. It was as if it had been subdued by the presence of this child, as if this little child of all the children in the world, might lead it towards a peaceable kingdom where it need not eat meat. But only 'as if'. All we could see was, it knelt. A crackle of shock ran through the tent; the tiger was acting out of character.

Its mind remained, however, a law unto itself. We did not know what it was thinking. How could we?

It stopped roaring. Instead it started to emit a rattling purr. Time somersaulted. Space diminished to the field of attractive force between the child and the tiger. All that existed in the whole world now were Lizzie and the tiger.

Then, oh! Then . . . it came towards her, as if she were winding it to her on an invisible string by the exercise of pure will. I cannot tell you how much she loved the tiger, nor how wonderful she thought it was. It was the power of her love that forced it to come to her, on its knees, like a penitent. It dragged its pale belly across the dirty straw towards the bars where the little soft creature hung by its hooked fingers. Behind it followed the serpentine length of its ceaselessly twitching tail.

There was a wrinkle in its nose and it buzzed and rumbled and they never took their eyes off one another, though neither had the least idea what the other meant.

The boy holding Lizzie got scared and pummelled her little fists, but she would not let go a grip as tight and senseless as that of the newborn.

Crack! The spell broke.

The world bounded into the ring.

A lash cracked round the tiger's carnivorous head, and a glorious hero sprang into the cage brandishing in the hand that did not hold the whip a three-legged stool. He wore fawn breeches, black boots, a bright red jacket frogged with gold, a tall hat. A dervish, he; he beckoned, crouched, pointed with the whip, menaced with the stool, leaped and twirled in a brilliant ballet of mimic ferocity, the dance of the Taming of the Tiger, to whom the tamer gave no chance to fight at all.

The great cat unpeeled its eyes off Lizzie's in a trice, rose up on its hind legs and feinted at the whip like our puss Ginger feints at a piece of paper dangled from a string. He batted at the tamer with its enormous paws, but the whip continued to confuse, irritate and torment it and, what with the shouting, the sudden, excited baying of the crowd, the dreadful confusion of the signs surrounding it, habitual custom, a lifetime's training, the tiger whimpered, laid back its ears and scampered away from the whirling man to an obscure corner of the stage, there to cower, while its flanks heaved, the picture of humiliation.

Lizzie let go of the bars and clung, mud stains and all, to her young protector for comfort. She was shaken to the roots by the attack of the trainer upon the tiger and her four-year-old roots were very near the surface.

The tamer gave his whip a final, contemptuous ripple around his adversary's whiskers that made it sink its huge head on the floor. Then he placed one booted foot on the tiger's skull and cleared his throat for speech. He was a hero. He was a tiger himself, but even more so, because he was a man.

'Ladies and gentlemen, boys and girls, this incomparable TIGER known as the Scourge of Bengal, and brought alive-oh to Boston from its native jungle but three short months before this present time, now, at my imperious command, offers you a perfect imitation of docility and obedience. But do not let the brute deceive you. Brute it was, and brute it remains. Not for nothing did it receive the soubriquet of Scourge for, in its native habitat, it thought nothing of consuming a dozen brown-skinned heathens for its breakfast and following up with a couple of dozen more for dinner!'

A pleasing shudder tingled through the crowd.

'This tiger,' and the beast whickered ingratiatingly when he named it, 'is the veritable incarnation of blood lust and fury; in a single instant, it can turn from furry quiescence into three-hundred pounds, yes, three-hundred POUNDS of death-dealing fury. The tiger is the cat's revenge.'

Oh, Miss Ginger, Miss Ginger Cuddles, who sat mewing

censoriously on the gate-post as Lizzie passed by; who would have thought you seethed with such resentment!

The man's voice dropped to a confidential whisper and Lizzie, although she was in such a state, such nerves, recognised this was the same man as the one she had met behind the cider stall, although now he exhibited such erect mastery, not a single person in the tent would have thought he had been drinking.

'What is the nature of the bond between us, between the Beast and Man? Let me tell you. It is fear. Fear! Nothing but fear. Do you know how insomnia is the plague of the tamer of cats? How all night long, every night, we pace our quarters, impossible to close our eyes for brooding on what day, what hour, what moment the fatal beast will choose to strike?

'Don't think I cannot bleed, or that they have not wounded me. Under my clothes, my body is a palimpsest of scars, scar upon scar. I heal only to be once more broken open. No skin of mine that is not scar tissue. And I am always afraid, always; all the time in the ring, in the cage, now, this moment – this very moment, boys and girls, ladies and gentlemen, you see before you a man in the grip of mortal fear.

'Here and now I am in terror of my life.

'At this moment I am in this cage within a perfect death trap.'

Theatrical pause.

'But,' and here he knocked the tiger's nose with his whip-stock, so that it howled with pain and affront, 'but . . .' and Lizzie saw the secret frog he kept within his trousers shift a little, '. . . BUT I'm not half so scared of the big brute as it is of me!'

He showed his red maw in a laugh.

'For I bring to bear upon its killer instinct a rational man's knowledge of the power of fear. The whip, the stool, are instruments of bluff with which I create his fear in my arena. In my cage, among my cats, I have established a hierarchy of FEAR and among my cats you might well say I am TOP DOG, because I know that all the time they want to kill me, that is their project, that is their intention . . . but as for them, they just don't know what I might do next. No, sir!'

As if enchanted by the notion, he laughed out loud again, but by now, the tiger, perhaps incensed by the unexpected blow on the nose, rumbled out a clear and incontrovertible message of disaffection and, with a quick jerk of its sculptured head, flung the man's foot away so that, caught off balance, he half toppled over. And then the tiger was no longer a thing of stillness, of hard edges and clear outlines, but a whizz of black and red, maw and canines, in the air. On him.

The crowd immediately bayed.

But the tamer, with enormous presence of mind, seeing as how he was drunk, and, in the circumstances, with almost uncanny physical agility, bounced backwards on his boot-heels and thrust the stool he carried in his left hand into the fierce tiger's jaws, leaving the tiger worrying, gnawing, destroying the harmless thing, as a ragged black boy quickly unlatched the cage door and out the tamer leaped, unscathed, amidst hurrahs.

Lizzie's stunned little face was now mottled all over with a curious reddish purple, with the heat of the tent, wth passion, with the sudden access of enlightenment.

To see the rest of the stupendous cat act, the audience would have had to buy another ticket for the Big Top, besides the ticket for the menagerie, for which it had already paid, so, reluctant on the whole to do that, in spite of the promise of clowns and dancing ladies, it soon got bored with watching the tiger splintering the wooden stool, and drifted off.

'*Eh bien, ma petite,*' said her boy-nurse to her in a sweet, singsong, crooning voice. '*Tu as vue la bête! La bête du cauchemar!*'

The baby in the lace bonnet had slept peacefully through all this, but now began to stir and mumble. Its mother nudged her husband with her elbow.

'*On va, Papa?*'

The crooning, smiling boy brought his bright pink lips down on Lizzie's forehead for a farewell kiss. She could not bear that; she struggled furiously and shouted to be put down. With that, her cover broke and she burst out of her disguise of dirt and silence; half the remaining gawpers in the tent had kin who had been bleakly buried by her father, the rest owed him money. She was the most famous daughter in all Fall River.

'Well, if it ain't Andrew Borden's little girl! What are they Canucks doing with little Lizzie Borden?'

The Mermaid

DAVID CONSTANTINE

JACK WOKE, EV was snoring, but above that sound he could hear the sea, the wind had got up, there was a big sea, the sound of it made his heart beat faster. Gently, gently, he slid out from beside her, crept to the window, parted the curtains a fraction, enough for one eye: no rain, only the wind, a sliver of draught, the sash was trembling and across the street, across the field, there was the sea coming nearer and higher, the white sea. He thought: There'll be some wreck, the breakers coming in like friendly hounds with timbers in their mouths. Glancing down Jack saw that his John Thomas was out, up and out, sticking its head out of his pyjamas into the cold room, stiff as a chairleg. Always the same when a man wakes, especially in the middle of the night if he wakes then, he mentioned it to Stan one day when they were sitting in the Folly Field watching the visitors, and Stan said his was the same whenever he woke, especially if he woke in the night, like a tableleg, so that you wondered what was going on down there when you were sleeping, all night long, something must be going on, in the mind at least, but you never remembered it, worse luck. Gently, gently Jack slid in again. The sea. He might get a nice piece of wood. What time was it? Ev had the clock on her side and her teeth, in a glass of water, guarded it, she knew the time and what time to get up and when the alarm went off Jack went downstairs and made the tea, at a quarter to eight. Ev wore a mobcap in her sleep, lay on her back and snored, her sharp little fingers gripping the eiderdown. Jack did the trick he had learned from Stan (it seemed to work): lifted and let fall back his head six times onto the pillow, to wake at six and be on the beach before anyone else, after the wood. Funny how the brain works. Jack was listening to the sea and going down nicely to where the mind whatever it thinks is not to blame, when Ev hit him suddenly on the nose with her hard elbow. The shock was frightful, his eyes wept, he felt at his upper lip whether blood was coming out. Ev snored, the clock was smiling faintly. Marvellous how a woman knows, deep down, even in her sleep, she always knows what's going on in her loved ones.

Jack went out the back way, down the garden, past his shed, into the back lane and round. It was still dark, there was nobody about. A car came by very slowly. He stood on the little street like a malefactor; then crossed, entered the field, hurried to the beach. The sea had withdrawn, the waves were milky white in a dozen layers where they spilled and ended, the widening beach was empty. Jack got to the tideline and struck along it into the wind, shingle and dunes on his right hand, the lights of town far ahead of him on the bay's long curve. The sky, lightening, was enough to see by, and new wood always showed up. He soon spotted a nice length of six by four, tugged it out of the slippy deadweight of thong and wrack, dragged it into hiding in the dunes. So he went on – a fishbox, a wicker chair, a useful pole – making caches in the dunes. Nothing like it, nothing else in his life was like getting up early after a wind in the night and scouring along a mile or so for what the sea had left. Everything pleased him, even the plastic bottles and tubes, the women's things in different languages. You never know. He had found a bed once, without its bedding, of course, but a bed all the same, thick with barnacles and weed, he couldn't budge it, there it stayed, for weeks, he felt sorry for it in the daylight and was glad when a gale took it away again, a bed on the sea, all rough and slippery and stinking.

At the seawall, that would have taken him as far as the railway station, Jack turned back. Ev would be waking and wanting her cup of tea. It was light. The first masters and mistresses were coming along the wall, out of town, and along the beach, out of the village, with their dogs. Jack took up his best piece, a plank, and shouldered it. Later he would get Stan to come down with the car and fetch the rest. The wet plank under his steadying hand, its rasping sand, its smell of brine and tar, he nestled it into his neck. He would have liked to find some wood he could carve, but mostly it was cheap timber used for packing, or it had been in the water too long. Once he had found a log he thought he might do something with, four or five feet long and about nine inches thick, very smooth, he carried it home, it was surprisingly light. The worms were in it, shipworm, he split it and all the naked creatures, as squelchy as oysters, were brought to light in their honeycomb. Soon the two lengths, leaning against the wall, began to stink, and Ev made him take them back to the beach. He went to the trouble of throwing them back into the water at high tide, but by then, needless to say, the worms in their wooden cells were dead.

Stan said he would get Jack a nice piece of wood to carve. His neighbour had cut down a cherry tree, it was blocking the light. He cut it down one Sunday while it was flowering. Stan said the neighbour's wife was heartbroken. She was a very handsome woman, he visited her sometimes with little presents from the garden, her husband was away, driving around up country on financial business.

Stan and Jack met in the Folly Field and sat on a bench watching the visitors. In summer they liked to watch the girls going into the sea and coming out again. Stan had a word for the very short skirts they wore: he called them fanny-pelmets. Jack said the word to himself as he walked home and while he was doing woodwork in the shed. The next time he came into the Folly Field, Stan was already sitting there with a fat log of cherry wood between his knees. Mrs Wilberforce's compliments, he said. Most of the visitors had gone, there was nobody much to look at. Here, said Stan, take a look at this. And slid a pair of nutcrackers from his inside pocket, a carved black woman, naked, as a pair of nutcrackers. The nut goes in between her legs and when you squeeze, it cracks. Ethel won 'em at the Chapel ladies' whistdrive.

Jack came in the back way but Ev was at the kitchen window looking out. Jack had the log on his shoulder. He smiled, and pointed at it. Ev came into the garden, wiping her hands. That friend of yours, she said. He had it off a neighbour, Jack replied. They chopped it down, it was taking up too much light. Ev liked the look of the cherry wood. Make a nice something, she said. Take that filthy coat off before you come in. Jack laid the log on his workbench in the shed. Its bark was red and smooth. Such a beautiful length of tree. Jack stroked it, sniffed it, laid his cheek on it. Time you finished me that stool, said Ev when he came in. Nearly done, he said, one of the legs was wrong.

Next day Jack went out early picking mushrooms. They grew in the field across the street. Must have been horses in there years ago, he said to Stan. Funny to think of them nearly on the beach. Jack had a secretive way of picking mushrooms. He was sure he was the only one who knew they were growing in that field. He was out early, but other people might be out as well walking their dogs. He held a plastic bag under his old raincoat. He held on to it with his left hand through a big hole in the pocket. That way he could slip the mushrooms in and nobody noticed. Sometimes he had to stand over one and pretend to be looking out to sea. The Minister's wife was passing with her alsatian. She said: Good morning, Mr Little. Good morning, Mrs Blunt, said Jack. He picked a good lot and sorted out the best of them in his shed. They were for Mrs Wilberforce. The rest he took in for himself and Ev, to breakfast on. Not so many this morning, he said, I dunno why. Your eyesight's going, I shouldn't wonder, said Ev. She was partial to mushrooms with a bit of crispy bacon. When the tea was made and they sat down in the little kitchen by the fire she would become quite jovial and holding up a mouthful of mushroom on her fork would say, for a joke, that she hoped he wasn't poisoning her. How black the morsel looked when she held it up. No danger of that, said

Jack, eating his own with relish. He was so fond of the feel and smell of mushrooms when he was picking them and of their taste when he was eating them that he could scarcely believe they were not forbidden him. And what a strange thing to come of horse-piss! It was a miracle you could eat one and not die.

After breakfast Jack went out into his shed. To finish that stool, I hope, said Ev. Later he slipped out to the Folly Field with the mushrooms for Mrs Wilberforce in a little wicker basket. Give her these, he said to Stan. And thank her very much. She can keep the basket too. I found it on the beach. Stan set off at once. Always glad of an excuse to call on Mrs Wilberforce, he said.

Jack came in at dinner time with the stool. It was a four-legged one, quite low. I put a bit of decoration on it, he said, to brighten it up. Yes, he had carved the seat into the likeness of a smiling face. It's the sun, he said. Uncomfortable to sit on, I should think, said Ev. Still, I can always cover it with a cushion, and it will be handy for standing on, to reach the Christmas pudding down.

There was not much doing in the Folly Field, most of the visitors had gone. The little fair had shut, all but the roundabout. She's having her morning, said Jack. The house is full. I can tell you what they'll be talking about, said Stan. You heard the news? Jack hadn't. Councillor Rabbit exposing himself in Chapel. Jack shook his head. There's something wrong with us, he said. They were singing 'Love divine, all loves excelling' when Betty Creeble looked across the aisle and there he was with it out. Of course, when she'd seen it he hung his hat on it. But by then she was hysterical. He'd just been round for the collection too. Jack shook his head. Whatever's wrong with us? The Minister's having a word with him, said Stan. Stan's daughter was coming across the Folly Field with her boy and girl. Down for a week or so, said Stan. She got a husband yet? Jack asked. She was eating an ice cream cornet. Seems not, said Stan, doesn't seem to want one either. The children ran to the roundabout and climbed into a fire engine together. They were the only customers. The girl began ringing the bell. Then they were off. Stan kept up with them and did the circuit several times, prancing and neighing like a little horse. Jack was glad their mother was not wearing a very short skirt, but her jacket was open on a pretty blouse. Dad'll give himself a heart attack, she said. Your ice cream's coming out the bottom, said Jack, if you don't mind my saying so. He felt for a handkerchief to wipe her blouse, but dared not bring it out. Never mind, she said, and put her mouth under the cone where it was leaking. Jack paid for the children to have another ride. Stan went on hands and knees in the opposite direction. The boy looked as dark as a southern Italian, the girl was as blonde as corn. Then the owner gave them a ride for nothing. Jack tugged his beret and said he'd better be off. Not going in, are you? said Stan. You must be mad. I'll be in my shed, said Jack, doing my carving. Tell Mrs W I'm doing a mermaid.

When he was carving Jack always thought of school. It was in the country, the boys came in from the farms. They were slow at words and figures, but it had happened every year that a boy in one or other of Jack's classes discovered he could use his hands. Never knew I had it in me, they used to say. They did some lovely work, Jack had some in the attic still, it was better than his own, and when they outdid him he was proud of them, he had shown them they could do it, that was his part and he was proud of that. They made serviceable things, he guessed there must be hundreds of useful household things still being used in that region of the country in the homes and perhaps even abroad. And if a boy ever asked him specially and they could get the wood, he let him carve whatever he liked, a bird or an animal, for a present. During the war there was a camp near the school, for prisoners of war, Italians, they were marvellously good with their hands. Jack slipped them pieces of wood whenever he dared and they gave him back what they had made of it with their clasp knives, in exchange for cigarettes. Once he had a crib given him at Christmas: an ox, an ass, the manger, the baby Jesus, Mother Mary and Joseph and a couple of shepherds, all simple, warm and true, they were lovely to feel in the hands. They must be still in the house somewhere, Ev had never liked them much, he thought every Christmas of giving them to somebody with children.

Jack knew that his own hands were not especially skilful. Mrs Wilberforce's log of cherry was too good for him. But he had an idea, he knew what he was trying to do. It was common knowledge what a mermaid looked like. She must have long hair and a fishy lower half and be carrying a comb and mirror. Jack thought he could do the fish scales pretty well, like leaves, like a low long skirt, and it was there that he had begun, below the waist, and she was taking shape. Time passed him quietly by. When Ev called him in for dinner he started like a guilty man and hid his carving under a pile of potato sacks.

I hear the illegits are down again, said Ev as they ate their cod. Jack admitted that he had seen them on the Folly Field. The man gave 'em a free ride, he said. I wonder she shows her face down here, said Ev. I wonder Ethel gives 'em house room. Seem nice enough to me, said Jack. They would to you, said Ev. But it's the mother I blame. Poor illegits, how'll they ever manage, I'd like to know. I wonder Ethel can look me in the face. Jack finished up his cod. He was thinking of the children on the roundabout, one blonde, one dark, and of the young woman's blouse and how she had stood next to him and given him a friendly smile. Then he wondered what Mrs Wilberforce would have to say about the illegits, and whether she was really interested in his carving. I see you put a cushion on my sun, he said. Looks better, said Ev. Behind her, on the wall, was a piece of marquetry he had done when they were married. It showed the church they were married in. He felt a crumpling sadness at the sight of it, and a sort of pity for them both. He rose. I'll see to these, he said, taking the plates, which were green and in the shape of obese fish. You'll want a nap after your morning with the ladies. There's pudding, said Ev. You know very well I always do a pudding. When she came in again – it was spotted dick – Jack said, wishing to smooth her: Bad business at the Chapel, so I hear. No woman's safe, said Ev, not even when she's singing hymns. Who told you anyway? That Stan, I suppose. I'll see to these, said Jack, as soon as he could. You'll be wanting a nap after your ladies.

Jack sent another gift of mushrooms to Mrs Wilberforce. Tell her she can keep the little box, he said. I found it on the beach. She says thank you very much, said Stan, and how's the mermaid coming on? Tell her she's coming on very well, said Jack. Her tail was done, he had even managed to give a flourish to the extremity. Then he dug out a little hole for her belly-button and that was it, all of the bottom half of her was done. Now for the rest. He admitted to Stan that he was going to find the upper half more difficult. I mean, he said, everyone knows what a fish looks like. He knew as soon as he came up to her hips and when he was making the hole and the little bulge (like half a cherry) for her belly-button that the rest of her was going to be difficult. The sea was quiet, the roundabout and every other amusement in the Folly Field had closed, on the beach the Minister's wife was unleashing her alsatian. No wreck, said Stan. Nothing, said Jack. What's Ethel say about you visiting Mrs W? Nothing, said Stan. I go in through the garden, behind the bonfire, she never misses me. You mean you do your visiting in your gardening coat? Doesn't bother her, said Stan. And what d'you do up there? Stan had the face of a childish devil when he grinned, and his hands, when he rubbed them together, sounded as though they felt like bark. Have a chat, he said, have a cup of tea. Nothing else besides? A saffron bun maybe, if I touch lucky. Jack did not know where Mrs Wilberforce lived exactly. Some days he might have gone that far and called on Stan, but his usual walk was along the beach as far as the seawall or along the front as far as the Folly Field. That way Ev knew where he was. What's she like? he asked. I've maybe seen her on Thursdays in the post office. Fullish, said Stan, and blonde.

The ladies Ev had when it was her turn to entertain were mostly grey, grey or white, but not an old colour, more like a frost and snow scene on a Christmas card. They came in talking and when they were in they began to shout. When it was over they shouted at the door, and went away again talking. They often wore blue, and jewellery, their mouths were done in red, and certainly one or two of them were fullish. Sometimes the noise they were making suddenly grew louder and Jack was worried in his shed that they might be coming out to visit him, to do him a serious mischief in a friendly sort of way. Mrs Blunt had a face which was massive and immensely powerful around the jaws, her tongue was like a steak. Betty Creeble (the lady whom Councillor Rabbit had offended) seemed to have fractured as a flint does, rather than to have worn as will, for example, chalk. Jack thought Ev's ladies fiercer than buffalo. Must be very nice, he said, at Mrs W's, I mean. Some conversation with a well-spoken woman must be very nice. Stan offered to take him along next time he went – Come up the ditch, he said, and meet me by the bonfire – or next time Ev had her ladies, to be on the safe side; but Jack declined. He was gazing at his hands. Using the chisels and the hammer so much had made them sore.

Half way. Jack decided to start at the top and work down to her middle. He gave her a round face, like the moon, but left it blank for the time being and did her hair which he imagined a golden blonde, he took it right down her back to where her fishy half began. She was lying face down, her front was unspoiled trunk of cherry tree, and he did her hair, spreading it so that her bare back was covered, streams of hair, plaited, in long knots, a semblance of wrack and thong, as was fitting. Then he hid her under the sacks and went in to wash his hands.

By the way, said Ev, as they ate their haddock, I've thought what you can do me with that nice piece of wood. The haddock was yellower than usual. Funny how very unlike a fish it looked. I'll have a lighthouse that lights up. That would be very unusual, don't you think? You mean with a flashing light? Jack asked. Yes, flashing, said Ev. And if we stand it in the corner no one'll see the wires. And do some waves around the bottom to make it look more real. I see what you mean, said Jack. But I think you'll need a longer piece, and not so fat. It's long enough, said Ev, and you can shave it if it's fat.

The bare lightbulb, the steam of his tea, the smells of wood and of the seashore. Jack lifted the mermaid out in her sacks and uncovered her. She was face up, a blank round face, her arms were still encased in the unquarried wood. He had decided she would be empty-handed after all. He had decided she would be hugging herself as though she were cold. The hair came down her shoulders as far as her waist like a cloak, but open, entirely open, at the front, so she was cold. Used to the sea, and cold? The air was colder. He gave her an open face, her smile was innocent and broad, but her eyes were so wide open it was shock her looks expressed. He roughed out her arms the way he wanted them. It was time to begin dividing and shaping her breasts. Happy valley, as Stan said. But the time was a quarter to eight and Ev had woken and would be expecting her cup of tea. Mushrooms, she said when he came in with the tray and wished her good morning. You haven't been out, I don't suppose. Just off, he said. But they're getting to the end, you know.

Soon there were no more mushrooms, neither for Ev nor for Mrs Wilberforce, the nights drew in, the mornings were darker. Jack walked on the beach as far as the seawall or sat with Stan in the deserted Folly Field. I'm doing her bust, he said. Get me some oil, will you, next time you're in town. And he gave him the money out of the pocket without a hole. Ev wants a lighthouse, he added, one that flashes.

Her bust, her breasts. Jack was doing them after an idea he had of a woman's breasts in perfection in his head. By her slim arms, vertical and horizontal, they were enclosed and given a lovely and entirely natural prominence. Day after day, in the early mornings as it grew light and in the late afternoons as it grew dark, Jack was working on the mermaid's breasts with a love and patience that were a wonder to him afterwards. He was glad to have finished with the necessary chisels and the knives. Now he eased the finer and finer sandpapers with oil to induce the wood to become as smooth as skin. Her hair was rough, as it should be, and all of her fishy half, and even her face he was happy to leave like a doll's with broad features, but on her huddled shoulders, her hugging arms, and on her breasts that were like young creatures in a nest or fold, he worked, in the sweet wood, for the perfect smoothness of a human and living form. He was in a trance of work, under the bare bulb, his mug of tea absentmindedly to hand, the sky outside either lightening or darkening. It put him in mind of the best work ever done by the most gifted boys (surprising themselves) in all his years at school, and of the animals reached out through the wire by the prisoners of war in exchange for a couple of Woodbines or a twist of tea. The memory – the association – filled him with pride. After such work he came into his own house like a stranger.

There was a big sea. Jack lay awake, listening. He would wake himself early, but not to go looking for wood. His time before Ev woke was for the mermaid. He lay awake in the night, thinking. The sea came nearer. Jack was thinking of the illegits, and of their mother, Stan's daughter, who had stood beside him carelessly in the Folly Field.

Next morning after breakfast Jack climbed into the loft and found the nativity carvings. They were in a shoebox wrapped in brown paper. When he unwrapped them on the dining-room table they gave him a shock, it was years since he had had them out, and when he took the animals and the human figures one by one into his sore hands he felt a joy and a grief that bewildered him. He fitted the baby into the crib, set father and mother at the head, and crowded the shepherds and the ox and the ass around as though their curiosity were greater even than their reverence. The carving was rough, but every figure had its own liveliness, its dignity and an almost comical manifest good nature. Jack was entranced, like a child, he sat at the table staring, reached now and then for the ox or for Joseph or for the mother herself, as though by pressing them in his grip he could get a little way further into the feelings that were troubling him. He felt regret, but also a sort of gladness and gratitude that he was coming nearer to the source of his regret. Then Ev's voice said: What d'you want getting them out for? She startled him, she stood facing him across the table and her face had slipped, he had never seen such a look on her before, she looked momentarily disfigured as though a stroke had halted her and set her oddly in relation to the world. Well? she said. Well? Her voice had gone strange. Jack was balancing Joseph and Mary in either hand. Thought I'd give 'em to the illegits, he said. Thought they'd look nice where there's a Christmas tree. Ev screamed, once, then again, it was a sound that seemed to have in it nothing at all of personal volition, as though she were ripped. Then she sat at the table and began to weep. Jack put the figures back into the shoebox and the brown paper around it easily resumed its folds. It was paper of a kind no longer ever seen, thick and with an oily texture. Written on it in Ev's big capitals, in purple copy pencil, was the one word NATIVITY. I'll have to get some more string, said Jack.

As he stood up with the box in his hands Ev uncovered her face. And where's my lighthouse? she asked. That would have been nice for Christmas in the corner. It was an ordinary morning in November, a Thursday. Shan't I be going to the post office? said Jack. Don't change the subject, Ev replied. I want my lighthouse. Jack set down the nativity box again, went down the garden to his shed, took up the mermaid in her sacks and carried her thus into the living room. There he unwrapped her on the table, turned on the standard lamp and set her upright on the orange floral chair. I made this instead, he said. Ev stared, said nothing, only stared at the mermaid standing on her fishy tail and smiling foolishly and hugging her breasts as though she were very cold. Ev said: So that's what you've been down there doing. Yes, said Jack. What do you think? Nice, said Ev, very nice. A mermaid will be very unusual. Her voice was quiet, Jack was beginning to smile. So you don't mind then? Stan says he'll get me another log. He tells me Mrs W's got one left. Mrs W, eh? said Ev. So that's where you get your pieces of wood from, is it? Just the one, said Jack. But she'll very likely give me another, for your lighthouse.

Very nice, Ev said again. She was standing in the lamplight next to the floral chair on which the mermaid was standing. Only one little thing, she said: Her tits will have to come off. Pardon me? said Jack. Cut 'em off, said Ev. I have my ladies round. They can't be expected to look at things like that. It isn't fit. You'll cut 'em off. Then she'll be very nice. Quite unusual really. Jack was looking at his hands. They were calloused and sore from the work he had done on the mermaid. Ev, he said. Her face was remarkable for its infinite creases and wrinkles, but her hair was newly permed. She was smiling, she seemed on the verge of a sort of hilarity. It wouldn't be natural, said Jack. Who ever saw a mermaid without a bust? That's not the point, said Ev. You'll do as I say. Jack got to his feet. He found that his hands were trembling. He took up the mermaid and was wrapping her safely in the potato sacks. Ev said: And don't think I'm having her down there in your shed. She belongs in my front room. I'm having her on show. Jack backed away, hugging his burden.

When he came in again the table was laid for dinner. The nativity box was lying on the hearth empty. The fire was burning very fiercely. Ev set before him the pale-green fish-shaped plate. I've done you a nice piece of sole, she said.

Jack sat in the Folly Field with Stan. He was cold. She wants me to cut her bust off, he said. Hell hath no fury, said Stan. I don't follow, said Jack. I told her it wouldn't look natural, but she's adamant. He did not tell Stan about the nativity figures. He was ashamed. Stan finished his cigarette and tossed it away towards the empty beach. I'll tell you what, he said. Why don't you give her to Mrs Wilberforce? She's always asking how you're getting on. Jack was tempted, he was very tempted. His heart raced at the proposal. Though he could not be certain that he had ever seen Mrs Wilberforce, the idea of her, the idea in his head, which came not only when he sat with Stan in the Folly Field, was luminous and detailed. In spirit at least he often sat alongside Stan on the comfortable sofa in her parlour drinking tea and, on the luckiest days, eating one of her buns whilst the winter evening drew in. She lit the lamp, but left the big curtains open to watch the starlings hurtle past on a livid sky. And she might ask Stan would he mind throwing another log on the fire, and there they sat, making conversation without any difficulty, and she was indeed, as

Stan had often said, a handsome woman. No doubt about it, the mermaid would look very well in that room. The sea was not *so* far distant (you could hear it when the wind was right), and the noise the big trees made when there was a wind in them was very like the sea. And didn't the mermaid belong there after all, to make up for the flowering cherry tree which Mrs W had been so sorry to lose? She'd murder me, he said. She'd never know, said Stan. She would, said Jack. She finds out everything when her ladies come. Pity, said Stan. Would have made a nice present. Jack wondered whether his friend was deceiving him. Perhaps Mrs Wilberforce never asked after him, perhaps she had never heard he was making a mermaid, perhaps Stan would present it to her one evening as the work of his own hands. Suddenly Jack even doubted whether he had been given any credit for the mushrooms. Stan could be very sly. Jack recalled numerous instances of his slyness in the course of their long friendship. Jack had become very downhearted by the time he said goodbye.

Jack switched the light on and unwrapped the mermaid. She lay on her back, her face as round as the moon, a helpless smile, hugging herself for cold. He was amazed at his achievement; or call it luck, a once in a lifetime abundance of good luck. The way her breasts were was exactly how the idea of them was in his head. He laid his cheek on them, closed his eyes, took into the blood of his heart her scent of oil and wood. Then he left her uncovered on the workbench, under the bare bulb.

Ev was getting the tea ready, a nice salad. Well? she said, chopping a cucumber. What if I made 'em a bit smaller? said Jack. Ev put a hardboiled egg in the egg slicer. Cut 'em off, she said.

Next day, in the afternoon, Ev had her ladies. Jack took an unusual walk, away from the Folly Field. He walked through the village to the cemetery, and sat there for an hour or so looking out to sea. When it got dark he came home again, though he knew that the ladies would only just be having their tea. He could hear them from the kitchen, they were in the front room and the door was closed, their noise seemed greater than he had ever heard it. Were they more numerous? Had every lady in the Chapel come? He went a little way into the hall. The ladies were in the highest spirits. They beat at one another with their voices. Jack went a little nearer, applied his ear. But nothing vey distinct was audible. He bowed himself, he knelt, he applied his eye. He saw his mermaid. She had been brought out of the corner and was standing on her tail in an easy chair. She smiled her smile, without any hope of pleasing. It seemed to Jack that the space within her arms was cavernous. Then she was obscured by a welter of blue and silver and gold. The hairdos of the ladies fitted their heads like shining helmets, their mouths, open for an enormous hilarity, were as red as jam. Jack rose very slowly and out of habit made towards the back door and the garden – but bethought himself and turned and climbed the stairs to bed.

Jack woke in the night, there was a high wind, Ev was snoring by his side, but above that sound he could hear the sound of the sea, the sea had risen, he imagined it foaming white and slung across the bay from point to point. There'll be some wreck, he thought, and did the trick with his head he had learned from Stan. He rose secretly before first light and taking his old coat from the garden shed was soon on the beach along the high water mark. The tide had turned and was beginning to withdraw, it dragged down the shingle like a death rattle. The weed was a yard high, packed solid. The wind had scarcely lessened and there was rain on it. Jack's small exaltation left him at once. He could see no wood, nor anything else worth picking up. The lights of the railway station and the town looked infinitely beyond his strength, even the seawall was too far, he skidded and stumbled in the weed and on the pebbles. Then it was enough, and he halted. Rolled in weed there was a dead thing at his feet, a seal, and for no good reason he began to tug at the slippery stuff, to free it. He got the head clear and the flippers, then desisted. One eye had gone, the other was beaten in, the head, so shapely on a living beast in water, was monstrous. And all below was deadweight in a stinking winding sheet.

A wet light eastwards over home. Jack stood. In the narrow strip between the shingle and the surf a man and his dog were making their way. Jack moved from the cadaver as though he were guilty. The walker was Councillor Rabbit and his dog, a dachshund, trotted beside him on a lead. Meeting Jack, he cast down his eyes and halted to let him pass. But Jack addressed him. Wet, he said, I'm turning back. Councillor Rabbit was a big man in a trilby, which he had to clutch hold of or the wind would have taken it. He wore a very large herringbone overcoat and polished Oxford shoes. His face, when he allowed Jack to look into it, was as sorrowful as a bloodhound's. It had slipped, it had collapsed. Though Jack had hardly exchanged a word with him in all the years, he grasped him now almost familiarly by the elbow and turned him towards home. He did not want the dog to go sniffing at the seal.

Councillor Rabbit was easily led. There was enough room for the two men and the dachshund to walk side by side between the pebbles and the waves. You never let him off? said Jack, nodding down at the adipose dog. Safer the way he is, said the Councillor. Besides, he's going blind. From under the brim of his trilby he was glancing fearfully at Jack. They made their way, exchanging remarks about this and that. What's he called? Jack asked. Billy, said the Councillor. The little dog's belly left a trail on the wet sand. He's not much of a runner, said the Councillor. As they neared the dunes and the wider beach below the Folly Field other dogs and their masters and mistresses appeared. I generally come out early, said the Councillor. You'll maybe want to go ahead. No, no, said Jack. I'm in no hurry. And again he touched the Councillor amicably on the elbow. First came the Minister's wife, Mrs Blunt, and her alsatian. It was bounding free, in and out of the retreating tide, and others were advancing after her, more or less frolicsome and fierce. The Councillor was inclined to halt, it seemed he might have stared into the dunes until the trade and Chapel people had all passed, but Jack with gentle touches to the elbow kept him going. So they shuffled forwards, Jack and Councillor Rabbit and between them, on a tight lead, Billy the little wheezing dog.

Craigavon Bridge

SEAMUS DEANE

FATHER REGAN WAS lighting a candle in his dark classroom at the foot of the statue of the Blessed Virgin. Regan permitted no overhead lights when he gave his formal religious address at the beginning of our last year in school. Regan was small, neat, economical. After he said 'Boys,' he stopped for a bit and looked at us. Then he dropped his eyes and kept them down until he said, more loudly this time, 'Boys.' He had complete silence this time.

'Some of you here, one or two of you perhaps, know the man I am going to talk about today. You may not know you know him, but that doesn't matter.

'More than thirty years ago, during the troubles in Derry, this man was arrested and charged with the murder of a policeman. The policeman had been walking home one night over Craigavon Bridge. It was a bleak night, November, nineteen hundred and twenty-two. The time was two in the morning. The policeman was off duty; he was wearing civilian clothes. There were two men coming the other way, on the other side of the bridge. As the policeman neared the middle of the bridge, these two men crossed over to his side. They were strolling, talking casually. They had their hats pulled down over their faces and their coat collars turned up for it was wet and cold. As they passed the policeman, one of them said "Goodnight" and the policeman returned the greeting. And then suddenly he found himself grabbed from behind and lifted off his feet. He tried to kick but one of the men held his legs. "This is for Neil McLaughlin," said one. "May you rot in the hell you're going to, you murdering bastard." They lifted him to the parapet and held him there for a minute like a log and let him stare down at the water – seventy, eighty feet below. Then they pushed him over and he fell, with the street lights shining on his wet coat until he disappeared into the shadows with a splash. They heard him thrashing and he shouted once. Then he went under. His body was washed up three days later. No one saw them. They went home and they said nothing.

'A week later a man was arrested and charged with the murder. He was brought to trial. But the only evidence the police had was that he was the friend and workmate of Neil McLaughlin, who had been murdered by a policeman a month before. The story was that, before McLaughlin died on the street where he had been shot, coming out of the newspaper office where he worked, he had whispered the name of his killer to this man who had been arrested. And this man had been heard to swear revenge, to get the policeman – let's call him Mahon – in revenge for his friend's death. There was no point in going to the law, of course; justice would never be done; everyone knew that, especially in those years. So maybe the police thought they could beat an admission out of him, but he did not flinch from his story. That night he was not even in the city. He had been sent by his newspaper to Letterkenny twenty miles away, and he had several witnesses to prove it. The case was thrown out. People were surprised, even though they believed the man to be innocent. Innocence was no guarantee for a Catholic then. Nor is it now.

'Well, I wasn't even in the city in those days. But I met this man several times and we became friendly. I was then a young curate and this man was prominent in local sporting circles and he helped in various ways to raise money for the parish building fund. One night, in the sacristy of the Long Tower

Church, just down the road from here, he told me that he had not been to confession in twenty years. He had something on his conscience that no penance could relieve. I told him to trust in God's infinite mercy; I offered to hear his confession; I offered to find someone else, a monk I knew down in Portglenone, to whom he could go, in case he did not want to confess to me. But no, he wouldn't go. No penance, he said, would be any use, because, in his heart, he could not feel sorrow for what he had done. But he wanted to tell someone, not as a confession, but in confidence.

'So he told me about being arrested. He told me about the beatings he had been given – rubber truncheons, punches, kicks, threats to put him over the bridge. He told me how he had resisted these assaults and never wavered.

' "Oh," I said, "that's just a testimony to the strength you get from knowing you are in the right."

'He looked at me in amazement. "D'ye think that's what I wanted to tell you? The story of my innocence? For God's sake, Father, can't you see? I wasn't innocent. I was guilty. I killed Mahon and I'd kill him again if he came through that door this minute. That's why I can't confess. I have no sorrow, no resolve not to do it again. No pity. Mahon shot my best friend dead in the street, for nothing. He was a drunken policeman with a gun, looking for a Teague to kill, and he left that man's wife with two young children and would have got off scot-free for the rest of his days, probably promoted for sterling service. And Neil told me as he lay there, with the blood draining from him, that Mahon did it. 'Billy Mahon, Billy Mahon, the policeman,' that's what he said. And even then, I had to run back into the doorway and leave his body there in the street because they started shooting down the street from the city walls. And I'm not sorry I got Mahon and I told him what it was for before I threw him over that bridge and he knew, just too late, who I was when I said 'Goodnight' to him. It was goodnight all right. One murdering bastard less."

'Boys, that man went to the grave without confessing that sin. And think of all the wrongs that were done in that incident. Two men were murdered. Two men – three, for there was another man whose name was never mentioned – were murderers. Indeed maybe there was another murderer, for it's possible that Mahon was not the policeman involved. And there were perjurers who swore that the accused was elsewhere that night. And there were policemen who assaulted a man in custody. And there were judges who would certainly have acquitted any policeman, no matter how guilty, and would have found guilty any Catholic, no matter how innocent, on the slightest shred of evidence. The whole situation makes men evil. Evil men make the whole situation. And these days, similar things occur. Some of you boys may feel like getting involved when you leave school, because you sincerely believe that you would be on the side of justice, fighting for the truth. But, boys, let me tell you, there is a judge who sees all, knows all and is never unjust; there is a judge whose punishments and rewards are beyond the range of human imagining; there is a Law greater than the laws of human justice, far greater than the law of revenge, more enduring than the laws of any state whatsoever. That Judge is God, that Law is God's Law and the issue at stake is your immortal soul.

'We live, boys, in a world that will pass away. The shadows that candle throws upon the walls of this room are as substantial as we. Injustice, tyranny, freedom, national independence are realities that will fade too, for they are not ultimate realities and the only life worth living is a life lived in the light of the ultimate. I know there are some who believe that the poor man who committed that murder was justified, and that he will be forgiven by an all-merciful God for what he did. That may be. I fervently hope that it is so, for who would judge God's mercy? But it is true too of the policeman; he may have been as plagued by guilt as his own murderer; he may have justified himself too; he may have refused sorrow and known no peace of mind; he may have forgiven himself or he may have been forgiven by God. It is not for us to judge. But it is for us to distinguish, to see the difference between wrong done to us and equal wrong done by us; to know that our transient life, no matter how scarred, how broken, how miserable it may be, is also God's miracle and gift; that we may try to improve it, but we may not destroy it. If we destroy it in another, we destroy it in ourselves. Boys, as you enter upon your last year with us, you are on the brink of entering a world of wrong, insult, injury, unemployment, a world where the unjust hold power and the ignorant rule. But there is an inner peace nothing can reach; no insult can violate, no corruption can deprave. Hold to that; it is what your childish innocence once was and what your adult maturity must become. Hold to that. I bless you all.'

And he raised his hand and made the sign of the Cross above our heads and crossed the room, blew out the candle as the bell rang wildly in the chapel tower, and asked that the light be switched on. He left in silence with the candle smoking heavily behind him at the foot of the statue, stubby in its thick drapery of wax.

'That was your grandfather,' said McShane to me. 'I know that story too.'

I derided him. I had heard the story too, but I wasn't going to take it on before everyone else. Anyway, it was just folklore. I had heard it when I was much younger and lay on the landing at night listening to the grown-ups talking in the kitchen below and had leaned over the banisters and imagined it was the edge of the parapet and that I was falling, falling down to the river of the hallway, as deaf and shining as a log.

Love of Fat Men

HELEN DUNMORE

LOVE OF FAT men. Ulli would like to go and see a film with this title. She would buy herself a fistful of Panda liquorice and a daytime ticket and sit there and watch it through again and again, until the usherette sent for the manager.

And another good thing about films is that people who are of average weight in real life look dense, almost majestic, once they are on film. Because the camera loves absences. Flesh that isn't there. Hollows under cheekbones. A shadow under the jaw which writes a whole false story of intellect and suffering into the face of a man who spends all day wondering whether he has done right to have both ears pierced, or should he have left it at one? Speaking of ear-rings, she loves them too. She thinks of a man who was in a promising way to be fat one day. For now he makes do with a curve of the jowl, a faint trace that time will roll out in flesh. Around his lips there is a gloss of oil. He has always just finished eating spaghetti. And not cheap dried macaroni either. He has a pasta machine in his kitchen. He strips off long ribbons of slippery translucent dough and coats them in virgin green olive oil and eats them just as they are. He says it is a waste of time trying to make sauce with the tomatoes they grow in this country, which are only fit for throwing at dogs. Instead of this he makes anchovy spaghetti and tagliatelle with pesto for his friends, which they eat with strong sharp wine. An hour or two later they are hungry again. His name is Lucca, like the city. Or at least, this is what he calls himself. He has a family which is even more secret than her own. But she hopes that she will not discover one day that Lucca has a mother and father sitting in a one-bedroom apartment in the outskirts of Helsinki, dreaming of their summer house, and visits from Lucca. She likes small lies to remain as they are, lying, seductive, growing their own flesh out of hints and silences.

What a tombstone it would make, too. Here lies a liar.

Ulli knows she isn't Lucca's type. But he is fond of her. He is her friend. Ulli's not being his type means that he can come round to her room and sprawl on her bed eating packets of macaroons or Danish pastries which he has bought at a cakeshop in the city centre. He makes quite a long detour in order to buy these particular macaroons, fragile and yet chewy at the centre, flavoured with almonds rather than with almond essence. When Lucca has been spending the afternoon in Ulli's room there are frail crackling crumbs in the bed all night and transparent grease stains on the quilt cover. But she doesn't mind. He buys tiny triangular apricot pastries for her, and makes better coffee to go with them than she ever makes herself. Come to think of it that is the only time he stands up. When Lucca visits, he lies.

He asks Ulli about what he refers to as her love-life. In the hope that it will stop him using this expression, which she dislikes, Ulli has told him that her own grandmother used to ask exactly the same question, when Ulli was about sixteen.

'How's your love-life, Ulli?'

Ulli pictures her love-life as an elusive but rapacious animal which nobody else has ever seen. This is why they keep asking after it.

Lucca always smells so clean. He smells of clean cotton and sharp lemon soap and almonds and vanilla. Sometimes he smells of sugar, but she doesn't like that so much. Or he smells of garlic and wine, and the parsley he chews after meals to freshen his breath. Lucca is the only person she has ever seen eating a bunch of parsley sprig by sprig. It is full of iron, he tells her. If she eats enough garlic and parsley she will get through the whole winter without flu or a cold.

Ulli is not Lucca's type, but he likes her hair, because it is long and very soft, with a watery feel to it when it is newly-washed. He feels that he could look after it better than she does herself. So sometimes she'll give it over to him for the afternoon. Her head goes with it of course, but they don't mind that. She sits on the floor by the bed and Lucca rolls over so that he can spread the hair out over the quilt, lift it and brush it out and run his hands down it, then plait it again. He can do a French plait, and once he has done this Ulli wriggles away from him, because she likes this style and is not able to do it for herself. But as soon as he has done it he always wants to unplait it again, to stroke and weigh and twist the hair into new shapes, to let it drop free. Sometimes he plaits ribbons into it. Sometimes he puts it up and pins it on the top of her head. But it's too severe for her like that, he says. It will suit her better when she's older. He tells her how she will look when she is thirty, if she is lucky and things go well for her. He says that she's lazy and she ought to have her hair trimmed regularly at the hairdresser's instead of letting one of her girl-friends snip round the bottom of it with a pair of cheap sewing scissors.

'It saves money,' says Ulli, 'You aren't going to eat all that macaroon, are you? Let me have the outside bits.'

She is not Lucca's type, but he says that she reminds him of his sisters. He doesn't say much about them, but she has the impression that they are a little younger than she is, still at home, three girls with long hair and lively sliding eyes crammed into one bedroom with pictures of Switzerland on the wall. No popstars. They like Switzerland, for some reason. The eldest of them is planning to work there as an au-pair, before she goes to college. They are all bright girls, Lucca says, much brighter than he is. He says they adore speaking English.

Lucca's sisters do not live in jeans like Ulli. They make their own clothes: suits and skirts and fitted jackets. Then they lend them to one another, because they are all as near the same size as makes no difference, and they go out on summer evenings in jade green, in cerise, in butter-yellow, in soft cream. Ulli wonders if they are still virgins. Perhaps they would have to be, in one room. Or perhaps there is a system for sharing the men, as there is for sharing the clothes, so that no one gets over-attached to one garment, or one manner of making love.

Next week, Lucca says, he has been asked to a sauna party in the country about fifty kilometres away. Does Ulli want to come?

'Will your sisters be there?' asked Ulli.

'Of course not! What would my sisters be doing at such a party? They wouldn't know anybody.'

'Will I?'

'Oh, I should think so. One or two. And anyway you'll like the others. They'll be your type.'

'How do we get there? I'm not going on the bus.'

'I've fixed it. We're borrowing a car.'

'Whose?'

'I don't think you know him.'

'Come round on the Friday then, and put my hair in a French plait.'

'Not if you're going to wear those jeans.'

'Fine, I'll wear it loose.'

She stands up and nearly treads on their dirty coffee cups. Lucca smiles at her from the bed. Looking at him from this angle, she thinks that it is a pity she is not his type.

By midnight on Saturday Ulli knows that she's not going to meet anyone at the party. Only half an hour ago the rooms were thick with dancers. People were spilling out onto the wooden verandah and into the garden beyond to enjoy the mothy dusk of a summer night. Couples drifted under the trees, twining and consuming one another. If you blinked, they were gone.

And they've gone. Strangers, acquaintances, lovers, it's all one now. It doesn't matter. For those who've found some-body, all that matters is now. For those who've found somebody the night has narrowed to an intake of breath, and a little pulse of sweat. They laugh with eagerness. They sprawl

63

and ache on the sand down by the shore. They share a cigarette and blur each other's lips with dry whispers.

Ulli steps out onto the veranda and sips from her potent little glass of mesimarja.* The dew settles on her bare arms. The rail of the veranda is damp. Its paint peels under her hands. The family is not staying here this summer. There will be a party or two, a weekend, perhaps some sailing. But nobody will have time to sand down the veranda railings and coat them with primer and paint them so that they last through the winter ahead. That's the kind of job you do when you go to the summer house for weeks on end, the kind of job you do towards the middle of August when the days are already getting shorter and you are starting to think of berry-picking and mushroom gathering in the forest. And hauling the boat out of the water to clean the hull. Ulli has never been to this summer house before, but it's familiar to her as her own breath.

The air smells of raspberries, but it's still too dark for her to see where they are growing. She takes another sip of her drink. She's hardly drunk anything tonight, just a couple of glasses of white wine with blackcurrant syrup in them, and now this. She has eaten some birthday cake, a cake with TIMMO on it in dull silver pearls.

Someone whistles. She starts and looks round. A dark shape detaches itself from the door. It's Lucca. He comes over to her and stands very close, so close that she can smell his white cottony smell, and again the smell of raspberries.

'We're going fishing,' he said, 'Do you want to come?'

'Who's we?'

'Just me and Timmo. You remember, I introduced you to Timmo. It's his house.'

'Why don't they come here any more?'

Lucca shrugs.

'The kids are grown-up. And his mother's got something wrong with her. Multiple sclerosis. She can't get about.'

'Do you know her?'

* a liqueur made from berries.

'Oh yes.'

'It seems sad to leave it like this. The house.'

'Timmo comes here sometimes.'

'With you?'

'Sometimes.'

They walk down the path through the woods, to the little jetty. It is closer to one than twelve now, and the midsummer dawn's breaking. Timmo is sitting at the end of the jetty. He has cast his line already. The water is so still that Ulli can see his float, scarcely moving.

Ulli sits on the silvery wood, tucking her heels under her. A breeze draws across the surface of the lake, wrinkling it. It reminds Ulli of her mother making jam. She would drop a spoonful onto a clean saucer and blow on it. If it wrinkled, it was ready to pot.

Lucca and Timmo speak very softly so as not to frighten the fish. This is the best time for fishing, Timmo says.

They sit for a long time, fishing and catching nothing. Ulli is glad. She does not want to see the jetty bloodied with slippery, mauled fish. Lucca has a bar of dark bitter chocolate, which he breaks carefully in three pieces. They eat it, and Ulli throws tiny crumbs into the reedy water under the jetty.

'Come and sit here,' Lucca says to her, 'You can't see anything back there.'

He shifts sideways and makes room for her.

'Quite a party, wasn't it?' says Timmo.

'It was fine,' says Ulli, 'But a bit too couply for me.'

'I know what you mean,' says Timmo, 'Well this fishing is a dead loss. Never mind.'

Ulli's feet are getting cold. She shivers and rubs them together.

'Parties, parties,' says Lucca. 'Turn round, Ulli, and you can put your feet under Timmo's coat while I plait your hair.'

Timmo sighs and leans back, gripping the rod between his knees. He spreads out a fold of his coat and wraps it around Ulli's feet. It's one of those family coats that doesn't really belong to anyone, and is kept on a peg by the back door for people to grab as they go out of the house to fish or to chop wood in the chill of the early morning. It must have been an expensive coat once, but now it's scored with thorns and berry stains, and the lining's torn. It smells of moss. A few hundred metres downshore, where a bathing-hut's rimmed by the sunrise, Ulli sees a flicker of movement. A figure steps out onto a frail-looking jetty, like their own. It bends, unpacking fishing equipment. 'A serious fisherman, that one,' says Timmo, 'He's down here every morning.'

It's two-thirty. The sun's fully up now, hazily wrapped in blue. It's going to be hot again. Why sleep, why go back to the house, why waste a single hour of the summer's day that's just joined on flawlessly to the one before, thinks Ulli, as her feet begin to tingle with the warmth from under Timmo's coat. She smells moss and chocolate and the sharp mineral smell of lake-water. Why not stay all day? Later they'll bathe, the three of them. She'll find little wild raspberries, so ripe they are almost purple, the sort that dissolve in your mouth leaving only a grainy rub of seed against your teeth. She shuts her eyes. 'Lucca,' she says. She's going to tell him about the day ahead. There's no need to go home. They can stay here, just the three of them. . . .

'What?' asks Lucca, finishing off the plait. Each woven strand of hair is cold and perfect as the scale of a fish.

But Ulli doesn't answer. She's already asleep.

The Visitors' Book

STEPHEN GALLAGHER

'SOMEONE'S TORN A page out of this,' she said, turning the book toward me. 'Look, you can see.'

She was almost right. The page hadn't been torn, it had been cut; taken out with a blade that had been run down the middle of the book as close to the centre as it was possible to get. It was the kind of cut you make when you don't want your handiwork to be noticed. The only thing that gave it away was that when the book was closed, a slight gap appeared as if a bookmark had been lost in there somewhere. It made me faintly curious, but no more than that. I really didn't think that it was any big deal.

'So it has,' I said, and tried to look more interested than I was.

Some time later, I remember getting it out of the drawer to look at it again. It was a big book, album-sized, and it was two-thirds filled with handwritten entries by many of the families who'd stayed in the summerhouse before us. Only one or two of them were in a language I could understand, and they gave a few hints about the place – how to puzzle out how the circuit breakers worked, where to get English newspapers two days out of date – as well as the standard, had-a-lovely-time kinds of sentiments. There were some people from

Newcastle, others who'd come over from Dorset. Many of the others were Germans, a few French. Sally hadn't come across the book until we'd been in the place for three days already, and then she'd found it while rummaging around in the sitting-room furniture for maps and brochures. When I eventually went back and brought it out again, I turned to the place where the missing page had been and looked at the entries before and after. I couldn't remember anything of what had been written, but by then I was only interested in the dates. The gap seemed to correspond to a two-week period exactly one year before.

No, I remember thinking. *It can't have any significance.* All that it probably meant was that someone had messed up their entry and had taken the leaf out to try it again. The paper-cutter they'd used was still there at the back of the drawer, a little plastic block with just the corner of a razor blade showing.

When I turned the paper to the light, I could see that some of the missing writing had pressed through onto the next page. Not to the extent that I could make out any words, but enough to get an idea of the overall style. It was neat, it was rounded. A feminine hand.

And it didn't match with any of the entries that came before or after.

But that was later. Back on that third day, there was no reason for the Visitors' Book to bother me at all. I left Sally looking through the remaining pages, and went out onto the covered terrace on the front of the summerhouse.

'Watcha doing, Minx?' I said.

The Minx looked up at me from the table. On her birth certificate and by her grandparents she was called Victoria, but to us she'd been the Minx for so long that we had to make an effort to remember that she had any other name. She was four years old that autumn, and was due to start at school the following spring. She'd have her own books, nametabs, a uniform, everything. We'd always told ourselves that we could look forward to this – like all children she'd hit our lives like a hurricane, leaving us dazed and off-kilter and somehow feeling that we'd never quite be able to make up the ground again to become the people we'd once been – but I found that I wasn't quite anticipating the event in the way that I'd imagined. I suppose I was just beginning to realise how closely the growing and the going away were entwined, and would ever be so.

'I'm colouring,' she said.

She was, too. She'd coloured the page in her book and a good piece of the old vinyl tablecloth around it. She'd coloured a cow blue, and the sky behind it black.

I said, 'That looks really good. Are you going to do another?'

'I'll do another next Tuesday,' she said, next Tuesday being her way of indicating some undetermined time in the future. 'Let's go and look for froggies.'

'Clear your lunch away first,' I said, 'or you'll bring in all kinds of creepy-crawlies.'

She climbed down from the bench to the wooden planking of the terrace, and surprised me by doing what I'd asked of her. Then we set off down the steps and into the grounds to find some froggies.

It was a pretty good house. I'd felt a twinge of disappointment when we'd first rolled up the grassy drive after a long haul by road and ferry, but within a few hours of unpacking and beginning to unwind it had started to grow on me. It was bigger than we needed, but I liked the sense of space. So what if it was a little shabby round the edges and the shower arrangements were kind of spartan and the beds were dropped in the middle in a way that would have suited a hunchback perfectly and nobody else at all; after a while this only seemed to add to the atmosphere.

It was late, a quiet time of the year. Almost all of the other summerhouses, including the newer one that shared this grassy clearing in a thicket just a little way back from the beach, appeared to be unoccupied. When the road gate at the end of the driveway was closed, it was almost as if we were shutting ourselves into a private world. When the Minx had spotted the horde of tiny frogs that seemed to migrate across the drive at around four o'clock every afternoon, that more or less confirmed it. It seemed that we were going to be okay.

'Have you found any?' she asked brightly, but I had to tell her that I hadn't. She liked to hold them on her hand. By now they probably just sat toughing it out and thinking, *Oh, shit, not again* and *Why me, God, why me?*

'No,' I said. 'It's the wrong time of day. Look, I saw a bike in the garage yesterday. Why don't you ride it around the garden?'

'A big bike?' she said warily.

'No, just a little bike.'

So we spent the afternoon playing with the house's rusty old tricycle and a football that we'd picked up from Willi's Market about a half-mile down the shore road, and after we'd eaten picnic-style out on the terrace we all took a walk along the beach until it was too cold for everybody but the Minx, who had to be picked up out of the sandhole that she'd dug and carried home squalling.

And as we were tracing our way back through the upturned boats and then across the strip of coarse grassland that divided the shoreline from the shore road, I found myself thinking: *Maybe the people who wrote the page weren't the ones who took it out. Maybe it was something that the owners didn't want the rest of us to see.*

The owners.

Those shadowy people who weren't actually present but whose mark was everywhere, so that they seemed to stand just out of sight like a bunch of watchful ghosts. Their pictures, their ornaments, their old castoff furniture – their house. Maybe they came in after each new tenant and read the book, and there was something here that they'd censored.

Maybe.

Exactly what I had in mind, I couldn't have said. Something uncomplimentary, some insult even; written by someone who perhaps didn't have a good time and blamed the place and not themselves for it. Or worse. It could have been something worse. I was surprised to find that the possibility had been playing on my mind. I said nothing to Sally, but I decided there and then that I'd think about it no further. I mean, you worry at something to which you know you can never find the answer, and where does it get you?

Nowhere. So I thought I'd better stop.

That night, after the Minx had been installed in her room and had exhausted every avenue for stories and drinks and had eventually exhausted herself as well, we got a couple of the local beers out of the fridge and turned on the sitting-room lights. Sally flicked through some of the magazines that she'd picked up on the boat coming over, and I hunted around for the paperback I'd been reading. I'm not much of a reader, and thinking of the two weeks that lay ahead I'd bought the book for its size and weight as much as for any other reason. Every other page was dotted with CIA and MI5 and KGB, and the plot went on and on and had about as much grip as a wet handshake; after a while I gave up looking for it, and went over to the shelves instead.

There had to be something here I could read. There was a cabinet full of books and overseas editions of the *Reader's Digest*, most of them probably abandoned and accumulated from visitors over the years, but there wasn't much that was in the English language. There was a fat book by Leon Uris that I put back because it looked such heavy going and, besides, I'd already seen the movie, and an old and brittle Agatha Christie which, on a quick check, appeared to have lost its last ten pages. The only decent bet seemed to be a two-fisted private eye story titled *Dames Die First*.

When I pulled it out, a photograph dropped to the floor. It had been between the books. I picked it up and looked at it, and saw that there was the sign of a crease across the middle. At a guess, it had been slipped in between the volumes for the pressure to flatten it out, and then it had been forgotten. It was of a blonde girl of about six or seven, and if it had been taken anywhere around here I didn't recognise the spot. I carried the picture over to the chest of drawers and then started to go through them, much as Sally had earlier in the day. After a while I became aware of her watching me.

'What's the matter?' she said.

'Just checking on something.'

She didn't seem to think much of my answer, but it was the best one I had. As she was laying down her magazine to come over, I found what I was looking for; another, different photograph that lay in one of the drawers underneath some boxed games and out-of-date timetables.

It was a family group. Nothing formal, just a snapshot. The house was recognisable in the background, although they'd added to it since. These, I'd been guessing, were the people who actually owned the place and who let it out through an agency for the times when they didn't need it themselves.

I laid the two photographs side by side on top of the dresser. The girl who appeared in one didn't appear in the other.

Sally picked up the portrait shot and said, 'She doesn't look local,' before dropping it again and going on through the kitchen towards the bathroom.

Yeah, fine.

That's probably what I'd been thinking too.

Saturday came around.

I didn't actually realise that it was Saturday until I saw a strange car coming up the driveway that morning. At first I thought that it was somebody on their way to speak to us, but the car turned off and pulled in by the other of the two houses that shared the driveway and the private clearing at its end. Suddenly it didn't seem so private any more.

The family got out and we nodded to each other. They didn't seem to have brought much in the way of luggage and they went straight into the house as if they already knew their way around. My guess was that they were another set of owners, just up for the weekend. I went back into our own place and warned Sally and the Minx, just in case either of them happened to be wandering around after a shower in less than their underwear. There was just a stretch of open ground between the two buildings, nothing screening them at all. The other house was newer, neater. I know it was theirs, but I couldn't help thinking of them as intruders.

I looked at the two children. Neither of them was anything like the girl in the photograph.

So then I wondered if they might be able to tell me what had happened here, in this same week exactly one year before.

But I never asked.

On Sunday we took the Minx on a long drive to the zoo, where she acted up so much that we had to threaten to leave her there and halfway meant it. When we got back late in the afternoon, our short-term neighbours were apparently loading up to go. We nodded as we passed just as before, and then they went.

I gave it a few minutes after their departure and then I took a walk down the driveway to check that the gate was secure; the driveway curved and was lined with dense bushes, so the gate couldn't be seen directly from the house. The Minx came after me, on the prospect of froggies. She squatted down looking hopefully at the ground while I rattled the wide gate, but the bolt was secure.

'Why are you doing that?' she said.

'So that we can let you wander around without worrying about you getting onto the road where the cars are,' I told her. 'Haven't you noticed how one of us checks on it every morning?'

'I check on it too,' she said.

'Really?'

'Yes,' she said. 'Someone keeps coming in and leaving it open.'

Either the frogs had already been and gone, or else they were getting wiser and waiting. We walked back up to the house. The day was dying and the shadows were long and deep, and the houselights glowed yellow-on-blue like a twilit jack-o'-lantern. The Minx took hold of my hand as we climbed the wooden steps. Only a couple of hours before, she'd been winding me up to bursting point outside the monkey house and she'd known it. Now this. I couldn't help thinking, and not for the first time, that the worst thing in the world for me would be to lose her.

And, of course, eventually to lose her was one of the few things in my life that could fairly be called inevitable.

*

With only a few days left of our stay, we found ourselves less inclined towards loading up the car and going looking for late-season amusements and so instead we just stayed around the place. I'm not exactly sure what we did, but the time carried on leaking away from us anyway. Anything we needed, we could usually get from Willi's Market. The only problem was that we couldn't mention the name of the place when the Minx was in earshot without her latching onto it and getting us helpless with laughter.

Sometimes the Minx walked down with me. Thursday was one of the days when she didn't.

It was a rambling, one-storey building set back from the road with space for about half a dozen cars in front of it, and although it wasn't big it sold just about everything from fresh bread to padlocks. It was clean and it was bright and it was modern, and the only note that jarred when I compared it to similar places back home was the sales rack of shrink-wrapped pornography stuck in there by the checkout between the Disney comics and the chewing gum. One man seemed to run the place on his own, at least at this quiet time of year when there were only the few locals and late visitors like ourselves to keep it ticking over. He wore a sports shirt and glasses and combed his thinning hair straight back, and whenever I went in we communicated entirely by nods and signs and smiles.

As he was punching up my stuff on the till, I brought out the little girl's picture and showed it to him.

He paused in his work and looked at the picture. He wasn't certain of why I was doing this, and so he looked closely without any reaction other than mild puzzlement for a few moments. Then he glanced up at me.

He shook his head. There was sadness and sympathy in his eyes.

And he said something, and right there and then I'd have given almost anything to know what it was; but I just took the picture from him and stowed it away again, and I nodded my head as if I understood. The words meant nothing to me, but I thought I knew the tone of them.

It was the tone, I believed then, that one would use when speaking of someone else's tragedy.

As I was walking back along the side of the shore road, I felt as if the formless apprehensions of the past few days had suddenly come together and made a creature with a name. Its name was dread, and it sat in me like an angry prisoner with no sight of daylight. A few cars zipped by me, one with a windsurfing board on its rack. I knew I'd closed and bolted the gate behind me, I *knew* it, and yet . . .

In my mind's eye I could see the Minx running hell-for-leather down the drive, giggling in mischief the way she often did, with Sally screaming a warning and falling behind and the Minx too giddy to realise what she was being told . . . *Someone keeps coming in and leaving it open*, she'd said, and I'd paid her no attention . . .

But who? Apart from our weekend neighbours, we were the only ones to be using the gateway at all. *Was* there someone who'd been prowling around the place, and I'd overlooked the evidence because it was the Minx who was telling me and I was so used to the workings of her imagination that I was dismissing the truth along with the usual dose of unreality?

Come to think of it, the garage door had been standing open when we'd gone to get the bike a few days before.

And I still hadn't found that damned paperback, even though I was pretty sure of where I'd left it.

And there was the Visitors' Book, which had planted the seed of my unease.

And the reaction of the checkout man in Willi's Market, that had brought it into flower . . .

Pretty thin fabric, I know.

But by the time I reached the house I was running.

Sally saw me coming up the drive. I must have been a sight. Breathless, my shirt half-out, the bag of groceries crushed up against my side. She was out on a sun lounger in front of the house, and she raised her head and squinted at me. I slowed. Everything seemed normal, and I was a dope. But I wasn't sorry.

'Where's the Minx?' I said.

'She's set herself up with a picnic on the porch,' she said. 'What's the matter with *you*?'

'Nothing,' I said, almost sharply, and I walked past her and up the steps to the covered entrance. As my eyes adjusted to the shade, I could see the Minx; in a world of her own as she so often was, with plates and crockery from the kitchen set out on the outdoor dining table and her all-time favourite doll, clothes long gone and the rest of her distinctly frayed around the edges, propped up outside. She'd hijacked the big tub of margarine and a packet of biscuits, and Sally must have opened a bottle of cola for her to round off the feast. She was just raising it to her lips and tilting it as I came into sight.

Nothing amiss here.

And then, in an instant, I saw that I was wrong.

I don't know exactly what happens when you're in a situation like that. You can see the most minor detail with the utmost clarity, and it burns itself deep into your awareness; but it's almost as if the sheer volume of information suddenly slows the speed of processing, so that you don't seem to act or react in any positive way at all. You see your own failure, even before it's had the chance to happen. Disaster's heading straight for you like a rocket, and your responses are moving like letters in the mail.

If I had any talent with a paintbrush, I could probably reproduce the scene exactly. The well-worn sheen on the checkered vinyl cloth. The sunlight, backlighting the Minx's hair as she raised the bottle. The mismatched china and the scattering of crumbs. The open margarine tub, its contents churned like an angry sea. The last inch of flat cola.

And the live wasp in the bottle, floating towards the neck as the bottle was tilted.

She screamed and dropped the bottle, and clapped both her hands to her face. The wasp was on the deckboards now, buzzing furiously but too wet or too damaged to rise; she'd squeezed it between her mouth and the rim of the bottle as it had tried to escape, and it had reacted the only way it knew how. Which got no sympathy out of me at all. I stepped on it quickly, and it popped like a grape.

The Minx was still screaming as I hauled her up and onto my knee. Sally was already on her way up the steps. I tried to pull the Minx's hands away, but she was hysterical. Sally was saying 'What is it, what's happened?' and I remember thinking, completely unfairly but in the lash-out, bite-anything manner of a run-over dog, that she should have been right there and this should never have been allowed to happen. Which makes no sense, of course, but that's the way I was thinking. I don't think it showed on the outside, but I was in a panic. I didn't know what to do. We were in the middle of nowhere in a place where we didn't speak the language, and there was a crisis here and I *didn't know what to do*.

The stinger was still in the Minx's lip, like a tiny yellow thumbtack. I managed to pick it out carefully with my thumbnail. And what then? I tried to have a go at sucking out the poison, but the Minx beat me away. Sally ran to the kitchen and brought back half an onion to rub the wound, but the Minx batted that away too. She was screaming for a plaster, the little-kids' answer to every hurt. I handed her over and went for the first-aid kit in the car.

There were Band-aids, there were bandages, there was a folded-up sling for a broken arm. I'd bought the kit as a ready-made box and I don't think I'd even looked into it since I'd taken a curious glance over the contents and then stowed it away in the car at least three years before. I fumbled it, and the contents went everywhere. I saw some antiseptic wipes and grabbed one up and went back to the covered terrace.

The Minx, still tearful, was quieter. Sally was rocking her and whispering *Sshh, sshh*, and the Minx was sobbing. I tore open the sachet and crouched down before them both and managed to get a few dabs in with the wipe. Her lip was already beginning to swell.

I was scared.

When the swelling grew steadily worse over the next half-hour, we loaded her into the car and went out looking for a hospital. I had no idea. We were already on the road and moving when I thought that I should have checked through the old brochures and guides for an area map which might have some indication on it. I had a terrific sense of desperation, as if there were a bomb ticking in the back of the car. I hardly knew what I was doing. In the end it was the cashier at a big Shell service area who marked the nearest hospital on a tourist map and then waved me away when I tried to pay for it.

Carrying the Minx into the Emergency Room, I felt like a wrecked sailor reaching the shore. I mean, for all I knew, she could have *died* – she could have been dying right then, and I'd have been no more useful. As it was they checked her over, gave her a couple of shots, painted the sting site with something, and then sent us away. The Minx stayed quiet in the back with Sally as I drove us all home. It was dusk when we got there, and it was to find that we'd gone off leaving every door and window of the place wide open. Even the gate at the end of the drive was swinging to and fro, and I knew that I'd stopped and jumped out of the car to close it behind us.

I knew that I'd never feel quite the same again, about anything. I'd crossed a line. I'd peeped into the abyss.

Nothing much more happened those last couple of days. I put the child's photograph back on the shelf where I'd found it, and I made no further enquiries. The Minx looked like a defeated boxer, five rounds and then out for the count, but by the next morning we were even able to make jokes about it. They were morale-boosters, not the real thing, and I suppose they must have sounded pretty hollow to both of us. The camera stayed in its case for the rest of the trip. Nothing was said or agreed, but I think that this was something that none of us would ever want to be reminded of.

So, no more photographs.

We'd probably have gone home early if we could, but the boat ticket couldn't be transferred. And, besides, there was so little time remaining. The weather held good, but we stuck around the house killing time as if on the rainiest of rainy days.

On the last day we packed almost in silence, and the Minx went for one last froggie-hunt while I loaded up the car. Sally stayed in the house. When I went inside to bring out the last few items – the boots, the overcoats, the radio . . . all the stuff that didn't belong in any particular box or bag – I found her at the big table in the sitting room. The Visitors' Book was open on the table before her. She looked up, and she seemed almost defensive.

'We've got to write something,' she said. 'It's not the house's fault. Not to put anything at all would be rude.'

I shrugged, and didn't say anything. We hadn't been saying much of anything to each other since the accident, at least not directly. I picked up the stuff that I'd come for and went out to the car.

Half an hour later, with everything loaded away and the house locked up for the last time behind us, we rolled down the driveway and out through the open gate.

'Say goodbye, house,' Sally told the Minx, and the Minx turned and waved through the back window and said, 'Bye!'

I stopped the car.

'I just realised, I left my sunglasses,' I said.

'I checked everywhere before we locked up,' Sally said. 'Are you sure?'

'I only meant to put them down for a second,' I said. 'I know where they are. Let me have the keys.'

The keys were to be dropped off at the agents' office in the nearest town as we drove on by to the ferry. Sally got them out of the big envelope and passed them forward to me, and I got out of the car and walked back up the drive. I left the engine running. This wasn't going to take very long.

Already the house seemed different. No longer ours, it was a place of strangers again. I felt out-of-place, almost observed, as I walked up the steps with the door key in my hand. I could hear the car's engine running at the end of the driveway, over on the far side of the bushes.

I entered the newly regained silence of the place. There was no sign of my sunglasses but then, I'd known there wouldn't be; they were in their case, safe inside my jacket.

I didn't have much time. I crossed the room to the chest of drawers and crouched, pulling open the one which I knew held the Visitors' Book. It was uppermost on all the brochures, and I took it out and laid it on top of the chest before feeling around at the back of the drawer. Then I straightened, and opened the book to the latest entry.

I didn't want to read it. In fact I'd turned the book around so that all of the entries were upside-down to me, on purpose. I didn't know whether Sally had mentioned anything about how the visit had ended, and I didn't want to. I spread the pages flat and I took a grip on the little cutter and I ran it, firmly and neatly, down the final page as close to the spine as I could get.

A firm tug, and it came out cleanly. I screwed it up and stuffed it into my pocket, for quiet disposal at a stopover point somewhere on the journey ahead.

And then I closed the book, returned it to the drawer, locked up the house, and walked away.

Forever.

Forain

MAVIS GALLANT

ABOUT AN HOUR before the funeral service for Adam Tremski, snow mixed with rain began to fall, and by the time the first of the mourners arrived the stone steps of the church were dangerously wet. Blaise Forain, Tremski's French publisher, now his literary executor, was not surprised when, later, an elderly woman slipped and fell and had to be carried by ambulance to the Hôtel-Dieu hospital. Forain, in an attempt to promote Cartesian order over Slavic frenzy, sent for the ambulance, then found himself obliged to accompany the patient to the emergency section and fork over a deposit. The old lady had no social security.

Taken together, façade and steps formed an escarpment – looming, abrupt, above all unfamiliar. The friends of Tremski's last years had been Polish, Jewish, a few French. Of the French, only Forain was used to a variety of last rites. He was expected to attend the funerals not only of his authors but of their wives. He knew all the Polish churches of Paris, the Hungarian mission, the synagogues on the Rue Copernic and the Rue de la Victoire, and the mock chapel of the crematorium at Père Lachaise cemetery. For nonbelievers a few words at the graveside sufficed. Their friends said, by way of a greeting, 'Another one gone'. However, no one they knew ever had been buried from this particular church. The parish was said to be the oldest in the city, yet the edifice built on the ancient site looked forbidding and cold. Tremski for some forty years had occupied the same walkup flat on the fringe of Montparnasse. What was he doing over here, on the wrong side of the Seine?

Four months before this, Forain had been present for the last blessing of Barbara, Tremski's wife, at the Polish church on the Rue Saint-Honoré. The church, a chapel really, was round in shape, with no fixed pews – just rows of chairs pushed together. The dome was a mistake – too imposing for the squat structure – but it had stood for centuries, and only the very nervous could consider it a threat. Here, Forain had noticed, tears came easily, not only for the lost friend but for all the broken ties and old, unwilling journeys. The tears of strangers around him, that is; grief, when it reached him, was pale and dry. He was thirty-eight, divorced, had a daughter of twelve who lived in Nice with her mother and the mother's lover. Only one or two of Forain's friends had ever met the girl. Most people, when told, found it hard to believe he had ever been married. The service for Tremski's wife had been disrupted by the late entrance of *her* daughter – child of her first husband – who had made a show of arriving late, kneeling alone in the aisle, kissing the velvet pall over the coffin, and noisily marching out. Halina was her name. She had straight, greying hair and a cross face with small features. Forain knew that some of the older mourners could remember her as a pretty, unsmiling, not too clever child. A few perhaps thought Tremski was her father and wondered if he had been unkind to his wife. Tremski, sitting with his head bowed, may not have noticed. At any rate, he had never mentioned anything.

Tremski was Jewish. His wife had been born a Catholic, though no one was certain what had come next. To be blunt, was she in or out? The fact was that she had lived in adultery –if one wanted to be specific – with Tremski until her husband had obliged the pair by dying. There had been no question of a divorce; probably she had never asked for one. For his wedding to Barbara, Tremski had bought a dark–blue suit at a

good place, Creed or Lanvin Hommes, which he had on at her
funeral, and in which he would be buried. He had never
owned another, had shambled around Paris looking as though
he slept under restaurant tables, on a bed of cigarette ashes and
crumbs. It would have taken a team of devoted women, not
just one wife, to keep him spruce.

Forain knew only from hearsay about the wedding ceremony in one of the town halls of Paris (Tremski was still
untranslated then, had a job in a book-store near the Jardin des
Plantes, had paid back the advance for the dark-blue suit over
eleven months) – the names signed in a register, the daughter's
refusal to attend, the wine drunk with friends in a café on the
Avenue du Maine. It was a cheerless place, but Tremski knew
the owner. He had talked of throwing a party but never got
round to it; his flat was too small. Any day now he would
move to larger quarters and invite two hundred and fifty
intimate friends to a banquet. In the meantime, he stuck to his
rented flat, a standard émigré dwelling of the nineteen-fifties,
almost a period piece now: two rooms on a court, windowless
kitchen, splintered floors, unheatable bathroom, no elevator,
intimidating landlord – a figure central to his comic anecdotes
and private worries. What did his wife think? Nobody knew,
though if he had sent two hundred and fifty invitations she
would undoubtedly have started to borrow two hundred and
fifty glasses and plates. Even after Tremski could afford to
move, he remained anchored to his seedy rooms: there were
all those books, and the boxes filled with unanswered mail,
and the important documents he would not let anyone file.
Snapshots and group portraits of novelists and poets, wearing
the clothes and haircuts of the fifties and sixties, took up much
of a wall. A new desire to sort out the past, put its artifacts in
order, had occupied Tremski's conversation on his wedding
day. His friends had soon grown bored, although his wife
seemed to be listening. Tremski, married at last, was off on an
oblique course, preaching the need for discipline and a
thought-out future. It didn't last.

At Forain's first meeting with Barbara, they drank harsh tea
from mismatched cups and appraised each other in the grey

83

light that filtered in from the court. She asked him, gently, about his fitness to translate and publish Tremski – then still at the bookstore, selling wartime memoirs and paperbacks and addressing parcels. Did Forain have close ties with the Nobel Prize committee? How many of his authors had received important awards, gone on to international fame? She was warm and friendly and made him think of a large buttercup. He was about the age of her daughter, Halina; so Barbara said. He felt paternal, wise, rid of mistaken ideals. He would become Tremski's guide and father. He thought, This is the sort of woman I should have married – although most probably he should never have married anyone.

Only a few of the mourners mounting the treacherous steps can have had a thought to spare for Tremski's private affairs. His wife's flight from a brave and decent husband, dragging by the hand a child of three, belonged to the folklore, not the history, of mid-century emigration. The chronicle of two generations, displaced and dispossessed, had come to a stop. The evaluation could begin; had already started. Scholars who looked dismayingly youthful, speaking the same language, but with a new jarring vocabulary, were trekking to Western capitals – taping reminiscences, copying old letters. History turned out to be a plodding science. What most émigrés settled for now was the haphazard accuracy of a memory like Tremski's. In the end it was always a poem that ran through the mind – not a string of dates.

Some may have wondered why Tremski was entitled to a Christian service; or, to apply another kind of reasoning, why it had been thrust upon him. Given his shifting views on eternity and the afterlife, a simple get-together might have done, with remarks from admirers, a poem or two read aloud, a priest wearing a turtleneck sweater, or a young rabbi with a literary bent. Or one of each, offering prayers and tributes in turn. Tremski had nothing against prayers. He had spent half his life inventing them.

As it turned out, the steep church was not as severe as it looked from the street. It was in the hands of a small charismatic order, perhaps full of high spirits but by no means schismatic. No one had bothered to ask if Tremski was a true convert or just a writer who sometimes sounded like one. His sole relative was his stepdaughter. She had made an arrangement that suited her: she lived nearby, in a street until recently classed as a slum, now renovated and highly prized. Between her seventeenth-century flat and the venerable site was a large, comfortable, cluttered department store, where, over the years, Tremski's friends had bought their pots of paint and rollers, their sturdy plates and cups, their burglarproof door locks, their long-lasting cardigan sweaters. The store was more familiar than the church. The stepdaughter was a stranger.

She was also Tremski's heir and she did not understand Forain's role, taking executor to mean an honorary function, godfather to the dead. She had told Forain that Tremski had destroyed her father and blighted her childhood. He had enslaved her mother, spoken loud Polish in restaurants, had tried to keep Halina from achieving a French social identity. Made responsible, by his astonishing will, for organising a suitable funeral, she had chosen a French sendoff, to be followed by burial in a Polish cemetery outside Paris. Because of the weather and because there was a shortage of cars, friends were excused from attending the burial. Most of them were thankful: more than one fatal cold had been brought on by standing in the icy mud of a graveyard. When she had complained she was doing her best, that Tremski had never said what he wanted, she was probably speaking the truth. He could claim one thing and its opposite in the same sentence. Only God could keep track. If today's rite was a cosmic error, Forain decided, it was up to Him to erase Tremski's name from the ledger and enter it in the proper column. If He cared.

The mourners climbed the church steps slowly. Some were helped by younger relatives, who had taken time off from work. A few had migrated to high-rise apartments in the outer suburbs, to deeper loneliness but cheaper rents. They had set out early, as if they still believed no day could start without them, and after a long journey underground and a difficult change of direction had emerged from the Hôtel de Ville métro station. They held their umbrellas at a slant, as if countering some force of nature arriving head-on. Actually, there was not the least stir in the air, although strong winds and sleet were forecast. The snow and rain came down in thin soft strings, clung to fur or woollen hats, and became a meagre amount of slush underfoot.

Forain was just inside the doors, accepting murmured sympathy and handshakes. He was not usurping a family role but trying to make up for the absence of Halina. Perhaps she would stride in late, as at her mother's funeral, driving home some private grudge. He had on a long cashmere overcoat, the only black garment he owned. A friend had left it to him. More exactly, the friend, aware that he was to die very soon, had told Forain to collect it at the tailor's. It had been fitted, finished, paid for, never worn. Forain knew there was a mean joke abroad about his wearing dead men's clothes. It also applied to his professional life: he was supposed to have said he preferred the backlist of any dead writer to the stress and tension of trying to deal with a live one.

His hair and shoes felt damp. The hand he gave to be shaken must have chilled all those it touched. He was squarely in the path of one of those church drafts that become gales anywhere close to a door. He wondered if Halina had been put off coming because of some firm remarks of his, the day before (he had defended Tremski against the charge of shouting in restaurants), or even had decided it was undignified to pretend she cared for a second how Tremski was dispatched; but at the last minute she turned up, with her French husband – a reporter of French political affairs on a weekly – and a daughter of fourteen in jacket and jeans. These two had not been able to read a word of Tremski's until Forain had published a novel in translation about six years before. Tremski believed they had never looked at it – to be fair, the girl was only eight at the time – or any of the books that had followed; although the girl clipped and saved reviews. It was remarkable, Tremski had said, the way literate people, reasonably well travelled and educated, comfortably off, could live adequate lives without wanting to know what had gone before or happened elsewhere. Even the husband, the political journalist, was like that: a few names, a date looked up, a notion of geography satisfied him.

Forain could tell Tremski minded. He had wanted Halina to think well of him at least on one count, his life's work. She was the daughter of a former Army officer who had died – like Barbara, like Tremski – in a foreign city. She considered herself, no less than her father, the victim of a selfish adventure. She also believed she was made of better stuff than Tremski, by descent and status, and that was harder to take. In Tremski's own view, comparisons were not up for debate.

For the moment, the three were behaving well. It was as much as Forain expected from anybody. He had given up measuring social conduct, except where it ran its course in fiction. His firm made a speciality of translating and publishing work from Eastern and Central Europe; it kept him at a remove. Halina seemed tamed now, even thanked him for standing in and welcoming all those strangers. She had a story to explain why she was late, but it was farfetched, and Forain forgot it immediately. The delay most likely had been caused by a knockdown argument over the jacket and jeans. Halina was a cold skirmisher, narrow in scope but heavily principled. She wore a fur-and-leather coat, a pale grey hat with a brim, and a scarf – authentic Hermès? Taiwan fake? Forain could have told by rubbing the silk between his fingers, but it was a wild idea, and he kept his distance.

The girl had about her a look of Barbara: for that reason, no other, Forain found her appealing. Blaise ought to sit with the family, she said – using his first name, the way young people did now. A front pew had been kept just for the three of them. There was plenty of room. Forain thought that Halina might begin to wrangle, in whispers, within earshot (so to speak) of the dead. He said yes, which was easier than to refuse, and decided no. He left them at the door, greeting stragglers, and found a place at the end of a pew halfway down the aisle. If Halina mentioned anything later, he would say he had been afraid he might have to leave before the end. She walked by without noticing and, once settled, did not look around.

The pale hat had belonged to Halina's mother. Forain was sure he remembered it. When his wife died, Tremski had let Halina and her husband ransack the flat. Halina made several trips while the husband waited downstairs. He had come up only to help carry a crate of papers belonging to Tremski. It contained, among other documents, some of them rubbish, a number of manuscripts not quite complete. Since Barbara's funeral Tremski had not bothered to shave or even put his teeth in. He sat in the room she had used, wearing a dressing gown torn at the elbows. Her wardrobe stood empty, the door wide, just a few hangers inside. He clutched Forain by the sleeve and said that Halina had taken some things of his away. As soon as she realised her error she would bring them back.

Forain would have preferred to cross the Seine on horseback, lashing at anyone who resembled Halina or her husband, but he had driven to her street by taxi, past the old, reassuring, unchanging department store. No warning, no telephone call: he walked up a curving stone staircase, newly sandblasted and scrubbed, and pressed the doorbell on a continued note until someone came running.

She let him in, just so far. 'Adam can't be trusted to look after his own affairs,' she said. 'He was always careless and dirty, but now the place smells of dirt. Did you look at the kitchen table? He must keep eating from the same plate. As for my mother's letters, if that's what you're after, he had already started to tear them up.'

'Did you save any?'

'They belong to me.'

How like a ferret she looked, just then; and she was the child of such handsome parents. A studio portrait of her father, the Polish officer, taken in London, in civilian clothes, smoking a long cigarette, stood on a table in the entrance hall. (Forain was admitted no further.) Forain took in the likeness of the man who had fought a war for nothing. Barbara had deserted that composed, distinguished, somewhat careful face for

Tremski. She must have forced Tremski's hand, arrived on his doorstep, bag, baggage, and child. He had never come to a resolution about anything in his life.

Forain had retrieved every scrap of paper, of course – all but the letters. Fired by a mixture of duty and self-interest, he was unbeatable. Halina had nothing on her side but a desire to reclaim her mother, remove the Tremski influence, return her – if only her shoes and blouses and skirts – to the patient and defeated man with his frozen cigarette. Her entitlement seemed to include a portion of Tremski, too; but she had resented him, which weakened her grasp. Replaying every move, Forain saw how strong her case might have been if she had acknowledged Tremski as her mother's choice. Denying it, she became – almost became; Forain stopped her in time – the defendant in a cheap sort of litigation.

Tremski's friends sat with their shoes in puddles. They kept their gloves on and pulled their knitted scarves tight. Some had spent all these years in France without social security or health insurance, either for want of means or because they had never found their feet in the right sort of employment. Possibly they believed that a long life was in itself full payment for a safe old age. Should the end turn out to be costly and prolonged, then, please, allow us to dream and float in the thickest, deepest darkness, unaware of the inconvenience and clerical work we may cause. So, Forain guessed, ran their prayers.

Funerals came along in close ranks now, especially in bronchial winters. One of Forain's earliest recollections was the Mass in Latin, but he could not say he missed it: he associated Latin with early-morning hunger, and sitting still. The charismatic movement seemed to have replaced incomprehension and mystery with theatricals. He observed the five priests in full regalia, sitting to the right of the altar. One had a bad cold and kept taking a handkerchief from his sleeve. Another more than once glanced at his watch. A choir, concealed or on tape, sang 'Jesu, bleibet meine Freude', after which a smooth, trained voice began to recite the Twenty-fifth

Psalm. The voice seemed to emanate from Tremski's coffin but was too perfectly French to be his. In the middle of Verse 7, just after 'Remember not the sins of my youth', the speaker wavered and broke off. A man seated in front of Forain got up and walked down the aisle, in a solemn and ponderous way. The coffin was on a trestle, draped in purple and white, heaped with roses, tulips, and chrysanthemums. He edged past it, picked up a black box lying on the ground, and pressed two clicking buttons. 'Jesu' started up, from the beginning. Returning, the stranger gave Forain an angry stare, as if he had created the mishap.

Forain knew that some of Tremski's friends thought he was unreliable. He had a reputation for not paying authors their due. There were writers who complained they had never received the price of a postage stamp; they could not make sense of his elegant hand-written statements. Actually, Tremski had been the exception. Forain had arranged his foreign rights, when they began to occur, on a half-and-half basis. Tremski thought of money as a useful substance that covered rent and cigarettes. His wife didn't see it that way. Her forefinger at the end of a column of figures, her quiet, seductive voice saying, 'Blaise, what's this?' called for a thought-out answer.

She had never bothered to visit Forain's office, but made him take her to tea at Angelina's, on the Rue de Rivoli. After her strawberry tart had been eaten and the plate removed, she would bring out of her handbag the folded, annotated account. Outdone, outclassed, slipping the tearoom cheque into his wallet to be dissolved in general expenses, he would look around and obtain at least one satisfaction: she was still the best-looking woman in sight, of any age. He had not been tripped up by someone of inferior appearance and quality. The more he felt harassed by larger issues, the more he made of small compensations. He ran his business with a staff of loyal, worn-out women, connected to him by a belief in what he was doing, or some lapsed personal tie, or because it was too late and they had nowhere to go. At eight o'clock this morning, the day of the funeral, his staunch Lisette, at his side from the beginning of the venture, had called to tell him she had enough social-security points for retirement. He saw the points as splashes of ink on a clean page. All he could think to answer was that she would soon get bored, having no reason to get up each day. Lisette had replied, not disagreeably, that she planned to spend the next ten years in bed. He could not even coax her to stay by improving her salary: except for the reserve of capital required by law, he had next to no money, had to scrape to pay the monthly settlement on his daughter, and was in continual debt to printers and banks.

He was often described in the trade as poor but selfless. He had performed an immeasurable service to world culture, bringing to the West voices that had been muffled for decades in the East. Well, of course, his thimble-size firm had not been able to attract the leviathan prophets, the booming novelists, the great mentors and tireless definers. Tremski had been at the very limit of Forain's financial reach – good Tremski, who had stuck to Forain even after he could have moved on. Common sense had kept Forain from approaching the next-best, second-level oracles, articulate and attractive, subsidised to the ears, chain-smoking and explaining, still wandering the universities and congresses of the West. Their travel requirements were beyond him: no grant could cover the unassuming but ruinous little hotel on the Left Bank, the long afternoons and evenings spent in bars with leather armchairs, where the visitors expected to meet clever and cultivated people in order to exchange ideas.

Forain's own little flock, by contrast, seemed to have entered the world with no expectations. Apart from the odd, rare, humble complaint, they were content to be put up on the top storey of a hotel with a steep, neglected staircase, a wealth of literary associations, and one bath to a floor. For recreation, they went to the café across the street, made a pot of hot water and a tea bag last two and a half hours, and, as Forain encouraged them to keep in mind, could watch the Market Economy saunter by. Docile, holding only a modest estimation of their own gifts, they still provided a handicap: their names, like those of their characters, all sounded alike to barbaric Western ears. It had been a triumph of perseverance on the part of Forain to get notice taken of their books. He wanted every work he published to survive in collective memory, even when the paper it was printed on had been pulped, burned in the city's vast incinerators, or lay mouldering at the bottom of the Seine.

Season after season, his stomach eaten up with anxiety, his heart pounding out hope, hope, hope, he produced a satirical novella set in Odessa; a dense, sober private journal, translated from the Romanian, best understood by the author and his friends; or another wry glance at the harebrained makers of history. (There were few women. In that particular part of Europe they seemed to figure as brusque, flirtatious mistresses or uncomplaining wives.) At least once a year he committed the near-suicide of short stories and poetry. There were rewards, none financial. A few critics thought it a safe bet occasionally to mention a book he sent along for review: he was considered sound in an area no one knew much about, and too hard up to sponsor a pure disaster. Any day now some stumbling, tender, newborn calf of his could turn into a literary water ox. As a result, it was not unusual for one of his writers to receive a sheaf of tiny clippings, sometimes even illustrated by a miniature photograph, taken at the Place de la Bastille, with traffic whirling around. A clutch of large banknotes would have been good, too, but only Tremski's wife had held out for both.

Money! Forain's opinion was the same as that of any poet striving to be read in translation. He never said so. The name of the firm, Blaise Éditions, rang with an honest chime in spheres where trade and literature are supposed to have no connection. When the Minister of Culture had decorated him, not long before, mentioning in encouraging terms Forain's addition to the House of Europe, Forain had tried to look diffident but essential. It seemed to him at that instant that his reputation for voluntary self-denial was a stone memorial pinning him to earth. He wanted to cry out for help – to the Minister? It would look terrible. He felt honoured but confused. Again, summoned to the refurbished embassy of a new democracy, welcomed by an ambassador and a cultural attaché recently arrived (the working staff was unchanged), Forain had dared say to himself, 'Why don't they just give me the cheque for whatever all this is costing?' – the champagne, the exquisite catering, the medal in a velvet box – all the while hoping his thoughts would not show on his face.

The truth was that the destruction of the Wall – radiant paradigm – had all but demolished Forain. The difference was that Forain could not be hammered to still smaller pieces and sold all over the world. In much the same way Vatican II had reduced to bankruptcy more than one publisher of prayer books in Latin. A couple of them had tried to recoup by dumping the obsolete missals on congregations in Asia and Africa, but by the time the Third World began to ask for its money back the publishers had gone down with all hands. Briefly, Forain pondered the possibility of unloading on readers in Senegal and Cameroon the entire edition of a subtle and allusive study of corruption in Minsk, set in 1973. Could one still get away with it – better yet, charge it off to cultural cooperation? He answered himself: No. Not after November, 1989. Gone were the stories in which socialist incoherence was matched by Western irrelevance. Gone from Forain's intention to publish, that is: his flock continued to turn them in. He had instructed his underpaid, patient professional readers – teachers of foreign languages, for the most part – to look only at the first three and last two pages of any manuscript. If they promised another version of the East-West dilemma, disguised as a fresh look at the recent past, he did not want to see so much as a one-sentence summary.

By leaning into the aisle he could watch the last blessing. A line of mourners, Halina and her sobbing daughter at the head, shuffled around the coffin, each person ready to add an individual appeal for God's mercy. Forain stayed where he was. He neither pestered nor tried to influence imponderables; not since the death of the friend who had owned the cashmere coat. If the firm went into deeper decline, if it took the slide from shaky to foundering, he would turn to writing. Why not? At least he knew what he wanted to publish. It would get rid of any further need of dealing with living authors: their rent, their divorces, their abscessed teeth, not to speak of that new craze in the East – their psychiatrists. His first novel – what would he call it? He allowed a title to rise from his dormant unconscious imagination. It emerged, black and strong, on the cover of a book propped up in a store window. 'The Cherry Orchard'. His mind accepted the challenge. What about a sly, quiet novel, teasingly based on the play? A former property owner, after forty-seven years of exile, returns to Karl-Marx-Stadt to reclaim the family home. It now houses sixteen hardworking couples and thirty-eight small children. He throws them out, and the novel winds down with a moody description of curses and fistfights as imported workers try to install a satellite dish in the garden, where the children's swings used to be. It would keep a foot in the old territory, Forain thought, but with a radical shift of focus. He had to move sidelong: he could not all of a sudden start to publish poems about North Sea pollution and the threat to the herring catch.

Here was a joke he could have shared with Tremski. The stepdaughter had disconnected the telephone while Tremski was still in hospital, waiting to die; not that Forain wanted to dial an extinct number and let it ring. Even in Tremski's mortal grief over Barbara, the thought of Forain as his own author would have made him smile. He had accepted Forain, would listen to nothing said against him – just as he could not be dislodged from his fusty apartment and had remained faithful to his wife – but he had considered Forain's best efforts to be a kind of amateur, Western fiddling, and all his bright ideas to be false dawns. Forain lived a publisher's dream life, Tremski believed – head of a platoon of self-effacing, flat-broke writers who asked only to be read, believing they had something to say that was crucial to the West, that might even goad it into action. What sort of action? Forain still wondered. The intelligent fellow whose remains had just been committed to eternity was no different. He knew Forain was poor but believed he was rich. He thought a great new war would leave

Central Europe untouched. The liberating missiles would sail across without ruffling the topmost leaf of a poplar tree. As for the contenders, well, perhaps their time was up.

The congregation had risen. Instead of a last prayer, diffuse and anonymous, Forain chose to offer up a firmer reminder of Tremski: the final inventory of his flat. First, the entrance, where a faint light under a blue shade revealed layers of coats on pegs but not the boots and umbrellas over which visitors tripped. Barbara had never interfered, never scolded, never tried to clean things up. It was Tremski's place. Through an archway, the room Barbara had used. In a corner, the chair piled with newspapers and journals that Tremski still intended to read. Next, unpainted shelves containing files, some empty, some spilling foolscap not to be touched until Tremski had a chance to sort everything out. Another bookcase, this time with books. Above it, the spread of photographs of his old friends. A window, and the sort of view that prisoners see. In front of the window, a drop-leaf table that had to be cleared for meals. The narrow couch, still spread with a blanket, where Halina had slept until she ran away. (To the end, Barbara had expected her to return saying, 'It was a mistake.' Tremski would have made her welcome and even bought another sofa, at the flea market, for the child.) The dark-red armchair in which Forain had sat during his first meeting with Barbara. Her own straight-backed chair and the small desk where she wrote business letters for Tremski. On the wall, a charcoal drawing of Tremski – by an amateur artist, probably – dated June, 1945. It was a face that had come through; only just.

Mourners accustomed to the ceremonial turned to a neighbour to exchange the kiss of peace. Those who were not shrank slightly, as if the touch without warmth was a new form of aggression. Forain found unfocused, symbolised love positively terrifying. He refused the universal coming-together, rammed his hands in his pockets – like a rebellious child – and joined the untidy lines shuffling out into the rain.

Two hours later, the time between amply filled by the

accident, the arrival and departure of the ambulance, the long admittance procedure, and the waiting around natural to a service called Emergency, Forain left the hospital. The old lady was too stunned to have much to say for herself, but she could enunciate clearly, 'No family, no insurance.' He had left his address and, with even less inclination, a cheque he sincerely hoped was not a dud. The wind and sleet promised earlier in the day battered and drenched him. He skirted the building and, across a narrow street, caught sight of lines of immigrants standing along the north side of central police headquarters. Algerians stood in a separate queue.

There were no taxis. He was too hungry and wet to cross the bridge to the Place Saint-Michel – a three-minute walk. In a café on the Boulevard du Palais he hung his coat where he could keep an eye on it and ordered a toasted ham-and-cheese sandwich, a glass of Badoit mineral water, and small carafe of wine, and black coffee – all at once. The waiter forgot the wine. When he finally remembered, Forain was ready to leave. He wanted to argue about the bill but saw that the waiter looked frightened. He was young, with clumsy hands, feverish red streaks under his eyes, and coarse fair hair: foreign, probably working without papers, in the shadow of the most powerful police in France. All right, Forain said to himself, but no tip. He noticed how the waiter kept glancing towards someone or something at the far end of the room: his employer, Forain guessed. He felt, as he had felt much of the day, baited, badgered, and trapped. He dropped a tin of random coins on the tray and pulled on his coat. The waiter grinned but did not thank him, put the coins in his pocket, and carried the untouched wine back to the kitchen.

Shoulders hunched, collar turned up, Forain made his way to the taxi rank at the Place Saint-Michel. Six or seven people under streaming umbrellas waited along the curb. Around the corner a cab suddenly drew up and a woman got out. Forain took her place, as if it were the most natural thing in the world. He had stopped feeling hungry, but seemed to be wearing layers of damp towels. The driver, in a heavy accent, probably Portuguese, told Forain to quit the taxi. He was not allowed to pick up a passenger at that particular spot, close to a stand. Forain pointed out that the stand was empty. He snapped the lock shut – as if that made a difference – folded his arms, and sat shivering. He wished the driver the worst fate he could think of – to stand on the north side of police headquarters and wait for nothing.

'You're lucky to be working,' he suddenly said. 'You should see all those people without jobs, without papers, just over there, across the Seine.'

'I've seen them,' the driver said. 'I could be out of a job just for picking you up. You should be waiting your turn next to that sign, around the corner.'

They sat for some seconds without speaking. Forain studied the set of the man's neck and shoulders; it was rigid, tense. An afternoon quiz show on the radio seemed to take his attention, or perhaps he was pretending to listen and trying to decide if it was a good idea to appeal to a policeman. Such an encounter could rebound against the driver, should Forain turn out to be someone important – assistant to the office manager of a Cabinet minister, say.

Forain knew he had won. It was a matter of seconds now. He heard 'What was the name of the Queen of Sheba?' 'Which one?' 'The one who paid a visit to King Solomon.' 'Can you give me a letter?' 'B.' 'Brigitte?'

The driver moved his head back and forth. His shoulders dropped slightly. Using a low, pleasant voice, Forain gave the address of his office, offering the St Vincent de Paul convent as a landmark. He had thought of going straight home and changing his shoes, but catching pneumonia was nothing to the loss of the staunch Lisette; the sooner he could talk to her, the better. She should have come to the funeral. He could start with that. He realised that he had not given a thought to Tremski for almost three hours now. He continued the inventory, his substitute for a prayer. He was not sure where he had broken off – with the telephone on Barbara's desk? Tremski would not have a telephone in the room where he worked, but at the first ring he would call through the wall, 'Who is it?' Then 'What does he want? . . . He met me

97

where? . . . When we were in high school? . . . Tell him I'm too busy. No – let me talk to him.'

The driver turned the radio up, then down. 'I could have lost my job,' he said.

Every light in the city was ablaze in the dark rain. Seen through rivulets on a window, the least promising streets showed glitter and well-being. It seemed to Forain that in Tremski's dark entry there had been a Charlie Chaplin poster, relic of some Polish film festival. There had been crates and boxes, too, that had never been unpacked. Tremski would not move out, but in a sense he had never moved in. Suddenly, although he had not really forgotten them, Forain remembered the manuscripts he had snatched back from Halina. She had said none was actually finished, but what did she know? What if there were only a little, very little, left to be composed? The first thing to do was have them read by someone competent – not his usual painstaking and very slow professional readers but a bright young Polish critic, who could tell at a glance what was required. Filling gaps was a question of style and logic, and could just as well take place after translation.

When they reached the Rue du Bac the driver drew up as closely as he could to the entrance, even tried to wedge the cab between two parked cars, so that Forain would not have to step into a gutter filled with running water. Forain could not decide what to do about the tip, whether to give the man something extra (it was true that he could have refused to take him anywhere) or make him aware he had been aggressive. 'You should be waiting your turn . . .' still rankled. In the end, he made a Tremski-like gesture, waving aside change that must have amounted to thirty-five per cent of the fare. He asked for a receipt. It was not until after the man had driven away that Forain saw he had not included the tip in the total sum. No Tremski flourish was ever likely to carry a reward. That was another lesson of the day.

More than a year later, Lisette – now working only part-time – mentioned that Halina had neglected to publish in *Le Monde* the anniversary notice of Tremski's death. Did Forain want one to appear, in the name of the firm? Yes, of course. It would be wrong to say he had forgotten the apartment and everything in it, but the inventory, the imaginary camera moving around the rooms, filled him with impatience and a sense of useless effort. His mind stopped at the narrow couch with the brown blanket, Halina's bed, and he said to himself, What a pair those two were. The girl was right to run away. As soon as he had finished the thought he placed his hand over his mouth, as if to prevent the words from emerging. He went one further – bowed his head, like Tremski at Barbara's funeral, promising himself he would keep in mind things as they once were, not as they seemed to him now. But the apartment was vacated, and Tremski had disappeared. He had been prayed over thoroughly by a great number of people, and the only enjoyment he might have had from the present scene was to watch Forain make a fool of himself to no purpose.

There were changes in the office, too. Lisette had agreed to stay for the time it would take to train a new hand: a thin, pretty girl, part of the recent, nonpolitical imigration – wore a short leather skirt, said she did not care about money but loved literature and did not want to waste her life working on something dull. She got on with Halina and had even spared Forain the odd difficult meeting. As she began to get the hang of her new life, she lost no time spreading the story that Forain had been the lover of Barbara and would not let go a handsome and expensive coat that had belonged to Tremski. A posthumous, novel-length manuscript of Tremski's was almost ready for the printer, with a last chapter knitted up from fragments he had left trailing. The new girl, gifted in languages, compared the two versions and said he would have approved; and when Forain showed a moment of doubt and hesitation she was able to remind him of how, in the long run, Tremski had never known what he wanted.

Five Paintings of the New Japan

STEVEN HEIGHTON

A National Gallery

I Sunflowers

I WAS THE first foreigner to wait tables in the *Yumei no ato*. Summer enrolment was down at the English school where I taught so I needed to earn some extra money, and since I'd been eating at the restaurant on and off for months it was the first place I thought of applying. It was a small establishment built just after the war in a bombed-out section of the city, but when I saw it the area was studded with bank towers, slick boutiques, coffee shops and flourishing bars and the *Yumei no ato* was one of the oldest and most venerable places around. I was there most of the summer and I wish I could go back. I heard the other day from Nori, the dishwasher, who works part-time now in a camera store, that our ex-boss Mr Onishi has just fought and lost a battle with cancer.

'We have problems here every summer,' Mr Onishi sighed during my interview, 'with a foreign tourist people.' He peered up at me from behind his desk, two shadowy half-moons drooping under his eyes. 'Especially the Americans. If I hire you, you can deal to them.'

'With them,' I said automatically.

'You have experienced waitering?'

'A little,' I lied.

'You understand Japanese?'

'I took a course.'

'Say something to me in Japanese.'

I froze for a moment, then was ambushed by a phrase from my primer. '*Niwa ni wa furu-ike ga arimasu.*'

'In the garden,' translated Mr Onishi, 'there is an old pond.'

I stared abjectly at his bald patch.

'You cannot say a sentence more difficult than that?'

I told Mr Onishi it was a beginner's course. He glanced up at me and ran his fingers through a greying Vandyke beard.

'How well do you know the Japanese cuisine?'

'Not so well,' I answered in a light bantering tone that I hoped would disarm him, 'but I know what I like.'

He frowned and checked his watch, then darted a glance at the bank calendar on the wall by his desk.

'Morinaga speaks a little English,' he said. 'He will be your trainer. Tomorrow at 1600 hours you start.'

'You won't be sorry, sir,' I told him.

'I shall exploit you,' he said, 'until someone more qualitied applies.'

Nori Morinaga leaned against the steam table and picked his nose with the languid, luxurious gestures of an epicure enjoying an after-dinner cigar. He was the biggest Japanese I'd ever seen and the coke-bottle glasses perched above his huge nose seemed comically small.

'Ah, *gaijin-san!*' he exclaimed as he saw me, collecting himself and inflating to his full height. 'Welcome in! Hail fellow well-hung!'

I wondered if I'd heard him correctly.

'It gives me great pressure!'

I had. I had.

Nori Morinaga offered me his hand at the same moment I

tried to bow. Nervously we grinned at each other, then began to laugh. He was a full head taller than I was, burly as a linebacker but prematurely hunched as if stooping in doorways and under low ceilings had already affected his spine. He couldn't have been over twenty-five. His hair was brush-cut like a Marine's and when he spoke English his voice and manner seemed earnest and irreverent at the same time.

'Onishi-San tells me I will help *throw you the ropes*,' he chuckled. 'Ah, I like that expression. Do you know it? I study English at the University but the *gaijin-sensei* always says Japanese students must be more idiomatic so I picked up this book' – his giant hand brandished a thick paperback – 'and I study it *like a rat out of hell*.'

He grinned enigmatically, then giggled. I couldn't tell if he was serious or making fun of me.

Nori pronounced his idiomatic gleanings with savage enthusiasm, his magnified eyes widening and big shoulders bunching for emphasis as if to ensure his scholarship did not pass unseen. I took the book and examined it: a dog-eared, discount edition of UP-TO-DATE ENGLISH PHRASES FOR JAPANESE STUDENTS – in the 1955 edition.

'We open in an hour,' he said. 'We are *oppressed for time*. Come on, *I'm going to show you what's what*.'

Situated in a basement, under a popular *karaoke* bar, the *Yumei na ato*'s two small rooms were dimly lit and the atmosphere under the low ceiling was damp and cool, as in an air-raid shelter or submarine. I wondered if this cramped, covert aura hadn't disturbed some of the earliest patrons, whose memories of the air-raids would still have been fresh – but I didn't ask Nori about that. The place had always been popular, he said, especially in summer, when it was one of the coolest spots in Ōsaka.

A stairway descended from street level directly into the dining room so on summer days, after the heat and bright sunshine of the city, guests would sink into a cool aquatic atmosphere of dim light and swaying shadows. The stairway was flanked on one side by a small bar and on the other by the sushi counter where I'd eaten before. An adjoining room contained a larger, more formal dining space which gave onto the kitchen through a swinging door at the back. Despite the rather western-style seating arrangements (tables and chairs instead of the traditional *zabuton* and *tatami*) the dining area was decorated in authentic Japanese fashion with hanging lanterns, calligraphic scrolls, a *tokonoma* containing an empty *maki-e* vase, *bonsai* and *noren* and several framed, original *sumi-e* prints. The only unindigenous ornament was a large reproduction of Van Gogh's 'Sunflowers' hung conspicuously on the wall behind the sushi bar.

'Onishi–San says it's for the behoof of the American tourists,' Nori explained, 'but I'd *bet my bottom* he put it there for the bankers who come in *the wee-wee hours*. It's the bankers who are really interested in that stuff.' He sniffed and gestured contemptuously towards 'Sunflowers' and towards the *sumi-e* prints as well, as if wanting me to see he considered all art frivolous and dispensible, no matter where it came from.

I didn't realise till much later the gesture meant something else.

Nori showed me around the kitchen and introduced me to the cooks, who were just arriving. Kenji Komatsu was head chef. Before returning to Japan and starting a family he'd worked for a few years in Vancouver and Montreal and his memories of that time were good, so he was delighted to hear I was Canadian. He insisted I call him Mat. 'And don't listen to anything this big whale tells you,' he warned me affably, poking Nori in the stomach. 'So much sugar and McDonald's the young ones are eating these days. . . This one should be in the *sumo* ring, not my kitchen.'

'*Sumo* is for old folk,' Nori said, tightening his gut and ironically saluting a small, aproned man who had just emerged from the walk-in fridge.

'*Time is on the march,*' Nori intoned. '*Nothing can stop it now!*'

Second chef Yukio Miyoshi glared at Nori, then at me with frank disgust and muttered to himself in Japanese. He marched towards the back of the kitchen and began gutting a large fish. 'Doesn't like the foreigners,' Nori grinned indifferently. 'So it is. You can't pleasure everybody.'

The swinging door burst open and a small dark form hurtled into the kitchen and disappeared behind the steam table. Nori grabbed me by the arm.

'It's Oh-San, the sushi chef – come, we must hurry.'

Mr Oh was a jittery middle-aged man who scurried through the restaurant, both hands frantically embracing a mug of fresh coffee. Like all the elder folks, Nori explained, Mr Oh worked too hard. . .

We finally cornered him by the walk-in fridge and Nori introduced us. Clearly he had not heard of Mr Onishi's latest hiring decision – he flung down his mug and gawked as if I were a health inspector who'd just told him twenty of last night's customers were in the hospital with food poisoning.

The *yukata* which Mr Oh insisted I try on looked all right, and in the changeroom I finally gave in and let him brylcreem and comb back my curly hair into the slick, shining facsimile of a typical Japanese cut. As he worked with the comb, his face close to mine, I could see the tic in his left eye and smell his breath, pungent with coffee.

'You look *marvellous*,' Nori laughed on my return, 'and you know who you are!' He winked and blew me a kiss.

Mr Onishi entered and snapped some brusque truculent command. When the others had fled to their stations he addressed me in English.

'I hope you are ready for your first shift. We will have many guests tonight. Come – you will have to serve the aliens.'

From the corner of my eye I could see Nori clowning behind the grille, two chopsticks pressed to his forehead like antennae.

As I trailed Mr Onishi into the dining room two men and a woman, all young, tall, clad smartly in *yukata*, issued from behind the bar and lined up for inspection. One of the men wore a pearl earring and his hair was unusually long for a Japanese, while the woman had a rich, brown, luminous skin and plump, attractive features. Mr Onishi introduced the other man as Akiburo. He was a college student and looked the part with his regulation haircut and sly, wisecracking expression.

With patent distaste Mr Onishi billed the long-haired man

as 'your bartender, who likes to be known as Johnny Walker.'
The man fingered his earring and smiled out of the side of his
mouth. 'And this is Suzuki Michiko, a waitress.' She bowed
awkwardly and studied her plump, brown hands, the pale skin
on the underside of her wrists.

My comrades, as Mr Onishi called them, had been expecting me, and now they would show me to my sector of the
restaurant – three small tables in the corner of the second
room. In this occidental ghetto, it seemed, Mr Onishi thought
I would do the least possible damage to the restaurant's
ambience and reputation. Michiko explained in simple
Japanese that since my tables were right by the kitchen door I
could ask Nori for help as soon as I got in trouble.

The *tokonoma*, I now saw, had been decorated with a spray
of poppies.

'We open shortly,' Mr Onishi declared, striding towards us.
His manner was vigorous and forceful but his eyes seemed
tired, their light extinguished. 'We probably will have some
American guests tonight. Your job will be to service them.'

'I'll do my best sir.'

'And coffee – you will now take over from Michiko and
bring Mr Oh his coffee. He will want a fresh supply every
half-hour. Do not forget!'

For the first hour the second room remained empty, as did
the tables of the front room, but the sushi bar was overrun
within minutes by an army of ravenous, demanding guests.
'Coffee,' cried Mr Oh, and I brought him cup after cup while
the customers gaped at me and hurled at Mr Oh questions I
could not understand. The coffee yellowed his tongue and
reddened his eyes, which took on a weird, narcotic glaze,
while steam mixed with sweat and stood out in bold clear
beads on his cheeks and upper lip. Orders were called out as
more guests arrived. Mr Oh's small red hands scuttled like
sand crabs over the counter, making predatory forays into the
display case to seize hapless chunks of smelt or salmon or eel
and then wielding above them a fish-silver knife, replacing
the knife deftly, swooping down on speckled quail eggs and
snapping shells between thumb and forefinger and squeezing

the yolk onto bricks of rice the other hand had just formed. Then, with fingers dangling, the hands would hover above an almost-completed dish, and they would waver slightly like squid or octopuses in currents over the ocean floor, then pounce, abrupt and accurate, on an errant grain of rice or any garnish or strip of ginger imperfectly arranged, and an instant later the finished work, irreproachable and beyond time like a still-life or a great sculpture, would appear on the glass above the display case from which it was snatched within seconds by the grateful customers or attentive staff.

The process was dizzying. I was keenly aware of my ignorance and when I was not airlifting coffee to the sushi bar I was busy in my own sector studying the menu and straightening tables.

Around eight o'clock Mr Onishi entered the second room, carrying menus, followed by a man and woman who were both heavyset, tall and fair-haired. The man wore a tailored navy suit and carried a briefcase. The woman's hair was piled high in a steep bun that resembled the nose-cone of a rocket, and her lipstick, like her dress, was a pushy, persistent shade of red.

'Take good care with Mr and Mrs Cruikshank,' Onishi-San murmured as he passed me and showed them to their seats. 'Mr Cruikshank is a very important man – a diplomat, from America. Bring two martinis to begin.'

Mr Cruikshank's voice was genteel and collected, his manner smooth as good brandy. 'How long have you been working in this place?' he inquired.

'Two hours,' I told him, serving the martinis.

'Surprised they'd have an American working here.' With one hand he yanked a small plastic sabre from his olive, then pinched the olive and held it aloft like a tiny globe.

'I'm not American,' I said.

There was a pause while Mr and Mrs Cruikshank processed this unlooked-for information.

'Well surely you're not Japanese?' Mrs Cruikshank asked, slurring her words a little. 'Maybe half?'

Mr Cruikshank swallowed his olive then impaled his wife's

with the plastic sword. He turned to me, inadvertently aiming the harmless tip at my throat.

'*Nihongo wakaru?*' he asked in plain, masculine speech. *You understand Japanese?* I recognised his accent as outstanding.

'Only a little,' I said.

'I'll bet he's Dutch,' Mrs Cruikshank wagered. 'The Dutch speak such beautiful English – hardly any accent at all.'

'You'll find it hard here without any Japanese,' Mr Cruikshank advised me, ignoring his wife, drawing the sword from his teeth so the gleaming olive stayed clenched between them.

'*Coffee,*' Mr Oh called from the sushi bar.

'I'll only be serving the foreign customers, sir.'

Mr Cruikshank bit into his olive. 'Some of the foreign customers,' he said, 'prefer being served in Japanese.'

'Or maybe German,' said Mrs Cruikshank.

'I can speak some German,' I said. 'Would you like it if – '

'*Coffee,*' cried Mr Oh from the sushi bar.

Mrs Cruikshank was beaming. 'I was right,' she said, lifting her martini glass in a kind of toast. '*Wie geht's?*'

'We'd like some sushi,' Mr Cruikshank interrupted his wife, who was now grimacing at her drink as if trying to recall another German phrase.

I fumbled with my pad.

'An order each of *maguro, saba, hamachi*, and – why not? – some sea urchin. Hear it's full of mercury these days, but hell, we've got to eat something.'

'Yes, sir.'

'And two more martinis.' He pointed at his glass with the plastic sword.

'Got it.'

'*Danke schön,*' roared Mrs Cruikshank as I hurried from the room. . .

While waiting for Johnny Walker to finish the martinis I noticed an older guest rise from the sushi bar and stumble towards the washrooms. As he saw me, his red eyes widened and he lost his footing and crashed into the bar, slamming a frail elbow against the cash register. He righted himself with quick slapstick dignity and stood blushing. When I moved to help him he waved me off.

Johnny Walker smirked and muttered as he shook the martinis and for a moment the words and the rattling ice took on a primitive, mocking rhythm, like a chant. The older man began to swear at him and reached out as if to grab his earring, his long hair. *Shin jin rui*, the old man muttered – *strange inscrutable creature*! I'd heard it was a new phrase coined by the old to describe the young.

'Wake up, old man,' Johnny snapped in plain Japanese as he poured the martinis. 'Watch out where you're going.'

The man lurched off.

'Always drunk, or fast asleep in their chairs.'

'*Coffee*,' cried Mr Oh from the sushi bar.

II The Dream

'Tell me something about the restaurant,' I said to Nori, sweeping my hand in a half-circle and nodding at the closed bar. 'How old is the place?'

Nori finished his Budweiser and balanced the empty can on a growing tower of empties. 'It was built after the war ends,' he belched – and I couldn't help noticing how casually he used the word *war*. His expression was unchanged, his voice was still firm, his eyes had not recoiled as if shamed by some unspeakable profanity. That was how my older students reacted when The War came up in a lesson. No doubt Mr Onishi would react the same way. But not Nori. For him the war was history, fiction – as unreal and insubstantial as a dimly remembered dream, a dream of jungles, the faded memory of a picture in a storybook. He wasn't much younger than me.

'What about the name,' I said, '*Yumei no ato?* I mean, I can figure out the individual words, but I can't make sense of the whole thing.' *Yumei*, I knew, meant 'dream', *no* signified possession, like an apostrophe and an 's', and *ato*, I thought, meant 'after'.

Nori lit a cigarette and trained a mischievous gaze on my hairline. His capacity for drink was larger than average for a

Japanese but now after four tins of beer he was flushed, theatrical and giddy. He wrinkled his broad nose, as if at a whiff of something rotten, and spat out, 'It's a line from a poem we had to study in the high school. Ah, Steve-San, University is so much better, we have fun in the sun, we make whoopee, we live for the present tense and forget all our yesterdays and tomorrows – I hated high school, so much work. We had to study this famous poem.'

He stood and recited the lines with mock gravity:

> *'Natsu kusa ya!*
> *Tsuamono domo ga*
> *Yumei no ato.'*

'It's a *haiku*,' I said.

'Aye, aye, captain.' He slumped down and the tower of beer cans wobbled. 'Do you watch Star Trek?'

'I'm not sure,' I said, 'that I understand it.'

'Oh, well, it's just a TV show – about the future and the stars.'

'I mean the poem, Nori, the *haiku*.'

'Ah, the poem – naturally you don't understand. It's old Japanese – old Japanese language, old Japanese mind – not so easy for us to understand either. It's Matsuo Bashō, dead like Shakespeare over three hundred years. Tomorrow and tomorrow and tomorrow. We had to study them both in school. Full fathom five and all that.'

'But about that last line. . . '

'*Yumei no ato?*'

I nodded.

'That's the name of the restaurant. You see, when Mr Onishi's uncle built the place after the war he gave it that name. It's a very strange name for a restaurant! Mr Onishi was just a boy then.'

'What does it mean?'

'I don't think Mr Onishi would have called it that, but when his uncle went over the bucket he didn't want to change the name. Out of respect.'

I finished my own beer and contributed to the tower of cans. The other staff had gone upstairs to the *karaoke* place but they'd drunk a lot of Bud and Kirin beforehand and the tower was growing high.

'I wonder,' I said, 'if the words mean "when the dream is over"?'

Nori took a long drag on his cigarette. 'I don't think they do,' he finally said. 'And besides, the dream had only just begun. . . The uncle was smart and he built *Yumei no ato* to attract foreigners as well as Japanese and it's done really well, as you can see.' His eyes brightened. '*We're going great guns.*'

Mr Onishi's telephone began to ring from the back of the restaurant, where he was still working. We heard his answer.

'The first line,' I said, 'is "Ah! Summer grasses", right?'

Nori seemed to be weighing this, then blurted out, '*Yumei no ato* means . . . it means what's left over after a dream.'

Mr Onishi's voice could be heard faintly. I surveyed the shaky tower, the ashtrays, the skeletons of fish beached on the sides of our empty plates.

'Leftovers' I said, ironically.

'There's another word.'

'What about vestige? No? Remnant?'

Nori stubbed out his cigarette like a game-show panelist pressing a buzzer. '*Remnant!*' he cried, '*your choice is absolutely correct, for five thousand dollars and a dream home!*' Suddenly he grew calm, thoughtful. 'So many foreign words sound alike,' he mused. 'There's a famous Dutch painter with that name.'

'Rembrandt?' I said.

'That's him. A bank here in Umeda just bought a Remnant for nine hundred million yen.'

'*Yumei no ato*,' I said, 'must mean "the remnant of dreams".'

Nori furrowed his brow, then nodded.

'Funny name for a restaurant,' I said. 'You like game shows?'

As if in a fresh wind the paper *noren* in the doorway behind the sushi bar blew open and a haggard phantom came in. Mr Onishi. He seemed to look right through us. Nori suggested we clean up and leave. We began to pile the chopsticks and empty plates onto a tray. I glanced up and saw Mr Onishi beckoning Nori.

'Please go examine the guest toilet,' Nori told me.

The guest washroom was immaculate – I'd cleaned it myself two hours before – but I spent a few minutes checking it again so Nori and Mr Onishi would know I was thorough. For the second time that night I was intrigued by a notice in the stall, pencilled on the back of an old menu and taped to the door –

TO ALL FOREIGNERS:
OUR TUBES ARE IN ILL REPAIR, PLEASE
DO NOT THROW YOUR PEEPERS
IN THE TOILET.

When I came out of the washroom Mr Onishi was gone. 'The boss looks awful,' I whispered to Nori, my smile forced. 'When he was on the phone before – maybe a guest was calling to complain about the new waiter, eh?'

'Possibly,' Nori said, 'but more likely it was a banker.'

'What, at this time of night?'

Nori shrugged. 'The elder folks, I told you, they're working late. And early, too – there was a banker here first thing this morning to talk at Mr Onishi.'

'Bankers,' I scoffed, shaking my head. 'Not trouble, I hope. . . .'

Nori laughed abruptly. Arm tensed karate-style he approached the tower of cans.

III The Kermess

CAMPAI!

A month has gone past and the whole staff, *gaijin-san* included, are relaxing after a manic Saturday night in the *Yumei no ato*. August in Ōsaka: with other waiters and students and salarymen we sit in a beer garden under the full moon above twenty-two storeys of department store merchandise, imported clothing and cologne and books and records, Japanese-made electronics, wedding supplies,

Persian carpets and French cigarettes and aquariums full of swordfish and coral and casino-pink sand from the Arabian Sea, appliances and appliqué, blue-china chopstick-holders, computers, patio-furniture, coffee-shops, chefs and friendly clerks and full-colour reproductions of well-known Western portraits, etchings, sketches, sculptures, landscapes that Japanese banks are buying like real estate and bringing back to Ōsaka, anything, anything at all, SPEND AND IT SHALL BE GIVEN, endless armies of customers and ah, summer tourists billowing like grain through the grounds of Ōsaka's most famous department store. SURELY, quoth the tele-vangelist from the multitudinous screens, SURELY THE PEOPLE IS GRASS.

(For a moment the tables shudder as a tremour ripples through toxic earth under the Bargain Basement, and passes.)

CAMPAI! Western rock and roll music blasts from hidden speakers. In a few minutes the *O-bon* fireworks are due to start and we've got the best seats in the house. The plastic table sags and may soon buckle as another round of draft materialises and is swiftly distributed. A toast to this, a toast to that, *campai, CAMPAI*, every time we lift our steins to take a drink, someone is proposing another toast: in a rare gesture Komatsu toasts the wait-staff (Akiburo and Johnny and Michiko and me) because (this in English) we were really on the balls tonight and made no errors at all. *Campai!* Akiburo toasts Komatsu and Mr Oh and second chief Miyoshi in return, presumably for turning out so much good food on such a busy night and making it all look easy. *Campai!* Mr Oh raises his glass of ice-coffee in thanks while second chef Miyoshi, drunk and expansive, in a rare good mood, toasts Nori for not smacking his head in the storeroom when he went back for extra soy sauce, *CAMPAI*, (this translated by the delighted Nori, who immediately hefts his stein and decrees a toast to Michiko, the waitress, simply because he's mad about her and isn't it lucky she doesn't speak English?).

The blushing Michiko lifts her heavy stein with soft plump hands and meekly suggests, in Japanese, that it might be possible, perhaps, to maybe if it isn't too much trouble drink a toast to our skilful bartender, Johnny Walker, without whom we could hardly have survived the night, it seems to me, after all, or maybe we might have? *Campai! Campai!* The flesh of Johnny's ear lobe reddens around his pearl stud. He smirks and belts back another slug of whiskey.

'To Onishi–San,' he says in English. 'To *Yumei no ato.*' And he quickly adds some other remark in harsh, stacatto Japanese.

'*CAMPAI!*' I holler, hoisting my stein triumphantly so that beer froths up and sloshes over the lip of the glass. But no one elsc has followed suit. They are all gazing without expression at the table or into their drinks. Johnny Walker's head hangs lowest, his features hidden.

Komatsu glances at his watch and predicts that the fireworks will start in thirty seconds.

I turn to Nori. 'Did I do something wrong?'

Miyoshi and Mr Oh both snap something at him. I can't make out a word.

'Well, not at all,' says Nori softly, 'I guess people just don't feel like talking about work after a busy night.'

I purse my lips. 'I have the feeling you're not being completely honest with me.'

'Of course I'm not!' Nori protests, and I wonder if we've understood each other.

At that moment the fireworks start. Everyone at our table looks up, relieved. '*O-bon,*' Nori says to me, relaxed again. 'Tonight, the ancestors return.' Flippantly he rolls his eyes, or only seems to – I can't be sure because his coke–bottle lenses reflect the moonlight and the fierce red glare of the first rockets. One after another they are up out of the dark expanse of Nagai Park, miles to the north, then slow down and pause at their zenith and explode in corollas of violet, emerald, coral, cream, apricot and indigo. *Hanabi*, they call them in Japanese: fire–flowers. The steins are raised again, glasses rammed together, toasts made and spirits drawn skyward by the aerial barrage.

My flat is somewhere down there on the far side of Nagai Park and now I picture a defective missile veering off course and buzzing my neighbourhood, terrifying the old folks,

113

plunging with a shriek like an air-raid siren through the roof of
my flat. . .

Nori grabs my arm with steely fingers. 'Steve-san, listen –
do you hear what I hear?' I'm still concentrating on the look
and sound of the exploding flowers, but suddenly I pick it out,
the bouncy unmistakable opening bars of 'Like a Virgin.'

'It's the Madonna!'

'I hear it, Nori.'

He lumbers to his feet. 'You want to dance? Hey, get up!
Come off it!'

Michiko and Johnny Walker are already up beside the table,
strobe-lit by the fireworks, shaking themselves to the beat,
Michiko with a timid, tentative look and Johnny with self-
conscious abandon. The older staff sit motionless and watch
the exploding rockets. Nori glances at them, at Michiko, at
me, and I can tell he doesn't want to lose her. As she dances her
small hands seem to catch and juggle the light.

'Life is so curt,' he pleads. 'You only lived once!' He gives
me a half-smile, a sly wink, and I'm no longer sure he doesn't
know exactly what he's saying.

CAMPAI! Nori hauls me to my feet and heaves me from the
table in a blind teetering polka, out towards Johnny and
Michiko, his big boorish feet beating a mad tattoo on my toes.
Komatsu and Mr Oh, the elders in the crowd, link arms and
start keening some old Japanese song. Steins raised, they sway
together to a stately rhythm much slower than Madonna's,
their voices rolling mournfully over the antique minors and
archaic words. The rockets keep exploding. Their sound takes
on a rhythm which seems to fall between the beats of the
opposing songs – then as I watch, one of the rockets fails to
burst. Like a falling star it streaks earthward in silence and
disappears over the city.

IV Guernica

I woke early the next morning with a headache and a burning
stomach. I'd been dreaming. I dreamed Michiko had come
home with me to my flat and we stood together hand-in-hand

on the threshold, staring in at a gutted interior. The guilty rocket, however, had not actually exploded – it was resting in perfect condition, very comfortably, on an unburnt, freshly-made *futon* in the centre of the room.

Michiko took me by the hand and led me into the ruin. When the smoke began to drown me she covered my mouth with her own. Her breath was clean and renewing as wind off an early-morning sea and when she pulled away the smell of burning was gone. She removed her flowered kimono and stood naked before me. The nipples of her firm small breasts were now the accusing eyes of a seduced and betrayed woman – then I was naked too, and utterly absolved, and we were lying side by side amid the acrid wreckage by the futon. She climbed atop me and took me inside her, slowly, making small articulate sighs and rolling her head back and forth so her dark bangs rippled like a midnight waterfall across my nipples, and the blue-black hair was curved as space-time and full of sparks like the Milky Way, which in the Japanese tongue is called *ama no gawa*, the river of heaven.

I wanted to come, to fill the gathering space inside her, and I wanted to run my tongue down the soft pale line of hair from her breasts to her belly and on up the wooded mound of Venus and lick the nectar from her tender orchid, as the Japanese poets say, but then it came to me that Nori had meant to tell me something important – about Michiko? About a poem? Or was there something I'd asked him that he hadn't answered?

Summer grasses. . . Something left over after dreams. . .

What a stupid time to be thinking about poetry.

I woke embarrassed, but with a feeling of desperate tenderness for Michiko, to whom I'd hardly ever spoken and who had inspired, I thought, no more than a generic interest on my part. It was like missing a lover who'd slept beside me all night and had just left and gone home before I woke. . .

Well, I reflected, a dream like that was better than the waitering nightmares I'd had all the time till recently, and still woke from now and then. Usually I'd enter the restaurant and be told I was two hours late and none of the other wait-staff had shown up and the restaurant was full and we were booked solid till midnight. Other times I would realise I'd forgotten a couple or threesome who'd been seated two hours ago in the back corner of the second room and would they believe now it was just an honest mistake and I'd been really busy and meaning to get to them all along? Sometimes they were the Cruikshanks, and sometimes Mr Sato who (Nori had told me) was a professor at the University in Kyōto but had been demoted and now taught primary kids in Nagai, and that was why he drank so much and was so cold and pedantic when he spoke to you. In fact the unrequited dream-diners could be just about anyone, because the summer had been busy and now I was serving both foreigners and Japanese alike.

It had been the busiest summer in years, Komatsu said, and we were attracting more tourists than ever before – so why the visible anxiety whenever talk after-hours came round to the restaurant? Mr Onishi did not look like a man with a flourishing business. Perhaps he was ill and everyone was worried? I'd been reading articles lately about the soaring incidence of cancer in Japan, the spread of big business and factories into the countryside, toxins in the soil, polluted water, poisonous seafood. . .

'I think you'd better level with me,' I told Nori the night of my dream.

Miyoshi was standing by the walk-in, reading the *Sangyo Keizai*, and Komatsu was behind the steam table chopping onion. But I had the feeling they were listening to us, and so did Nori.

'*Not here,*' he whispered.

'Ah, such good news,' growled Miyoshi, lowering his paper with an unpleasant smile. Since he hardly ever spoke English I knew the remark was meant for me. 'Such good news about the yen!'

Nori shook his head. 'For some the war has never ended.'

'*Nihon ichiban!*' Miyoshi cried. 'Japan is number one!'

'And he wasn't even born till after,' Nori grumbled. 'I don't understand.'

'Maybe we should talk somewhere else,' I said.

Nori nodded, but Komatsu set down his knife and said quickly. 'No. It's all right. Steve-san is part of the restaurant now – we should tell him the truth.' Eyes pink and glistening, he walked out from behind the steam table and pulled the newspaper from Miyoshi's hands.

Miyoshi scowled, did an about-face and marched into the fridge.

'Look at this,' Komatsu sniffled, handing me the paper.

'You know I can't read Japanese.'

'Of course. Don't read, just look – the pictures.'

In the lower right-hand corner of the front page several well-known pieces of European art were reproduced in hazy black and white. One was a Rousseau, the second a Gauguin, the third a Brueghel. I couldn't read the caption beneath but I could make out the name of a prominent Ōsaka bank, written in *romaji*.

'And Van Gogh,' Komatsu said, frowning. 'I hear they just bought another costly painting by Van Gogh – so many paintings they are buying and bringing to Japan.'

We could hear Miyoshi in the fridge, muttering to himself, furiously shifting things around.

'They're buying everything in their sights,' Nori said, his usual gusto tangibly absent.

I told them I knew a bit about these purchases, but didn't see what they had to do with us.

'Well,' Komatsu started, 'they need some place to put these paintings. . .' His voice tapered off on the last words. I sensed I was being counted on, in customary Japanese fashion, to finish the sentence mentally so that everyone would be spared embarrassment.

'Chagall, too,' Komatsu resumed, 'and Rembrandt and Picasso.' *Big-asshole*, it sounded like, but I knew who he meant. 'Costly things . . . they need to find a place to put them all. . .'

'Like an art gallery,' I said.

Komatsu rubbed his eyes with a corner of his apron. 'I'm afraid so.'

It had been just like Dallas, Nori groaned, describing how

the bank had first made polite offers to the dozen businesses operating in the block where they meant to build, and most were politely accepted. But several proprietors (including Mr Onishi and the owner of the Idaho Caffeine Palace, a large coffee shop dating to the late forties) had refused to consider them. Secretly the bank made more attractive offers, then a final offer which the firm's representative begged Mr Onishi to accept, because if a negotiated settlement proved necessary then payment would revert to the level of the initial sum – or, conceivably, somewhat less.

Mr Onishi had ignored the bank's covert threats and a negotiated settlement proved necessary. Unfortunately it did not involve negotiation. The bank produced lawyers who showed that actual title to the land had belonged to the bank till the end of the war and they argued that the transfer of deeds had been improperly handled by the over-worked civil authorities of the time.

The young lawyers (I could just hear them) moved further that since the art gallery would be a public facility of great benefit to all citizens of the prefecture and would attract hundreds of thousands of foreigners to Ōsaka, it was in effect a civic institution, albeit privately owned, and the city should urge Mr Onishi to come to terms.

'The court is asking Mr Onishi to accept,' Nori said, 'but he just says no.'

Nihon ichiban, we heard faintly from the fridge.

Komatsu took the newspaper from me and walked back around the steam table. He began to giggle, like a bad comedian setting up a punchline. 'They're going to tear us down,' he said, laughing openly. 'Soon!'

Nori was chuckling, too, as the Japanese often will when speaking of their own misfortunes. Komatsu was laughing harder than I'd ever seen him, so I knew he must really be upset.

I paused respectfully. 'Listen, I'm really sorry to hear this.'

Komatsu roared with laughter. Nori continued to cackle. I asked them if they knew when these things were going to happen.

'There's no time like presently,' Nori said, slapping me on the shoulder a bit harder than he needed to. 'Come on, it's a busy night tonight, we'd better get happening.'

'Please take coffee now to Mr Oh-San,' Komatsu giggled.

Miyoshi was still marching around in the fridge.

V The Starry Night

September in Ōsaka is just as hot as July or August and this year it was worse. Though many of the tourists were gone, the *Yumei no ato* was busier than ever – Mr Onishi's struggle with the bank was now common knowledge, so old customers came often to show their support and the sushi bar was crowded with curious locals. Meanwhile enrolment was picking up at the school and I had to cut back on my hours as a waiter.

Mr Onishi was upset when I told him, but since I knew now of the epic struggle he was waging each day in the courts (Nori got the details from Komatsu and passed them on to me) I found it hard to feel angry in return. The boss, after all, was showing tremendous pluck. Sure, he was of another generation, a hardy breed of industrious survivors, and as a child he would have absorbed with his mother's milk the bracing formula of *bushido*, but this was valour way beyond the call of duty. He was giving Japan's second biggest bank the fight of its life. Already the original date for demolition was three weeks in arrears. . .

I heard that after receiving the court's final decision, Mr Onishi sighed and said '*Yappari nah*. It is as I expected. They will build a museum and a new country and fill both with foreign things.'

The demolition was set for the end of September and the *Yumei no ato* was to close a week before.

On the last night, a Saturday, the dining room was booked solid from five till closing with regular customers, both Japanese and foreign. We assembled by the bar a few minutes before five to wait for Mr Onishi and at five sharp he emerged from his office. He marched up to us, a menu tucked under one arm like a swagger stick, then briefed us in a formal and highly nuanced Japanese that I could not follow, though the general tenor of his speech was easy enough to guess. Or was it? Sometimes I wondered if I'd ever done more than misimagine what these people felt and believed.

A current of laughter rippled through the staff and Nori nudged me appreciatively, forgetting for a moment I did not understand.

Mr Onishi dismissed us and we hurried off to complete our preparations as he climbed the stairs and opened the door. A long shaft of dirty sunlight pierced the cool gloom, and a few seconds later our guests began to descend, bringing with them the hot muggy air of the street.

'Meet me in the back,' I told Nori.

We stood in the kitchen on either side of the open rice machine, slowly filling it with the contents of two clay cooking pots. Thick billows of steam rose between us and Nori's face was intermittently clouded, his eyes nacreous, indistinct, like a man under a foot of water.

'So what did Onishi-San say,' I asked, scooping the soft, sweet-smelling grains into the machine.

'He was apologising.'

'Apologising,' I said.

'Sure. He was apologising for letting the bank close the *Yumei no ato*. He says it's all on his shoulders. He feels responsible for the jobs we will lose. He says he is sorry because he has felled us.'

The steam was thinning and I could see Nori clearly. His big face was pink and sweating.

'He says his uncle was a soldier in the old navy and after the war he built this restaurant with his own two hands. So he says that by losing the restaurant he has felled his uncle, too.'

'But isn't his uncle dead?'

Nori put down his pot and gave me a faintly disappointed look.

'For many years. But so the old people believe – they can fell the dead as well as the breathing. Like being caught *between the devil and the deep blue sea, neh*?'

I nodded and stared into the rice cooker, its churning steam spectral and hypnotic.

'I feel sorry for him,' I said.

'So it is, all the while. The big fish eat the little.'

There was a harsh grating sound as he scraped rice from the bottom of his pot.

It was the busiest night of the summer but the customers were gentle and undemanding and the atmosphere, as at a funeral reception, was chastened and sadly festive and thick with solidarity. The foreigners left huge tips and Mr Oh grunted graciously whenever I freshened his coffee. It fell to Michiko to serve the disagreeable Mr Sato for the last time and though he usually deplored the grammar and fashions of her generation, he was tolerant tonight and even remarked at one point on her resemblance to his own daughter. The Cruik-shanks were among the last to arrive. When they left, just before closing, Mrs Cruikshank said she trusted I wouldn't have to go home to Germany just yet and surely with my good English I could land another job. . .

The last guests, our oldest customers, intoxicated and teary-eyed, staggered up the stairs around midnight and we dragged together a few tables and sank down for a last meal. Mat and Nori and second chef Miyoshi filed from the kitchen bearing platters of steaming rice and salmon teriyaki; at Mr Onishi's behest Johnny Walker opened the bar to all staff. And now, though I'd felt more and more a part of things over the last months, I sensed my saddened colleagues closing ranks, retreating into dialect, resorting to nuance, idiom and silence, a semaphore of glances and tics and nods. Nori loomed on the far side of the table with Michiko beside him. They were talking quietly. In the shadows by their chair-legs I could see two hands linked, like sinuous sea-creatures, twined and mating in the deep.

Johnny had finished the last of the Johnny Walker Red and was now working on a bottle of Old Granddad. Mr Oh was not drinking. He sat mutely, his agile hands wrapped around one beer tin after another, crushing them and laying them to rest among the plates and ashtrays. Komatsu and second chef

Miyoshi were smoking side by side, eyes half-closed, meditating on the fumes that rose and spread outward over their heads.

Mr Onishi, I suppose, was in his office. At one-thirty he came out and told everyone it was time to leave. There were some last half-hearted toasts and deep bowing and then we all stumbled upstairs and outside. The night air was cool and fresh. We looked, I thought, like a beaten rabble. As if wounded, Nori tottered over and proffered a scrap of paper the size of a cheque or phone bill. 'Here,' he said, his speech slurred, 'I almost forgot. That poem they called the restaurant for. . . Remember?'

He and Michiko swayed before me, their features painted a smooth flawless amber by the gentle light of the doorway. Behind them the brooding profiles of bank and office towers and beyond those in long swirling ranks the constellations of early autumn.

I took the slip of paper and held it to the light:

Ah! summer grass/this group of warriors'/remnant of
    dream
(this poem by Matsuo Bashō, lived same time as
    Shakespeare)
    So long and take care of yourself. Nori.

He shrugged when I thanked him. 'We had to study it back then. A real pin in the ass.'

'Drop by the school sometime,' I said. 'Please, both of you. . .'

I knew they wouldn't come.

Gradually the rest straggled off alone or in pairs and I headed for the station. Waves of heat rising from sewers, smokestacks and vacant pavement set the stars quivering, like the scales of small fish in dark water. In the late-summer heat of 1945, after the surrender, Japanese armies trudged back through the remains of Ōsaka and there was little where these buildings now stood but rubble, refuse, dust and blowing ash. A stubble of fireweed and wildflowers bloomed on the ruins, rippled in the hot wind. There was nothing for the children to eat. I heard these things from a neighbour, a toothless old man who had been a soldier at that time, and I heard other things as well: how faceless Japan had been, how for a while it had been a different place – beaten, levelled and overrun, unable to rise – waiting for the first touch of a foreign hand. For a sea change, into something rich, and strange.

On the train to Nagai I had a half-hour to experiment with the words of Nori's farewell card. By the time I got home I had the translation done, though the line 'yumei no ato' was still troublesome and I found it hard to focus on the page.

Ah, summer grass!
All that survives
Of the warrior's dream. . .

I keep thinking I should send a copy to Nori.

The End-of-the-line End-of-the-world Disco

JANETTE TURNER HOSPITAL

FLUTIE RECKONS IT'S an even chance the world will end before the shearing cuts out, and therefore they shouldn't wait, they should have the party tonight. Sure, a train is coming from Brisbane, volunteers are coming, sandbags and sandbaggers, a train's on the way, but will it arrive in time? Already vultures hover, a sure sign. When Mike leans out the pub window, their shadows blacken him and his hurricane hair whips across his face. 'Hey, vultures!' he calls. He hoists his beer and gives them the finger, gives it to the helicopter pilots, to the Sydney producers, to the cameramen dangling from slings, to the whole bang lot of them. 'Hey, vultures! Stuff that up your TVs and poke it!' Grinning, grinning. 'Gonna be on *The 7.30 Report* tonight, mates,' he laughs, as he winds himself back inside.

'River's reached Warrabunga already.' Flutie pushes the phone back across the bar. 'She's coming down like a seven-foot wall, Paddy Shay says. How about another one, love?'

'Cooper's, is it?' Gladys asks, as though she hasn't been serving him beer in the Millennium Hotel every day and night for six months, as though in the last ten minutes she's forgotten every relevant detail about him.

'Drive a man to drink, Gladdie.' Flutie is baffled,

exasperated, because she really is waiting for an answer. She really is not certain, in spite of the small regiment of empty Cooper's stubbies at his elbow. Or maybe she can't quite believe that a man in these parts would ask for anything but Four-X, and maybe she needs confirmation each time. Or maybe, as Mike maintains, she's just *slow*; but Flutie doesn't think that's the reason. She's still standing there with her watery blue eyes looking at him but not quite seeing him, blinking and waiting.

Waiting.

'Yeah,' he says, awkward. 'Cooper's.'

Mike rolls up his eyes, taps his forehead, grins at Flutie, but Flutie frowns. It drives him crazy, the way he feels protective of Gladys, and he's damned if he knows why, because she's no spring chicken, she's not a looker, she's skinny as a bloody fencepost, almost no tits at all. He thinks – for a reason he can't fathom out – that it's got something to do with the tired way she rubs the back of her hand across her eyes, and with that strand of faded hair which is always falling out of the loose bun she twists it into, always falling down behind her ear into a hollow of her shoulder-blade, and he always wants to brush it off her neck, tuck it into the elastic band, and let the pad of his thumb rest very lightly in the hollow below the bone. Jesus. He must be going soft in thc head. It's almost frightening, that hollow, it's deep as a bloody egg cup. He wants to put his tongue in it.

She's staring at the spigot in her right hand, the spigot on the Four-X keg, having run him off a pot of draught without thinking. 'Oh fuck,' she says mildly. 'Sorry.' She reaches for a clean glass. 'Cooper's, wasn't it?'

'Wake up, Australia,' Mike says. 'You'll miss the end of the world if you don't watch out.'

'Why don't you bloody leave her alone?'

'What?'

'You heard me.'

'Jesus, mate. Keep yer shirt on.' There's a gleam in Mike's eye though. Flutie with the hots, well well.

Flutie scowls, embarrassed. He knocks back the Cooper's to

clear a space, start fresh. 'Anyway,' he says, 'Paddy Shay climbed up to his roof last thing, saw the water coming. He's got the wife and kids in the ute, gonna run for it, should be here by dark. That's if he makes it. Another day, he reckons, and goodbye Charleville.'

Goodbye Charleville, good riddance, Gladys thinks. She leans against the glass doors of the refrigerator and closes her eyes and sees the swollen black snake of the river nosing south. A little higher than her head, preserved as curio, is the last flood souvenir, a decade old but still a clear corroded rust-brown line, threading its way across the white enamel wall behind the stubbies: the high-water mark.

Last time, the high-water level stayed exactly there for six whole weeks. Nothing moved. Not so much as a damn cockatoo moved upon the face of the waters, and all flesh died, both of fowl and of cattle that moved upon the Queensland earth anywhere west of the Warrego. And the flood was forty days and forty nights upon the earth – so Mike says, and so Flutie says, and they can prove it from the *Courier-Mail*, though the figures were disputed in the Sydney papers – and every living thing upon the ground was destroyed, both man and cattle and crops and creeping things (except for the bloody mosquitos and flies, it goes without saying). And only Noah O'Rourke the publican remained alive, and they that were with him in the ark of the Millennium Hotel, a regular zoo. And for forty days and forty nights the waters prevailed. Those are the nine last words on the subject from Flutie and Mike, who tell only the gospel truth.

Then Queensland unplugged her drains, glug glug. Ssschloop. There was a swift season of sucking back. The regulars haven't stopped talking about the 'afterwards' party yet – there will always, damn it, *always* be an afterwards, Gladys thinks wearily. Oh, the regulars can trot out befores and afters from 1880 on, but the last afterwards party is particularly vivid. It was more or less yesterday, that resurrection party, that wild fishing-for-stubbies-in-the-mud party, that jamboree, wangaree, rainbow time. Wheee! what a way to come home.

'This hotel,' Mike will tell every visitor who leans across the bar, 'the river took 'er clear down to Cunnamulla in 1990, and then she came floating home on the backwash.' Hallelujah, is the standard response, and don't let the pint pot stand there. 'What we got,' Mike explains, 'is life everlasting. What we got is the Hotel Indestructible, we gonna outlive the millenium itself in this here pub.'

Gladys presses back against the slick flood-surviving glass of the Millennium Hotel's stock of beer, feels the blessed frigidaire-coolness through her cotton shift, feels it sweet as a lover against her sweaty buttocks and thighs, feels herself go heavy between the legs. The wet blunt snout of the river is past Warrabunga. Here, baby, she murmurs, moving her hips.

Wavelets slap against the mirrored wall of the disco and the dance floor is two inches awash but in any case the musicians are on an island dais. Confidence is high. Some tried to flee – in cars, on horseback – but there was nowhere to go, with all the rivers running in packs and the creeks gone brumby. Water water everywhere, it's a bloody stampede.

The mirror tiles are pocked with black holes. A glittering rind of alum peels from the damp edges and leaves streaks that might be read as a map of the watercourses that are rising in convocation. Revellers arrive and arrive. Under the watchful eye of the helicopter, trucks and utes and horses and drays are still fanning out and then fanning in again like ants, for the disco lures them and where else can they go? This is the place of refuge, the end of the line.

This is the day and the hour.

The great inland sea, vouchsafed in vision to the prophet-explorers, has come into its own, so everyone's giving up. One by one, they are turning back for the Millennium. For a while, the regulars could watch themselves on TV in the upstairs lounge. There's Paddy Shay's ute, they could say. See? With that box thing he built on the back. He's turning back, keep a Four-X good and cold for 'im, Gladdie.

But now the power has gone.

The power went hours ago.

Gladys has strung up the hurricane lanterns, and volunteers have been working in shifts to see the beer safely stowed in iceboxes on the wide upper verandas. It's party time. No worries, mate. As for the sandbags and sandbaggers, the train was last seen, glugging at the windows, going slowly under somewhere west of Muckadilla. No question, this is the safest place to be. The beer is safe, and high time too, with the years spilling over the Warrego embankment, the years welling up and over like the zeros in an old Holden odometer, the century shifting, the party in full swing.

Oh when the saints . . . plays the motley band (one trumpet, one bass, three guitars, four harmonicas tuned to four different pitches, one Jew's harp, real drums, saucepan drums, about twenty people playing the spoons) . . . *go marchin' in* . . . The cymbals, two rubbish-bin lids, are banged with gusto by Noah O'Rourke himself.

'Marching? We're gonna *float* across the New South Wales border,' sings Mike. 'We're gonna float to kingdom come. We're gonna float into the next century, mates.'

Oh when the saints, booms the bar-room chorus, *go floating in* . . .

'Amen,' says Flutie. He watches Gladys coming downstairs with more beer. 'Put that bloody tray down,' he calls. 'It's every man for himself now, let 'em nick up and get it for themselves.' He can feel a sort of bright madness in his voice, he can see it dancing above the heads of every last one of them, tongues of fire, disaster excitement. He takes the stairs two at a time, whisks the tray from Gladys, puts it on the landing, and grabs Gladys round the waist. 'Come a-waltzing with *me*, Gladdie darling.'

He knows there's no way in the world she can resist him. He can feel the revving like a dynamo, the cyclone of final possibilities gallumphing down from the Gulf of Carpentaria, an irresistible force that sweeps her down the last steps, past the bar, into the swampy space around the musicians. For just a half-second he feels her body stiffen, then she moves against him and with him. They're both barefoot, everyone's barefoot, and they stomp and splash like children at a wading-pool party. Big Bill, the Maori shearer playing guitar, leans from the dais and booms the words in their ears. *Oh when the saints* . . .

Go barging in, Gladys sings back, and Flutie hears again that edge of wild and dangerous pleasure.

In the mirror, he sees musicians turning into dancers, dancers leaping on stage to have a go on drums or at the spoons. If the water doesn't weaken the foundations, he thinks, the stomping and clapping will. Any minute, the hotel could slip its moorings.

Oh when the saints . . . Flutie sing-shouts into the hollow in Gladys's shoulderblade.

'How come,' she gasps, breathless, slapping up a fan of water with the balls of her feet, 'they call you Flutie?'

'It's my baritone, my incredible bloody beautiful voice.'

'Come off it.'

'Hey,' he says aggrieved. 'Listen. You're talking to a winner of a Bundaberg eisteddfod. The nuns made me perform as a boy soprano, a fate worse than death. When me voice was breaking, I swung a punch at every kid who called me Flutie, but I never managed to beat off the name.' He puts his tongue into the dip of her shoulder. 'You've been here five months. Six maybe? You run away from a husband, or what?'

In the mirror, he sees her throw back her head and laugh. Her bun has come loose and all her faded red hair flies free. She cannot stop laughing. Flutie thinks they might all drown in her laughter.

Now the ground floor has been surrendered, the revelry transposed up several notches. Although it's far too hot and humid for sleeping, couples are disappearing into the rooms off the veranda. Flutie's looking for Gladys. Pacing the old veranda boards, he can hear the fizz and spit of concentrated life, it's like walking the deck beside a row of pressure cookers just before they blow. It's sensible, he thinks, telling death to fuck off. Where's Gladys?

At the veranda railing, interest in the swooping flotsam is intense. Will the milk can pass the bucking sheet of corrugated roof-iron? Will that green thing (is it the top of someone's ute?) beat the fencepost down to Corones? Will the black water kiss the veranda in one hour, two, three, tonight, tomorrow night, or never? Bets are formally laid.

'Vultures!' Mike shouts, and yes, the whirlybirds are back but what are they dangling? Not cameramen. No. It's a fat sausage-string of rubber dinghies.

They know something we don't, Flutie thinks. The water's still rising. In slow astonishment, because he has always, deep down, believed himself immortal, he says to no one: 'You know, we just mightn't make it.'

'Hey, Flutie!' It's Big Bill, the Maori shearer, strumming his guitar at the railing. Flutie has traded punches with Big Bill on the issue of wide combs or narrow combs for shearing. He can't believe his own life. 'This is it, Flutie,' the Maori says.

'We gonna make it, d'you think?'

'Dunno, Flutie. This is it, the Big Water.' He plucks at the strings of his guitar. *Oh when the saints* . . . 'Hey, Flutie,' he grins. 'You remember that fight at Reardon's shed?'

A funnel of laughter descends on Flutie like a willy-willy and sucks him inside. 'The combs . . .' he tries to say. 'We bet you Kiwis would never . . .' But his voice goes spiralling upwards, round and round, faster, faster, beyond the reach of his breath and into the high whooping grace-notes of absurdity. And Big Bill enters the funnel with him, they are dizzy with glee.

'Jesus,' Big Bill bleats, in pain with mirth. 'You silly fuckers bet us . . . You fuckers claimed that New Zealand wool . . . You dumb fuckers lost your fucking *pants*.'

Through the fog of vertigo and laughter, Flutie sees Gladys fishing for dinghies with a pole. He sets his compass and strikes out for her shore.

Gladys thinks that at last has come a day with real *juice* to it, a day she can sink her teeth into. God, how come the bloody water's so cold when they're all sweating like pigs from the heat? She's got it now, she's hooked one of the dinghies. She'll have to share, damn it.

What she'd really like to do is stand in the dinghy and spread her arms and descend on New South Wales like one of the Furies, singing at the top of her lungs. Dimly she senses there'd be a letdown somewhere. There always is.

'Gladys,' Flutie says, encircling her from behind with his arms. 'Tell me why you came here. Because there's no time left, you know. You confess and I'll confess. I wanna know the lot.'

'Jesus, Flutie.' She can't believe men, she really can't. Boss cocky to the very last second.

'Where'd you come from?' he persists. 'Brisbane? Sydney?'

Because he can smell a city girl, yes, that's partly what's been grabbing him, that dazed state of the city slicker in the bush, that *Where am I? What am I doing here?* bemusement, he's a sucker for that.

'Brisbane,' she says. 'If you must know.'

What will she tell him? She ticks off items in her mind: married twenty-seven years, three kids all grown up and married, Mum dying of cancer in Toowoomba; and while she sits at Mum's bedside, her old man buggers off with the neighbour's daughter. End of story.

How boring, how *embarrassing* a life is, once it slides down inside the tacky skin of words. Cheap skin, sharkskin, vulgar. Who could bear to say them? They had to be shoved away somewhere, in a suitcase under a bed. Goodbye words, good riddance; because what you felt afterwards, after the disorientation, when your clumsy tongue got free of dead explanations, was an immense and intoxicating freedom. You felt like singing your new self without any words at all.

You felt like a snake discarding the skins of past lives, sleek, unimpeded.

'When Mum died,' she says absently, smiling, 'I hopped on a train and bought a ticket for the end of the line.'

'Amen,' says Flutie.

'I didn't bring any luggage,' she says. 'No luggage at all.'

'Amen,' he says again. It doesn't matter if she tells him anything or not, they're both end-of-the-liners. Compatible histories is something he can taste, and he moves his tongue into the warm currents of her mouth.

When there's a space, she says mildly: 'I don't mind fucking you, Flutie, but I'm never going back.'

To a man, she means. To routine. To luggage. To intolerable ordinary life.

Then he realises, *of course*, it's her sheer indifference, her unreachability, that's been driving him crazy.

'Hey,' he says sharply. 'Hey, your dinghy!' – because floating rubble, like a tank on the move, is ramming the rubber boat against the railing, ramming the lattice, ramming the shipwrecked veranda, oh Jesus, are they in the water or swamped on the deck? Chaos. He swallows an ocean. Veranda posts approach, an anchor holds, he is wrapped around something vertical and he can see her scudding out of reach, body-riding the dinghy like a surf-board queen.

'Gladysssss. . . !' He dingo-howls across the water.

She waves, or so he wishes to believe. Yes, she waves.

Gladys waves. But what she is seeing is the swooping green of the mango tree in Brisbane. The leaf canopy parts for her and she keeps flying. She is on that wild delicious arc of the swing, soaring up, up, and out from the broken rope. A sound barrier breaks. There are shouts, but they reach her only faintly through the pure rush of bliss, they are a distant and wordy murmuring of bees in mangoes.

We *begged* you not to swing so high . . . We told you the rope was frayed, we warned, we warned, we promised we'd fix it but you just can't wait, you can't ever wait, you foolish stubborn little girl . . . you wilful impetuous . . . *Buzz buzz* to reckless ears.

'I don't care! I don't care!' she shouts. She has flown beyond the farthest branch of the mango tree, she is higher than the clothes line, euphoria bears her upward, she is free as a bird. Any second now the broken legs waiting on the lawn will come rushing to meet her, but she doesn't care. This is worth it.

She waves. But all that comes back to Flutie is her laughter, the wild clear rapturous sound of a child on the last Big Dipper.

The Sandcastle

MATTHEW KRAMER

'LET'S WAIT HERE,' said my cousin, who was one year older. There was an intervening mesh of bushes between us and the mild drop, at the foot of which they stood, two women, also holiday makers. 'They might undress.' So we waited. Beyond them the ground bucked again, quite steeply, then fell away one final time to merge with the beach. It was a concealed cavity and my cousin was hopeful. The two women sat down. One was young and one old. They wore identical hats, butter-coloured, broad and round as shields. They kept their bags to themselves, their narrow backs to us, upright and dignified, observing the rim of the sea, like two sunflowers without colour. Occasionally one or other of the hats would move, but slightly, an immediately corrected twitch, oblivious of us, the silently breathing spies crouching in the bushes. Hats like dumb wheels. My cousin would have liked to reach into that crevice with enormous arms and pluck them off.

'I don't think they're going to,' I said. I looked at my cousin. He had grown broader and redder with expectation, or frustration. Puffing up like a toad, silently willing the two bleached sunflowers to rise, unfold, turn towards his furious demanding eyes.

'I don't think they're going to.'

'Wait a bit longer, can't you, wait a bit longer.'

Thirty years later he is still waiting for that moment. Only he is wider and redder now, and no longer expectant, no, merely resigned, with his collapsed chin and his heavy spectacles, and if he ever comes back here, on his bachelor holidays (he faded out of my family's life years ago, and none of us know) he wouldn't stand again over that cavity expecting to see any slender sunflowers, just an empty and arid space.

Wait a bit longer wait a bit longer wait a bit longer.

Briefly, a bare arm was extended, down in the hollow. Then, leisurely, it was withdrawn.

We descended to the beach. My cousin was discomforted by the sun. Flinched and squinted behind his glasses. My younger brother came up, running with difficulty through the sand. He stopped beside us.

'Go away,' I said.

'There's a man,' he said, looking up at us, 'who's building this enormous sandcastle. He wants us to help.'

'Where?' demanded my cousin.

'Over there.' And he pointed, but we couldn't see anything, apart from the beach, monotonously unrolling, white and then a slick, dark brown where the sea reached each time it slid in and away at the edge of its advance. 'No, not there, *there*.'

But the beach was utterly empty, as was the sea.

Earlier, that morning, we had played a game, my cousin and I, to see how quickly, without touching him, we could make my brother cry. First we had hidden his recently-acquired watch. Then produced it, only to dangle the thing (a hand-me-down from an uncle) in front of him, bringing it nearer, then away, until he almost danced in front of us, trying to lure tears of frustration up into those simple eyes. Please give it. All the previous day he had touched and polished and cosseted the thing, as if the ticking circle was alive. He would kneel, watch resting on his open palm, and follow the second hand's repetitive journey, mesmerised. He still could not tell the time. Please give it. I tossed the watch to my cousin. My brother leapt instinctively, but was far too small. Now my cousin tempted him. For some reason my brother could never learn, never see how to undercut our game – and kept on reaching for the toy, predictable as a small dog. Eventually, they came. Huge shining tears. My cousin, seeing his radiant eyes, dropped the watch into my brother's cupped uplifted hands.

My brother ran away. We knew he would never tell on us. 'Five minutes,' my cousin said, looking at his own watch, and slumped down heavily, like a weary grown-up, in one of the hotel arm chairs.

But, needless to say, my brother had come back. Had earnestly followed us across the sand. I noticed the watch was now strapped to his arm, above the elbow.

'He's lying,' said our cousin. 'Liars have to be punished because lying is a sin.'

He reached out an upholstered, clumsy hand. My brother dodged. 'I'm not. Please. It's over there. He wants us to help.'

Our cousin grabbed at him again. My little brother ducked once more and this time our cousin, unbalanced, fell badly. He lay there for a moment in his own crater of loose sand.

'I'm sorry,' said my brother.

But he understood our cousin's expression. Our cousin's size had given him a precocious sense of his own dignity. He knew that, lying there, he appeared ridiculous. My brother started to run.

We chased him. He ran stubbornly, compact, the pistons of his elbows moving just like a grown-up runner, but he had only a small stride, and I gained on him while our cousin lumbered further and further behind.

The beach curved. I could hear his panting. Our cousin shouted after me, 'You've got him.'

And then I saw the tower. It was one foot high, with strangely detailed battlements and minute, arched windows carved delicately into the damp compacted sand. A wall of sand ran from the sand tower for maybe ten yards, a few inches high. Where it ended someone had thrust a spade deep into the ground.

My brother faced me from the other side of the tiny wall.

'I don't know where he is now,' he said, gasping repeatedly.

'Who?'

'The man.'

It was an alcove of the beach, above which reared black slimy rock. There was no one there to claim responsibility for that nascent fortress. Several other walls had been raised. One of them had a moat. Numerous lines had been patiently traced, like a ground plan. There was a man-made hump of sand at the centre, perhaps intended for the building of a keep.

'Who's been doing all this then?' Our cousin had caught up now. He was considering, almost greedily, the ambitious scale of this unexplained development in the sand. He let a bare, bruised foot hover teasingly over the tower, and looked at me with the beginnings of a smirk.

'Don't,' said my brother.

The wide foot swayed with fake indecision above the battlement.

'I told you it was true.'

We were three explorers who had broken through an eternity of jungle to find the mute, subsided ruins of an ancient race unspread in front of us. That was the fantasy which briefly shone in my mind. The domes of pith helmets, imperial and white, blotting out with shadow our sun-grilled childish faces.

'I wasn't making nothing up.' My brother spoke quietly, without looking at us. He had knelt and was gently touching the crenellated walls.

There was a scampering sound, then the dog was in front of us, tensed and black and open-mouthed by the hump reserved for the keep. Its great head turned slowly; its eyes were sly and cold.

My brother stood up and automatically approached it, one hand held out, already spread.

'Don't go near it, you idiot.' Our cousin looked smaller now, because of the dog. 'It's vicious.'

And the animal, as if to concur, softly snarled, black eyes encompassing all of us.

My little brother stopped. 'I only wanted to stroke it.' He lowered his arm sadly.

'Fatso, ge' away from that tower. An' you, come 'ere.' That was meant for the dog, which moved obediently forward; its powerful body brushed me.

'I only wanted to stroke it, sir.' My little brother was looking past me, addressing the stranger.

'I's a fightin' dog . . . Yer don' stroke fightin' dogs. Yer control 'em, or yer run away.'

I turned round. The man was almost old, on the border of middle age, with a reddened, pitted nose, a pin-head of dirt in each tiny pit, feral eyes and the thickened arms of a wrestler. He wore a T-shirt, so the arms were bare. It did not look right for a man of that age to show his arms in that way, however hard and tanned.

The dog came up to him. The man rested his free hand on the wide collar, then pressed what was left of his cigarette into its hide. The dog squealed.

'Has it been naughty?' said my brother.

The dog was trying to lick the burn, it turned around and around, stupidly, futilely trying to reach with its tongue the source of the torment, twisting furiously its neck as the body unsteadily revolved in an apparently independent act of volition. There was something maddened about its movements, about the persistence of that effort.

My little brother went up to it with an extended hand.

'Yer let it sort i'self out,' said the man flatly, uninterested in the turning, stumbling dog.

My brother obediently stopped. He patiently looked up at the man, allowing him the initiative.

The man seemed to have stirred his hair in lard, or something equally gelatinous, to have let it luxuriate in, absorb the mixture. It shone unhealthily, an overrich, slippery gleam. Suddenly, thinking of the texture of that hair, I felt sick. If he'd grabbed me, forced me to touch it, let it slide away through my hand, I would have vomited.

'This all yer could find?'

'Yes,' said my brother.

'No, no, this won't do.' Now he sounded his age, or older, almost a crabby old man. A crabby old man with lines set in lines like a tree and hippy-length hair. I noticed that he wore steep-heeled boots and leather trousers, tight to his legs, and a wide studded belt. An almost old man's face lost in hippy hair and on a hardened, honed body. Now my eyes were taking in his hands. There were rings on two of the fingers.

'This won't do.' He pulled the spade out of the ground. Then he offered it to my brother. It was taller than him. '. . . You start diggin' along this line. See? See this line?'

'Yes.'

My brother had difficulty with the spade because of its length and weight; he couldn't come to terms with it, as if it was alive. The rest of us watched. The dog had stopped. It was now very still.

'Fatty. There's another spade over there . . . You. This is what I wan' yer to do.'

Then one hard hand was pushing me down, making my legs concertina, and I was on my haunches, quite abruptly, with him hunkered down beside me. He was not particularly large, but for the first time I felt the terrible strength in that body. Its strength and its core of cold purpose. Yes, I think that was what I felt, coming from him, even if I couldn't understand, the two of us on our haunches in the centre of his castle. That close, despite the old tobacco smell and the unpleasant odour of the leather, for the first time I felt comfortable with him. He felt in control of himself, almost reasonable, and I relaxed and succumbed to that control.

'This is what I wan' you to do,' he said. I didn't look at him. I looked at his hand, at the extended forefinger, familiar now with his warm, stale smell.

The finger, quite delicately, using the long scoop of its upturned and cultivated nail – I mean he had grown it, for the thing was yellow-edged, black and hard – began to sculpt the flank of the low wall. It made indents and shaped them. Windows and battlements formed before my eyes.

'Think yer can do that, kid?'

'Yes,' I said.

And I tried, and while I tried, he rested a hand on my shoulder.

And, after a while, 'not clumsy, are you,' in a quiet voice.

The hand remained on my shoulder. I had become tremendously aware of it.

While the sun's heat intensified, I worked. I drew windows and shaped battlements. At first there was a certain excitement in participating. I took great care, though my nail was too short and forefinger too clumsy, down on my knees, bare legs clamped by the hot sand. I drifted into the world of that wall, its miniature grandeur and, in my imagination, peopled it. My fat cousin meanwhile was helping with the creation of the keep, packing wet sand into buckets which the man would then upturn, and rap smartly on the base to disgorge their contents, now solid and smooth. My little brother had somehow conquered the spade and, holding it half way down its handle, was slowly digging into the ground, a patient, trance-like excavation, almost tenderly taking the moat around the swollen base of a tower. An enormous castle was growing up around us.

The man stopped working. He casually lit a cigarette. Briefly he hummed some pop song – currently doing well, courtesy of excited teenagers – to himself, and nodded his head in time to his music, smoke curling up from his hand.

After the fag had sufficiently revived him, he said, 'You're doin' well, lads.'

My little brother said, 'Thank you.'

My cousin said, 'I want to build more towers over there to guard that wall.'

He marched away with his bucket. With one hardened hand, the man brushed his long fringe away from his eyes, smoothing down the lank side of his hair and then giving a curious, abrupt shake of his head as if to finally settle or restore the hang of it. I had seen girls with long tanned legs and red lipstick doing that before. I wondered briefly why he didn't care about his dirty nails.

My little brother accidentally backed into one of the towers my cousin had built. 'You idiot.' He pushed him down and kicked a dirty shower of sand over his body.

After a moment, my brother stood up.

'I'm sorry.' He knelt in front of the crumbled stump. 'I'll put it better.'

Perhaps because of the heat, I had lost interest in the wall. My fantasy had waned, and the bustle I'd imagined for it, people and packhorses moving alongside it, through it, like a medieval picture seething with life, all that had ebbed away, back into the dry sand. All I was left with was that dry sand. And the beginnings of an ache in both my legs. The sea now began to glitter and tempt me. Everything there seemed simpler, easier. Strangest of all, looking at it from within that half-finished sand fortress, my mouth began to water.

I stood up. I'd had enough. My little brother was standing with the man and saying quietly, 'It's bigger than in my dream.'

''Course it is,' said the man. 'This is goin' ter be fucking enormous.' My brother nodded gravely. He did not yet understand bad words.

'What do you do?' continued my brother. He would ask adult questions without realising it.

'Never yer mind, never yer mind . . . I's be'er a secret. Can yer keep a secret?'

'I think so.'

'Very important, though, very important . . . More important than your dad. I seen your dad. Rich man, rich man. Is your dad important?'

'No.'

'Bu' i's be'er kept a secret . . . Not fer everyone to know.'

'No,' said my brother with great seriousness.

Our fat cousin interrupted. 'I'm going to be the general commanding this side.'

'Are you now?'

'This will be the strong side.'

The man looked gravely at my little brother as if it was necessary first for them to confer.

I said, 'I'm tired. I'm going to swim.'

The man quietly turned. He sucked in his lips; considered me.

'I'm tired. I'm going to swim.'

'Are you?'

I was brushing sand from my legs.

The man looked at my brother. 'Do you think 'e should?'

After a moment my brother shook his head.

Our cousin loudly agreed. 'I'm in command of this wall.
No one crosses it without my permission.'

The man clicked his fingers and the dog padded to him.

'Why don' your big brother wan' to help any more?'

My little brother thought for a moment. Then he said,
'Because he doesn't dream enough.'

'No,' agreed the man, eventually, as if slightly suspicious of
that answer. Briefly, there was puzzlement in his eyes. Then he
laid a hard, scarred hand on the scruff of the dog's neck and
latched a chain to its collar. Immediately the dog pulled away,
went the full length of the chain, straining and being restrained.

'Do you think 'e should stay?'

My little brother nodded. But then turned away, to
concentrate instead on what had been built, no longer
interested in us. He repeated softly, happily, 'It's bigger than
in my dream.'

Meanwhile, I was looking at the dog. Now that it was a
prisoner of the chain, it had developed a cold and thoughtful
interest in me. Where the man looked, the dog looked. I
imagined my gentle brother's empty shining eyes and
wondered what he would do if the man let the dog advance.

The dog pulled, and the links of the taut chain scraped
together. But my little brother remained with his back to us.

Our cousin said, 'He's got to stay until it's finished. Until
it's all finished.' He had the spade resting upright against his
shoulder, the base of the long handle in his waist-high palm.

'All right, kids,' the man said eventually. 'Now we're
gonna work harder, much harder.'

And then he smoothed his hair, smoothed it at the back and
on top, carefully, as if facing a mirror, like a model about to
posture for the camera, and then after that, with the end of the
chain coiled thickly around his wrist, hooked his thumbs in his
belt. An old face with hippy hair and teeth brown from too

many cigarettes. 'We're goin' ter build the biggest castle yer fuckin' dad ever saw.'

It rose up out of the beach. It surrounded us and walled us in. It acquired admirers. Two small boys who stared longingly and shuffled about for a while at a respectful distance. An American couple who took a photograph. A wino in the remnants of a raincoat. He hovered doubtfully and then approached and was frightened away by the man and the dog. I worked on in a mood of resentful obedience, and forgot both the time and myself in the heat.

The man meanwhile swaggered around within the walls, advising, ordering, sometimes making moderately approving noises, at other times shaking his head, repeating, 'This won' do, this won' do; will it?' At one point he shook my cousin roughly. My cousin accepted this correction and promised to improve. Later, the man said to my saucer-eyed brother, 'After. I may show you wha' I really do, son. If I'm satisfied yer really can keep a secret.'

My little brother nodded dumbly, gazing upward, intensely serious.

'Here,' said the man, and produced an ancient handkerchief. It was large and discoloured, nearer yellow than white. 'I 'ave ter look my best, now tha' i's almost done.'

And then my brother knelt in front of the man, having accepted the handkerchief. I looked at it, suddenly felt it in my hand. It felt as if it had been thinly buttered.

'Give 'em a good spit, le's see 'ow yer do as a shoeshine boy.'

My brother concentrated and spattered bright spittle over both boots. A shining thread of saliva hung tremulously from his chin. Gently, carefully, he began to rub.

I heard a familiar female voice, and then another, just as familiar. I started and was on my feet immediately, guiltily lowering my hands even before I'd had time to put names to those two sharp voices.

My mother and my aunt had turned together into the alcove.

'Hullo, been playing?' was the first thing my aunt said, on seeing me. Then immediately after, or perhaps as she spoke, my little brother and the man they didn't know, still in that pose, registered on them.

My mother gasped my brother's name. He turned his head, still crouching, and smiled.

'What are you doing? Who are you?' The two sentences almost overlapped.

At the same time my aunt barked to her son, 'Come here.'

I was nervous, but my principal interest was to see how the man responded.

He said, 'I know your husband, lady.'

'Do you?'

'Fine man, fine man.' Now he came towards them, abandoning my still kneeling brother, moving lightly over the sand with a swing of his upholstered shoulders; the dog wanted to go the other way but he yanked fiercely on the chain and the animal dutifully followed.

He faced my mother and my aunt from behind his tiny wall. I was surprised to realise that both women were taller than him.

He now nodded thoughtfully, several times, lips bunched up together, although nothing further had been said and so there was nothing to agree with or to consider.

My aunt said to my cousin, 'We were looking for you. You disappeared.'

'Who are you?' my mother persisted. 'What have you been doing?'

'Well you're lookin' at it, lady.'

'I want to know who you are and what you've been doing.'

The man continued to nod, to bunch up his lips as he did so. None of these gestures accorded with what my mother and aunt were saying.

'Who are you? What have you done to them?'

Then my mother stepped over the wall and strode through the castle to where my brother still knelt. She pulled him up roughly and began to slap the sand from his body. He accepted all this without any reaction.

My aunt followed, looking hard at the man as she stepped over the wall, as if daring him to block her, oh just you try, and marched as purposefully as had my mother towards my fat cousin. I knew he was going to get hit and so did he.

While he was yelping and protesting his innocence, my mother came back, leading my beatific little brother by the hand. Crossing two parallel inner walls, her impatient heel demolished a tower. She didn't notice. My aunt's impact, while busy with her noisy act of correction, was equally dramatic. The side of the fortress my cousin had aspired to command was laid waste by her flip-flops.

The women led us away. We were the remnants of a defeated army. They said nothing to the man as we were marched from the sandcastle and its alcove of slimy rock. My brother tried once to look back, but his small head was rudely pushed back round, to face the way he was going, or being led.

The man said nothing, nor did the dog respond to this maternal counter-attack. I didn't dare look round for fear of getting a slap as we hurried back along the beach, listening to the angry, clumsy sound of my aunt's flip-flops. But I imagined him, a lean, dwindling figure, following us with his eyes from his violated castle. It was early evening now, and the sea made a soothing, susurrating sound. Our noisy progress across the beach, with smacks and crying and the irate adult tones of the two sisters as they talked about what had happened above our bent, shamed heads, seemed an ugly counterpoint to that immense peace. I kept on wanting all the time to look back.

I did hear stories about him later, on other visits, though we never met him again. Once I saw him from a bus. He was standing with some other men, selling newspapers. 'It's to do with sending the coloureds home,' said the old woman behind me. That was the last sighting, though I heard later he was charged with touching a small boy on his private parts. And on hearing that I saw him again, with a clarity which had previously eluded me throughout those intervening years. I saw his kneeling form and hard, tobacco-tipped fingers and imagined him saying, this won't do, this won't do, I don't know why he would have said that, down on his knees before a shivering exposed confused little boy. I think he got six months or maybe a year for that. The beach is still popular in summer. He never came back. I have two sons of my own now. Lying on my back I watch them running screaming with their little buckets and spades along the sea's edge. They are not interested in the sunset, on which I am trying to concentrate, recognising it is beautiful.

Meng's Pool

ISOBEL LUSTED

IT WAS THE boy's first outing alone with his father. He stood stolid and still while the yoke with its buckets was fixed across his shoulders. The women, his mother, his grandmother, stood close together, watching, saying nothing.

His father led the way ignoring the track to the village. The boy followed pushing against the strong northwest wind.

'We're on our way to the Wall,' the man called back. The boy did not ask why, but plodded on trying to close the distance between the two, wanting company, perhaps even reassurance now that the women had been left behind. The brittle dust carried on the wind stung and scratched his uncovered face and hands. A few fields away tiny figures swathed head to foot bent low in the thin dust of their ploughs. The man passed by quickly.

They walked alone, the man and boy, across the dry riverbed and on. The boy gave no thought to the Wall, what it could mean, or how long it would take to reach it. He knew nothing of distance, or perspective so that when they arrived at the Wall he was unsurprised at the way it stood over the land, abrupt and dark like pictures on tins in the village store, boats on boats, mountains on men's heads.

He showed no astonishment when he found himself

walking on top of it, level with the tops of the jacaranda trees in the old Keep. The distance between him and his father widened. His shoulders ached. His buckets clanged against the stone wall when he stepped from the track. The brown mountains behind him disappeared in the noonday smog. The birds were silent. The frogs slept.

His father waited impatiently, his finger stabbing the air at the edge of the Wall. 'Here,' he said, 'this is the place.' The boy followed his father's pointing finger to the ridge of rock where water seeped from invisible fissures, gathering itself into a tiny fall, rustling and splashing down the rock face to a clear, round pool at the base of the Wall. 'This pool never runs dry. The buffalo found it. Years ago. She'd strayed. I was scared she'd died, but she turned up here and I've been coming here ever since. We'd have starved in the drought but for this water.' He unyoked his own buckets. 'This will be your job, getting the water. Do you know what I'm saying?'

The boy nodded as he always did. His father's words spun in the air, one after another, but enough of them settled for the boy to take in the message. He was to carry water home.

'The others go to the village well,' his father went on, 'but the water's too low to reach in the dry season. They have to wait for the cart from Qinhandao. Just you remember, not a word.' He rubbed his hands.

The boy nodded again. It was all that was required of him. He did not know about wells and secrets.

The old man filled his buckets, yoked them across his shoulders and walked away across the brown earth. The boy, copying his father, bent to the pool and came face to face with a woman. She spoke.

'I am Meng Jiangii. This is the pool of my tears. I allowed your father to find it many moons ago when the land was parched and he was concerned for his buffalo. But he has become greedy. You are too young and frail to do his work for him. You do not realise what he asks of you, do you?'

The boy stood quite still, one bucket hanging just above the water. He did not speak.

'Don't be afraid. I am here to help you.' And she reached out of the pool and took his hand.

The boy had never experienced anything outside his family, their day to day chores, the silences, the grim task of survival; if he had never come across the speaking face of a woman in water it did not mean that this was in any way special. He had listened to his grandmother's tales of ghosts, but he did not know what ghosts were, what they represented. His own world was flat, two dimensional, sepia, ochre, restricted by the very lack of that dimension, thought.

As he gazed into the pool his father called, 'Get a move on. You mustn't waste time.' But the child could not lower the bucket onto the face. Then the face said, 'Hand them down to me one by one and I'll fill them for you.'

He did as he was told following her directions one at a time, working jerkily like a stringed puppet. When the buckets were safely chained to the yoke he raised himself to his full height, slowly, carefully as the voice directed, and with just one glance back to the pool he trotted after his father, sometimes side-stepping the stones, sometimes stubbing his toes. Behind him the light in the pool went out, the sky's reflection which had moved across it when Meng withdrew, seeped away with the water and the pool became just one more hollow in the rocks.

The buckets were as light as they had been when he carried them empty to the pool. Back home his father waited. When the boy reached him he took the yolk from the child's shoulders and tipped the water into the wooden tub. 'You've done well. More careful than I thought you could be. I've never known the journey completed without spills. And the buckets are brim full. You have a gift. From now on you are the water carrier.'

The boy was pleased that his father was pleased, but that was as far as he was able to think about the subject. He did not even wonder how he had completed the journey so easily.

The next day he went alone. 'Remember, avoid the village. Use the fields,' his father told him. 'This secret of ours is all that lies between starvation and life.' He watched the boy until he was sure his feet were set in the right direction, then winding the cloths about his head he went back to his plough.

Meng was waiting for the boy when he reached the pool, but this time she was sitting on a rock beside the water. Now she had become real, looking at her made the boy shy. She did not look like either his mother or grandmother. She was young. Her skin was clear, her cheeks pink, her eyes bright. Her clothes were different too. Where they wore dark blues and faded greys, she wore shiny reds and golds with embroidered flowers and birds that winked in the sunlight until they flew over the pool like summer demoiselles.

Meng took the yoke from the boy's shoulders, filled the buckets and yoked him up again. Every day for a week the boy went to the pool and Meng filled his buckets and started him on the homeward journey. His family was pleased at the way he had remembered what to do and how to do it and no one, not one of them, his father, mother nor grandmother could even begin to suspect the way Meng removed the water for the journey to replace it as he tipped the first bucket above the tub.

His father began to reach out. In his mind he saw his son bringing them a better living, even wealth. He would not be content to let his son's skill for water-carrying remain his only gift, although when he thought about it he felt bewildered by what the boy had achieved when he could not dress himself unaided, nor remember how to speak more than a few words. He sensed the presence of magic somewhere near the boy, and so being a practical man, he scolded himself for letting his imagination soar so high and told himself to accept what the boy could do and not expect too much. He knew how it was with boys when they were praised. He would become cocksure and their secret would lie exposed to the village.

He never spoke of this to his wife. The women were proud of the boy. His new prowess proved somehow that their wisdom in keeping him when he was born had paid off. The father noticed the extra tidbits saved for the child. He wanted to remonstrate with the women; in times of want they should share alike, at least he and his wife, the workers, should eat as well as possible, the old lady and the boy could do with less;

149

but the amounts were small and the boy doing so well that he let it pass, meanwhile watching closely to see that the gifts did not increase and that his own portion at least, did not decrease.

On the eighth morning when the boy started out for the pool the earth had exchanged its tired brown face for a film of hazy green like the green of the celadon pot which was his grandmother's treasure and which she unwrapped every evening after their meal so that she could stroke the smooth, rounded shoulders and speak of the times when she lived with her husband in the great market of Dailen.

It was a strange morning altogether. The boy's feet flew over the ground. In no time at all he was standing before Meng Jiangii at the pool. She unyoked the buckets and turned him to face her. 'Your eagerness has tired you and made you too warm. Come with me.' And taking his hand she led him along the base of the Wall until they came to an endless pool of water fringed with white lace. The boy tried to back away but was restrained by Meng's hand. He stood stiffly, awkwardly, unable to place this new experience. His head whirled. His stomach churned. Until this thing, objects, fields, rooms were there – or they were not. They did not come and go. They made no noise. Oh, he was used to the wind waves that ran through the growing rice in summer, but this green pool scared him. It moved on its own without the help of the wind.

He tried to run but Meng's arms were round him. 'This is the sea, silly.' She smiled to take the sharpness from her words. 'Sit here beside me. See those rocks?' She turned his head and pointed to the rocks glistening black in the sunlight. 'They are called Waiting-for-Husband Rocks. I live there.'

She waited but the boy did not speak. He did not look at the rocks. She had made no sense. She said too much, too fast. His brain worked in a special way, do-this-do-that, orders which it followed reasonably well, but explanations were beyond its scope.

It Meng had expected bewilderment she was disappointed. There was nothing in the black pools fixed on her face. She tried again. 'I hoped we could swim together in the sea, but you won't, will you? Instead I shall tell you my story and then we shall see.

'Hundreds of years ago when the Wall was building I came here to Shaihanguan as the bride of Young-Husband. He lived with his father and they farmed the land where you now live. We were happy – too happy. We loved as no others before or since have ever done, although Young-Husband had moments of despair when he worried that the evil spirits of the North would darken our lives, but I did not care about evil. There was too much that was good with us, besides we had been told that the north wind came to us pure, unblemished since the Great Wall built to protect us from the Northern tribes also safeguarded us from the spirits; flung against the rough outer stone, they perished, so it was said. It was to be the ultimate answer to wealth and longevity. I believed all this. I tried to take the fear of Happiness-Reprisal from Young-Husband's shoulders, but he knew more than I did of the ways of evil. He knew of its disguises. He knew it could wear a different cloak each day, how it could come rolling down the Wall, disturbing, distressing and deadly.

'He was right. I should have listened to him. Evil did come. It came in the guise of forced labour. Even then I did not know it for what it was. Our young neighbours had long left their farms and fields to hide in the hills until the Wall should be finished. I pooh-poohed that idea when Young-Husband suggested it. We were exempt from mundane worries by the very strength of our love. How blind I was. Young-Husband was press-ganged from our bed one night as we lay together. The Emperor's overseers had no respect for love. They marched Young-Husband away to serve his time building the last of the great Van Li Wall. When he called to me to wait, I believed him. I thought it would be soon over. The Wall, I thought, was almost finished. Many months went by before I realised he might never come back.'

Meng Jiangii looked out to sea and back to the child again. He watched her as closely now as he had when they first sat down. 'Do you know what I am saying?' she asked him, but he did not reply and she went on.

'But Young-Husband had promised. And I hoped as I went about my duties as a wife, tending the water buffalo and the fields. I saw the loosening earth caught between the melt and the small monsoons. I saw it washing out the uncertain grains trying to roothold in the dusty soil. I tied white cloths to the cairn that guarded Young-Husband's mother's bones. Day upon day of scorching heat followed the rains. The sun moved south: the birds gathered, wheeling under slate skies, then they too flew south. Hung shadows lay across the dark and empty earth. Then the snow began. It was time to go. I packed a bundle of warm clothes for my husband, said goodbye to his old father, and left.'

Meng looked once again at the boy. His black eyes, darker than any snow-filled cloud, looked back. She put her arms around him and he relaxed, leaning into her softness.

'The snow was falling thickly on the wall, but the overseers had not called a halt to the work. I searched the faces and knew none of them, but on the third, dark afternoon when I put my hand below the chin of yet another man and lifted his face to the remaining light, I recognised him as Loo Sing Fah from the village. He was pitifully thin. "Young-Husband?" I asked him. He turned away, bent and shifted the stone at his feet, but I had to have an answer and I tore at his poor, emaciated shoulders. "Where is he?" He touched my arm and I saw the blood on his fingers. "He's not here any longer. He died some days ago." And he went back to his work.

'I wept and wept. I wept so much that the stones began to crumble and wash away.' She paused and the boy saw tears roll from her eyes and splash to the rocks on which they sat.

The boy stirred suddenly and turned his head away. Meng turned too, catching the expression that flitted across his face. 'You are rested now. Take the water home.' Hearing the command in her voice the boy went.

This time he did not walk so easily. Perhaps because he tried to hurry, he stumbled more. The journey seemed long. At home he delivered his brimful buckets, but instead of sitting in the doorway as he usually did, he went to stand beside his grandmother as she pounded the rice. She was surprised to find him there, so much so that she spoke to him, asking, 'What is it?' and was more surprised when he answered, 'The woman.'

The old lady put the beater down on the rice cloth and wiped her hands. 'Which woman?' she asked in an unconcerned voice, wary of scaring the boy's thoughts back to wherever they had come from.

'Water woman.'

'Oh yes? You saw her today?'

'Yes.'

His grandmother searched quickly for words that would break the tension in the boy's voice. 'And she was crying?'

'She took me to the big pool.'

'Ah.' The old woman plucked a piece of cold dumpling from a dish and pushed it into the boy's hand. 'Go. Eat.' And the boy went back to the doorway, relieved for the present of the strange sense of dread which had sent him scurrying home.

That evening as he lay on the edge of sleep, he heard voices arguing, but it was not unusual and he did not listen to what he said. By the morning he had forgotten the day before. His father and mother had left for the fields and his grandmother was collecting firewood. He ate the spare food left for him and began the walk to the pool.

It was another very hot day. He did not hurry. Meng was there – only a face in the pool this morning. She filled his buckets and he walked home at his usual slow pace. His grandmother was raking a pile of small stones into a heap with a cleft stick. She looked hard at the boy, but said nothing. The next day it was the same. On the third morning the old lady said, 'I want you to make two trips today, or the scallion and kaolung will wilt and die.'

The boy shuffled off as though he had not heard her and she stepped close behind him. 'Don't waste your time talking with her. You hurry.'

At that moment the father appeared: at this time of day he should have been in the fields, but he walked with the boy. They did not speak. When they reached the pool it was lying blue beneath the sky. The man filled the buckets, then yoked them to the boy and they went home. The grandmother received the water without comment, but before he left them the father grumbled, 'The boy was dreaming.'

Meng was sitting beside the pool when the boy returned. She took the yoke from his shoulders and placed it beside the buckets near the water. 'Come,' she said, taking his hand, 'come.'

The boy walked beside her. He had forgotten the uneasiness of their previous meeting. Meng shone. She sparkled. The tears on her face were precious stones. Her small white feet barely touched the ground.

She took the boy to the bluff above the sea and they sat while she told him how her tears had opened a runnel through the stones and how they had revealed Young-Husband's body. 'It was the end for me. I could not live without him as he had not been able to live without me.

'They came, the overseers and whipped the labour into patching the damage. My tears fell faster and faster. The runnel widened. The Army Chief of that section arrived and told the men to drag me away, but wherever I went my tears ran unstopped and found their way back to Young-Husband. The Chief changed his tactics. He ordered the men from me and sought to drive me away with soft talk. I spat at him. That was it. If I had not shown such spirit, he might have had me killed then and there, but he appreciated courage, so he said, admired a woman who did not cower. He announced that he loved me and would do anything in the world for me. He sent some of his men straight away to the garrison town to procure flowers and fruits for me. I did not want his gifts. I did not want him. I wanted Young-Husband's body and presently I saw a way to get it.

"My only wish," I told him, "is to see my husband's body placed on a litter and taken to the sea which he loved almost as much as he loved me."

"Very well," the General, for that was his rank, agreed. "We shall take his body to the sea."

'I could not look at him. The desire in his eyes would have set alight all the land. I had to get rid of him once I had my

wish. We set off for the Bohai Sea. I walked beside the litter.
The General walked beside me. How to lose him? Then I had
it, the idea. For a little while I used my feminine wiles. I played
for a moment, the coquette, entrancing him, addling his
brains; then I pretended alarm. Oh! I covered my mouth with
my hand.

"What is it my loved one?"

' "Turn back your men. Turn back at once. Please. I have a
vision. There is an attack coming from the north and now that
you are here, so kindly attending to my wants, there is no one
to repel them. Please. Before it is too late."

'I wept even harder. I knew what he was thinking. "Women,
fanciful creatures." But common sense also whispered in his ear
that women were prophetic creatures. He wanted to ignore what
I had to say, but he could not afford to. My tears became a
deluge, and fearing the effect of them on the Wall and more
fearful of being cut off from the main army by the northern
tribes, he called his men and turned back. The men placed the
litter on a rock above the sea and followed their General.'

When Meng looked into the boy's face she found her own
face mirrored in his eyes. She saw the tears streaming down
her cheeks. And she saw something else. She saw her own
attraction in his eyes. She began speaking again, watching
herself all the while. Her words when they came, were slow
and measured.

'I waited beside the litter, saying my earthly farewells. I
knew that once we left this earth he would never know the son
who had been held back from coming to us because of the
Emperor's Wall. I knew that would be Young-Husband's
greatest regret, greater even than losing me. My tears spilled
down the rockface and mingled with the salt waters of the
incoming tide. I watched it swell into the cove below, just as it
is doing now. Look. Do not be afraid. See the water swelling,
reaching up to us?'

They leapt together, down into the deepest part way
beyond the frilly, white lace. Silt swirled like a dust storm as
they pierced the surface. Then the water that was not blue, not
green, not yellow, closed over them.

When the boy's father went to the pool it had doubled in size. He was a thrifty man – a hard worker. There was not much talk when, after the next winter he bought another buffalo and two young pigs.

Say Something

BRIAN McCABE

WAIT FOR ME Pete, will you, *wait*. Stop running away, will you, *wait*! Look, Pete, it's a doll. Somebody's gone and lost their dolly, Pete. *Pete*. Look, it's one of those dolls that can talk, Pete, I used to have one exactly like this. You pull the cord, see, like this . . . Hear what she says, Pete? She says she's thirsty, Mummy. I'm thirsty too, Pete. Hear what she says, Pete? She says she wants a dwinkie. I wanna *dwinkie* too, Pete. A *big dwinkie*, daddy! *I wanna gweat big dwinkie*! I want . . . I want to sit down, Pete. I've got to . . . sit down. Just for a minute. I'm sorry, I'm really, really sorry but . . . I've just got to sit down for a minute. I just want . . . one cigarette, Pete, then I'll come upstairs, okay? *Okay*, Pete?

Shit. Oh fuck. Look at that. I've gone and dropped my make-up things all over the stairs!

Say something, will you, don't just stand there. *Pete*! You don't care, do you? You don't. I've dropped my make-up things all over the stairs. Somebody's gone and lost their dolly. A little girl's gone and lost her dolly, but you don't care. Do you, Pete? No, you don't care. You just stand there. You just stand there looking like . . . like *you*. There's nothing else like it. You. You in a huff. You in a black, black mood. Oh say *something*, will you, for Pete's sake!

157

For *Pete's* sake! That's a good one!

She's laughing too, Pete! Did you hear her? She thought it was funny, didn't you dolly? It made you laugh, eh dolly? *Yes*. Funny Mummy. But it didn't make Daddy laugh, did it dolly? *No*. Because nothing makes old huffy Daddy laugh tonight, does it? *No*. 'Cause old Daddy-waddy's gone into a gweat big huffy-wuffy, hasn't he? *Yes*. Shall I tell you why, baby? He's gone into a gweat big huffy-wuffy 'cause funny Mummy went and got boozy-woozy at Daddy's little de-part-mental party! *Naughty* Mummy! And now old huffy-Daddy isn't going to speak to her for *days*! Is he, baby? *No*! Isn't that a terrible thing, baby? It is. It is a terrible thing, isn't it? Not to speak to somebody for days. Isn't it, Pete? *Pete*?

Please, Pete, say something, anything. Tell me I'm drunk as a skunk. All right, I'm drunk as a skunk. I know I'm drunk as a skunk. So what? Am I not s'posed to get drunk any more, hmm? Am I not s'posed to enjoy the party? That's what parties are for, isn't it Pete? For enjoying getting drunk as a skunk. You said so yourself, Pete, you know you did. You said just enjoy it, just be yourself. You said just enjoy the party Isabel, just be yourself *Isabel*. You called me Isabel, you know you did. That's why I got drunk. I was nervous, Pete. I'm sorry, I'm really . . . really sorry. Oh, shit. Oh, fuck. I couldn't help it. I got nervous cause you called me Isabel. You did. Instead of Izzy like you usually do. So I knew you didn't really mean enjoy the party, you didn't really mean be yourself. You meant don't you dare do any such thing. You meant behave yourself *or else*.

Or else *what*?

You meant be decorative, that's what you meant. Be the New Blood's dec'rative fiancée! Be my formal little fiancée, wear the frilly, floral thing I bought you for that purpose! Yes! Act like a wifeling, be the New Blood's pretty wife-to-be! If she's lucky! If she behaves herself! As long as she doesn't get drunk as a skunk at the departmental party, eh Pete? As long as she doesn't go and do something really inconsiderate, like get herself pregnant again, for instance! Oh, that would really be the end, wouldn't it Pete?

That's what you meant, you know you did. You meant speak when you're spoken to, otherwise keep your mouth shut. You meant don't be yourself. For christsake, don't be *Izzy*! Not tonight! Not at the departmental party! Don't be natural, don't be relaxed! Not with the professor, at all costs! For Godsake, don't say what you *think*! Don't disagree with the professor! Not about *literature*! Heaven forbid! Not about the role . . . the *portrayal* of women – that's the word, isn't it, portrayal? – of women in Victorian fiction. Oh no. That's the professor's speciality. Women in Victorian fiction. Women in bloomers, in stays! He's an expert on bloomers and stays! That's his baby! Don't shoot your mouth off about the suffragettes, he's much too learned to disagree with! Learned! Old letch. His eyes were all over me, you *fool*! And the others, the others were worse. Your so-called colleagues, Pete. And that young one with the little beard he was trying to grow, the little pubic beard – what was he called again? You know the one I mean, Pete, the one wearing the jeans. The one with the cock in his jeans and the little pubic beard, the one you thought I fancied, Pete – who was he, and how come you've never mentioned him before? No you don't have to tell me, Pete, I remember. His name was Mike. He told me, he introduced himself over the vol-au-vents. He must be about the same age as you, Pete. Or is he younger? Another of the new bloods, eh? Is that where you got the idea of growing a beard, Pete? So that you and Mike could scratch your pubic beards together in the staff club over a couple of mature malts?

I don't like you with a beard, Pete. I know I said it suited you, but that doesn't mean I like it, right? Oh, it suits you. It suits you too much, just like the pipe. And I mean, you have to look older than the students to have some authority over them, eh Pete? Maybe you should get a walking stick, that would do the trick, wouldn't it, Pete? A knobbly old walking stick, and you could use it like the pipe, Pete, use it to point to things. Things like students. I mean, you've only had the job for a month, it's a one-year contract, but already you look like you're in with the bricks. That jacket, Pete, that tweed jacket. I never thought I would live with a man who wore a tweed jacket. You are really boring, Pete, you know that? I feel sorry for myself, I really do.

Come on, Pete, you can tell me about Mike – is he a friend or an enemy? A rival? You should watch him, Pete, he's got horrible little close-set eyes like a ferret. What he was doing to me with his ferrety little eyes. And the wives, did you notice the wives, Pete? Christ, Pete, you don't really want me to look like one of them, do you? The professor's wife – did you see what she was wearing, Pete? She was wearing the fucking curtains, Pete! And the shoes – Jesus, Pete, who the fuck did she think she was – Shirley Temple on acid? And the others, did you look at them, at what they were wearing, Pete? Have you ever seen so many cardigans in one room? Like a fucking cardigan convention, if you ask me. I looked at them, Pete, and they looked at me. Oh yes, they incinerated me with their eyes. That's a good word, eh Pete? Incinerated? I know where I learnt that word, Pete, I learnt it in hospital.

Say something, Pete. Please say something.

I'm not s'posed to say a word. I'm not s'posed to get drunk. I'm not s'posed to try, to *try* to *enjoy* . . . Admit it, that's what you meant, isn't it Pete? You meant don't dare enjoy the departmental party, or else. Or else I'd pay for it. All right, I'm paying for it now. And I'll go on paying for it for days. Won't I, Pete? *Pete?*

You meant be Isabel. Be a good little dolly. I tried, Pete. I really did, but I s'pose I'm just Izzy, I'm fed up trying to be Isabel, so there. Put that in your PHD and smoke it.

Somebody's gone and lost their dolly. Look at her, Pete. Isn't she pretty? And she can talk. Listen.

She says she's hungry, Mummy! I'm hungry too, Pete. Seriously, Pete, I was expecting something real to eat, not a cube of cheese and a chipolata impaled on a fucking toothpick. And the vol-au-vents, I still don't know what was in those vol-au-vents, but it tasted like cold tapioca, like wallpaper paste. Ugh! I'm ravenous, Pete, I've never been as hungry in my life. Come over here and I'll show you how hungry I am. No? What is it, are you scared I'll bite?

Say *something*. Go on, tell me I'm a drunken slut. Tell me

how terrible I've been. How mortified you were when I dropped my wine. All over the white linen tablecloth, all over my new flowery dress, all over the stinking rotten carpet. I spoiled it all, didn't I Pete? The tablecloth, the dress, the carpet . . . Your chances of a ruined new . . . I mean a *renewed* contract. Ruined your career, didn't I Pete? Just because I spilled a little wine, a little red wine. A little red wine isn't so bad, is it, Pete? It isn't as bad as blood, not as bad as spilling blood, new blood. You're the New Blood lecturer, aren't you? So you should know. Tell me then, I need to know. Really I do . . . I really do need to know, Pete. It's worse, isn't it, to spill new blood?

Get your old ethics textbook out and tell me.

Okay, don't. Don't say anything at all. Just stand there. Just stand there looking like you.

Your glasses are steaming up again, Pete.

I wonder why they do that. You know what, Pete, why is it that no one has ever invented windshield-wipers for glasses? I mean, when your glasses got wet tonight, I mean when I threw that glass of wine over you, that other glass of wine somebody gave me to replace the one I'd spilled all over your career, well, remember how it went all over your glasses? Well Pete, now think about this. If you'd had a little button in your pocket you could've pressed to activate the wipers, maybe it wouldn't have been so bad for you, eh Pete? You men like pushing buttons, I've noticed that. You've pushed my button, Pete, and now it's time to drop the bomb. The only kind of bomb we women ever drop, Pete.

I'm really sorry for throwing that wine at you, Pete, but it was the way you were talking to me, through clenched teeth like that, the way you were gripping my arm and leading me out of the room . . . You were hurting me, Pete. At least no one saw me do that, eh? Isn't that something to be thankful for? At least you'd got me out of the room before I threw the wine at you. It would've been worse if you'd been wearing your contacts. How are your contacts, Pete?

Oh, yes, I forgot. I'm sorry I stood on one of your contacts, Pete. But that's what happens in the Academic business, isn't it? You end up with a fiancée who stands on your contacts.

Do your contacts get steamed up the way your glasses do? No, really, Pete, I'm curious, I'm interested to know. I remember being with you somewhere, Pete. Either the botanical gardens or a café with a lot of pot plants. Anyway, when we went in, your glasses steamed up, and I looked at you Pete, and you know what you looked like? You looked like a dalek, Pete. A steamed-up academic dalek. If you think I'm going to spend the rest of my life with a steamed up academic dalek like you, you've got another think coming.

You've always got another think coming. That's what you're paid to do. You're paid to think, Pete, and you know it! But you don't think, you don't really think at all. You mouth your footnotes like fleabitten animals grunting at each other in the zoo. That professor of yours looks exactly like a Yak, don't you think?

Why are you gripping the bannister like that? Hmm? Your knuckles've gone all white. You've gone white all over, Pete. What d'you think you're doing, palely loitering? Palely loitering. It's unhealthy. You've been taking too many of those tutorials. You look like a ghost. Worse, you're as white as a thesis. An unwritten one, one that just can't seem to get written. That one you kept telling me about the first time I got pregnant, that one you had to get finished then! That one you still have to finish! *Then* we'll move out of this dump. Then we'll get a bigger flat, have a baby! Not yet though, oh no! You just stand there looking like a silent seminar, like the ghost of an unwritten thesis, looking down at me like—

All right, go ahead and look! This is me, Pete, this is who I am!

At least I can still do that, Pete. I can still look at myself. Can you do that, eh? What do you think you see when you look in the mirror, Pete? Apart from a bit of designer pubic beard and a thorough understanding of your period?

I have a thorough understanding of my period as well. Don't you think I didn't want it to come? Don't you think I've been praying for it to arrive?

You don't know what it was like for me to grow up. At the school I went to, I was expelled. That's what happened to me,

Pete. I got fucking well expelled. All right, I know you know about that, I know I've told you about that before, but I haven't told you why, not really. You know why I got expelled, Pete? I want to tell you this, I have to tell somebody this so I suppose it'll have to be you. I got expelled because . . . they had this school council, a kind of mini-parliament, except we were all girls of course because it was a girls' school – can you follow that, Pete? Just stop me if there's anything you don't understand – and so anyway, I was expelled because I brought up the subject of our periods at the school council. Seriously. You know what we had to do? If a girl was caught unawares by her period, which happened all the time, because girls of that age aren't always all that regular as I'm sure you'll remember if you think hard, Pete. But I'm forgetting – you don't think, do you, Pete? Oh well, just let me think for you and give your brain a rest. Anyway, the girl in question had to go through this great rigmarole to get a sanitary towel, right? She had to request permission to leave the classroom, she had to go to the games teacher, who had the key to the cupboard, the cupboard where the sanitary towels were kept. I'm sorry if this is disgusting you, Pete, but it's true. The truth is disgusting sometimes, the truth is never pleasant, otherwise it wouldn't be the truth. I expect you've read a book or two about the truth, Pete, eh? Your kind of truth. Anyway, to get back to my kind of truth, this sanitary towel from the games mistress had to last you all fucking day. And the thing was, of course, everybody knew, when they saw you being led through the corridors by the games mistress to the cupboard, everybody *knew* . . . But that wasn't the worst of it, the worst of it was that when you'd finished with your sanitary towel, you had to put it in this disposal bag and *give it to the janitor*! Can you believe it, Pete? Can you understand what I'm telling you? That was why I was 'asked to leave' school. I raised the issue of the issue, and the disposal of, the sanitary towels with the School Council.

Aren't you proud of me, Peter?

You fucking should be.

See? I called you Peter. I did. I called you Peter, Pete, so that's what you are to me now. Peter. All right, Peter, although I never thought I'd live with anybody called Peter, what about sex then, Peter? Isn't that what you want now? To atone for my sins at the departmental party in bed. And how.

Why don't you edit a volume on the subject, Peter? I could do your research for you, I could *be* your fucking research, *and* type out your boring footnotes, make the coffee, dress up as a schoolgirl-whore-nun who demands to be dominated. What d'you think? Isn't there a monogram in it somewhere? All right, Peter, come on, dominate me. I demand to be dominated. Come on, Pete, dominate me, all over. Really, it would make a fucking change!

No? Oh, so that's how it is, is it? No sex, please, we're English Literature. We'd rather interpret the Wife of Bath's Tale again, in the original! Of course, we wouldn't touch a real Wife of Bath with a fucking barge-pole, oh no!

Don't look at me like that!

Don't. Please. I'm sorry. I'm really . . . really. You know I can't stand it when you look at me like that. Like I'm some kind of despicable . . . *thing*. I'm not a thing, I'm Izzy. Don't you understand? Don't you like Izzy? You used to. You used to say . . . You didn't look at me like a thing. Maybe that's what you want me to be, Pete, is that it? A plaything. And a work-thing. And a sex-thing. And a little wifeling-thing. I can't be all those fucking things! Not any more, Pete. That's what you want all your so-called colleagues to think, isn't it Pete? Oh here's the New Blood, with his *thing*! She's quite sexy, quite pretty, pretty good in the sack I imagine, I imagine she's quite the *thing*! Good for the New Blood, well done the New Blood!

This is what you really want, Pete. A doll. A doll called Isabel. Dress her up in a pretty floral thing. Take her to the departmental party. Then undress her again, take her to bed. That isn't all you want from me, is it Pete?

It's a pity she talks so much, isn't it Pete? Listen. She says she's sleepy, Mummy. I'm sleepy too, Pete. I'm so tired I could sleep for a hundred years, a hundred years, a hundred years. I could do that, Pete, but you wouldn't chop the trees down, would you? You wouldn't wake me with a kiss. No, because your kiss, with that little pubic beard of yours, would send me into a fucking coma!

Okay, turn your back on me, if you can't stand to look at me. Turn your back on everything, go on. Everything you can't deal with. It's yourself you can't deal with, not me.

A little girl's gone and lost her dolly, but you don't care, do you Pete?

I want you to care. Everyone has to care. I want to care for it. I don't want to lose it. Not this time, Pete. I want to keep it, to hold it, to care. I don't want to have to . . . You shouldn't make me have to . . . No one should be made to have to . . .

Cybernetics

DAVID MACKENZIE

Part One: Learning to Walk

THE MAN LYING on his side at the bottom of the steps leading into the underground station is still moving his legs in long slow strides. The intermittent contact of the sides of his scuffed shoes with the grey concrete floor engages his body in a curious turning motion, his feet treading the circumference of a circle, his hips at the centre, his head and upper body moving backwards in awkward but relentless geometry.

The legs of the people rushing past him are involved in quick, accurate, effective movements, propelling bodies into the tunnel which opens out, farther on, into the station forecourt. Some of these people pause for a moment as they reach the man, glance down at him for a second or two to take in his young face and his brown, dusty coat. The stream of commuters parts, moves round on either side, joins again, moves on.

The place where the man is lying, the very point around which his body is slowly pivoting, is no more than fifteen feet from the road above the underpass. This road is also full of movement, manufactured and metallic, all four lanes braiding and rebraiding into a spillway of grimed metal and chrome.

From the tunnel entrance the noise that is generated by these vehicles is rich and aggressive, an almost monotonous white roar into which individual mechanical sounds merge and submerge.

A tall slim man wearing a grey business suit and carrying an overfull briefcase comes down the steps, sees the young man lying on his side, passes him, walks quickly on for another ten or fifteen yards and then stops. He stands for a few moments, still facing his direction of travel. Then he turns and tries to make his way back to the tunnel entrance. This is difficult for him as he is going against the flow of people but he reaches the man eventually and leans down over him until their faces almost touch. The tall man's position further restricts movement into and out of the tunnel. He places his briefcase on the floor beside the young man whose cycling leg movements have almost ceased. Other briefcases brush the backs of the tall man's legs as he stands there, bent over, and tries to speak to the young man whose eyes, unfocused, stare directly ahead of him. The noise from the roadway overhead and the bustle all round them makes communication between the two men very difficult. There appears to be no response at all from the young man. The tall man bends his knees and crouches down. He reaches out and takes hold of the young man's left shoulder. He begins to shake it, gently at first and then with gathering force as he notes no change in the condition of the young man's eyes, still staring ahead, fixed, if on anything, on an advertising poster which has been pasted to the tiny grey tiles of the tunnel wall.

A girl with short-cropped, pale blonde hair and wearing a white low-cut blouse is enjoying a bar of dark chocolate. Her bright red lips on which every tiny crease and fold of skin is visible, fit neatly round the end of the narrow chocolate bar from which the silver wrapping has been peeled back.

The tall man speaks again and this time there is a response in that the young man turns his head and tries to look at his new companion. The tall man takes hold of the young man's left arm and hauls him quickly to his feet. As he does this he notices a small white plastic bag on the floor, previously trapped under the young man's body. He leans the young man against the tunnel wall and steps back to the centre of the walkway to retrieve his own briefcase and this plastic bag in which there seem to be only a few light possessions. This manoeuvre requires him to step twice across the flow of people heading into the station and he receives two or three bumps and nudges.

Meanwhile the young man, only a matter of five or six feet away, begins to slip gently down the wall. His back remains vertical but his knees buckle very slowly so his descent is little more than a gradual and measured lessening of height until he is sitting on his heels. His eyes are still open, however, and he appears to be staring across at the blonde woman with the chocolate bar who can be glimpsed intermittently between the rushing bodies. The tall man sets the briefcase and the plastic bag down and, taking hold of the lapels of the young man's brown overcoat, pulls him to his feet again. The young man begins to tilt forward but a restraining hand pushes him gently back against the wall. With his upper arm thrust under the young man's left armpit trapping the left arm against his body, the tall man grasps the briefcase in his free hand and sets off into the tunnel. After two uncertain steps he halts, sets the briefcase down and presses the swaying figure of the young man back against the wall once more. He dashes back two or three yards to collect the plastic bag which he had failed to pick up. By the time he returns, the young man's knees have given way again and he has begun sliding towards the concrete floor. The tall man whisks him up, shifts the plastic bag to his other hand, grabs the briefcase in the same hand, whirls the young man round, pinions his arm in a strong grip and launches the two of them into the tunnel once again.

Their pace is dictated by the rate of the body flow around them and the uncertain movements of the young man who takes a few short steps followed by much longer ones. This disables any rhythm the tall man has managed to build up and changes them into a strange sideways tandem creature apparently struggling to find its feet.

They reach the bright station forecourt. The concrete floor

gives way to speckled grey tiles, scuffed by thousands of feet. The sound of the traffic above has subsided but is replaced, below them, by the clatter of the silver-grey underground trains as they burst from the tunnels. There is more movement too as another pedestrian entryway can be seen from which even more people are disgorged into the forecourt. These people bring with them a hundred conversations which break, restart and break again as the several pathways cross and recross on the way to the ticket barrier. Automatic gates feed the passengers through to the crowded upper area from which the steps lead down on either side to the two platforms.

The tall man leans the young man against the small free area of wall near a kiosk where cigarettes and confectionery are on sale. The blonde woman is there, behind him, still consuming her chocolate. The young man's head, lolling backwards, strikes her on the nose. The tall man places the briefcase and plastic bag on the floor. He steps over to the kiosk and makes a purchase. By the time he retraces these few steps from the kiosk, the young man is sitting once again on his heels. The tall man leans over and holds out a chocolate bar in front of the young man's face. A few words come from the young man. The tall man straightens up, unwraps the chocolate bar completely and offers it to the young man. The sight of the chocolate bar galvanises him. He grabs it with his right hand and stuffs it into his mouth. Within a few seconds it has gone. A minimum of chewing has been employed. The tall man speaks again and the young man, still sitting on his heels and leaning against the wall with his knees at the level of his chin, nods. The tall man returns to the kiosk. The young man notices that there are crumbs of chocolate smeared on the fingers of his right hand. It is not clear whether he has caught sight of them – his eyes appear to be looking straight ahead, as before – or sensed the presence through his fingertips. He raises his hand to his face, thrusts all four fingers and thumb into his mouth and sucks them. Then he sucks each finger separately, licking the tips in turn, ending with the thumb. By the time he has completed this exercise the tall man has returned from the kiosk bearing another bar of chocolate. This is consumed only slightly more slowly than the first.

The tall man waits patiently as the procedure of licking the fingers takes place as carefully and as methodically as before. Then he speaks again and the young man shakes his head. This interchange is repeated two or three times. The tall man squats down and talks in an earnest manner. At one point he opens the white plastic bag and looks through it. The young man's eyes close and his head slips to one side. The tall man reaches forward and grabs his collar. He gives it a shake but fails to get any response. He takes hold of each of the young man's ankles in turn and draws them forward so that he is now sitting on the grey speckled tiles with his legs stretched out before him.

The tall man rises and turns, apparently to go towards the ticket barrier. The kiosk owner notices this and shouts something at him. His few words are lost in the din as, below them, a train pulls into the station. There is a loud hiss as the doors are released and a hard rolling sound as they spring apart. The train is almost empty but a large crowd of commuters is waiting to board it.

At the door nearest the exit stairs a man in a grey tracksuit and holding a bicycle tries to get off the train against the crush of people trying to get on. One pedal of the bicycle snags a shopping basket which is pulled from the grasp of the middle-aged lady who is carrying it. The basket is dumped on the slatted wooden floor of the tube train. It contains mostly vegetables, including a plastic two-pound bag of new potatoes. This bag is ejected from the basket and splits as it hits the floor. The potatoes are all quite small and round and they scatter among the feet of those getting on the train.

One passenger, a businessman carrying a briefcase, steps on a potato which is squashed between the wooden slats of the floor but exudes enough juice to lubricate the sole of the highly polished shoe which pressurises it. The man slides sharply to the right, recovers momentarily and then pitches forward. He lets go of his briefcase and puts his hands out to break his fall. One corner of the briefcase strikes the floor first, the clips at the top spring apart with the shock and the briefcase flies open. The contents are deposited across the floor of the rapidly filling carriage.

A copy of the *Financial Times*, three pens, two pencils, a red and yellow packet containing thirty six photographs, a collapsible umbrella, a metal spectacle case, a dog-eared copy of *The Wilt Alternative*, a small plastic dispenser of Panadol tablets, a report on the Relative Processing Power of the IBM E, S and J series of multiprocessors, an out of date British Rail ticket to Milton Keynes, a keyring with five keys and a leather tab with 'Thailand' embossed on it, a small brown paper bag containing a wooden pepper mill and two tickets for the following evening's performance of 'Shirley Valentine' at the Empire Cinema, Leicester Square are all strewn over the floor along with at least half a dozen paper clips.

Three or four passengers bend down to help retrieve the contents of both the briefcase and the shopping basket while someone else helps the man who has fallen to get to his feet. He inspects his hands which are scuffed and bruised but not bleeding.

The cyclist, meanwhile, has managed to extricate himself from the crowd and is standing at the back of the platform waiting for the crush to subside. He has seen nothing of the incident with the shopping basket and the briefcase. He leans his bicycle against the wall and inspects it for signs of damage. The man in the train has now recovered his briefcase and all its contents except the paper clips. From his position in the centre of the space between the doors of the carriage he looks out over the heads of those latecomers still struggling to get on and sees the cyclist over by the wall, or rather, predominantly the cyclist's backside as he leans over to check the chain and gearing. Growing out of the cyclist's back is a large chocolate bar, partly unwrapped and angled towards the red lips of the blonde girl, her eyes apparently fixed on the man on the train.

The public address system barks a warning.

The lady with the shopping basket is still missing some items, notably most of the potatoes, at least one of which has been trampled on. She tries to look round for some of these but the carriage is now completely full of people and no further movement is possible.

There is a hiss as the doors prepare to close. One potato has lodged in the door runnel. The left hand door reaches it first and sends it tumbling along the groove until it meets the right hand door and is abruptly squashed quite flat.

From the platform the cyclist looks up the steps to the ticket barrier and station concourse above. When there appears to be a lull in the number of commuters descending the steps he picks up his bicycle and makes his way up. He takes it slowly and there is no further incident. When he reaches the top, however, he is faced with the problem of negotiating the automatic ticket gates as there is no ticket collector at either of the ticket barriers, both of which are firmly closed. He looks around and finally catches sight of the ticket collector who is standing by the kiosk in a group which includes three other figures. These are the tall man, the kiosk owner and the young man who is still sitting upright on the floor but with his head leaning over on his shoulder.

The tall man and the kiosk owner are both talking at the same time and both are gesticulating though the gestures of the kiosk owner are more abrupt and agitated. The ticket collector has his hands in his pockets. He is standing with his feet apart and he occasionally goes over on his ankles so that his full weight is taken on the outer edges of sole and heel.

The young man slips to one side and as he steadies himself with his hand he knocks over the tall man's briefcase. A young boy, perhaps twelve or thirteen years old, trips over the briefcase and sprawls on the floor. As he falls he makes a grab for the nearest object which is a display bin of chocolate bars positioned to one side of the kiosk. His hand rakes the top of the display and several chocolate bars are flung to the floor. The kiosk owner turns to yell at the boy. The boy picks up himself and three chocolate bars and sprints for one of the exits. One of the other dislodged bars has struck the young man on the knee and landed on the tiled floor at his side. He gives a long, slow shrug and reaches for the bar. The kiosk owner, intent on picking up the other bars scattered on the floor, does not notice the one which the young man is now struggling to unwrap.

The kiosk owner rejoins the tall man and the ticket collector and continues to argue. His voice rises to a shout but is lost in the clamour as another train pulls into the station. The young man continues to work at the wrappings of the chocolate bar but its pressed and glued seams are too much for his awkward and uncoordinated fingers. The bar falls to the floor between his legs two or three times and he appears to pick it up with less enthusiasm on each occasion.

Finally, with a dismissive gesture, the kiosk owner turns abruptly from the tall man and re-enters his kiosk. The tall man now fixes his attention on the ticket collector but he has already turned away as the cyclist has finally managed to catch his eye. The tall man is left alone with the young man. He crouches down in front of him again but as he does so the young man's upper body slowly keels over and he slumps onto the floor beside the kiosk.

The still unwrapped chocolate bar falls from his lap onto the floor. The kiosk owner, a witness to the young man's collapse, comes from his kiosk and stands over the two figures, the tall man crouched down and the young man recumbent. The tall man looks up and he and the kiosk owner exchange a look but no words. Then the kiosk owner leans over and retrieves the chocolate bar from beside the young man's knees. He returns to the kiosk, replacing the bar on the display bin as he does so.

The ticket collector opens the barrier to allow the cyclist and his bicycle through onto the station forecourt. He checks the cyclist's ticket and returns it to him. Seeing the barrier open, a number of passengers who have just got off the most recent train move away from the automatic ticket gates and attempt to follow the cyclist. The ticket collector tries to close the barrier against them but he is too late. As the train clanks and wheezes its way out of the station below them he shouts at the passengers and points over to the automatic gates. He is ignored. So many people rush past him that he has difficulty checking more than a few tickets. The tall man approaches the ticket collector from behind and speaks into his ear. Without turning round the ticket collector waves him away. The tall man moves round until he is at the ticket collector's shoulder, partly blocking the exit through which passengers continue to push and shove their way. He speaks earnestly, perhaps heatedly, to the ticket collector who has given up any attempt to close the barrier and is concentrating hard on grabbing as many tickets as possible. The tall man persists, gesticulating towards the young man lying motionless beside the kiosk. His manner is becoming almost violent and he is beginning to shout.

A woman of about twenty, wearing a black sweater and faded blue jeans and with her brown hair braided into a long pigtail, rushes through the barrier, passing as far away from the ticket collector as the narrow exit will allow. The ticket collector spots her, turns, pushes the tall man roughly out of the way and yells at her to stop. She continues to move away, however, walking as fast as she can without actually breaking into a run. She heads for one of the station exits, sees the young man on the floor by the kiosk and stops abruptly.

She goes over to him, crouches down in front of him and sniffs the air before his face. She looks round and catches the eye of the tall man who is standing behind the ticket collector again as more people veer away from the automatic gates and make for the ticket barrier. The tall man walks quickly over to her and leans towards her, hands on knees, to talk to her. Together they pull the young man into an upright position and the tall man tries to prop him up by taking his heavy briefcase and setting it on end underneath the young man's right arm.

A few moments later they are joined by the ticket collector who has seen the rush of passengers through and has managed to close the ticket barrier. He grabs the girl by the arm and yanks her to her feet. She gives a little scream of surprise and wrenches her arm free.

The ticket collector starts shouting. The tall man stands between them, facing the ticket collector. He holds his hands up, palms outward, and seems about to place them on the ticket collector's shoulders.

The next train clatters into the station. The ticket collector continues to shout, though a little less loudly, and keeps pointing past the tall man at the girl behind. There are moments when he seems about to reach round and grab the girl but the tall man keeps his body between the two and carries on talking in a soft voice which at times is lost in the background noise of the newly arrived train, the ticket gates, the announcements and the movement of hundreds of people. His right hand touches lightly the ticket collector's left shoulder. The ticket collector stops talking and appears to be listening. The tall man puts his head to one side and talks calmly.

The first passengers from the most recent train arrive at the automatic gates.

The young girl cowers behind the tall man.

The young man slips sideways to his left.

The ticket collector folds his arms across his chest.

Someone shouts from the ticket barrier.

Amid the din, the ticket collector says something quite quietly.

The tall man takes some coins from his pocket and hands them over to the ticket collector.

The train grinds its way out of the station.

There are more shouts from the ticket barrier.

The girl pokes her head round from behind the tall man. She points over to the young man who is slumped on the floor again.

The kiosk owner shouts something as another train bursts from the tunnel.

The ticket collector turns and walks slowly towards the ticket barrier. He opens it, steps back and lets the crowd of people rush through. He makes no attempt to check any tickets. He leaves the gate wide open and walks slowly to a small wooden cubicle at the far side of the forecourt. Inside the cubicle there is a stool and a ledge. On the ledge there is a telephone. The ticket collector taps the wall above the phone twice with his knuckle. Then he picks up the receiver and begins to dial.

Sing, Milo, Sing!

BRYAN MACMAHON

THIS IS A simple class of story and the chances are that it isn't worth the telling. It's about a man's wife asking him to sing her a song, and his singing it. Only, as far as it is possible to know, she didn't hear it – for she was dead when he sang it.

The husband's name was Milo Burke and the wife's name was Norrie. Milo was tall, heavy-jowled, bushy-haired and dark-complexioned. He was a noted local singer. He slouched rather than walked. He drank, and his reason for drinking was not really apparent. He was no good for the world. His age was twenty-nine and his wife's twenty-five. She was small – delicately but strongly made. She was flaxen-haired, and when she smiled she resembled a Norwegian. To see her face when it was smiling was to see it at its best. When she was standing she had a trick of placing one shoe down squarely and raising the other shoe-sole so that only the back of the heel rested on the floor. They had one daughter, Nora, a heavy child of six who resembled her father.

These three people lived in a broken-down public-house at the end of the village of Teerla. The village street was wide, and Burke's house lay at one end of it. The house gave one the impression that it had been built elsewhere on a frame with wheels beneath it and then drawn directly athwart the village street. That is, until one saw where the roadway had escaped to the right just before running right under the building. There was a small grimy shop-window, over which precariously hung a board with the name Burke printed dismally on it. The whole village smelled of decay.

When Nora was six years of age, Norrie Burke gave birth to a second child – a baby girl who survived birth by three days. Then there was the little doll's funeral, the playing at laying out, the tiny candles, the tiny dress, the white doll's coffin with tapes to carry it, and the pathetic grave that a man would dig in ten or twelve minutes. What people attended the funeral attended more from curiosity than from sympathy or respect.

Norrie took the child's death badly. After a few days she found herself caught up in a disease that only women should discuss. She suspected her imminent death in her cold sweating members. Finally she read her death-warrant in the doctor's face. When he had gone she composed herself as best she could, then called 'Milo! Milo!'

The heavy boots came up the squeaking stairs. Now more than ever this thundering in the narrow house offended her. The noise made her wince. Hard on her husband's heels came a neighbouring woman who was in and out tending the sick woman.

'Tis all right, Mary,' she said to the woman. 'I want to talk to Milo.'

Mary punched the pillows and arranged them behind her.

'Don't wear yourself out, leanav,' she said.

'Shut the door behind you, Mary, and don't let little Nora come up.'

When they were alone the sick woman turned to her husband who was standing awkwardly at the bedside.

'Sit down, Milo; I want to talk to you.'

He sat gingerly on a finely made chair.

'Move closer, Milo.' He did so.

After a pause, 'I'm going my road, Milo. You know that. The doctor told you.'

Milo examined his large stupid hands. His face was

indicative of little emotion. After an effort he began in a colourless voice, 'I wasn't such a good husband, Norrie.'

The sick head coquetted wanly: 'Who said you weren't, Milo? Did I say it? Answer me, Milo?'

Again in a voice that was incapable of lustre: 'I didn't bring you luck, Norrie. What with the drink and everything. What did I bring you but misfortune?'

'You brought me your singing.'

The man was silent and kept examining his hands as if they were novel to him.

'Milo?'

'Well, Norrie?'

'Do you remember the day I met you first? It was on the pier of Inver. Seven years ago last 26th of July at a quarter-past four in the evening. Do you remember, Milo? Myself and Kitty Dawson were sitting on the pier wall, and the quiet waves were slapping the cement behind us. A canoe was going out to the islands. In front of it was a big bundle of hay. The mountains far away stood up out of the heat-mist. You come down the pier with all the other girls and fellows. One of them had a concertina. I took particular note of you – you were trailing behind like a sheep. Your big mohall of hair, your blundering boots, your heavy lugs and your stone-dead eyes. Do you remember, Milo?'

The man tired of looking at his palms. He turned over his hands and began examining the large hairs on the backs of them.

'Kitty Dawson nudged me and you passin'. I skitted right into your face. Even then your eyes didn't come alive. You passed out and trailed after the others as they went to the end of the pier. You looked more awkward from the back than you did from the front. And then I lost interest in you until all the fellows and girls gathered in a ring around you. I heard them saying, "Sing, Milo, sing!"'

'And then, Holy God, you sang. Out into the sea. Do you remember, Milo?'

The man kept turning his hands to see all sides of them. He said nothing. His face was utterly composed.

'I followed you then, Milo, until I got you. And through drink and misfortune and trouble I had no payment but your singing. I was well paid, Milo.'

The man said stolidly, 'I wasn't a good husband, Norrie . . .'

'No, no, Milo. How many times did we talk all night long until the green morning walked in the windows. And now and again, if I asked you, you sang with your head under the bedclothes so as not to wake the child.

'And how many times did I walk home from the concerts with you after you had sung. And all the women were jealous of me and I having hold of you by the sleeve.

'And how many times did we go into the woods together and walk by the path under the hazels until we came out on a lump of white gravel over the river. And then you sang against the snarling water.

'Milo!'

'Well, Norrie?'

'I want you to promise me something.'

The man did not answer.

'It isn't the drink – it isn't fair to cage a man in that sort of a promise. Not 'tisn't about getting married again, because that's not fair but a slittle. Nor it isn't about the child, because I know that whatever happens it's your nature to be good to her. It's a different thing entirely.' The woman checked her swallowing and said: 'The night I'm being waked, Milo . . .' She stopped.

Milo looked at her bovinely as if her terrible emotions had not the power to hinder or hurt him. Steadied by his non-display of grief she began again in a steadier voice:

'The night I'm waking . . . you'll sing for me. Won't you, Milo?'

'I will, Norrie.'

'You promise, Milo?'

'I promise, Norrie.'

'As sure as God is your judge?'

'As sure as God is my judge!'

In Teerla, gentle and simple can tell you how Milo Burke kept his word to his wife. The night of the wake was still and

windless – such a night for singing had never been before. She
was laid out in her blue Child o' Mary cloak and white veil.
She looked contented. Small wonder that, since the stones of
the road know that a woman dying out of childbirth is certain
sure of Glory. By some means or another it had become public
property that Milo was going to sing. No one begrudged him
doing so, no more than they begrudged the cat her mew or the
sheep her bleat. The wake-house was thronged. The very last
of the drink of the shop was going – Milo himself drank but he
didn't get drunk. Out in the village the people who had
remained at home to mind the houses kept coming to the
doors to watch Burke's casement windows. The windows
were open, and the watchers could see the mourners passing
and re-passing in the lighted wake-room.

About half-past ten Milo came into the wake-room and,
standing with his awkward hands more or less by his side,
began to sing:

> *I'll take you home again, Kathleen,*
> *Across the ocean, wild and wide,*
> *To where your heart has ever been,*
> *Since first you were my bonnie bride.*

The first note he uttered sliced to silence the speaking house.
In the back bedroom his child leaped straight from sleep to
wakefulness, and beating down those who had come in to pin
her, said, 'Hush! I want to hear my Da singing.'

So divorced from his song was the singer that his voice took
on a body of its own. The people listening in the village
included an old man standing before a pergola and a girl and
her lover who stood beneath some poplars.

The song called the dead woman jewel, darling, treasure,
calf, secret, share and bright white love.

It told the people how to be beautiful though ugly, how to
be rich though poor, how to be happy though sad, how to be
young though old.

When the song was finished, Milo retreated into a corner of
the room and remained there for the rest of the night, quite
silent.

Bears in Mourning

ADAM MARS-JONES

WHEN I THINK about it, it was terrible the way we behaved when Victor died. We behaved as if we were ashamed of him, or angry. It didn't show us at our best – we didn't cope at all well. We all knew Victor was 'ill', obviously, but none of us really took on board how bad things had got.

He was in the middle of our little group, our sect, but somehow he got lost all the same. I suppose each of us paid him some token attention – his conversation tended to go round in circles, particularly with the drink – and then left it to somebody else to do the real work: supporting him and talking him through the dark days. He was our brother Bear, but the fraternity didn't do well by him.

We Bears are a varied crowd. There's an organist, a social worker, a travel agent, an osteopath. That's not the full list, of course, that's off the top of my head. If it wasn't for membership of the Bear nation we would have nothing in common. Somehow we always thought that would be enough.

It's amazing that Victor was able to hold down his job for as long as he did, but then he'd done it for a long time. He was working with friends, people who would make allowances. In any case there was a structure set up, and within limits it ran itself. Every few months Victor, or rather the company that employed him, put out the first issue of a magazine devoted to some sure-fire subject – French cookery, classic cars, sixties pop. When I say the first issue, I mean of course Parts One and Two, Part Two coming free.

It doesn't take long, with a half-way decent picture researcher, to get enough stuff from reference books to fill a few magazine pages. Tasters for future issues take care of the rest. Part Three never arrives, and maybe people wonder why not. Maybe they think, shame nobody bought Parts One and Two – it was such a good idea. Pity it didn't catch on.

I used to wonder what would have happened if one of Victor's magazines had really taken off, had sold and sold off the news-stands. Would there have come a time when Part Three became inevitable? I don't think so. I think Victor's employers would have carried on repackaging their little stack of ideas for ever. With a little redesign, they could put out the same Parts One and Two every two years or so. Which they did.

Victor was prime Bear, Bear absolute. I know I haven't explained just what a Bear is, and it's not an easy thing to define. There have always been tubby men, but I can't think they ever formed a little self-conscious tribe before. *Tubby* isn't even the right word, but at least it's better than *chubby*. *Chubby* is hopeless, and *chubby-chaser* is a joke category.

To be a Bear you need, let's see, two essential characteristics, a beard and a bit of flesh to spare, preferably some body hair. But it's a more mysterious business than that. Some men will never be Bears however hairy they are, however much surplus weight they carry. They just look like hairy thin guys who've let themselves run to seed, thin men who could stand to lose a few pounds. A true Bear has a wholeness you can't miss – at least if you're looking for it.

It's a great thing to watch a Bear become aware of himself. All his life he's been made to feel like a lump, and then he meets a person, and then a whole group, that thinks he's heaven on legs. On tree-trunk legs. He's been struggling all his life against his body, and suddenly it's perfect. There have been quite a few lapsed health-club memberships in our little circle, I can tell you.

One of them was mine. I remember the first time I was hugged by a Bear, as a Bear. We were Bear to Bear. I remember how his hand squeezed my tummy – *tummy*'s a childish word but the others are worse – and I realised I didn't need to hold it in. He wasn't looking for a wash-board stomach, the sort you can see in the magazines. He was happy with a wash-tub stomach like mine. He liked me just the way I was.

And Aids, Aids. Where does Aids come into this?

All of us were involved in the epidemic in some way, socially, politically, rattling collection buckets at benefit shows if nothing else. And of course we were all terrified of getting sick. But that's not what I'm getting at.

Aids is like the weather. It doesn't cause everything, but the things it doesn't cause it causes the causes of. So, yes, you'd think there'd be a link between a group of men who like their lovers to have a bit of meat on their bones, who like men with curves, and a disease that makes people shrivel away into a straight line up and down.

But I don't really think so. The Bear idea would have happened with or without Aids. The English language had a hand in it, by putting the words *bear* and *beard* so close to each other in the dictionary. Perhaps it's a sexual style that works differently in other languages. Has anyone in history ever really enjoyed beards, let alone based a little erotic religion around them? I suppose Victorian wives were the people in history most exposed to facial hair, and they weren't in much of a position to shop around or compare notes.

The beard is a mystery worn on the face. There are beards of silk and beards of wire, each with its charge of static, and it isn't easy to tell them apart without a nuzzle, or at least a touch of the hand.

We in our group are great observers of the way a beard shows up different pigments from the rest of the head hair. Ginger tints are common; less often, we see magical combinations of darkness and blondness. Beards age unpredictably, sometimes greying before the head hair, sometimes retaining a strong shade when all colour has drained from the scalp. The first frost may appear evenly across the beard, or locally in the sideboards, or on the chin, or at the corners of the mouth.

We in our group are tolerant of tufty beards, wispy beards, beards with asymmetrical holes. There are beards that Nature more or less insists on, to cover up her blotches. Only a few bearers of the beard, we feel, positively bring it into disrepute, usually by reason of fancy razorwork. The beard to us is more than a sexual trigger, not far short of a sexual organ. Some of us even defend jazzman beards, goatees, beards that look like a few eyebrows stuck together. As a group, we particularly admire a beard that rides high on the cheeks, or one that runs down the neck unshaven.

Bears don't discriminate against age. It's just the other way about. We often say that someone is too young for his beard – he'll have to grow into it.

A man with a pure-white beard can expect as many looks of appreciation, still tinged with lust, as someone twenty, thirty years younger. There are many couples in our group, though few of them even try to be monogamous, and some of them are made up of figures who we might describe as Bear and Cub, Daddy Bear and Baby Bear – but even they don't take their roles very seriously. Neither of them tries too hard to play the grown-up.

It's as if in every generation of boy children there are a few who put their fingers in their ears during tellings of *Goldilocks*, filtering out the female elements in the story, until what they are left with is a fuzzy fable of furry sleepers, of rumpled beds and porridge.

Every happy period is a sort of childhood, and the last ten years have been a happy period for the Bears, in spite of everything.

So when I say that Victor was an absolute Bear, I mean that he had pale skin, heavy eyebrows and a startlingly dark beard, full but trimmed. No human hair is black, even Chinese or Japanese, and Raven Black hair dye is sold as a cruel joke to people who know no better, but Victor's came close. He was forty-two or three then, I suppose, and five foot eight, ideal Bear height. He pointed his feet out a bit, as if his tummy was a new thing and needed a new arrangement of posture to balance it.

We met in a bar. Under artificial light the drama of his colouring wasn't immediately obvious, and I mistook him for a German who had been rude to me in another bar a couple of months before. I suppose my body language expressed a preemptive rejection, which in the event Victor found attractive. After a while he came over to me and said, 'You win. You've stared me down. Let me buy you a drink.'

I went home with him in his old Rover to Bromley, an unexpectedly long journey, and a suburban setting that didn't seem to fit with the man who took me there. Later I learned that this had been his childhood home. When his mother died, Victor had let go a West End flat so as to keep his father company. It was a doomed gesture, as things turned out – one of a series – because his father soon found some company of his own. The companion may in fact have dated back to days before Victor's mother died.

It was late when we arrived at Bromley. I assumed we were alone in the house, in which case Victor's father was stopping out with his lady friend, but perhaps he was asleep in a bedroom I didn't see. If so, he slept soundly, and got up either before or after we did.

The bedroom was in chaos, but not knowing Victor it didn't occur to me to wonder whether it was an ebullient chaos or a despairing one. There was a big bulletin board on the mantelpiece, with photographs, letters and business cards pinned up on it, but there was still an overflow of paper and magazines. There was the inevitable shelf of Paddingtons, Poohs and koalas, and a single Snoopy to show breadth of mind.

Victor wanted first to be hugged and then fucked. He mentioned that this second desire was a rarity with him, and I could believe him. He was vague about the location of condoms. Eventually I found a single protective in a bedside drawer, of an unfamiliar brand (the writing on the packet seemed to be Dutch) and elderly appearance. I could find no lubricant that wouldn't dissolve it. I put it on anyway, to show willing, and lay down on top of Victor. I enjoyed the heat and mass of the man beneath me; I made only the most tentative pelvic movements, just vigorous enough to tear the dry condom. Then Victor remembered that he had some lubricant after all, under the bed.

Victor was apologetic about the confusion of our sexual transaction, but looking back I find it appropriate. He was both in and out of the world, even then, and he could summon up separately the elements of love-making, desire, caution, tenderness, but not string them together.

At some stage I noticed he was crying, and he went on for over an hour before he stopped. I hugged him some more, but I can't say that I took his distress very seriously. I didn't make anything of the fact that we didn't have a particularly good time in bed. Good sex isn't very Bear, somehow. I was already well used to awkwardness, lapses of concentration, sudden emotional outpourings. What could be more Bear than a fatherly man on a crying jag?

Bears are never far from tears, or wild laughter come to that. I have seen Bears cry just as hard as Victor did that night, beards matted with their tears, and be cheered up by a bowl of cereal or a cartoon on television. But of course Victor only stopped crying when he fell asleep. The curtains were open, and it was already beginning to get light. I hate sleeping like that – this Bear likes his cave dark – but I didn't stay awake long enough to do anything about it.

That was my only intimate contact with Victor, but the Bear community continued to revolve in its eccentric orbit around him. Everybody I met seemed to know him, and I ended up keeping track of him without making any great effort. Victor's father died a few months after we met, which I think was the great event in Victor's life. After that he had a succession of room-mates at the house – Bears, inevitably. They didn't stay long. Victor was hard going by then, even for Bears. But while they stayed, and while he stayed coherent,

Victor took a fatherly interest in them, and would try to fix them up with compatible Bruins. That's a nice characteristic – that's a good thing to remember.

I invited Victor to dinner once about that time, and he phoned me on the evening arranged to warn me he'd be late. He never arrived. From friends on the Bear grape-vine I learned that this pattern was typical.

After Victor died, the room-mate at the time wanted everything of Victor's, everything that was even reminiscent of Victor, cleared away at once. He wasn't being heartless, he just couldn't cope with a dead man's presence being imprinted so strongly on the rooms. I went along to help out, but it wasn't as straightforward a job as I had thought when we started. Apparently neutral objects kept leaping into hurtful life.

It turned out that Victor used to offer himself as a photographic model for his magazines and their stable-mates. Surprising that a man with low self-esteem should so much enjoy being photographed. But apparently he used to tease the company's photographic editor about the scarcity of bearded images in the media, and offered himself to make good the lack. So as we cleared the room we found that the slippered individual on the cover of a mid-seventies hi-fi magazine, head cocked while he stroked a spaniel and listened to a hulking array of quadrophonic speakers, was a mid-seventies Victor. The genial chef on another cover, stirring a golden sauce in a kitchen hung with gleaming copper pans, was also Victor. Victor was even a tasteful Adam on the cover of a pop-psychology mag, Parts One and Two, receiving a glossy apple from an Eve with scheming eyes. Finally all the traces of Victor's presence were gone, stuffed under beds or bundled into bin-bags.

The worst part of the visit, though, was finding in Victor's waste-paper basket something that was like the opposite of a suicide note. It was the note he would have left for his roommate if Victor had managed to decide to go on living. *Dear Bear*, it started, and it said

Sorry I've been so hard to be around lately, that's the last thing you need. Thanks for bearing it anyway (bad joke), and I think I've turned the corner. I'll leave the car tomorrow – no point in taking it – and I'll see you in the p.m. Don't chuck the *Guardian*, there may be some jobs in it. Love Victor.

I had known that Victor was due to appear in court the next day for drunk driving (not his first offence) and was certain to lose his licence. I hadn't heard that he had also lost his job, which was probably because of his general unreliability, although the pretext had to do with fiddling expenses or paying somebody who was already on the staff to do piecework under another name.

Instead of turning up in court, and instead of leaving the note, which he crumpled up and threw in the waste-paper basket, Victor took the car and drove down to the country, Kent somewhere, I'm afraid I've blotted out the details. I think it was where his parents met, or had their first date, or went on their honeymoon. It had a private significance, but I've forgotten exactly what. I imagine it was a beauty spot, and that he reached it in the early hours. He must have waited a bit, after he arrived, for the crumbling exhaust pipe of the old Rover to cool down from the journey. He wouldn't have wanted to burn his hands or melt the hose. Perhaps he waited again afterwards, before he restarted the engine.

He didn't leave a note, but he hardly needed to. For weeks he had been sitting around drinking and listening to a record – the first single he had bought for years, I dare say. It was called *The Living Years* by Mike and the Mechanics, and by bad luck it was at number one. For a few weeks it was impossible to avoid it on the radio. It was all about not telling your father you loved him while he was alive, and Victor played it over and over again. Mike of the Mechanics is one of the very few beards in pop music, but I don't think that had anything to do with it. Far too lanky to be a Bear.

Victor had a little bag of runes, a sort of Celtic *I Ching*, given him by an Irish Bear who used them to make every decision, and he would draw a rune from the bag every now and then when he was drinking. He seemed to draw the blank tile rather a lot, or so I heard, from the black suede draw-string bag. The draw-string bag of fate. The blank rune means death, according to the little booklet that comes with the set, but I hope he read a little further and learned that it could also mean the absolute end of something. The blank tile can actually be a positive sign: new beginning. Still, I don't expect it would have mattered what tile he drew, or what he thought it meant.

I don't expect it occurred to Victor to think of that old magazine cover, with a younger and hopeful-looking him patting a dog and listening with an expression of neutral pleasure to an unspecified music. But I find myself thinking, as I didn't when Victor's death was fresh, of the two images, the one of posed contentment, and the other of real-life squalor and misery – a middle-aged man letting a pretentious pop single contain and enlarge all his sense of failure.

Suicide rates go down in wartime. Isn't that a fascinating fact? Except that I can never work out what it means. Does it mean that people with a self-destructive streak volunteer for dangerous jobs or missions, so they don't need to go to the trouble of topping themselves – they're either killed or cured? Or does it mean that people forget to be self-obsessed when there's a genuine crisis out there in the world?

You'd think there'd be a lot of Aids-related suicides, but there aren't. It can't just be a matter of being British, not wanting to make a fuss, all that. There must be a few people who freak out when they're diagnosed HIV-positive out of a clear blue sky; they're the most likely to lay hands on themselves. But anyone who's already shown symptoms must at least have considered the possibility. Knowing the worst can even calm people down, in a certain sense.

It's different for people who are really sick. They're faced with a series of days only fractionally better or worse than the one before, and suicide is such an all-or-nothing business. It's really tricky deciding what individual trial finally tips a life over into being not worth the living, and then sticking to your decision. It's like a problem in algebra. What is x, such that x *plus 1* is unbearable?

But how do the survivors feel if someone does commit suicide in the middle of a war? That was the problem for the Bears – that was what we were dropped in. We knew damn well that Victor wasn't physically sick. He couldn't have taken an HIV test without our knowing. It seemed to us that he'd just thrown away a body that any of our sick friends, any dwindling Bear, would have jumped at. OK, so Victor was short of puff, no great shakes when it came to running up stairs. There are plenty of skinny people who could have learned to put up with that.

We were angry. Didn't Victor know there was a war on? We Bears had given bouquets that had appeared at the graveside stripped of their messages. We had laboured to clean the bathrooms of the dead, so that their heirs found nothing so much as a stain to alarm them – and had had our names forgotten however many times we were introduced to them. We had held our candles high at Trafalgar Square vigils, year after year, forming helpful compositional groups on cue, for press photographs that never got published. And there was Victor beautiful in his coffin, plump in his coffin, his poison-blued face hardly presenting a challenge to the undertaker's cosmetician.

Everywhere we look we see Aids. We can be driving along, not thinking of anything. We stop at the traffic lights and there's a cyclist waiting there too, foot flexed on the pedal, ready to shoot off first. The picture of health. Except that he's wearing a mask to filter the city air that makes us think of an oxygen mask, and there's a personal stereo fastened by a strap to his bicep that reminds us of a drip feed – as if he was taking music intravenously.

So how could Victor see anything but Aids? What gave him the right to follow his obsession with his father so far? Somehow while we were all busy he found the time to invent his own illness. Wasn't Aids good enough for him? We loved his flesh, but it was unnatural that he died with it unmelted. Dying fat is an obscenity, these days. You're not supposed to be able to take it with you.

★

These days I understand Victor a little better. His anti-suicide note has made me understand suicide in a way that no suicide note could ever do. His father dying made his failure final. When we finally worked out the the access code for his home computer, we found it was full of rambling journal entries saying so. But in another way he must have been relieved. With both his parents dead, he didn't need to resist the temptation of suicide any more, for their sake. He had no loyalty to life. He felt no patriotism for the mortal country.

I realise now that Victor's life only amounted to a little loop of track, like a child's first model railway layout. There was only one set of points in the whole circuit, and every time Victor passed it he had to decide whether to commit himself to going round again. But even if he did, he knew that he'd be passing the points again soon. Sooner or later he was bound to make the other choice.

He didn't steer the way we do. He wasn't affected by our weather. His despair was a gyroscope. But any other time, we would have grieved for him.

I didn't go to the memorial service, though I know that one or two of the Bears did, along with a couple of colleagues from work. But all the Bears turned up to a funeral feast at the Bromley house. We had a sort of picnic, but there was an ugly feeling behind it all, a resentment we didn't quite come out with. Most of us got a little drunk, which didn't help. I remember wandering through the house, looking for signs of Victor, even though I had helped so recently to clear such things away. I found a photo of him in a drawer, and slipped it into a pocket. Then a little later, someone dragged out the bin-bags of Victor's papers and possessions, and a little after that we made a bonfire.

Possibilities

MARY MORRISSY

AT 41, Grace Davey's biggest fear was that she would dry up. When she rose in the morning she would be relieved and delighted to find her loins pleasingly damp. The milky secretion of mid-cycle was a cause for secret celebration. So, when she discovered a greenish discharge she was not at all alarmed. It reminded her of the sap that oozes from the barks of pine trees – strong, pungent, fertile. The workings of her own body were a mystery to her. She took great trouble with her appearance. Her chestnut hair, streaked here and there with grey, was swept back in a coil from her lightly lined face and pale green eyes. She had a slender neck, graceful shoulders, girlish hips. Yet of her innards she had only the vaguest notion – an impression of oiled, livid organs performing languid, primitive rituals unquestioningly – which was why the discharge did not at first bother her. She certainly didn't relate it to Lucas. Her body was merely dispelling something nasty and sharp-smelling which it needed to get rid of. She bowed to its wisdom.

She took to bathing more often, aware that the acrid odours of one's own body are always more pleasing to oneself than others. She dabbed lavender water on her wrists and behind her ears to distract attention. But as the weeks wore on she would panic if anyone so much as wrinkled a nose in her presence. Once, on a particularly muggy day in late August, Mr Weatherby paused in the middle of dictation and started sniffing noisily.

'Don't you get it?' he asked rising from the desk and wandering around the room.

His penthouse office was all glass, the smoky tinted kind which threw a bronzed blanket on the sky and over the city far below. The air conditioner was whirring noisily but the room was still stuffy.

'Get what?' she asked sliding her hand furtively into her handbag for the lavender water.

'That smell, like seaweed, rotting seaweed.'

Grace sat in a damp pool.

'Perhaps it's the river,' she suggested willing him to move away. He was poised like a hound. She was afraid he would catch the smell of fear from her which was now stronger than the other smell. 'It was at low tide this morning and it always stinks in the summer.'

He paced up and down in his glassy cage. He was a small, soft man with the contours of a baby. A paunch, a soft sagging chin, plum-like hands as if knuckles had never formed.

'You must be right,' he said, 'it looks pretty foul from here and there's all that greenish stuff clinging to the banks. Ugh, disgusting. . . !'

He stretched up and fiddled wth the knob on the air-conditioning box.

Then he thumped it impatiently.

'Damn thing isn't worth a jot!'

Grace sighed with relief.

Lucas Spalding's hand appeared first through the hatch. Next came a head with dark, spiky hair, then a bare spindly torso. He had the sort of looks that until a certain age seem handsome and then suddenly become malevolent – when a dark eye turns beady, an arched eyebrow becomes demonic and a strand of brilliantined hair or tufts escaping from the nostrils seem like small fragments of evil. He hauled himself out onto the deck of the barge and sat with his legs, clad in a shiny pair of dark pants, dangling over the edge. He scratched his stubbly chin irritably and yawned. It was midday. He surveyed his world. The bridge forming a surprised O with its counterpart in the still, scummy water, the juggled backsides of houses on the far bank, the stone wall along the tow path with little back doors set into it and dark, glabrous ivy clinging to its crevices. On the near bank, a heap of rusting junk – an old-fashioned mangle, an upended wheelbarrow, a gaping cast-iron fireplace, all sprouting great green tufts of weeds. Like everything else in his life, Lucas had come upon this home by chance. The dilapidated barge had lain idle on the canal for years. It had been there for so long that it had become part of the geography of the place. The sight of its rust-red gangrenous hull sinking into the water would have been missed as much as the elm trees on the banks were they to be felled. Lucas had moved in stealthily and taken possession. He knew how to insinuate himself into other people's lives; his trade required it. He had worked once in a photographic laboratory developing holiday snaps. He had seen it all there. Ugly, naked pendulous men smiling bare-facedly at the camera; fat women splayed on bedspreads showing off bluish, mottled bottoms. People assumed that only a machine shared their tacky secrets, but they were wrong. Lucas Spalding knew them too. Sometimes, by chance, he would pass those same people on the street and he would flash a viperish grin at them. They often mistook his glee for friendliness and would wave gaily, if uncertainly, back at him as if he were someone they had met at a party and couldn't quite put a name to. But, in fact, it was the other way round.

He worked now only when he had to. When he was short of cash he would take his camera down to the Merchants Bridge in the city. He wore a sign around his neck which read 'INSTANT PHOTOS'. The summer season was the best. The heat drove people to all sorts of vanity. The trick was to stop them as they linked one another across the bridge – usually young couples in the first flush of romance – and offer them something to remember their night by. The funny thing was that they were always flattered to be chosen, not realising that he chose them for one reason only, that they were easy prey. Suckers!

It was on the bridge that he had met Grace on a warm, thundery summer's night. The sky was a deep inky blue. She approached wearing a pale raincoat which flapped accommodatingly to show a lozenge of floral thigh. He did not usually stop lone women; they were either sullen or scathing and were not likely to buy. But there was something in her buoyant stride, her hair and coat afloat like one of those young girls on bicycles, that dared to be interrupted.

'Photo, madam?' he called out, bowing into her path.

She came to such a quick halt that his temple brushed against her breast as he straightened himself. He quivered. Quickly he drew a chipped mirror from his breast pocket. For the undecided this was usually the clincher. They rarely resisted this ritual presentation of their own image. She did not demur. Lucas brushed a stray hair from her cheek. Then, catching her firmly by the shoulder, he guided her back to the spot where he had first seen her. Holding the camera close to his chest he beckoned to her with a grubby hand. She walked towards him. His coat billowed around him as he reversed. A ghostly blue flash went zig-zagging between feet and legs and into the silent shadows of the river below. Minutes later the wet, curling print came lolling out of the camera, black at first, then grey and cloudy before finally clearing into a bright exposure. She took the print, still damp, and held it delicately by its edges. The flash had made her chestnut hair seem brighter, her smile more moist, the blue night more electric.

'So, this is how I look,' she said.

'The camera never lies,' he replied.

Suddenly a large drop of rain fell on the print like a fat childish tear. The trees rustled in a fit of restlessness. Thunder rumbled in the sky. Lucas looked up.

'Better shelter, there's going to be an almighty downpour,' he said, touching her fleetingly in the small of her back.

'Look, over there . . .'

He grasped her hand. She ran along beside him feeling

suddenly girlish, her light summer shoes clacking on the pavement. They tumbled into a doorway. There was already a crowd there, huddled together mournfully watching the shower. Arrows of rain lanced the kerbside puddles. A gutter nearby streamed blue and gold. In the crush she found herself pressed up against him but even when the rain had eased and the other people had gingerly ventured out, Lucas and Grace still stood close together, their warm damp breaths mingling, their fingertips just touching.

There were many things Grace liked about Lucas. He had the smell of a farmer, milky and slightly rancid. There was grit beneath his nails and a dirty rim around his neck. The collars of his shirts were frayed. She liked these things because she knew they would never have to be accommodated. For Grace the word 'we' was a strange and impossible notion. There had been other men, of course, but always unsuitable. There were some people whom one couldn't accommodate in one's life, she had discovered, who just wouldn't fit in. Like the lame carpenter she had been seeing who squirmed in company and could only talk about joists and dovetails. She had found men's needs for closeness irksome; she did not want to be troubled by their small grievances and petty outrages. And it was easy, so easy, to embarrass Grace. She had a finely tuned sense of embarrassment which, at times, was as acute as physical pain. It was to this that the men before Lucas had fallen prey.

Grace visited the barge three times a week. Lucas would wait for her in the dark. There were rarely any preliminaries. He would light the little gas bracket and put the kettle on the stove. By the time it had boiled Lucas would have already come. Sometimes there would not even be time to take their clothes off so that they would end up in odd states of dishevelment, Lucas with his pants round his ankles, Grace with a breast exposed above a strangled bra. They would smile gratefully at one another with wet teeth and swollen mouths without the slightest hint of foolishness. He called her Gracie. She was surprised to find it neither bleak nor dispiriting. Lucas was the only man who had ever made her feel wanton. Once he asked her to come to the barge with as few clothes on as possible. She travelled on the train wearing only a raincoat, buttoned and belted, but the thought that she was naked underneath drove her to such excitement that Lucas's first touch produced a wet spasm of sheer delight.

'There's nothing like it,' he would say, 'pure sex.'

Grace was inclined to agree. Afterwards she would dress and settle her hair while Lucas made tea. They would sit by the stove sipping from enamel mugs, snug as a pair of pensioners. He never pleaded with her to stay. They were as wary of one another's territory as a pair of animals might have been. Nightly, Grace returned to her scented bed while Lucas rearranged the divan and fell asleep in a nest of blankets which bore the tart smell of their union. And if she passed Lucas on the bridge the only acknowledgement between them was the flutter of an eyelid and that anarchic sense of conspiracy that accompanies any act of intimacy between two people.

It was only when the sores appeared that Grace began to worry. She went to the clinic. She was issued with a number and told to sit in the crowded waiting-room. She could feel her cheeks burning with shame. She fixed her eyes on the floor and studied the creases in her shoes. Nobody spoke and the only time a head was raised was when the door to the surgery opened and a new number was called.

He was a young doctor with sandy hair and an air of discreet disappointment. And why not, Grace thought. Her kind of illness was a failing, after all. It showed an absence of care and good taste. The treatment, he reassured her, was a hundred per cent effective. It would, of course, mean abstinence for some time, but in a monogamous relationship like hers, some accommodation could surely be made. Of course, there might be some side-effects, he went on. Nothing dramatic, no facial hair or anything like that. But she might notice a certain dryness – in the vaginal area. Absolutely nothing to worry about. Most women were actually quite glad of it, he said. He fixed her with a candid gaze.

'The main thing,' he said, 'is to cut down on the possibilities, to ensure that this sort of thing doesn't happen again . . .'

Carried Away

ALICE MUNRO

Letters

IN THE DINING room of the Commercial Hotel, Louisa
opened the letter that had arrived that day from overseas. She
ate steak and potatoes, her usual meal, and drank a glass of
wine. There were a few travellers in the room, and the dentist
who ate there every night because he was a widower. He had
shown an interest in her in the beginning but had told her he
had never before seen a woman touch wine or spirits.

'It is for my health,' said Louisa gravely.

The white tablecloths were changed every week and in the
meantime were protected by oilcloth mats. In winter, the
dining room smelled of these mats wiped by a kitchen rag, and
of coal fumes from the furnace, and beef gravy and dried
potatoes and onions – a smell not unpleasant to anybody
coming in hungry from the cold. On each table was a little
cruet stand with the bottle of brown sauce, the bottle of
tomato sauce, and the pot of horseradish.

The letter was addressed to 'The Librarian, Carstairs Public
Library, Carstairs, Ontario.' It was dated six weeks before –
January 4, 1917.

Perhaps you will be surprised to hear from a person you don't know and that doesn't remember your name. I hope you are still the same Librarian though enough time has gone by that you could have moved on.

What has landed me here in Hospital is not too serious. I see worse all around me and get my mind off of all that by picturing things and wondering for instance if you are still there in the Library. If you are the one I mean, you are about of medium size or perhaps not quite, with light brownish hair. You came a few months before it was time for me to go in the Army following on from Miss Tamblyn who had been there since I first became a user aged nine or ten. In her time the books were pretty much every which way, and it was as much as your life was worth to ask her for the least help or anything since she was quite a dragon. Then when you came what a change, it was all put into sections of Fiction and Non-Fiction and History and Travel and you got the magazines arranged in order and put out as soon as they arrived, not left to moulder away till everything in them was stale. I felt gratitude but did not know how to say so. Also I wondered what brought you there, you were an educated person.

My name is Jack Agnew and my card is in the drawer. The last book I took out was very good – H. G. Wells, Mankind in the Making. My education was to Second Form in High School, then I went into Doud's as many did. I didn't join up right away when I was eighteen so you will not see me as a Brave Man. I am a person tending to have my own ideas always. My only relative in Carstairs, or anyplace, is my father Patrick Agnew. He works for Douds not at the factory but at the house doing the gardening. He is a lone wolf even more than me and goes out to the country fishing every chance he gets. I write him a letter sometimes but I doubt if he reads it.

After supper Louisa went up to the Ladies' Parlour on the second floor, and sat down at the desk to write her reply.

I am very glad to hear that you appreciated what I did in the Library, though it was just the normal organisation, nothing special.

I am sure you would like to hear news of home, but I am a poor person for the job, being an outsider here. I do talk to people in the Library and in the Hotel. The travellers in the Hotel mostly talk about how business is (it is brisk if you can get the goods) and a little about sickness, and a lot about the War. There are rumours on rumours and opinions galore, which I'm sure would make you laugh if they didn't make you angry. I will not bother to write them down because I am sure there is a Censor reading this who would cut my letter to ribbons.

You ask how I came here. There is no interesting story. My parents are both dead. My father worked for Eaton's in Toronto in the Furniture Department, and after his death my Mother worked there too in Linens. And I also worked there for a while in Books. Perhaps you could say Eaton's was our Doud's. I graduated from Jarvis Collegiate. I had some sickness which put me in hospital for a long time, but I am quite well now. I had a great deal of time to read, and my favourite authors are Thomas Hardy – who is accused of being gloomy but I think is very true to life – and Willa Cather. I just happened to be in this town when I heard the Librarian had died and I thought, perhaps that is a job for me.

A good thing your letter reached me today as I am about to be discharged from here and don't know if it would have been sent on to where I am going. I am glad you did not think my letter was too foolish.

If you run into my father or anybody you do not need to say anything about the fact we are writing to each other. It is nobody's business and I know there are plenty of people who would laugh at me writing to the Librarian as they did at me going to the Library even, why give them the satisfaction?

I am glad to be getting out of here. So much luckier than some I see that will never walk or have their sight and will have to hide themselves away from the world.

You asked where did I live in Carstairs. Well, it was not anyplace to be proud of. If you know where Vinegar Hill is and you turned off on Flowers Road it is the last house on the right, yellow paint once upon a time. My father grows potatoes, or did. I used to take them around town with my wagon, and got five cents to keep for every load I sold.

You mention favourite authors. At one time I was fond of Zane Grey, but I drifted away from reading Fiction stories to reading

History or Travel. I sometimes read books away over my head, I know, but I do get something out of them. H. G. Wells I mentioned is one and Robert Ingersoll who writes about religion. They have given me a lot to think about. If you are very religious I hope I have not offended you.

One day when I got to the Library it was a Saturday afternoon and you had just unlocked the door and were putting the lights on as it was dark and raining out. You had been caught out with no hat or umbrella and your hair had got wet. You took the pins out of it and let it come down. Is it too personal a thing to ask if you have it long still or have you cut it? You went over and stood by the radiator and shook your hair on it and the water sizzled like grease in the frying pan. I was sitting reading in the Illustrated London News *about the War. We exchanged a smile. (I didn't mean to say your hair was greasy when I wrote that!)*

I have not cut my hair though I often think about it. I do not know if it is vanity or laziness that prevents me.

I am not very religious.

I walked up Vinegar Hill and found your house. The potatoes are looking healthy. A Police Dog disputed with me, is he yours?

The weather is getting quite warm. We have had the flood on the river, which I gather is an annual Spring event. The water got into the Hotel basement and somehow contaminated our drinking supply so that we were given free beer or ginger ale. But only if we lived or were staying there. You can imagine there were plenty of jokes.

I should ask if there is anything that I could send you.

I am not in need of anything particular. I get the tobacco and other bits of things the ladies in Carstairs do up for us. I would like to read some books by the authors you have mentioned but I doubt whether I would get the chance here.

The other day there was a man died of a heart attack. It was the News of all time. Did you hear about the man who died of a heart attack? That was all you heard about day and night here. Then everybody would laugh which seems hard-hearted but it just seemed so strange. It was not even a hot time so you couldn't say maybe he was scared. (As a matter of fact he was writing a letter at the time so I had better look out.) Before and after him others have died being shot up or blown up but he is the famous one, to die of a heart attack. Everybody is saying what a long way to come and a lot of expense for the Army to go to, for that.

The summer has been so dry the watering tank has been doing the streets every day, trying to lay the dust. The children would dance along behind it. There was also a new thing in town – a cart with a little bell that went along selling ice cream, and the children were pretty attentive to this as well. It was pushed by the man who had an accident at the factory – you know who I mean, though I can't recall his name. He lost his arm to the elbow. My room at the Hotel, being on the third floor, was like an oven, and I often walked about till after midnight. So did many other people, sometimes in pyjamas. It was like a dream. There was still a little water in the river, enough so that you could go out in a rowboat, and the Methodist minister did that on a Sunday in August. He was praying for rain in a public service. But there was a small leak in the boat and the water came in and wet his feet, and eventually the boat sank and left him standing in the water, which did not nearly reach his waist. Was it an accident or a malicious trick? The talk was all that his prayers were answered but from the wrong direction.

I often pass the Douds' place on my walks. Your father keeps the lawns and hedges looking beautiful. I like the house, so original and airy-looking. But it may not have been cool even there, because I heard the voice of the mother and little girl late at night as if they were out on the lawn.

Though I told you there is nothing I need, there is one thing I would like. That is a photograph of you. I hope you will not think I am overstepping the bounds to ask for it. Maybe you are engaged to somebody or have a sweetheart over here you are writing to as well as me. You are a cut above the ordinary and it would not surprise me if some Officer had spoken for you. But now that I have asked I cannot take it back and will just leave it up to you to think what you like of me.

Louisa was twenty-five years old and had been in love once,

with a doctor she had known in the sanatorium. Her love was returned, eventually, costing the doctor his job. There was some harsh doubt in her mind about whether he had been told to leave the sanatorium or had left of his own accord, being weary of the entanglement. He was married, he had children. Letters had played a part that time, too. After he left, they were still writing to one another. And they wrote once or twice after she was released. Then she asked him not to write any more, and he didn't. But the failure of his letters to arrive drove her out of Toronto and made her take a travelling job. Then there would be only the one disappointment in the week, when she got back on Friday or Saturday night. Her last letter had been firm and stoical, and some consciousness of herself as a heroine of love's tragedy went with her around the country, as she hauled her display cases up and down the stairs of small hotels, and talked about Paris styles and said that her sample hats were bewitching, and drank her solitary glass of wine. If she'd had anybody to tell, though, she would have laughed at just that notion. She would have said love was all hocus-pocus, a deception, and she believed that. But at the prospect she still felt a hush, a flutter along the nerves, a bowing down of sense, a flagrant prostration.

She had a picture taken. She knew how she wanted it to be. She would have liked to wear a simple white blouse, a peasant girl's smock with the string open at the neck. She did not own a blouse of that description and in fact had seen them only in pictures. And she would have liked to let her hair down. Or if it had to be up, she would have liked it piled very loosely and bound with strings of pearls.

Instead she wore her blue silk shirt-waist and bound her hair as usual. She thought the picture made her look rather pale, hollow-eyed. Her expression was sterner and more forbidding than she had intended. She sent it anyway.

I am not engaged, and do not have a sweetheart. I was in love once and it had to be broken off. I was upset at the time but I knew I must bear it, and now I believe that it was all for the best.

She had racked her brains, of course, to remember him. She could not remember shaking out her hair, as he said she had done, or smiling at any young man when the raindrops fell on the radiator. He might as well have dreamed all that, and perhaps he had.

She began to follow the war in a more detailed way than she had done previously. She did not try to ignore it anymore. She went along the street with a sense that her head was filled with the same exciting and troubling information as everybody else's. Saint-Quentin, Arras, Montdidier, Amiens, and then there was a battle going on at the Somme River, where surely there had been one before? She spread open on her desk the maps of the war that appeared in the centrefolds of magazines. She saw in coloured lines the German drive to the Marne, the first thrust of the Americans at Château-Thierry. She looked at the artist's brown pictures of a horse rearing up during an air attack, of some soldiers in East Africa drinking out of coconuts, and of a line of German prisoners with bandaged heads or limbs and bleak, sullen expressions. Now she felt what everybody else did – a constant fear and misgiving and at the same time this addictive excitement. You could look up from your life of the moment and feel the world crackling beyond the walls.

I am glad to hear you do not have a sweetheart although I know that is selfish of me. I do not think you and I will ever meet again. I don't say that because I've had a dream about what will happen or am a gloomy person always looking for the worst. It just seems to me it is the most probable thing to happen, though I don't dwell on it and go along every day doing the best I can to stay alive. I am not trying to worry you or get your sympathy either but just explain how the idea I won't ever see Carstairs again makes me think I can say anything I want. I guess it's like being sick with a fever. So I will say I love you. I think of you up on a stool at the Library reaching to put a book away and I come up and put my hands on your waist and lift you down, and you turning around inside my arms as if we agreed about everything.

Every Tuesday afternoon the ladies and girls of the Red Cross met in the Council chambers, which were just down the hall from the library. When the library was empty for a few moments Louisa went down the hall and entered the room full of women. She had decided to knit a scarf. At the sanatorium she had learned how to knit a basic stitch, but she had never learned, or had forgotten, how to cast on or off.

The older women were all busy packing boxes or cutting up and folding bandages from sheets of heavy cotton which were spread on the tables. But a lot of girls near the door were eating buns and drinking tea. One was holding a skein of wool on her arms for another to wind.

Louisa told them what she needed to know.

'So what do you want to knit, then?' said one of the girls, with some bun still in her mouth.

Louisa said, 'A muffler. For a soldier.'

'Oh, you'll want the regulation wool,' another said, more politely, and jumped off the table. She came back with some balls of brown wool, and fished a spare pair of needles out of her bag, telling Louisa they could be hers.

'I'll just get you started,' she said. 'It's a regulation width, too.'

Other girls gathered around and teased this girl, whose name was Corrie. They told her she was doing it all wrong.

'Oh, I am, am I?' said Corrie. 'How would you like a knitting needle in your eye?' Then she said solicitously to Louisa, 'Is it for a friend? A friend overseas?'

'Yes,' said Louisa. Of course they would think of her as an old maid, they would laugh at her or feel sorry for her, according to which show they put on – of being brazen or kind.

'So knit up good and tight,' said the one who had been eating the bun. 'Knit up good and tight to keep him warm!'

One of the girls in this group was Grace Horne. She did not say anything. She was a shy but resolute-looking girl, nineteen years old, with a broad face, thin lips often pressed together, brown hair cut in a straight bang, and an attractively mature body. She had become engaged to Jack Agnew before he went overseas, but they had agreed not to say anything about it.

Spanish Flu

Louisa had made friends with some of the travellers who stayed regularly at the hotel. One of these was Jim Frarey, who sold typewriters and office equipment and books and all sorts of stationery supplies. He was a fair-haired, rather round-shouldered but strongly built man in his middle forties. You would think by the look of him that he sold something heavier and more important in the masculine world, like farm implements.

Jim Frarey kept travelling all through the Spanish-flu epidemic, though you never knew then if stores would be open for business or not. Occasionally the hotels, too, would be closed, like the schools and movie houses and even – Jim Frarey thought this a scandal – the churches.

'They ought to be ashamed of themselves, the cowards,' he said to Louisa. 'What good does it do anybody to lurk around home and wait for it to strike? Now, you never closed the library, did you?'

Louisa said only when she herself had been sick. A mild case, hardly lasting a week, but of course she had to go to the hospital. They wouldn't let her stay in the hotel.

'Cowards,' he said. 'If you're going to be taken you'll be taken. Don't you agree?'

They discussed the crush in the hospitals, the deaths of doctors and nurses, the unceasing dreary spectacle of the funerals. Jim Frarey lived down the street from an undertaking establishment in Toronto. He said they still got out the black horses, the black carriage, the works, to bury such personages as warranted a fuss.

'Day and night they went on,' he said. 'Day and night.' He raised his glass and said, 'Here's to health, then. You look well yourself.'

He thought that in fact Louisa was looking better than she used to. Maybe she had started putting on rouge. She had a pale olive skin, and it seemed to him that her cheeks used to be without colour. She dressed with more dash, too, and took more trouble to be friendly. She used to be very on-again,

207

off-again, just as she chose. She was drinking whisky now, too, though she would not try it without drowning it in water. It used to be only a glass of wine. He wondered if it was a boyfriend that had made the difference. But a boyfriend might perk up her looks without increasing her interest in all and sundry, which was what he was pretty sure had happened. It was more likely time running out and the husband prospects being thinned out so dreadfully by the war. That could set a woman stirring. She was smarter and better company and better-looking, too, than most of the married ones. What happened with a woman like that? Sometimes just bad luck. Or bad judgement at a time when it mattered. A little too sharp and self-assured, in the old days, making the men uneasy?

'Life can't be brought to a standstill all the same,' he said. 'You did the right thing, keeping the library open.'

This was in the early winter of 1919, when there had been a fresh outbreak of flu after the danger was supposed to be past. They seemed to be all alone in the hotel. It was only about nine o'clock but the hotelkeeper had gone to bed. His wife was in the hospital with the flu. Jim Frarey had brought the bottle of whisky from the bar, which was closed for fear of contagion – and they sat at a table beside the window, in the dining room. A winter fog had collected outside and was pressing against the window. You could barely see the street lights or the few cars that trundled cautiously over the bridge.

'Oh, it was not a matter of principle,' Louisa said, 'that I kept the library open. It was a more personal reason than you think.'

Then she laughed and promised him a peculiar story. 'Oh, the whisky must have loosened my tongue,' she said.

'I am not a gossip,' said Jim Frarey.

She gave him a hard, laughing look and said that when a person announced they weren't a gossip, they almost invariably were. The same when they promised never to tell a soul.

'You can tell this where and when you like just as long as you leave out the real names and don't tell it around here,' she said. 'That I hope I can trust you not to do. Though at the moment I don't feel as if I cared. I'll probably feel otherwise when the drink wears off. It's a lesson, this story. It's a lesson in what fools women can make of themselves. "So," you say, "what's new about that? You can learn it every day!" '

She began to tell him about a soldier who had started writing letters to her from overseas. The soldier remembered her from when he used to go into the library. But she didn't remember him. However, she replied in a friendly way to his first letter, and a correspondence sprang up between them. He told her where he had lived in the town and she walked past the house so that she could tell him how things looked there. He told her what books he'd read and she gave some of the same kind of information. In short, they both revealed something of themselves, and feelings warmed up on either side. On his side first, as far as any declarations went. She was not one to rush in like a fool. At first she thought she was simply being kind. Even later, she didn't want to reject and embarrass him. He asked for a picture. She had one taken; it was not to her liking, but she sent it. He asked if she had a sweetheart and she replied truthfully that she did not. He did not send any picture of himself nor did she ask for one, though of course she was curious as to what he looked like. It would be no easy matter for him to have a picture taken in the middle of a war. Furthermore, she did not want to seem like the sort of woman who would withdraw kindness if looks did not come up to scratch.

He wrote that he did not expect to come home. He said he was not so afraid of dying as he was of ending up like some of the men he had seen when he was in the hospital, wounded. He did not elaborate, but she supposed he meant the cases they were just getting to know about now – the stumps of men, the blinded, the ones made monstrous with burns. He was not whining about his fate, she did not mean to imply that. It was just that he expected to die and picked death over some other options, and he thought about her, and wrote to her as men do to a sweetheart in such a situation.

When the war ended, it was a while since she had heard from him. She went on expecting a letter every day, and nothing came. Nothing came. She was afraid that he might have been one of those unluckiest of soldiers – one of those killed in the last week, or on the last day, or even in the last hour. She searched the local paper every week, and the names of new casualties were still being printed there till after New Year's, but his was not among them. Now the paper began to list, as well, the names of those returning home, often printing a photo with the name, and a little account of rejoicing. When the soldiers were returning thick and fast there was less room for these additions. And then she saw his name, another name on the list. He had not been killed, he had not been wounded, he was coming home to Carstairs, perhaps he was already here.

It was then that she decided to keep the library open, though the flu was raging. Every day she was sure he would come, every day she was prepared for him. Sundays were a torment. When she entered the town hall she always felt he might be there before her, leaning up against the wall awaiting her arrival. She felt this so strongly that sometimes she mistook a shadow for a man. She understood now how people believed they had seen ghosts. Whenever the door opened she expected to look up into his face. Sometimes she made a pact with herself not to look up till she had counted to ten. Few people came in, because of the flu. She set herself jobs of rearranging things, else she would have gone mad. She never locked up until five or ten minutes after closing time. And then she fancied that he might be across the street on the post-office steps, watching her, being too shy to make a move. She worried of course that he might be ill; she always sought in conversation for news of the latest cases. No one spoke his name.

It was at this time that she entirely gave up on reading. The covers of books looked like coffins to her, either shabby or ornate, and what was inside them might as well have been dust.

She had to be forgiven, didn't she – she had to be forgiven for thinking, after such letters, that the one thing that could never happen was that he wouldn't approach her, wouldn't get in touch with her at all? Never cross her threshold, after such avowals? Funerals passed by her window and she gave no thought to them, because they were not his. Even when she was sick in the hospital her only thought was that she must get back, she must get out of bed, the door must not stay locked against him. She staggered to her feet and back to work. On a hot afternoon she was arranging fresh newspapers on the racks, and his name jumped out at her like something in her feverish dreams.

She read a short notice of his marriage to a Miss Grace Horne. Not a girl she knew. Not a library user.

The bride wore fawn silk crêpe with brown-and-cream piping, and a beige straw hat with brown velvet streamers.

There was no picture. Brown-and-cream piping. Such was the end, and had to be, to her romance.

But on her desk at the library, a matter of a few weeks ago, on a Saturday night after everybody had gone and she had locked the door and was turning out the lights, she discovered a scrap of paper. A few words written on it. *I was engaged before I went overseas.* No name, not his or hers. And there was her photograph, partly shoved under the blotter.

He had been in the library that very evening. It had been a busy time, she had often left the desk to find a book for somebody or to straighten up the papers or to put some books on the shelves. He had been in the same room with her, watched her, and taken his chance. But never made himself known.

I was engaged before I went overseas.

'Do you think it was all a joke on me?' Louisa said. 'Do you think a man could be so diabolical?'

'In my experience, tricks like that are far more often indulged in by the women. No, no. Don't you think such a thing. Far more likely he was sincere. He got a little carried away. It's all just the way it looks on the surface. He was engaged before he went overseas, he never expected to get back in one piece but he did. And when he did, there is the fiancée waiting, what else could he do?'

'What indeed?' said Louisa.

'He bit off more than he could chew.'

'Ah, that's so, that's so!' Louisa said. 'And what was it in my case but vanity, which deserves to get slapped down!' Her eyes were glassy and her expression was roguish. 'You don't think he'd had a good look at me any one time and thought the original was even worse than that poor picture, so he backed off?'

'I do not!' said Jim Frarey. 'And don't you so belittle yourself.'

'I don't want you to think I am stupid,' she said. 'I am not so stupid and inexperienced as that story makes me sound.'

'Indeed, I don't think you are stupid at all.'

'But perhaps you think I am inexperienced?'

This was it, he thought – the usual. Women after they have told one story on themselves cannot keep from telling another. Drink upsets them in a radical way, prudence is out the window.

She had confided in him once before that she had been a patient in a sanatorium. Now she told about being in love with a doctor there. The sanatorium was on beautiful grounds up on Hamilton Mountain, and they used to meet there along the hedged walks. Shelves of limestone formed the steps and in sheltered spots there were such plants as you do not commonly see in Ontario – azaleas, rhododendrons, magnolias. The doctor knew something about botany and he told her this was the Carolinian vegetation. Very different from here, lusher, and there were little bits of woodland, too, wonderful trees, paths worn under the trees. Tulip trees.

'Tulips!' said Jim Frarey. 'Tulips on the trees!'

'No, no, it is the shape of their leaves!'

She laughed at him challengingly, then bit her lip. He saw fit to continue the dialogue, saying, 'Tulips on the trees!' while she said, 'No, it is the leaves that are shaped like tulips, no, I never said that, stop!' So they passed into a state of gingerly evaluation – which he knew well and could only hope she did – full of small, pleasant surprises, half-sardonic signals, a welling up of impudent hopes, and a fateful sort of kindness.

'All to ourselves,' Jim Frarey said. 'Never happened before, did it? Maybe it never will again.'

She let him take her hands, half lift her from her chair. He turned out the dining-room lights as they went out. Up the stairs they went, that they had so often climbed separately. Past the picture of the dog on his master's grave, and Highland Mary singing in the field, and the old king with his bulgy eyes, his look of indulgence and repletion.

'It's a foggy, foggy night, and my heart is in a fright,' Jim Frarey was half singing, half humming as they climbed. He kept an assured hand on Louisa's back. 'All's well, all's well,' he said as he steered her round the turn of the stairs. And when they took the narrow flight of steps to the third floor he said, 'Never climbed so close to heaven in this place before!'

But later in the night Jim Frarey gave a concluding groan and roused himself to deliver a sleepy scolding. 'Louisa, Louisa, why didn't you tell me that was the way it was?'

'I told you everything,' said Louisa in a faint and drifting voice.

'I got a wrong impression, then,' he said. 'I never intended for this to make a difference to you.'

She said that it hadn't. Now, without him pinning her down and steadying her, she felt herself whirling around in an irresistible way, as if the mattress had turned into a child's top and were carrying her off. She tried to explain that the traces of blood on the sheets could be credited to her period, but her words came out with a luxurious nonchalance and could not be fitted together.

Accidents

When Arthur came home from the factory, a little before noon, he shouted, 'Stay out of my way till I wash! There's been an accident over at the works!' Nobody answered. Mrs Groves, the housekeeper, was in the kitchen talking on the telephone so loudly that she could not hear him, and his daughter was, of course, at school. He washed, and stuffed everything he had been wearing into the hamper, and scrubbed up the bathroom, like a murderer. He started out clean, with even his hair slicked and patted, to drive to the man's house. He had had to ask where it was. He thought it was up Vinegar Hill but they said no, that was the father – the young fellow and his wife live on the other side of town, past where the Apple Evaporator used to be, before the war.

He found the two brick cottages side by side, and picked the left-hand one, as he'd been told. It wouldn't have been hard to pick which house, anyway. News had come before him. The door to the house was open, and children too young to be in school yet hung about in the yard. A small girl sat on a kiddie car, not going anywhere, just blocking his path. He stepped around her. As he did so an older girl spoke to him in a formal way – a warning. 'Her dad's dead. Hers!'

A young woman came out of the front room carrying an armload of curtains, which she gave to another woman standing in the hall. The woman who received the curtains was grey-haired, with a pleading face. She had no upper teeth. She probably took her plate out, for comfort, at home. The woman who passed the curtains to her was stout but young, with fresh skin.

'You tell her not to get up on that stepladder,' the grey-haired woman said to Arthur. 'She's going to break her neck taking down curtains. She thinks we need to get everything washed. Are you the undertaker? Oh, no, excuse me! You're Mr Doud. Grace, come out here! Grace! It's Mr Doud!'

'Don't trouble her,' Arthur said.

'She thinks she's going to get the curtains all down and washed and up again by tomorrow, because he's going to have to go in the front room. She's my daughter. I can't tell her anything.'

'She'll quiet down presently,' said a sombre but comfortable-looking man in a clerical collar, coming through from the back of the house. Their minister. But not from one of the churches Arthur knew. Baptist? Pentecostal? Plymouth Brethren? He was drinking tea.

Some other woman came and briskly removed the curtains. 'We got the machine filled and going,' she said. 'A day like this, they'll dry like nobody's business. Just keep the kids out of here.'

The minister had to stand aside and lift his teacup high, to avoid her and her bundle. He said, 'Aren't any of you ladies going to offer Mr Doud a cup of tea?'

Arthur said, 'No, no, don't trouble.'

'The funeral expenses,' he said to the grey-haired woman. 'If you could let her know – '

'Lillian wet her pants!' said a triumphant child at the door. 'Mrs Agnew! Lillian peed her pants!'

'Yes,' said the minister. 'Yes, they will be very grateful.'

'The plot and the stone, everything,' Arthur said. 'You'll make sure they understand that. Whatever they want on the stone.'

The grey-haired woman had gone out into the yard. She came back with a squalling child in her arms. 'Poor lamb,' she said. 'They told her she wasn't supposed to come in the house, so where could she go? What could she do but have an accident?'

The young woman came out of the front room dragging a rug.

'I want this put on the line and beat,' she said.

'Grace, here is Mr Doud come to offer his condolences,' the minister said.

'And to ask if there is anything I can do,' said Arthur.

The grey-haired woman started upstairs with the wet child in her arms and a couple of others following.

Grace spotted them. 'Oh, no, you don't! You get back outside!'

'My mom's in here.'

'Yes, and your mom's good and busy, she don't need to be bothered with you. She's here helping me out. Don't you know Lillian's dad's dead?'

'Is there anything I can do for you?' Arthur said, meaning to clear out.

Grace stared at him with her mouth open. Sounds of the washing machine filled the house.

'Yes, there is,' she said. 'You wait here.'

'She's overwhelmed,' the minister said. 'It's not that she means to be rude.'

Grace came back with a load of books. 'These here,' she said. 'He had them out of the library. I don't want to have to pay fines on them. He went every Saturday night, so I guess they are due back tomorrow. I don't want to get in trouble about them.'

'I'll look after them,' Arthur said. 'I'd be glad to.'

'I just don't want to get in any trouble about them.'

'Mr Doud was saying about taking care of the funeral,' the minister said to her, gently admonishing. 'Everything including the stone. Whatever you want on the stone.'

'Oh, I don't want anything fancy,' Grace said.

'On Friday morning last there occurred in the sawmill operation of Doud's Factory a particularly ghastly and tragic accident. Mr Jack Agnew, in reaching under the main shaft, had the misfortune to have his sleeve caught by a setscrew in an adjoining flunge, so that his arm and shoulder were drawn under the shaft. His head in consequence was brought in contact with the circular saw, that saw being about one foot in diameter. In an instant the unfortunate young man's head was separated from his body, being severed at an angle below the left ear and through the neck. His death is believed to have been instantaneous. He never spoke or uttered a cry so it was not by any sound of his but by the spurt and shower of his blood that his fellow-workers were horribly alerted to the disaster.'

This account was reprinted in the paper a week later, for those who might have missed it or who wished to have an extra copy to send to friends or relations out of town (particularly to people who used to live in Carstairs and did not anymore). The misspelling of 'flange' was corrected the next week. There was a note apologising for the mistake. There was also a description of a very large funeral, attended even by people from neighbouring towns and as far away as Walley. They came by car and train, and some by horse and buggy. They had not known Jack Agnew when he was alive, but, as the paper said, they wished to pay tribute to the sensational and tragic manner of his death. All the stores in

Carstairs were closed for two hours that afternoon. The hotel did not close its doors, but that was because all the visitors needed somewhere to eat and drink.

The survivors were a wife, Grace, and a four-year-old daughter, Lillian. The victim had fought bravely in the Great War and had only been wounded once, not seriously. Many had commented on this irony.

The paper's failure to mention a surviving father was not deliberate. The editor of the paper was not a native of Carstairs, and people forgot to tell him about the father until it was too late.

The father himself did not complain about the omission. The day of the funeral was very fine, and he headed out of town as he would have done ordinarily on a day he had decided not to spend at Doud's. He was wearing a felt hat and a long coat that would do for a rug if he wanted to take a nap. His overshoes were neatly held on his feet with the rubber rings from sealing jars. He was going out to fish for suckers. The season hadn't opened yet, but he always managed to be a bit ahead of it. He fished through the spring and early summer and cooked and ate what he caught. He had a frying pan and a pot hidden out on the riverbank. The pot was for boiling corn that he snatched out of the fields later in the year, when he was also eating the fruit of wild apple trees and grapevines. He was quite sane but abhorred conversation. He could not altogether avoid it in the weeks following his son's death, but he had a way of cutting it short.

'Should've watched out what he was doing.'

Walking in the country that day, he met another person who was not at the funeral. A woman. She did not try to start any conversation and in fact seemed as fierce in her solitude as himself, whipping the air past her with long fervent strides.

The factory stretched along the west side of town, like a medieval town wall. There were two long buildings like the inner and outer ramparts, with a closed-in bridge between them where the main offices were. And reaching up into the town and the streets of workers' houses were the kilns and the sawmill and the lumber-yard and storage sheds. The factory whistle dictated the time for many to get up, blowing at six o'clock in the morning. It blew again for work to start, at seven, and at twelve for dinnertime, and at one in the afternoon for work to recommence, and then at five-thirty for the men to lay down their tools and go home.

Rules were posted beside the time clock, under glass. The first two rules were:

ONE MINUTE LATE IS FIFTEEN MINUTES PAY. BE PROMPT.

DON'T TAKE SAFETY FOR GRANTED. WATCH OUT FOR YOURSELF AND THE NEXT MAN.

There had been accidents in the factory and, in fact, a man had been killed when a load of lumber fell on him. That had happened before Arthur's time. And once, during the war, a man had lost an arm, or part of an arm. On the day that happened Arthur was away in Toronto. So he had never seen an accident – nothing serious, anyway. But it was often at the back of his mind now, that something might happen.

Perhaps he no longer felt so sure that trouble wouldn't come near him as he had before his wife died. She had died in 1919, in the last flurry of the Spanish flu, when everyone had got over being frightened. Even she had not been frightened. That was nearly five years ago and it still seemed to Arthur like the end of a carefree time in his life. But to other people he had always seemed very responsible and serious – nobody had noticed much difference in him.

In his dreams of an accident there was a spreading silence, everything was shut down. Every machine in the place stopped making its customary noise and every man's voice was removed, and when Arthur looked out of the office window he understood that doom had fallen. He never could remember any particular thing that he saw that told him this. It was just the space, the dust in the factory yard, that said to him *now*.

The books stayed on the floor of his car for a week or so. His daughter, Bea, said, 'What are those books doing here?' And then he remembered.

Bea read out the titles and the authors. 'Sir John Franklin and the Romance of the Northwest Passage,' by G. B. Smith. 'What's Wrong with the World,' G. K. Chesterton. 'The Taking of Quebec,' Archibald Hendry. 'The Practice and Theory of Bolshevism,' by Lord Bertrand Russell.

'Bol-*shev*-ism,' Bea said, and Arthur told her how to pronounce it correctly. She asked what it was, and he said, 'It's something they've got in Russia that I don't understand so well myself. But from what I hear of it, it's a disgrace.'

Bea was thirteen at this time. She had heard about the Russian Ballet and also about dervishes. She believed for the next couple of years that Bolshevism was some sort of diabolical and maybe indecent dance. At least this was the story she told when she was grown-up.

She did not mention that the books were connected with the man who had had the accident. That would have made the story less amusing. Perhaps she had really forgotten.

The librarian was perturbed. The books still had their cards in them, which meant they had never been checked out, just removed from the shelves and taken away.

'The one by Lord Russell has been missing a long time.'

Arthur was not used to such reproofs, but he said, mildly, 'I am returning them on behalf of somebody else. The chap who was killed. In the accident at the factory.'

The librarian had the Franklin book open. She was looking at a picture of the boat trapped in the ice.

'His wife asked me to,' Arthur said.

She picked up each book separately, and shook it, as if she expected something to fall out. She ran her fingers between the pages. The bottom part of her face was working in an unsightly way, as if she was chewing at the inside of her cheeks.

'I guess he just took them home as he felt like it,' Arthur said.

'I'm sorry?' she said in a minute. 'What did you say? I'm sorry.'

It was the accident, he thought. The idea that the man who

had died in such a way had been the last person to open these books, turn these pages. The thought that he might have left a bit of his life in them, a scrap of paper or a pipe cleaner as a marker, or even a few shreds of tobacco. That unhinged her.

'No matter,' he said. 'I just dropped by to bring them back.'

He turned away from her desk but did not immediately leave the library. He had not been in it for years. There was his father's picture between the two front windows, where it would always be.

'A. V. Doud, Founder of the Doud Organ Factory and Patron of This Library. A Believer in Progress, Culture, and Education. A True Friend of the Town of Carstairs and of the Working Man.'

The librarian's desk was in the archway between the front and back rooms. The books were on shelves set in rows in the back room. Green-shaded lamps, with long pull cords, dangled down in the aisles between. Arthur remembered years ago some matter brought up at the Council meeting about buying sixty-watt bulbs instead of forty. This librarian was the one who had requested that, and they had done it.

In the front room, there were newspapers and magazines on wooden racks, and some round heavy tables, with chairs, so that people could sit and read, and rows of thick, dark books behind glass. Dictionaries, probably, and atlases and encyclo-pedias. Two handsome high windows looking out on the main street, with Arthur's father hanging between them. Other pictures around the room hung too high, and were too dim and crowded with figures for the person down below to interpret them easily. (Later, when Arthur had spent many hours in the library and had discussed these pictures with the librarian, he knew that one of them represented the Battle of Flodden Field, with the King of Scotland charging down the hill into a pall of smoke, one the funeral of the Boy King of Rome, and one the Quarrel of Oberon and Titania, from 'A Midsummer Night's Dream'.)

He sat down at a reading table, where he could look out the window. He picked up an old copy of *The National Geographic* which was lying there. He had his back to the librarian. He thought this the tactful thing to do, since she seemed somewhat wrought up. Other people came in, and he heard her speak to them. Her voice sounded normal enough now. He kept thinking he would leave, but did not.

He liked the high bare window full of the light of the spring evening, and he liked the dignity and order of these rooms. He was pleasantly mystified by the thought of grown people coming and going here, steadily reading books. Week after week, one book after another, a whole life long. He himself read a book once in a while, when somebody recommended it, and usually he enjoyed it, and then he read magazines, to keep up with things, and never thought about reading a book until another one came along, in this almost accidental way. There would be little spells when nobody was in the library but himself and the librarian.

During one of these she came over and stood near him, replacing some newspapers on the rack. When she finished doing this she spoke to him, with a controlled urgency.

'The account of the accident that was printed in the paper – I take it that was more or less accurate?'

Arthur said that it was possibly too accurate.

'Why? Why do you say that?'

He mentioned the public's endless appetite for horrific details. Ought the paper to pander to that?

'Oh, I think it's natural,' the librarian said. 'I think it's natural, to want to know the worst. People do want to picture it. I do myself. I am very ignorant of machinery. It's hard for me to imagine what happened. Even with the paper's help. Did the machine do something unexpected?'

'No,' Arthur said. 'It wasn't the machine grabbing him and pulling him in, like an animal. He made a wrong move or at any rate a careless move. Then he was done for.'

She said nothing but did not move away.

'You have to keep your wits about you,' Arthur said. 'Never let up for a second. A machine is your servant and it is an excellent servant, but it makes an imbecile master.'

He wondered if he had read that somewhere or had thought it up himself.

'And I suppose there are no ways of protecting people?' the librarian said. 'But you must know all about that.'

She left him then. Somebody had come in.

The accident was followed by a rush of warm weather. The length of the evenings and the heat of the balmy days seemed sudden and surprising, as if this were not the way winter finally ended in that part of the country, almost every year. The sheets of floodwater shrank magically back into the bogs and the leaves shot out of the reddened branches and barnyard smells drifted into town and were wrapped in the smell of lilacs.

Instead of wanting to be outdoors on such evenings, Arthur found himself thinking of the library, and he would often end up there, sitting on the spot he had chosen on his first visit. He would sit for half an hour, or an hour. He looked at the *Illustrated London News*, or *The National Geographic*, or *Saturday Night*, or *Collier's*. All of these magazines arrived at his own house, and he could have been sitting there, in the den, looking out at his hedged lawns, which old Agnew kept in tolerable condition, and the flower beds now full of tulips of every vivid colour and combination. It seemed that he preferred the view of the main street, where the occasional brisk-looking new Ford went by, or some stuttering older model car with a dusty cloth top. He preferred the post office, with its clock tower telling four different times in four different directions – and, as people liked to say, all wrong. Also the passing and loitering on the sidewalk. People trying to get the drinking fountain to work, although it wasn't turned on till the first of July.

It was not that he felt the need of sociability. He was not there for chat, though he would greet people if he knew them by name, and he did know most. And he might exchange a few words with the librarian, though often it was only 'Good evening' when he came in, and 'Good night' when he went out. He made no demands on anybody. He felt his presence to be genial, reassuring, and, above all, natural. By sitting here, reading and reflecting, here instead of at home, he seemed to himself to be providing something. People could count on it.

There was an expression he liked. *Public servant.* His father, who looked out at him here with tinted baby-pink cheeks and glassy blue eyes and an old man's petulant mouth, had never thought of himself so. He had thought of himself more as a public character and benefactor. He had operated by whims and decrees, and he had got away with it. He would go around the factory when business was slow, and say to one man and another, 'Go home. Go on home now. Go home and stay there till I can use you again.' And they would go. They would work in their gardens or go out shooting rabbits and run up bills for whatever they had to buy, and accept it couldn't be otherwise. It was still a joke with them, to imitate his bark. *Go on home!* He was their hero more than Arthur could ever be, but they were not prepared to take the same treatment today. During the war they had got used to the good wages and to being always in demand. They never thought of the glut of labour the soldiers had created when they came home, never thought about how a business like this was kept going by luck and ingenuity from one year to the next, even from one season to the next. They didn't like changes – they were not happy about the switch now to player pianos, which Arthur believed were the hope of the future. But Arthur would do what he had to, though his way of proceeding was quite the opposite of his father's. Think everything over and then think it over again. Stay in the background except when you have to come forward. Keep your dignity. Try always to be fair.

They expected all to be provided. The whole town expected it. Work would be provided just as the sun would rise in the mornings. And the taxes on the factory were raised, too, and rates were charged for the water that used to come free. Maintenance of the access roads was now the factory's responsibility instead of the town's. The Methodist church requesting a hefty sum to build the new Sunday school. The town hockey team needing new uniforms. The stone gate-posts for the War Memorial Park. And every year the smartest boy in the senior class to be sent to university, courtesy of Doud's.

Ask, and ye shall receive.

Expectations at home were not lacking, either. Bea was agitating to go away to private school and Mrs Groves had her eye on some new mixing apparatus for the kitchen, also a new washing machine. All the trim on the house was due to be painted this year. All that wedding-cake decoration that consumed paint by the gallon. And in the midst of this what had Arthur done but order himself a new car – a Chrysler sedan.

It was necessary, he had to drive a new car. He had to drive a new car, Bea had to go away to school, Mrs Groves had to have the latest, and the trim had to be as fresh as Christmas snow. Else they would lose respect, they would lose confidence, they would start to wonder if things were going downhill. And it could be managed – with luck it could all be managed.

For years after his father's death, he had felt like an impostor. Not steadily, but from time to time, he had felt that. And now the feeling was gone. It was gone. He could sit here and feel that it was gone.

He had been in the office when the accident happened, consulting with a veneer salesman. Some change in noise registered with him, but it was more of an increase than a hush. It was nothing that alerted him – just an irritation. Because it happened in the sawmill, nobody knew about the accident immediately in the shops or in the kilns or in the yard, and work in some places continued for several minutes. In fact Arthur, bending over the veneer samples on his desk, might have been one of the last people to understand that there had been an intervention. He asked the salesman a question, and the salesman did not answer. Arthur looked up and saw the man's mouth open, his face frightened, his salesman's assurance wiped away.

Then he heard his own name being called – both 'Mr Doud!', as was customary, and 'Arthur, Arthur!' by such of the older men as had known him as a boy. Also he heard 'saw' and 'head' and 'Jesus, Jesus, Jesus!'

Arthur could have wished for the silence, the sounds and objects drawing back in that dreadful but releasing way to give him room. It was nothing like that. Yelling and questioning and running around, himself in the midst being propelled to the sawmill. One man had fainted, falling in such a way that if they had not got the saw turned off a moment before, it would have got him, too. It was his body, fallen but entire, that Arthur briefly mistook for the body of the victim. Oh no, no. They pushed him on. The sawdust was scarlet. It was drenched, brilliant. The pile of lumber here was all merrily spattered, and the blades. A heap of work clothes soaked in blood lay in the sawdust, and Arthur realised that it was the body, the trunk with limbs attached. So much blood had flowed as to make its shape not plain at first – to soften it, like a pudding.

The first thing he thought of was to cover that. He took off his jacket and did so. He had to step up close, his shoes squished in it. The reason no one else had done that was simply that no one else was wearing a jacket.

'Have they gone a-get the doctor?' somebody was yelling. 'Gone a-get the doctor!' a man quite close to Arthur said. 'Can't sew his head back on, doctor. Can he?'

But Arthur gave the order to get the doctor – he imagined it was necessary. You can't have a death without a doctor. That set the rest in motion. Doctor, undertaker, coffin, flowers, preacher. Get started on all that, give them something to do. Shovel up the sawdust, clean up the saw. Send the men who had been close by to wash themselves. Carry the man who had fainted to the lunchroom. Is he all right? Tell the office girl to make tea.

Brandy was what was needed, or whisky. But he had a rule against it, on the premises.

Something still lacking. Where was it? There, they said. Over there, Arthur heard the sound of vomiting, not far away. All right. Either pick it up or tell somebody to pick it up. The sound of vomiting saved him, steadied him, gave him an almost light-hearted determination. He picked it up. He carried it delicately and securely as you might carry an awkward but valuable jug. Pressing the face out of sight, as if comforting it, against his chest. Blood seeped through his shirt and stuck the material to his skin. Warm. He felt like a wounded man. He was aware of them watching him, and he was aware of himself as an actor must be, or a priest. What to do with it, now that he had it against his chest? The answer to that came, too. Set it down, put it back where it belongs, not, of course, fitted with exactness, not as if a seam could be closed. Just more or less in place, and lift the jacket and tug it into a new position.

He couldn't now ask the man's name. He would have to get it in some other way. After the intimacy of his services here, such ignorance would be an offence.

But he found he did know it, it came to him. As he edged the corner of his jacket over the ear that had lain and still lay upward, and so looked quite fresh and usable, he received a name. Son of the fellow who came and did the garden, who was not always reliable. A young man taken on again when he came back from the war. Married? He thought so. He would have to go and see her. As soon as possible. Clean clothes.

The librarian often wore a dark-red blouse. Her lips were reddened to match, and her hair was bobbed. She was not a young woman any more, but she maintained an eye-catching style. He remembered that when they had hired her, years ago, he had thought that she got herself up very soberly. Her hair was not bobbed in those days – it was wound around her head, in the old style. It was still the same colour – a warm and pleasant colour, like leaves – oak leaves, say – in the fall. He tried to think how much she was paid. Not much, certainly. She kept herself looking well on it. And where did she live? In one of the boarding houses – the one with the schoolteachers? No, not there. She lived in the Commercial Hotel.

And now something else was coming to mind. No definite story that he could remember. You could not say with any assurance that she had a bad reputation. But it was not quite a spotless reputation, either. She was said to take a drink with the travellers. Perhaps she had a boyfriend among them. A boyfriend or two.

Well, she was old enough to do as she liked. It wasn't quite the same as it was with a teacher – hired partly to set an example. As long as she did her job well – and anybody could see that she did. She had her life to live, like everyone else. Wouldn't you rather have a nice-looking woman in here than a crabby old affair like Mary Tamblyn? Strangers might drop in, they judge a town by what they see, you want a nice-looking woman with a nice manner.

Stop that. Who said you didn't? He was arguing in his head on her behalf just as if somebody had come along who wanted her chucked out, and he had no intimation at all that that was the case.

What about her question, on the first evening, regarding the machine? What did she mean by that? Was it a sly way of bringing blame?

He had talked to her about the pictures and the lighting and even told her how his father had sent his own workmen over here, paid them to build the library shelves, but he had never again spoken of the man who had taken the books out without letting her know. One at a time, probably. Under his coat? Brought back the same way. He must have brought them back, or else he'd have had a houseful, and his wife would never stand for that. Not stealing, except temporarily. Harmless behaviour, but peculiar. Was there any connection? Between thinking you could do things a little differently that way, and thinking you could get away with a careless move, which might catch your sleeve, and bring the saw down on your neck?

There might be, there might be some connection. A matter of attitude.

'That chap – you know the one – the accident – ' he said to the librarian one evening. 'The way he took off with the books he wanted. Why do you think he did that?'

'People do things,' the librarian said. 'They tear out pages. On account of something they don't like or something they do. They just do things. I don't know.'

'Did he ever tear out some pages? Did you ever give him a lecture? Ever make him scared to face you?'

He meant to tease her a little, implying that she would not be likely to scare anybody, but she did not take it that way.

'How could I when I never spoke to him?' she said. 'I never saw him. I never saw him, to know who he was.'

She moved away, putting an end to the conversation. So, she did not like to be teased. Was she one of those people full of mended cracks that you could only see close up? Some old misery troubling her, some secret? Maybe a sweetheart had been lost in the war.

On a later evening, a Saturday in the summer, she brought the subject up herself, that he would never have mentioned again.

'Do you remember our talking once about the man who had the accident?'

Arthur said he did.

'I have something to ask you, and you may think it strange.'

He nodded.

'And my asking it – I want you to – It is confidential.'

'Yes, indeed,' he said.

'What did he look like?'

Look like? Arthur was puzzled. He was puzzled by her making such a fuss and secret about it – surely it was natural to be interested in what a man might look like who had been coming in and making off with her books without her knowing about it – and because he could not help her he shook his head. He could not bring any picture of Jack Agnew to mind.

'Tall,' he said. 'I believe he was on the tall side. Otherwise I cannot tell you. I am really not such a good person to ask. I can recognise a man easily, but I can't ever give much of a physical description of them, even when it's someone I see on a daily basis.'

'But I thought you were the one – I heard you were the one – ' she said. 'Who picked him up. His head.'

Arthur said, stiffly, 'I didn't think that you could just leave it lying there.' He felt disappointed in the woman, uneasy and ashamed for her. But he tried to speak matter-of-factly, keeping reproach out of his voice. 'I could not even tell you the colour of his hair. It was all – all pretty much obliterated, by that time.'

She said nothing for a moment or two and he did not look at her. Then she said, 'It must seem as if I am one of those people – one of those people who are fascinated by these sorts of things.'

Arthur made a protesting noise, but it did, of course, seem to him that she must be like that.

'I should not have asked you,' she said. 'I should not have mentioned it. I can never explain to you why I did. I would like just to ask you, if you can help it, never to think that that is the kind of person I am.'

Arthur heard the word *never*. She could never explain to him. He was never to think. In the midst of his disappointment he picked up this suggestion, that their conversations were to continue, and perhaps on a less haphazard basis. He heard a humility in her voice, but it was a humility that was based on some kind of assurance. Surely that was sexual.

Or did he only think so because this was the evening it was? It was the Saturday evening in the month when he usually went to Walley. He was going there tonight, he had only dropped in here on his way, he had not meant to stay as long as he had done. It was the night when he went to visit a woman whose name was Jane MacFarlane. Jane MacFarlane lived apart from her husband, but she was not thinking of getting a divorce. She had no children. She earned her living as a dressmaker. Arthur had first met her when she came to his house to make clothes for his wife. Nothing had gone on at that time, and neither of them had thought of it. In some ways Jane MacFarlane was a woman like the librarian – good-looking, though not so young; plucky and stylish and good at her work. In other ways, not so like. He could not imagine Jane ever presenting a man with a mystery and following that up with the information that it would never be solved. Jane was a woman to give a man peace. The submerged dialogue he had with her – sensual, limited, kind – was very like the one he had had with his wife.

The librarian went to the switch by the door, and turned out the main light. She locked the door. She disappeared among the shelves, turning out the lights there, too, in a leisurely way. The town clock was striking nine. She must think that it was right. His own watch said three minutes to.

It was time to get up, time for him to leave, time to go to Walley.

When she had finished dealing with the lights she came and sat down at the table beside him.

He said, 'I would never think of you in any way that would make you unhappy.'

Turning out the lights shouldn't have made it so dark. They were in the middle of summer. But it seemed that heavy rain clouds had moved in. When Arthur had last paid attention to the street he had seen plenty of daylight left; country people shopping; boys squirting each other at the drinking fountain; and young girls walking up and down in their soft, cheap, flowery summer dresses, letting the young men watch them from wherever the young men congregated – the post-office steps, the front of the feedstore. And now that he looked again he saw the street in an uproar from the loud wind that already carried a few drops of rain. The girls were shrieking and laughing and holding their purses over their heads as they ran to shelter; store clerks were rolling up awnings and hauling in the baskets of fruit, the racks of summer shoes, the garden implements that had been displayed on the sidewalks. The doors of the town hall banged as the farm women ran inside, grabbing on to packages and children, to cram themselves into the ladies' rest room. Somebody tried the library door. The librarian looked over at it but did not move. And soon the rain was sweeping down like curtains across the street, and the wind battered the town-hall roof, and tore at the treetops. That roaring and danger lasted a few minutes, while the power of the wind went by. Then the sound left was the sound of the rain, which was now falling vertically and so heavily that they might have been under a waterfall.

If the same thing was happening at Walley, he thought, Jane would know enough not to expect him. This was the last thought he had of her for a long while.

'Mrs Groves wouldn't wash my clothes,' he said, to his own surprise. 'She was afraid to touch them.'

The librarian said in a peculiarly quivering, shamed, and determined voice, 'I think what you did – I think that was a remarkable thing to do.'

The rain made such a constant noise that he was released from answering. He found it easy then to turn and look at her. Her profile was dimly lit by the wash of rain down the windows. Her expression was calm and reckless. Or so it seemed to him. He realised that he knew hardly anything about her – what kind of person she really was or what kind of secrets she could have. He could not even estimate his own value to her. He only knew that he had some, and it wasn't the usual.

He could no more describe the feeling he got from her than you can describe a smell. It's like burnt kernels of wheat. No, it's like a bitter orange. I give up.

He had never imagined that he would find himself in a situation like this, visited by such a clear compulsion. But it seemed he was not unprepared. Without thinking twice or even once what he was letting himself in for he said, 'I wish –'

He had spoken too quietly, she did not hear him.

He raised his voice. He said, 'I wish we could get married.'

Then she looked at him. She laughed but controlled herself.

'I'm sorry,' she said. 'I'm sorry. It's just what went through my mind.'

'What was that?' he said.

'I thought, That's the last I'll see of him.'

Arthur said, 'You're mistaken.'

Tolpuddle Martyrs

The passenger trains from Carstairs had stopped running during the Second World War and even the rails were taken up. People said it was for the War Effort. When Louisa went to the city, to see the heart specialist, in the mid-fifties, she had to take the bus. She was not supposed to drive anymore.

The doctor, the heart specialist, said that her heart was a little wonky and her pulse inclined to be jumpy. She thought that made her heart sound like a comedian and her pulse like a puppy on a leash. She had not come fifty-seven miles to be treated with such playfulness, but she let it pass, because she was already distracted by something she had been reading in the doctor's waiting room. Perhaps it was what she had been reading that had made her pulse jumpy.

On an inside page of the local paper she had seen the headline, 'LOCAL MARTYRS HONOURED', and simply to pass the time she had read further. She read that there was to be some sort of ceremony that afternoon at Victoria Park. It was a ceremony to honour the Tolpuddle Martyrs. The paper said that few people had heard of the Tolpuddle Martyrs, and certainly Louisa had not. They were six men who had been tried and found guilty for administering illegal oaths. This peculiar offence, committed over one hundred years ago in the village of Tolpuddle, in Dorset, England, had got them transported to Australia, and later on some of them had ended up in Ontario, here in London, where they lived out the rest of their days and were buried without any special notice or commemoration. They were considered now to be among the earliest founders of the trade-union movement, and the Trade Unions Council, along with representatives of the Canadian Congress of Labour and the ministers of some local churches, had organised a ceremony that would take place today, the occasion of the hundred-and-twentieth anniversary of their arrest.

'Martyrs' is laying it on somewhat, thought Louisa. They were not executed, after all.

The ceremony was to take place at three o'clock, and the chief speakers were to be one of the local ministers and Mr John (Jack) Agnew, a union spokesman from Toronto.

It was a quarter after two when Louisa came out of the doctor's office. The bus to Carstairs did not leave until six o'clock. She had thought she would go and have tea and something to eat on the top floor of Simpsons, then shop for a wedding present at Birks, or if the time fitted go to an afternoon movie. Victoria Park lay between the doctor's office and Simpsons, and she decided to cut across it. The day was hot and the shade of the trees pleasant. She could not avoid seeing where the chairs had been set up and a small speakers' platform draped in yellow cloth, with a Canadian flag on one side and what she supposed must be a labour-union flag on the other. A group of people had collected, and she found herself changing course in order to get a look at them. Some were old people, very plainly but decently dressed, the women with kerchiefs around their heads on the hot day. Europeans, she thought. Others were factory workers, men in clean short-sleeved shirts and women in fresh blouses and slacks, let out early. A few women must have come from home, because they were wearing summer dresses and sandals and trying to keep track of small children. Louisa thought that they would not care at all for the way she was dressed – fashionably, as always, in beige shantung with a crimson silk tam – but she noticed, just then, a woman more elegantly got up than she was, in green silk with her dark hair drawn tightly back, tied with a green-and-gold scarf. She might have been forty – her face was worn, but beautiful. She came over to Louisa at once, smiling, and showed her a chair, and gave her a mimeographed paper. Louisa could not read the purple printing. She tried to get a look at some men who were talking beside the platform. Were the speakers among them?

The coincidence of the name was hardly even interesting. Neither the first name nor the last was all that unusual.

She did not know why she had sat down, or why she had come over here in the first place. She was beginning to feel a faintly sickening, familiar agitation. But once it got going, telling herself that it was over nothing did no good. The only thing to do was to get up and get away from here, before any more people sat down and hemmed her in.

The green woman intercepted her, asked if she was all right.

'I have to catch a bus,' said Louisa in a croaky voice. She cleared her throat. 'An out-of-town bus,' she said with better control, and marched away, not in the right direction for Simpsons. She thought in fact that she wouldn't go there, she wouldn't go to Birks for the wedding present or to a movie, either. She would just go and sit in the bus depot until it was time for her to go home.

★

Half a block from the bus depot she remembered that the bus had not taken her there that morning. The depot was being torn down and rebuilt – there was a temporary depot several blocks away. She had not paid quite enough attention to which street it was on – York Street, east of the real depot, or King? At any rate, she had to detour, because both of these streets were being torn up, and she had almost decided she was lost when she realised she had been lucky enough to come upon the temporary depot by the back way. It was an old house – one of those tall, yellow-grey brick houses dating from the time when this was a residential district. This was probably the last use it would be put to before being torn down. Houses all around it must have been torn down to make the large gravelled lot where the buses pulled in. There were still some trees at the edge of the lot and under them a few rows of chairs that she had not noticed when she got off the bus before noon. Two men were sitting on what used to be the veranda of the house, on old car seats. They wore brown shirts with the bus company's insignia, but they seemed to be half-hearted about their work, not getting up when she asked if the bus to Carstairs was leaving at six o'clock as scheduled and where could she get a soft drink.

Six o'clock, far as they knew.

Coffee shop down the street.

Cooler inside but only Coke and orange left.

She got herself a Coca-Cola out of the cooler in a dirty little indoor waiting room that smelled of a bad toilet. Moving the depot to this dilapidated house must have thrown everyone into a state of indolence and fecklessness. There was a fan set up in the room they used as an office, and as she went by on her way outside she saw some papers blow off the desk. 'Oh, shit,' said the office girl, and stamped her heel on them.

Coming out, Louisa saw that the chairs set up in the shade of the dusty city trees were straight-backed old wooden ones originally painted different colours – they looked as if they had come from various kitchens. Strips of old carpet and rubber bathroom mats were laid down in front of them, to keep your feet off the gravel. On the ground a little way off slept a white calf, which Louisa would not accept, so she squinted at it until it stirred and roused itself and turned into a dingy dog. It trotted over and looked at her for a moment in a grave, semi-official way, gave a brief sniff at her shoes, and trotted away.

She had not noticed if there were any drinking straws and did not feel like going back to look. She drank Coke from the bottle, tilting back her head and closing her eyes.

When she opened them, a man was sitting one chair away and was speaking to her.

'I got here as soon as I could,' he said. 'Nancy said you were going to catch a bus. As soon as I finished with the speech I took off. But the bus depot is all torn up.'

'Temporarily,' she said.

'I knew you right away,' he said. 'In spite of – well, many years. When I saw you, I was talking to somebody. Then I looked again and you'd disappeared.'

'I don't recognise you,' said Louisa.

'Well, no,' he said. 'I guess not. Of course. You wouldn't.'

He was wearing tan slacks, a pale-yellow short-sleeved shirt, a cream-and-yellow ascot. A bit of a dandy, for a union man. His hair was white but thick and wavy, the sort of springy hair that goes in ripples, up and back from the forehead. His skin was flushed and his face was deeply wrinkled from the efforts of speechmaking – and from talking to people privately, she supposed, with much of the fervour and persuasiveness of his public speeches. He wore tinted glasses, which he took off now, as if willing that she should see him better. His eyes were a light blue, slightly bloodshot and apprehensive. A good-looking man, trim except for a little authoritative bulge over the belt, but she did not find these serviceable, good looks – the careful, sporty clothes, the display of ripply hair, the effective expressions – very attractive. She preferred the kind of looks Arthur had had. The restraint, the dark-suited dignity that some people could call pompous but that seemed to her admirable and innocent.

'I always meant to break the ice,' he said. 'I meant to speak to you. I should have gone in and said goodbye at least. The opportunity to leave came up so suddenly.'

Louisa did not have any idea what to say to this.

He sighed. He said, 'You must have been mad at me. Are you still?'

'No,' she said, and fell back, ridiculously, on the usual courtesies. 'How is Grace? How is your daughter? Lillian?'

'Grace is not so well. She had some arthritis. Her weight doesn't help it. Lillian is all right. She's married but she still teaches high school. Mathematics. Not too usual for a woman.'

How could Louisa begin to correct him? Could she say, No, your wife, Grace, got married again, during the war, she married a farmer, a widower? Before that she used to come in and clean our house once a week. Mrs Groves had got too old. And Lillian never finished high school, how could she be a high-school teacher? She married young, she had some children, she works in the drugstore. She has your height and your hair, dyed blonde. I used to look at her and think she must be like you. When she was growing up I used to give her my step-daughter's outgrown clothes.

Instead of this, she said, 'Then the woman in the green dress – that was not Lillian?'

'Nancy? Oh no! Nancy is my guardian angel. She keeps track of where I'm going, and when, and have I got my speech, and what I drink and eat and have I taken my pills. I tend towards high blood pressure. Nothing too serious. But my way of life's no good. I'm on the go constantly. Tonight I've got to fly out of here to Ottawa, tomorrow I've got a tough meeting, tomorrow night I've got some fool banquet.'

Louisa felt it necessary to say, 'You knew that I got married? I married Arthur Doud.'

She thought he showed some surprise. But he said, 'Yes, I heard that. Yes.'

'We worked hard, too,' said Louisa sturdily. 'Arthur died six years ago. We kept the factory going all through the thirties, even though at times we were down to three men. We had no money for repairs, and I remember cutting up the office awnings so that Arthur could carry them up on a ladder and patch the roof. We tried making everything we could think of. Even outdoor bowling alleys for those amusement places. Then the war came, and we couldn't keep up with the work. We could sell all the pianos we could make, but we were also making radar cases for the Navy. I stayed in the office all through.'

'It must have been a change,' he said, in what seemed a tactful voice. 'A change from the library.'

'Work is work,' she said. 'I still work. My stepdaughter, Bea, is divorced, she keeps house for me after a fashion. My son has finally finished university. He is supposed to be learning about the business, but he has some excuse to go off in the middle of every afternoon. When I come home at supper time, so tired I could drop, I hear the ice tinkling in their glasses and them laughing behind the hedge. Oh, Mud, they say when they see me – oh, poor Mud, sit down here. Get her a drink! They call me Mud because that was my son's name for me when he was a baby. But they are neither of them babies now. The house is cool when I come home. It's a lovely house if you remember, built in three tiers like a wedding cake. Mosaic tiles in the entrance hall, and wooden trim that looks like lace edges and drinks up the paint. But I am always thinking about the factory – that is what fills my mind. What should we do to stay afloat? There are only five factories in Canada making pianos now, and three of them are in Quebec, with the low cost of labour. No doubt you know all about that. When I talk to Arthur in my head it is always about the same thing. I am very close to him still but it is hardly in a mystical way. You would think that as you get older your mind would fill up with what they call the spiritual side of things, but mine just seems to get more and more practical, trying to get something settled. What a thing to talk to a dead man about.'

She stopped, she was embarrassed. But she was not sure that he had listened to all of this and, in fact, she was not sure that she had said all of it.

'What started me off – ' he said. 'What got me going in the

first place, with whatever I have managed to do, was the library. So I owe you a great deal.'

He put his hands on his knees and looked down.

'Ah, rubbish,' he said.

He groaned, and ended up with a laugh.

'My father,' he said. 'You wouldn't remember my father?'

'Oh, yes,' Louisa said.

'Well. Sometimes I think he had the right idea.'

Then he lifted his eyes and made a pronouncement.

'Love never dies.'

At first, she felt impatient to the point of taking offence. This is what all the speechmaking turns you into, she thought – a person who can say things like that. Love dies all the time, or at any rate it becomes distracted, overlaid – it might as well be dead.

'Arthur used to come and sit in the library,' she said. 'In the beginning I was very provoked with him. I used to look at the back of his neck and think, Ha, what if something should hit you there! None of that would make sense to you. It wouldn't make sense. And it turned out to be something else entirely that I wanted. I wanted to marry him and get into a normal life.'

'A normal life,' she repeated – and a giddiness seemed to be taking over, an airy solemnity and widespread forgiveness, a tender notion of understanding between him and herself. 'What do you think I mean by that?'

Across the gravelled yard came a group of oddly dressed folk. They moved all together, a clump of black. The women did not show their hair – they had black shawls or bonnets covering their heads. The men wore broad hats and black braces. The children were dressed just like their elders, even to the bonnets and hats. How hot they all looked in those clothes – how hot and dusty and wary and shy.

'The Tolpuddle Martyrs,' he said, in a faintly joking, resigned, and compassionate voice. 'Ah, I guess I'd better go over. I'd better go over there and have a word with them.'

That edge of a joke, the uneasy kindness, made her think of somebody else. Who was it? When she saw the breadth of his shoulders from behind, and the broad flat buttocks, she knew who.

Jim Frarey.

Oh, what kind of a trick was being played on her, or what kind of trick was she playing on herself! She would not have it. She pulled herself up tightly, she saw all those black clothes blotted together. She was dizzy and humiliated. She would not have it.

But not all black, now that they were getting closer. She could see dark blue – those were the men's shirts – and dark blue and purple in some of the women's dresses. She could see faces – the men's behind beards, the women's in their deep-brimmed bonnets. And now she knew who they were. They were Mennonites.

Mennonites were living in this part of the country, where they never used to be. There were some of them around Bondy, a village north of Carstairs. They would be going home on the same bus she was taking.

He was not with them, or anywhere in sight.

A traitor, helplessly. A traveller.

Once she knew that these were Mennonites and not some lost unidentifiable strangers, they did not look so shy or dejected. In fact they seemed quite cheerful, passing around a bag of candy, the adults eating candy with the children. They settled on the chairs all around her.

No wonder she was feeling clammy. She had gone under a wave, which nobody else had noticed. You could say anything you liked about what had happened – but what it amounted to was going under a wave. She had gone under and through it and was left with a cold sheen on her skin, a beating in her ears, a cavity in her chest and revolt in her stomach. It was anarchy she was up against – a devouring muddle. Sudden holes and impromptu tricks and radiant vanishing consolations.

But these settlings of Mennonites, all around her, are a blessing. The plop of behinds on chairs, the crackling of the candy bag, the meditative sucking and soft conversations. Without looking at Louisa, a little girl holds out the bag, and

Louisa accepts a butterscotch mint. She is surprised to be able to hold it in her hand, to have her lips shape 'Thank you,' then to discover in her mouth just the taste that she expected. She sucks on it as they do on theirs, not in any hurry, and allows that taste to promise her some reasonable continuance.

Lights have come on, though it isn't yet evening. In the trees above the wooden chairs someone has strung lines of little coloured bulbs that she did not notice until now. They make her think of festivities. Carnivals. Boats of singers on the lake.

'What place is this?' she said to the woman beside her.

On the day of Miss Tamblyn's death it happened that Louisa was staying in the Commercial Hotel. She was a traveller then, for a company that sold hats, ribbons, handkerchiefs, trimmings, and ladies' underwear to retail stores. She heard the talk in the hotel, and it occurred to her that the town would soon need a new librarian. She was getting very tired of lugging her sample cases on and off trains, and showing her wares in hotels, packing and unpacking. She went at once and talked to the people in charge of the library. A Mr Doud and a Mr Macleod. They sounded like a vaudeville team but did not look it. The pay was poor, but she had not been doing so well on commission, either. She told them that she had finished high school, in Toronto, and had worked in Eaton's Book Department before she switched to travelling. She did not think it necessary to tell them that she had only worked there five months when she was discovered to have t.b., and that she had then spent four years in a sanatorium. The t.b. was cured, anyway – her spots were dry.

The hotel moved her to one of the rooms for permanent guests, on the third floor. She could see the snow-covered hills over the rooftops. The town of Carstairs was in a river valley. It had three or four thousand people and a long main street that ran downhill, over the river, and uphill again. There was a piano-and-organ factory.

The houses were built for lifetimes and the yards were wide and the streets were lined with mature elm and maple trees. She had never been here when the leaves were on the trees. It must make a great difference. So much that lay open now would be concealed.

She was glad of a fresh start, her spirits were hushed and grateful. She had made fresh starts before and things had not turned out as she had hoped, but she believed in the swift decision, the unforeseen intervention, the uniqueness of her fate.

The town was full of the smell of horses. As evening came on, big blinkered horses with feathered hooves pulled the sleighs across the bridge, past the hotel, beyond the street lights, down the dark side roads. Somewhere out in the country they would lose the sound of each other's bells.

Three Minute Egg

WENDY PERRIAM

CAROLINE ROLLED OVER on her back, tugging down her nightdress; lay hot and restless, listening to her husband's steady breathing – so regular, so dogged, it sounded like a metronome. George never snored or snuffled or broke his own smug rhythm. She nudged his blue-pyjamaed arm, hoping that he'd miss a breath, or startle her by wheezing, provide some wild variety, even shriek and tangle in a technicoloured nightmare. But there was no change at all in the measured inhalations, the monotonous rising and falling of his chest.

She sat up very gingerly, being careful not to wake him. George worked hard, needed sleep and regularity on their rare weekends away. She tiptoed to the window, pushed aside the heavy velvet curtain. The view was like the opening shot in an MGM spectacular. A full-frontal moon was throbbing in the sky, the waves heaving underneath it with a whoosh of shimmering foam. She pressed both hands against the pane, as if hoping it would break, let her slip outside to join the wild and bright convulsion.

'George,' she said, out loud.

No answer, but the breathing. In, out. In, out. In, out. Unwavering, polite. Suddenly, she dived across the room, fumbled in the darkness for her clothes. She had left them scattered on the chair, last night, while her husband tidied his away, placed shoe-trees in his brogues.

She closed the door as quietly as she could, crept along the corridor, feet lapped in soft pink pile. No sound from any other room, no revelry or laugh. It seemed wrong to use the lift, disturb that clotted silence, so she drifted down the majestic curving stairs. The night porter was yawning in a chair, looked at her accusingly, as if she had no right to break the rules, get up before the day staff had come in.

She paused a moment in the stifling hotel lobby, aware that she would need a coat, yet reluctant to go back for it. She shrugged and pushed the door, collided with the wind head-on. It knifed rudely through her Jaeger skirt, thrust cold unwelcome fingers beneath her blue crêpe blouse. She broke into a run, to try to cheat it; loping swiftly down the hill towards the pier, building up her own internal body-heat. Bournemouth looked impeccable, even in the anaemic pre-dawn light, basking in its high-sun, low-crime records, turning its back on sordid Brighton and puny Littlehampton. She preferred it out of season, before the summer razzmatazz set in, encrusting it with trippers, their litter and their candyfloss, their pale and paunchy rolls of flesh offered naked to the sun.

There was no sun as yet, this morning, only the moon still lounging in the sky, though fading now, and spent; the explosive thrill of black and gold dimmed to sober grey. Dawn doesn't break, she thought, as she stopped to watch the scene – it seeps. Yet the very word sunrise suggested flame and action, not this stifled monochrome, creeping up almost imperceptibly and diluting the night's brilliance.

She turned right, along the promenade which led eventually to Christchurch. She and George had strolled there the previous afternoon, admired the fierce insistent yellow of the gorse flowers, haloed by a weaker yellow sun; listened to the gulls, their mournful keening cries and thresh of wings. Yesterday's colour photograph was now a blurred grey negative, unclear and out of focus. Shapes strode out of the darkness and assembled themselves into beach-huts, wooden benches. Shadows hung like birds from posts and railings. Her ears were aching from the wind, assaulted by the thwack-thwack of the waves. The moon grew paler and smaller, as if someone were erasing it, bit by bit by bit; the rubber leaving smear-marks in the sky. It was no longer night, but not yet morning. Nothing-time.

At intervals along the beach were narrow breakwaters, running down into the sea. Groynes, George had called them, explaining how they held the beach firm against erosion, stopped it being swept or washed away. He always had an eye to her education, corrected her if she used the vague word 'gulls' for Arctic terns, or muddle gorse with broom. She jumped down from the promenade on to the crunch and ache of shingle, then made her way across the sand towards the hazy human-shape she could see sitting on a groyne. The figure gradually resolved itself into dark hair and a duffle coat; a lad of seventeen or so, slightly built, with a pinched and girlish face. He was holding an ancient split-cane rod, with the binding coming loose; fishing paraphernalia marshalled all around him – a canvas bag, a tackle box, a tin of bait, a clasp-knife. At his feet were two flounder and a school bass, their gills still gasping in and out.

She edged a little closer, prodded them with her shoe. 'Isn't it early for bass?' she asked. She never spoke to strangers.

'Easterly wind. Brings 'em in closer.'

He had answered mechanically, as if he grudged the words, flinging her a wary glance, his whole face closed, suspicious. She had expected approval, or at least, surprise. Not every woman could recognise a bass, or tell a dab from a flounder. George was a human encyclopaedia.

'Is that lugworm?' she persisted, as she watched him bait his hook, then cast into the wind.

'No, king rag.' His tone was barely civil. The words seemed to struggle up from the region of his feet, emerge rusty and half-formed.

He was tall and very bony, his face muddy in the pallid light, all his features smudged and undefined. He appeared to be deliberately ignoring her, sitting mute and motionless, only his eyes showing he was still alive; narrowed watchful eyes, following every tiny movement of his rod tip. 'What's your name?'

'Ric.'

'You're a local, I suppose.'

He didn't answer, clearly didn't want her there. She stared down at her damp Kurt Geiger shoes, their soft beige skin stained darker from the sand. *He* was wearing combat boots with broken tangled laces. One of his front teeth was blackened, slightly buckled; his hands long and thin, in keeping with the rest of him, though the bulky coat built him up, made him look larger than he was. He tightened the line an inch or two, against the play of the waves; his body also rigid, as if someone held it tautly on a string. She sat gingerly beside him on the breakwater, feeling buffeted and fragile like a piece of bobbing bladderwrack. The tide was coming in, spray spattering their faces, as the angry water slammed against the wood, then swirled and fretted back.

'You must get lonely on your own.'

Silence.

The wind had blown her words away, and was now tugging at her hair, reminding her how cold she was. Her husband would be snug in bed, or maybe up and shaving in the overheated bathroom, a soft white towel tucked beneath his chin. She glanced across at Ric, wondering if he shaved. His cheek looked smooth and virgin like a child's.

Suddenly, he shambled to his feet and strode to the end of the groyne, turning his back to the wind, fiddling with his flies. She watched his feet brace themselves, his knees bend and splay a little, shoulders hunching up; realised with a shock that he was peeing over the edge of the breakwater. She might as well have not been there. Yet she couldn't help but look, torn between revulsion and excitement, taking in the details; the tensed and powerful legs; the buttocks thrusting forward; the intense concentration on a private ritual. She watched the stream of urine, scattered by the wind, lost in the dirty sea. He slouched back towards her, eyes cast down, feet stumbling on the wood. He was so young, so graceless, and – no, he didn't shave. She could see the fine blond down, softening his upper lip, as he slumped back beside her on the breakwater.

Slowly, very slowly, she touched a finger to that lip and grazed the fledgling hairs. He froze, the knuckles tautening like marbles along one tight-clenched fist. She let the finger lap across his mouth and chin, down his neck and throat, then grope between the buttons of his shirt. He seemed to have lost all power to respond, his body someone else's, not under his control. She had to help him, teach him, as George was always teaching her.

Both her hands began to probe, across his chest, beneath his shirt, down towards his stomach. Still he didn't move, just let her heave his coat off, as if he were a child to be undressed. She struggled with the buckle of his belt. His flies were still undone. She glimpsed grubby underpants, and something stiffening under them, the off-white nylon fabric bulging through the open zip. He was too big for his jeans now – tight and tattered Levis, needing to come down, though the belt-buckle was obstinate, refusing to release him. He stared down at the ground, embarrassed and uncertain, a tiny muscle in his neck palpitating, like an insect on his skin. Her small and dainty shoes had crept up on his rough black boots and were trying to edge between them.

Suddenly, he shoved her round, then pushed her to her knees, clawing down her white silk pants, and trying to bunch her skirt up. The wind thrust between her legs, its icy blast replaced by clammy warmth as he covered her like a dog. The rough ridge of the breakwater snagged and scraped her flesh. Out of the corner of one eye, she could see the frilled fins of the flounder, still fluttering and twitching. The thing inside her was threshing like a fish, a rising salmon, plunging home to spawn. She tried to fix her whole attention on the wild pain in her knees, as he kept grinding them and grinding them against the jagged barnacles. He was moving really roughly, as if annoyed at the disruption; breaking his own rhythm, gripping with his nails. Everything was contracted to the judder of her knees, and the small square of ridged wood staring into her face. Her lips were nuzzling soft green slime, her nose breathing tar and seaweed. She closed her eyes. George would have finished shaving and be back in the bedroom now, pressing down his cuticles with the silver-handled hoof-stick; Scarlatti on the radio, Old Spice on his chin.

There was a tiny whimper, followed by a shudder, and Ric withdrew as abruptly as he'd entered. It was the only sound he had made. She slumped forward, laid her cheek against the groyne, heard him fidgeting behind her, fumbling with his jeans, jerking back the zip. When she looked up, he was sitting exactly as before, the duffle coat refastened, the butt of the rod held firm between his legs. Only the tide was a little further in.

He reached down for a thermos lying on the sand, unscrewed its dented cap, gulped the contents noisily, his throat pulsing as he swallowed, like the gills of a hooked fish. He had almost drained the flask before he offered it to her, his greasy fingermarks smearing the red plastic. She grimaced as she took a sip; never drank sweet tea.

The silence was uneasy; Ric staring at his hands pulling at a hangnail on his thumb. She glanced down at her own hands, stained greenish from the breakwater, the palms printed with a pattern of still throbbing whorls and ridges. A minute passed. Another. She scrabbled for her pants, dragged them on again. The silk felt limp and cold.

Ric rummaged in his canvas bag, drew out a package, wrapped clumsily in newspaper. He tossed the paper in the sea, revealed a pair of hard-boiled eggs. He cracked one against the tackle box, stripping off its shell; wolfed it down – two bites – then handed her the other. The egg felt heavy in her hands, soothed her reddened palms. She began to pick the shell off, exposing the swollen curve beneath, then took a small reluctant bite of shiny flabby white. It tasted cold and rubbery, and she could see the yolk, off-centre and black-edged, as if it had already begun to putrefy. The stubborn odour of hard-boiled egg seemed to have seeped into her body, soiled her pants. She could smell nothing else at all now. Even the sharp salt tang of the sea was completely blotted out.

Suddenly, Ric cannoned to his feet, and in one violent

movement flung himself back and pulled the rod above his head. The line was lunging furiously as he reeled it in, pressed the butt hard against his stomach. His eyes were blazing blue now, and his face had hatched at last from its chrysalis stare; every nerve and muscle strained as he fought the flailing fish. Caroline glimpsed a bulging eye, a spiked and jagged fin; recognised a sea bream, a good three pounds or more. She felt the shock in her own body as Ric hauled it in, dropped it on the groyne, tried to still its struggles with a piece of dirty sacking. It squirmed sickeningly beneath his hands, zigzagging and writhing in streaks of silver fury. He struck it on the head. Blood oozed from its gills as he removed the savage hook.

She took a second bite of egg, but couldn't force it down. Her whole stomach felt distended, as if the first small mouthful had swollen up inside her, in some instant monstrous pregnancy. She shuddered, turned away, began to retrace her steps across the beach, looking back a moment as she reached the promenade, her footprints already swallowed up by the devouring sucking sand. Ric hadn't even noticed she was gone. He was on his knees, fussing with the fish, his back towards her, head bent low. She broke into a run. The light was muted still, but a paler shade of grey now. The night had finally drained away, but there was no sun, no splash of colour.

The promenade seemed endless, the clang and whirr of dustcarts drowning the noise of the waves. She stopped to catch her breath beside the row of dustbin-bags, their blackly gaping mouths disgorging greasy papers, empty cans and bottles. A dustman whistled at her and she smiled back automatically. She could still smell hard-boiled egg.

The first locals were appearing – a lady with a poodle, both in matching tartan coats; a gnarled old man searching for fag-ends; two early-morning joggers slowing to a wheeze. The town was still concealed behind the cliffs. She was in no-man's-land, hemmed in by the sea on one side and the steeply rising ground on the other. The pavilions looked dingy and diminished, slumbering in the grudging light. She wished she, too, were sleeping, protected from the cold, buttressed by her husband's stocky form. Her legs ached; her feet drudged on; her face felt sore and smarting from the wind. She turned, at last, past the pier and up the hill; the clang of dustcarts changing key into the clatter of teacups as she entered the hotel. They were serving breakfast now, the smell of sizzling bacon swamping last night's stale aroma of cigar-smoke, forced carnations. It was a relief to shut the wind out, to step from open sea to greenhouse fug. The lift was waiting, empty. She pressed the button for the fourth floor, glancing at her face in its luxurious mirrored walls. The face looked strange, and wrong.

George was sitting up in bed with the Business News open on his lap; one fleck of forgotten shaving-foam gleaming on his cheekbone. His thinning hair was neatly combed; his smile easy and relaxed above the hip-length quilted dressing-gown he called his smoking jacket. He turned the radio down. Haydn, not Scarlatti.

'Hello, darling. Enjoyed your early-morning constitutional? You should have woken me as well. I've ordered breakfast, by the way. Boiled eggs.'

George was a creature of habit. Boiled eggs on Sunday mornings, roast beef for Sunday lunch. The pattern never changed, not even in hotels, when he was offered Loch Fyne kippers, or *Caneton à la Bigarade*. He was fussy about his eggs, insisted they should be soft-boiled, with the whites just barely firm. At home, she timed them to the dot, she and the pinger both counting down the seconds. Three minutes exactly – the same time, more or less, it had taken Ric to come. They could almost measure out their marriage in three-minute-eggs; Sunday after endless Sunday, dipping Normandy-buttered soldiers into runny free-range yolks.

'Come in,' called George, as someone knocked – the waiter with a tray. The elderly black-coated man set it down obsequiously, unloaded a silver coffee pot, two bone-china egg-cups, in the same attractive floral pattern as the plates. George chose his hotels for their attention to small details, their insistence on high standards and good service. He was right in that respect. Bone china did enhance an egg, and of course they should be soft. They smelt different then, not tainted.

These eggs were large and pale, their finely speckled shells half-hidden under caressing woolly cosies. The golden toast was shorn of all its crusts, the marmalade thick with chunks of peel. A single pink-blush rose floated in a crystal bowl.

Caroline joined her husband on the bed, lay back against the pillows, while he fussed with plates and spoons, removed the berets from the eggs, passed her three small fingers of neatly buttered toast, fanned out around her egg-cup. 'All right, my dear?' he asked.

She nodded, watched him rap his own egg, the soft yolk spilling over, dribbling down the shell. He scooped it back fastidiously, took his first small mouthful, dabbing his thin lips with the starched white damask napkin. She drew up her knees, startled as she saw them grazed and bleeding, marked with red weals beneath the shredded stockings; the grazes oozing slightly, the same tacky and transparent ooze she could feel slimy in her pants. She dragged her skirt down quickly, spread her napkin over them. Her husband hadn't noticed. His spoon was deep inside his egg, prising out the last warm curl of white.

At last, he pushed the plate away, took a sip of coffee. 'Aren't you eating, darling?'

'No,' she said, wincing at the pain in her knees. 'I've already breakfasted.'

Queen Mahatonga Retires for the Night

DON RODGERS

QUEEN MAHATONGA RETIRES for the night. Her husband, the Prince, kisses her on the cheek, so too do her children, the Prince and Princess. They all withdraw to their separate rooms in the palace.

Queen Mahatonga lays her tiara on the dressing-table and dismisses her ladies-in-waiting. She combs out her hair which is long and streaked with grey. She gazes at her night attire which is laid out and waiting on her bed, like a corpse.

Her husband wore gold-braided pyjamas. She wondered who chose them and where they were bought and by whom. As Queen she was not expected to buy her husband's pyjamas. They were maroon in colour with gold braid on the cuffs and the bottoms of the trouser legs. Somewhere, she supposed, there was a manufacturer of pyjamas who sported a crest on his letterhead: by royal appointment.

Queen Mahatonga undressed very slowly. It was no longer a pleasure as it had been in her youth. Then she could hardly wait to strip herself of those ugly garments and to see her beauty emerge like a butterfly out of a pupa. She had strode around the room feeling the movement of air against her body. Sometimes she had slept naked in the white silken sheets.

Now Queen Mahatonga found undressing a wearisome chore. Her clothes were so heavy, so many brocaded items superimposed one on top of the other, so many things to be undone, unbuttoned, unclasped, unzipped, unpopped, unhooked, to be opened then dragged off the body, over the shoulders, or down the body to the floor, to be stepped out of, then picked up with a sigh and a stoop and a twinge of pain in the back or the hip.

She hated being undressed by her ladies-in-waiting. They were so servile, so efficient. They never sniggered or smirked or showed any feelings of repulsion like any ordinary human beings. It was humiliating. It was like being a baby all over again, any obscenity was permissible, everything would be overlooked.

Queen Mahatonga stood in her full regalia, her nakedness, and forced herself to look in the full-length mirror on the wall as she forced herself to look at herself every evening. She detested that mirror. The frame was gold, of course gold, the palace was laden with gold, even the lavatory chain was gold with a ball of onyx suspended at the end for the hand to hold. No doubt if ever, out of absent-mindedness, she forgot to pull on the onyx ball suspended on the golden chain, one of her ladies-in-waiting would see to it in her stead, without a blush or a retch or the slightest twinge of disgust. Somewhere, she supposed, there was a manufacturer of lavatories which sported on its letterhead: by royal appointment. Or perhaps not only on the letterhead. Perhaps on the bowl of the object itself, she would have to look next time, it would give added zest to the daily routine of purging the bowels.

There was no doubt, Queen Mahatonga concluded, that she was in need of more exercise. So many banquets equalled so much flab. Unfortunately there were some things she found it hard to resist. Like swans. She adored eating swans. Her mouth watered at the thought of the last swan she had eaten. The succulence of the flesh, the juices running between her teeth, filling her mouth – ah, what a swan that had been! Prepared, of course, in the manner she preferred: the head and neck unplucked, erect, the plumage on the neck perfect, white, regal – oh yes, there was no denying it, regal was the word. The body cooked to perfection, brown, lightly crisp outside, succulent within. The legs and webbed feet folded beneath the body so that it sat on its silver platter. She always had the first cut, the choicest cut, so many times she had wished she could do it herself, sharpen the long wicked knife, then plunge it into the side of the breast, plunge it in deep, then withdraw it slowly with a downwards motion, so the hank of flesh loosened and came away from the body.

And it wasn't only swans, oh no. What about strawberry jam, made with real strawberries, no artificial flavourings or colourings, by appointment to Her Majesty Queen Mahatonga, manufacturer of preserves, spread thickly on buttered muffins, wholemeal muffins, by appointment to Her Majesty Queen Mahatonga, manufacturer of muffins. The way the butter melted into the muffin, dribbled down one's chin. Not during state banquets, of course. There was such a thing as decorum. No, when having tea out of one's silver cup on one's own – or with the Prince Consort, which was pretty much the same thing – dropping crumbs on the carpet for the nearest lady-in-waiting to sweep up with her little silver dustpan and brush. They were getting so good at it that sometimes they would catch the crumbs on the way down, before they even reached the carpet. Yes, they were un-nervingly quick on the draw these ladies-in-waiting. And of course, completely impassive. Buster Keaton had nothing on her ladies-in-waiting.

There was no avoiding it in the end, Queen Mahatonga had to contemplate her ugly obesity in the gold-framed mirror. She made herself do it. It was good for her soul, she was convinced of that. Not that she hadn't done her best on that score either. The number of indulgences she had purchased. On her current reckoning, she would be exempt from 534,631 years, ten months, three weeks, four days, nine hours and thirty-five minutes of purgatory. It was more or less the only thing of importance her accountant had to calculate. Horrible, mousey little man with lank grey hair and a shiny black frock-coat. It irritated her no end, that frock-coat. It was impregnated with arithmetic, you could smell it, a sour, stale smell, and so old; so that although one could not justifiably impeach its respectability, one was constantly reminded that one's accountant had seven children and a wife whose appetite for rollmop herrings was truly monstrous. 'I assure you, your majesty' the odious little man had been emboldened to confide to her one day, 'we would all be living in the lap of luxury were it not for these rollmop herrings. They will be the ruin of me and my entire family.' What did he expect her to do? Issue a decree? It is hereby decreed that no rollmop herrings shall be manufactured or sold in our entire kingdom, by order of Her Gracious Majesty Queen Mahatonga? Ridiculous little man. In the end, as a compromise, she had ordered her dressmaker, by royal appointment to Her Majesty Queen Mahatonga, to make a new frock-coat for her accountant. Perhaps that would at least stop him whingeing on and on about rollmop herrings. The accountant had worn his new coat only once. The occasion was memorable. It was the last time Queen Mahatonga had enjoyed a really good, whole-hearted, whole-bodied belly laugh. She had laughed till she had ached, tears had coursed down her cheeks, the works. The fault of course lay with her, not with the execrable little accountant, for once. She ought to have placed the order with her husband's tailor, by royal appointment to His Majesty the Prince Consort, rather than with her own dressmaker. The thought had not occurred to her at the time. No doubt her dressmaker had done his best, he was such a nice man, always bowing and scraping and such a charmingly ingratiating smile. The way he took her measurements, it gave her a shiver of pleasure just thinking about it. Such tact, such a light touch, but a touch nonetheless, he always managed a light touch in all the right places, the sly old devil. That was about the only advantage to accrue from her steady gain in weight. She needed re-measuring for her robes nearly every week. The measuring was done in a room in the palace set aside for the purpose and used for no other. It was bare of furniture, not a stick to be seen, there was no carpet, just bare floorboards, by royal decree, all that there was in the room was mirrors: the walls and ceiling were covered with mirrors so that there was not a chink of wall or ceiling to be seen between them. It had been the dressmaker's idea, the sly fox. That way she could see herself on all sides when trying on her dresses. And it was so royal, didn't she think? Just like Louis Quatorze.

Those mirrors were not like this mirror, this mirror that belonged to a fairground hall of mirrors, the sort of mirrors that distort, that enlarge you to impossible dimensions. Oh no, they were nothing like this mirror. They were mirrors of the soul. They reflected back not accidental flesh, not contingent, superfluous, irrelevant flesh. What they showed in all their lovely surfaces, was her real, quintessential beauty, the real Queen Mahatonga, the lithe, svelte, graceful, light-as-a-feather Queen Mahatonga, the Queen Mahatonga who was a 'deliciously juicy morsel', a phrase that delighted her, that her dressmaker had let slip one night when in his cups, the sly old fox, she was sure he knew she was passing. Lovely and light and slender and dancing, she stood like a candle flame in the centre of the fitting-room, for her private exclusive use, her room of mirrors, while the dressmaker by royal appointment flitted round her like a moth, the lightest touch here, the merest whisper of a breath there, taking her measurements while she watched in her mirrors, while she blossomed like a rose in her mirrors and the dressmaker hovered in the atmosphere of her scent, flitted in and out of her radiance, a measurement here, a measurement there. If she looked up, she saw herself in the middle of a dark space, a brilliant shining figure like the sun, around which moved, in his elliptical orbit, her dressmaker, her planet, whirling round her heavenly body. Of course he had to measure her undressed, that was understood, if the garments were to fit properly, not to sag, the measurements must be exact. There was nothing shameful about it, a dressmaker is like a doctor or a priest, he has the right to one's nakedness, for how else is he to see the truth, how else can he absolve one of one's illness, one's body, one's sin?

Queen Mahatonga had more than once regretted that she had not had the bedroom mirror manufactured by the same mirror-maker who furnished the walls and ceiling of the fitting-room. Off with his head, is a phrase which came often to mind when she gazed in fascinated horror at the flab of her body in the bedroom mirror. She remembered very well the manufacturer of this mirror. A wizened sunburnt man with wisps of white hair, bent almost double so that at first one thought he was a hunchback. He had shuffled towards her up the strip of red carpet in the majestic audience chamber as she sat and waited, drumming her fingers with impatience on the armrest of her golden throne. His progress towards her royal presence had been interminable. The top of his head, for that was what was pointed towards her in his progress, approached with infuriating slowness, so that by the time he reached the foot of the three steps that led up to her golden throne, she knew the precise whereabouts of every strand of white hair on the pink pate, knew it better, it seemed to her, than the lines on the map of her own kingdom. When at last he arrived at the foot of the three steps, she told him, with as much graciousness as she could muster, that he could arise. What she had meant was that he could unstoop, unbow. She had presumed that it was out of deference to her majestic royalty that he had thus approached in so bowed a manner. The manufacturer of mirrors had misunderstood and had climbed, very slowly, with considerable effort, the three steps that led up to her golden throne. This was completely unheard of. This was against all protocol. It threw her into a complete tiz-waz. From the corner of one eye she saw a lady-in-waiting glide across towards her, ready, no doubt, to de-elevate the wizened manufacturer of mirrors. With a regal wave of her hand she had signalled the lady-in-waiting to stop. She was not going to be helped out of her predicament by one of those curtseying zombies. Presently the manufacturer of mirrors was standing on the top step, on a level with her throne. Fortunately, as he was so stooped, his head was on a level with Queen Mahatonga's, not higher, for had he been of a normal stance and height, some action would have had to be taken, for then he would have looked down on Queen Mahatonga. As it was, he stood in front of the throne, the top of his head on a level with the head of the seated Queen Mahatonga. Then, with considerable effort, he had raised his head and looked her in the face. His face was as brown and wrinkled as a dried walnut. But what had made Queen Mahatonga all but cry out, was the sight of his eyes. They were large, of an intense sky blue, with no discernible pupil at their centre. Blue, blank, of an alarming tranquillity, they gazed at her face, at her eyes, for a long time, until she had lost all notion of time and space, had felt herself lift off the throne, rise into the air like a piece of thistledown, as weightless as a piece of thistledown, she floated in a blue silence like a cloud in the blue sky, she floated, she floated, what bliss, what never-ending bliss!

'Your majesty' said the manufacturer of mirrors, and the never-ending bliss ended.

Make me a mirror, she had said, in which I shall see myself. What a foolish thing to say, it must have been because she was not yet restored to herself. A mirror in which I shall see myself. What other sort of mirror was there?

That was not what she had said to the manufacturer of mirrors who had fitted out her fitting-room. He was a tall, handsome man, young, with raven-black hair. What long, thin fingers he had had, the thought of them always made her shiver, as if she had been touched by the tips of icicles. And so pale, his face, his hands, so white; almost, she had thought, translucent. He had stood before her, beneath her, at the foot of the three steps he, in a black suit, his feet together, so thin, unmoving, like a flower rising up out of the red carpet, a black-stemmed flower topped by a white bloom. And his eyes? His eyes? Again and again she tried to remember his eyes, but failed each time. She could remember no eyes. It was as if he had had no eyes, as if he were totally eyeless, blind, standing, rising up out of her red carpet, swaying, yes, swaying ever so gently from side to side as if in a light breeze. She shivered.

Make me a mirror, she had said, just that: make me a mirror.

'What kind of mirror, your majesty' the black-stemmed, white-blossomed manufacturer of mirrors had asked her.

'What kind of mirror, your majesty?' The words were there in her memory, they whispered in her memory like flowers rustling against each other in a light breeze, but they were disembodied words, devoid of any voice, she could not remember the voice that had spoken the words. The words were there, whispering in her mind, the whispering frottage of white blooms.

'A mirror in which I shall see my beauty, of course,' she had sung out gaily, like a stupid schoolgirl, to silence the flowers, to be done with it. He had bowed and withdrawn. She supposed. For she had closed her eyes, she had had to close her eyes, and when she opened them again, he was gone.

Not so the wizened, stooped manufacturer of mirrors. She had followed each step he took as if her life depended on it; as he descended the three steps that led down from the golden throne, as he shuffled the length of the red carpet in her majestic audience chamber. She watched his receding figure as it slowly retreated along the strip of red carpet into the gloom, until it had become part of the gloom, until she was no longer sure if part of the gloom was moving, was moving away from her, an old wizened manufacturer of mirrors, or if the gloom was all one, was empty.

Off with his head. Off with his head bowed on his scrawny chicken's neck! How dearly she would have loved to have uttered the command, her voice booming impressively no doubt in an echoing chamber. Off with his head, his wretched nut-brown head; off especially with his clear blue eyes, the eyes that made one float like clouds, that made one forget that one was Queen of the Realm, Queen Mahatonga!

She was cold now. Her body in the mirror was all gooseflesh. Gooseflesh, creased, flabby gooseflesh wobbled on her thighs. Gooseflesh sagged on her nauseating belly; dangled, pathetically empty, from her chest; hung white and limp from her arms; and on her face: folds of putrefying gooseflesh, heavy drapes of it, so that she looked at once both blowsy and haggard.

Queen Mahatonga closed her eyes. She was tired of it all, so tired of it all.

'Princess Mahatonga, Princess Mahatonga,
  My love for you grows stronger and stronger.'

It was sheer doggerel, she knew, but still it filled her eyes with tears. It was the refrain of a love poem, a love poem written to her in her youth by one of her suitors, the Prince Trabakadabski. It was all nonsense of course, her eyes like the stars, her face like the moon, her belly like a pile of rice and so on and so forth. But it had meant such a lot to her. He was the only one of all her suitors to have shown any interest in her person. Yes, he had really cared for her, surely; loved her even? He had not been a strong youth, had been rather on the sickly side in fact. When her father had turned his offer down, he had gone off to the wars, had died a hero's death at the head of his men, his heart broken in twain, or some such thing.

Was that really all she had to look back on? After all these years? A memory of a glimmer of love in a pale breast? For her husband had never cared a jot about her, that had been obvious right from the start. He had done his 'duty by the kingdom', as he so tactfully called it, had sired two children; otherwise he spent all his time managing affairs of state, or so he said, what these affairs of state were she had never fathomed, she never seemed to have that many herself, apart from the banquets, and the audiences, and opening this and that and reciting her speech from time to time. Perhaps it was he who went round handing out royal appointments to manufacturers of every conceivable imaginable.

She had carried the poem about with her for years. In a little pouch sewn from golden thread that had hung between her breasts. Until one day, after a particularly boisterous banquet, she had taken it out and seen that her copious perspiration had caused the ink to run; it had seeped through the threads of the pouch and made a blue stain in the middle of her cleavage. She remembered standing stripped, like she was now, staring at the blue stain between her breasts. It was like a bruise. The poem had seeped through into her heart and left a bruise. She hadn't washed it off, but perspiration had done its work within a few days. Some of the ink had dribbled onto the left cup of her bra, she remembered. She had meant to tell the lady-in-waiting who ran the laundry not to have this particular item washed; but had forgotten, and it had come back clean, admittedly with a somewhat blue whiteness, but the manufacturers of the washing-powder, by appointment to the Princess Kazooma for some strange reason, said on the packet that this was the desired result of using their product. So presumably the last of the poem had been dissolved into the washing water. From there, who knows, might it not have journeyed to the sea, from thence been lifted into the air as a cloud, have floated light as thistledown through a clear blue sky?

That dratted little wizened manufacturer of mirrors! Ashamed, suddenly, beyond toleration, of the image of herself that she saw framed in the gold on the wall of her bedroom, Queen Mahatonga covered her nakedness with a dressing gown, maroon, like her husband's, with gold braid like her husband's, by royal appointment. She stole to the bedroom door, opened it a chink, peeped out to see if the coast was clear. Outside the corridor was long and dark. At intervals along the corridor, as along every interminable corridor of this wretched palace, propped up on a chair by each door that gave onto each corridor, slumped on a chair like a dead thing, slept a lady-in-waiting; they slept like dead things, like black dead things. Queen Mahatonga crept past them in the darkness along the dark corridors of this wretched palace, past the sleeping dead forms of the mindless ladies-in-waiting, until she reached the door of her private room of mirrors, for her sole exclusive use, by royal decree. She fitted the golden key that she kept suspended round her neck on golden thread into the golden lock, and went in. Inside, the room was lit up by an eerie glow, a pale bluish, whitish glow that emanated from the mirrors that covered the walls and the ceiling of the room. This was part of the magic of the tall, dark, white-petalled manufacturer of mirrors. Queen Mahatonga locked the door behind her, sliding the mirrored panel back over the keyhole so that there was no flaw in the flawless beautiful mirrors all around and above her. Queen Mahatonga let her dressing gown slip to the floor, stepped free of it, stepped into the middle of her room of mirrors. The flame was there once more, in the middle of the room, lithe and supple and dancing, incandescent in the light that emanated from the mirrors, the quintessential Queen Mahatonga, the beautiful, beautiful Queen Mahatonga!

Fuck that little wizened walnut of a hunchbacked manufacturer of mirrors! She had thought to fix him all right, oh yes, she would cook his goose for him. She had ordered him to appear before her, by royal decree of her Majesty Queen Mahatonga. She had waited for him here, here in her private fitting-room, her room of mirrors. She had ordered him to be escorted by one of those damnable ladies-in-waiting along the wretched corridors that dripped with gold on all sides, all around one; she sometimes wondered whether the spiders that spun webs in the corners of these royal corridors did not spin webs of gold out of their bulbous arses. He had been made to wait outside the door that led into the room of mirrors, the room that no one but herself and her dressmaker had ever been privileged to enter. Then she had unlocked the door with her golden key and had ordered him to enter, locking the door behind him after he had shuffled in, his head bowed as before. Now he would see what a true manufacturer of mirrors could produce! Now he would see how paltry, how shoddy his mirror was that he had manufactured for her bedroom by royal command! Let him see and be ashamed, let him cringe before the evidence of his incompetence in the art which was his life, the art of the manufacturing of mirrors. Behold, she had said to him when they were in the centre of the room of mirrors, lift up your head and see! The bowed, wizened manufacturer of mirrors had done as he was bid, had raised his head on his scrawny chicken's neck; and at once the world had become blue again, as blue as sky, on all sides and above, as far as the eye could see there was blue sky, blue sky, inviting her to float, light as a piece of thistledown, like a cloud, to float in the eternal wonderful blue. But Queen Mahatonga had resisted with all the strength of mind and body she had left, she had resisted the weightlessness, the joy, that even then was rising to her loins from the soles of her feet, was bidding her rise, rise up into clear blue sky. But she was having none of it, she, Queen Mahatonga, Queen of the Realm, was not to be imposed upon by one such as he, the bowed, wizened, walnut-brown manufacturer of mirrors, she would prevail, her will would prevail, her royal majestic will! And she had prevailed. The wonderfullest, intensest blue of sky, the joyful invitation to soar in the majestic blue, had withdrawn, departed. Leaving beside her, standing beside her, gently swaying as in a gentle breeze, the black-stemmed, white-blossomed manufacturer of mirrors, the eyeless, sightless manufacturer of mirrors. She had cried out, she, Queen Mahatonga though she be, had not been able to suppress a cry, of fear was it, of amazement, of anger at this wretched tomfoolery? And the words had whispered in her mind, the leaves and stems and flowers rattled together, rubbed against each other, nuzzled each other, licked each other, intertwined in her mind, had whispered in her mind:

'Queen Mahatonga, Queen Mahatonga,

I do not care for you any longer.'

Again and again the refrain was chanted in a whisper by a multitude of black-stemmed white-blossomed flowers, swaying in her mind, in her dark mind, stirred by who knows what breeze, to murmur, as if in sleep, as if entranced, in a hushed delirium of intertwining bodies:

'Queen Mahatonga, Queen Mahatonga,

I do not care for you any longer.'

Queen Mahatonga sat, a heap of quivering gooseflesh, on the bare boards of the floor of her room of mirrors, alone, quite alone. She wanted to weep, to wail, to wrap her face in her long grey hair, to rock her body, her fat ugly body, to and fro on the bare boards of the floor of her room of mirrors. She wanted to give herself up to her fantasy, a fantasy that had enticed her so often in her room of mirrors, a fantasy that thrilled her with fear, a thrill akin to the intimate shivery thrill of the thought of self-destruction. She wanted, at long last, to enter into this fantasy, to abandon herself to it once and for all: there she was, she, Queen Mahatonga, Queen of the Realm, a lithe and supple flame, a bluish whitish dancing flame, like the negative image of a wind-rippled cypress on the retina of a God, ethereal, sumptuous, undying, quivering with life, with energy, undulating in a light breeze, swaying to the music of a light wind, reflected from the walls, from the ceiling, of this room of mirrors, reflected a thousand, a million-fold in the tunnel of mirrors that burrowed back into each wall of this room of mirrors, an infinity of images, an infinity of Queen Mahatongas; while above her, the one, the pure, the absolute Queen Mahatonga, in all her heavenly splendour and radiance, all her unearthly loveliness, blossomed on the ceiling. And so she would remain, for ever and ever, the resplendent Queen Mahatonga in her room of mirrors, alone, majestic, eternal, unattainable, untouchable: the quintessential everlasting Queen Mahatonga.

Christopher Columbus and Queen Isabella of Spain Consummate Their Relationship, Santa Fe, January 1492

SALMAN RUSHDIE

COLUMBUS, A FOREIGNER, follows Queen Isabella for an eternity without entirely giving up hope.

In what characteristic postures?

Proud yet supplicant, the head held high but the knee bent. Fawning yet fearless; possessed of a certain saucy vulgarity, he gets away with it by virtue of his confidence-man's charm. However, as time passes, the ingratiating aspects of his stance are emphasised; the sea-dog raffishness wears a little thin. As do his shoes.

His hope. It is of what?

Obvious answers first: He hopes for preferment. He wants to tie the Queen's favour to his helmet, like a knight in a romance. (He owns no helmet.) He has hopes of cash, and of three tall ships, Niña Pinta Santa Maria; of, in fourteen hundred and ninety-two, sailing across the ocean blue. But, on his first arrival at court, when the Queen herself asked him what he desired, he bowed over her olive hand and, with his lips a millimetre away from the great ring of her power, murmured a single, dangerous word:

'Consummation.'

These unspeakable foreigners! The nerve! Consummation, indeed! And then following in her footsteps, month after month, as if he stood a chance. His coarse epistles, his tuneless serenades beneath her casement windows, obliging her to have them closed, shutting out the cooling breeze. She had better things to do, a world to conquer and so forth, who did he think he was? — Foreigners can be dogged. And can also, on account of language difficulties, fail to take a hint. Then again, let us not forget, it is considered de rigueur to keep a few foreigners around. They lend the place a certain cosmopolitan tone. They are often poor and consequently willing to perform divers necessary but dirty jobs. They are, moreover, a warning against complacency, their existence in our midst reminding us that there are quarters in which (hard as it is to accept) we ourselves would be considered foreigners. — But to speak so to the Queen! — Foreigners forget their place (having left it behind). Given time, they begin to think of themselves as our equals. It is an unavoidable hazard. They introduce into our austerities their Italianate blandishments. Nothing for it. Turn a deaf ear, look the other way. They rarely mean real harm, and go too far only infrequently. The Queen, be assured, can look after herself.

Columbus at Isabella's court is quickly burdened with the reputation of a crazy man. His clothes are excessively colourful and he drinks, also, to excess. When Isabella wins a military victory she celebrates it with eleven days of psalms and the sonorous severities of priests. Columbus crashes about outside the cathedral waving a wineskin. He is a one-man debauch.

See him, the drunkard, his huge, shaggy head filled with nonsenses! A fool with a glittering eye dreaming of a golden paradise beyond the western edge of things.

'Consummation.'

The Queen plays with Columbus.

At luncheon she promises him everything he wants and cuts him dead later the same afternoon, looking through him as if he were a veil.

On his saint's day she summons him into her inmost boudoir, dismisses her girls, permits him to braid her hair and,

265

for a moment, to fondle her breasts. Then she summons her guards. She banishes him to the stables and piggeries for forty days. He sits forlorn on horse-munched hay while his thoughts run on distant, fabled gold. He dreams of the Queen's perfumes but awakes, gagging, in a pigsty.

Toying with Columbus pleases the Queen.

And pleasing the Queen, he reminds himself, may help him to achieve his purposes. Pigs rootle by his feet. He grits his teeth. 'Pleasing the Queen is good.'

Does she torment him merely for sport?

Or: because he is foreign and she is unused to his ways and meanings.

Or: because her ring finger, still hot with the memory of his lips, his breath, has been – how-you-say? – *touched*. Tentacles of warmth spread backward from her fingers towards her heart. A turbulence has been aroused.

Or: because she is torn between the possibility of embracing his scheme with a lover's abandon, and the more conventional, and differently (maliciously) pleasurable option of destroying him by laughing, finally, after much foreplay, in his foolish supplicant face.

Columbus consoles himself with possibilities. Not all possibilities are consoling, however.

She is an absolute monarch. (Her husband is an absolute zero: a blank, couldn't be colder. We will not speak further of him.) She is a woman whose ring is often kissed. It means nothing to her. She is no stranger to blandishments. She resists them effortlessly. She is a tyrant, who numbers among her possessions a private menagerie of four hundred and nineteen fools, some grotesquely malformed, others as beauteous as the dawn. He, Columbus, is merely her four hundred and twentieth idiot. He is her clown, her performing flea. This, too, is a plausible scenario.

Either: she understands him, his dreams of a world beyond the world's end, so profoundly that she's spooked by it, and she turns first towards it, then away;

Or: she doesn't understand him at all, nor cares to understand.

Take your pick.

What's certain is that *he* doesn't understand *her*. Only the facts are plain. She is Isabella, all-conquering Queen. He is her invisible (though raucous, multicoloured, wine-bibbing) man.

'Consummation.'

The sexual appetites of the male decline; those of the female continue, with the advancing years, to grow. Isabella is Columbus's last hope. He is running out of possible patrons, sales talk, flirtatiousness, hair, steam. Time drags by. Isabella gallops around, winning battles, expelling Moors from strongholds, her appetites expanding by the week. The more of the land she swallows, the more warriors she engulfs, the hungrier she gets. Columbus, aware of a slow shrivelling inside him, scolds himself. He should see things as they are. He should come to his senses. What chance does he have here? Some days she makes him clean latrines. On other days he is on body-washing duty, and after a battle the bodies are not clean. Soldiers going to war wear man-size diapers under their armour because the fear of death will open the bowels, will do it every time. Columbus was not cut out for this sort of work. It is getting him nowhere. He tells himself to leave Isabella, once and for all.

But there are problems: his advancing years, the patron shortage. Once he decamps, he will have to forget the western voyage. The body of philosophical opinion which avers that life is absurd has never appealed to him. He is a man of action, revealing himself by deeds.

But without the possibility of the voyage he will be obliged to accept the meaninglessness of life. This, too, would be a defeat. Invisible in hot tropical colours, unrequited, he remains, dogging her footsteps, hoping for the ecstasy of her glance.

'The search for money and patronage,' Columbus says, 'is not so different from the quest for love.'

SALMAN RUSHDIE

*

*She is omnipotent. Castles fall at her feet. The Jews have been
expelled. The Moors prepare their last surrender. The Queen is at
Granada, riding at her armies' head. She overwhelms. Nothing she
has wanted has ever been refused. All her dreams are prophecies.
Acting upon information received while sleeping, she draws up her
invincible battle plans, foils the conspiracies of assassins, learns of the
infidelities and corruptions for which she blackmails both her loyalists
(to ensure their support) and her opponents (to ensure theirs). The
dreams help her forecast the weather, negotiate treaties, and invest
shrewdly in trade. – She eats like a horse and never gains an ounce.
The earth adores her footfall. Its shadows flee before the brilliance of
her eyes. Her face is a lush peninsula set in a sea of hair. Her treasure
chests are inexhaustible. Her ears are soft question marks, suggesting
some uncertainty. Her legs. – Her legs are not so great.*
   —*She is full of discontents.*
   —*No conquest satisfies her, no peak of ecstasy is high enough.*
   —*See: there at the gates of the Alhambra is Boabdil the Unlucky,
the last Sultan of the last redoubt of all the centuries of Arab Spain.
Behold: now, at this very instant, he surrenders the keys to the citadel
into her grasp: there! – And as the weight of the keys falls from his
hand into hers, she . . . she . . . yawns.*

Columbus gives up hope.
   While Isabella is entering the Alhambra in listless triumph,
he is saddling his mule. While she dawdles in the Court of the
Lions, he departs in a frenzy of whips, elbows, hooves, all
rapidly obscured by a dust cloud. Invisibility claims him. He
surrenders to its will. Knowing he is abandoning his destiny,
he abandons it. He rides away from Queen Isabella in hopeless
fury, rides day and night, and when his mule dies under him he
shoulders his ridiculous Gypsy-patchwork bags, their rowdy
colours muted now by dirt, and walks. Around him stretches
the lush plain her armies have subdued. Columbus sees none
of it, not the land's fertility or the sudden barrenness of the
vanquished castles looking down from their pinnacles. The
ghosts of defeated civilizations flow unnoticed down the rivers
whose names – Guadalthis and Guadalthat – retain an echo of
the annihilated past. Overhead, the arabesque wheelings of the

patient buzzards. Jews pass Columbus in long columns, but the tragedy of their expulsion makes no mark on him. Somebody tries to sell him a Toledo sword; he waves the man away. Having lost his own dreams of ships, Columbus leaves the Jews to the ships of their exile, waiting in the harbour of Cadiz. Exhaustion strips him of his senses. This old world is too old and the new world is an unfound land.

'The loss of money and patronage,' Columbus says, 'is as bitter as unrequited love.'

He walks beyond fatigue, beyond the limits of endurance and the frontiers of self, and somewhere along this path he loses his balance, falls off the edge of his sanity, and out here beyond his mind's rim he sees, for the first and only time in his life, a vision.

It's a dream of a dream. He dreams of Isabella, languidly exploring the Alhambra, the great jewel she has seized from Boabdil, last of the Nasrids. She is staring into a large stone bowl held aloft by stone lions. The bowl is filled with blood, and in it she sees (Columbus dreams her seeing) a vision of her own.

The bowl shows her that everything, all the known world, is now hers; everyone in it is in her hands, to do with as she pleases. And when she understands this (Columbus dreams) the blood at once congeals, becoming a thick and verminous sludge. Whereupon the Isabella of Columbus's weary, but also vengeful, imaginings is shaken to her very marrow by the realisation that she will never, *never*, NEVER! be satisfied by the possession of the known. Only the unknown, perhaps even the unknowable, can satisfy her. And at once she remembers Columbus (he envisions her remembering him), the invisible man who dreams of entering the invisible world, the unknown and perhaps even unknowable world beyond the edge of things, beyond the stone bowl of the everyday, beyond the thick blood of the sea. Columbus in this bitter dream makes Isabella see the truth at last, makes her accept that her need for him is as great as his for her. Yes! She knows it now! She must must must give him the money, the ships, anything, and he must must must carry her flag and her favour beyond the end of the end of the earth, into exaltation and immortality, linking her to him forever with bonds far harder to dissolve than those of any mortal love, the harsh and deifying ties of history.

'Consummation.'

Isabella, in Columbus's savage dream, tears her hair, runs from the Court of the Lions, screams for her heralds. 'Find him,' she commands. But Columbus in his dream refuses to be found. He wraps around himself the dusty patchwork cloak of his invisibility, and the heralds gallop hither and yon in vain. Isabella screeches, beseeches, implores.

Bitch! bitch! How do you like it now? Columbus sneers. By absenting himself from her court, by this final and suicidal invisibility, he has denied her her heart's desire. Serves her right. Bitch! She murdered his hopes, didn't she? Well, then. In doing so she has laid herself low as well. Poetic justice. Fair's fair.

At the dream's end he permits her messengers to find him. Their hoofbeats, their waving frantic arms. They plead, cajole, offer bribes. But it's too late. Only the sweet self-lacerating joy of murdering possibility remains. He answers the heralds: a shake of the head. *No.*

He comes to his senses. He is on his knees in the fertility of the plains, waiting for death. He hears the hoofbeats approaching and raises his eyes, half expecting to see the exterminating angel, riding towards him like a conqueror. Its black wings, the boredom on its face.

Isabella's heralds surround him. They offer him food, drink, a horse.

'Good news!' they shout. 'The Queen has summoned you. Your voyage: wonderful news. She saw a vision, and it scared her.'

All her dreams are prophecies.

'She ran from the Court of the Lions, shouting for you,' the heralds report. 'She will send you beyond the stone bowl of the known world, beyond the thick blood of the sea. She's waiting for you in Santa Fe. You must come at once.'

He stands up, like a requited lover, like a groom on his wedding day. he opens his mouth, and what almost spills out is the bitter refusal: no.

'Yes,' he tells the heralds. *Yes. I'll come.*

Dear George

HELEN SIMPSON

SHE WAS TRYING to write an essay on the various sorts of humour in *As You Like It* at the same time, which didn't help. To her right was a pad of file paper on which she scrawled scathing comments about Shakespeare as they occurred. In front of her was her mother's block of Basildon Bond. She had used four sheets so far.

Dear George, she wrote for the fifth time, and added a curly little comma like a tadpole. She sat back and admired the comma. That was pure luck when it turned out like that. Sometimes if you concentrated on something too hard you ruined it.

She sauntered over to the mirror and stared at herself for a few minutes. 'You gorgeous creature you,' she murmured, sly but sincere, ogling herself from sideways on. A yawn overtook her and she watched her tongue arch like a leaf. Then she performed a floozie's bump and grind back to the Complete Works.

    Jaq: What stature is she of?
    Orl: Just as high as my heart.

George was tall, that was the best thing about him. She

would be higher than his heart, of course, probably about level with his Adam's apple, but that was good enough for her. Already her feet were seven-and-a-halfs, and she was still not yet fifteen.

She turned back to her latest copy of the letter to George. She knew its phrases by heart now, and they were as spontaneous as two hours' effort could make them. 'Stephen Minter asked me to tell you that the Grindley match has been rearranged for the 16th because he thought you were coming back to the Bio Lab, but you didn't. So I thought I'd drop you a line to let you know. He asked me because I had to be there till 5 o'clock on the last day of term, collecting the results from our petri dishes.'

The handwriting was vital, that was what she was trying to perfect as she toiled over copy after copy. There must be nothing round or childish about it. She was dabbling now with italics like barbed wire. Sophistication was what she aimed for. A looped *f* would still creep in if she didn't watch it, or a silly swan-backed *s* .

There was her fat little sister, rattling the doorknob to be let in.

'I won't talk,' came the promises through the keyhole. 'I'll just sit on your bed and watch you.'

'Go away,' she drawled. 'You are banal.'

Silence. She thought of her sister's big baffled sheep's eyes and this made her giggle crossly and feel cruel.

'Banal!' she bellowed. 'Look it up in the dictionary.'

Her sister rushed heftily off downstairs towards the book-case. From another part of the house drifted a weak howl from their mother, who was trying to get the new baby to sleep.

Disgust jerked her out of her seat. How *could* she, at *her* age, it was so *selfish* of her. It was just showing off. As everyone at school had pointed out, she'd probably been trying for a boy this time, so *served her right*.

She would never be able to bring George home. It would be too awful. Her mother would probably try to breastfeed it in front of him. She started to wriggle and giggle in horror.

> Cel: I pray you, bear with me, I cannot go no further.
> Tou: For my part, I had rather bear with you than bear
>   you: yet I should bear no cross if I did bear you, for
>   I think you have no money in your purse.

She picked up her pen and scribbled. 'This is obviously meant to be funny, but it is not. It is rubbish. People only say this is good because it is Shakespeare. It is really boring. It is not even grammar, e.g. I cannot go no further.' The hexagonal plastic shaft of the biro turned noisily in the grip of her front teeth as she paused to read through what she had written. Then she crossed out 'boring' and printed 'banal' in its place.

'Commonplace. Trite. Hackneyed,' came through the keyhole with a lot of heavy breathing; then a pause and, 'What do *they* mean?'

'Go away,' she said. 'Ask mum.'

Served her mother right if she used up all the stamps and Basildon Bond. Spitefully she folded and inserted each of the four early drafts into separate envelopes, sealed them and wrote out George's address four times with self-conscious soppy relish. She had no intention of sending any of them, and stuck on the stamps in a spirit of wicked waste. Later today she would tear them up to show she had style, and send off this perfect fifth version.

She read it through again. It was making her cringe now, she couldn't see it fresh any more. She'd read those phrases so often, she couldn't tell whether they came across as casual or childish or too keen or what.

'I wish I was in 6B with you, all the O-levels out of the way. Hope you have a good holiday. If you would possibly feel like meeting for any reason, I am fairly free this holiday. Maybe hear from you soon. Ciao.'

Was ciao too trendy? She hadn't thought it was till this moment. She couldn't put Yours sincerely, and shook at the thought of Love. Cheers was what the boys in 6B said to each other, but she wouldn't stoop that low.

Dear George, she scribbled again, this time on a naughty impulse and a sheet of scrap paper, I don't know if I could stand to go out with you if Every Time We Said Goodbye you said Chiz instead. Why do you do it? It makes you all sound really thick. Chiz chiz chiz chiz chiz. Try Ciao, it's more stylish – it's Italian in case you didn't know and it means the same as chiz – you look a bit Italian which is partly why I fancy you.

The mournfulness of his image caught her, stopped her ticking for a second or two as a cameo of large, meaty nobility filled her mind's eye.

She reread what she had written, then, sniggering, clattering her teeth together in enamelled applause, dipping her head down so that her hair piled up on one side of the paper in a foresty rustle, she scrawled, 'You can't be *that* thick. Anyone can have bad luck in O-levels, ha ha, though two retakes in history is a bit much.'

Cupping her chin on the half shell of her hands, she made her mouth into a kissing shape. With the tip of her tongue she tenderly tapped inside each of the teeth in her upper jaw.

'I would like to feel your hands on the back of my waist (25″), with the thumbs round my sides,' she scrawled, chewing invisible gum, 'but only if they aren't sweaty. If you have wet hands it's all over before it's started, sorry Gorgeous George but that's the way I am.'

Holding her hands up in front of her, using them like boned fans to block the light, she spotted an incipient hangnail poking up from the cuticle of her left thumb and fell on it like a falcon, tearing at it with famished energy. When she had made it bleed she lost interest and stared out of the window.

There on the back lawn her gallumphing little sister was helping their mother hang out baby vests and babygros and other baby rubbish in the sun. Her mother had it strapped to her front in a hideous pink nylon sling.

'No style,' she muttered, curling her lip. She pulled the curtains on them and made a warm gloom.

Once the candle was lit and positioned on her homework table, she was able to ignore the worst aspects of her room, like the brainlessly 'cheerful' duvet cover with its sun, moon and poppy field. Her face's reflection was a blanched heart in the mirror on the back wall. When she came home on the last train she saw her reflection in the window like that, pale and pointed, looking sideways, fleering at the bugle eyes which were so very blot-like and black above cream-coloured cheeks. She had a vision of George coming up to her as she sat illegally alone in her accustomed first class carriage, and saw his difficult smile.

Hugging herself as she rocked to and fro on the folding chair, adjusting her balance as it threatened to jack-knife her thighs to stomach in its fold-up maw, her hands became George's, firm and pressing around her waist. She stood up. Now one crept forward and undid the buttons of her shirt, stroked her neck down past the collar bone. Catching sight of herself in the mirror tweaking her own breast, the silly lost expression left her face instantly.

She reached across for Shakespeare and flicked through until she came to her latest discovery in *Antony and Cleopatra*. Holding her left hand palm out to her reflection, she touched wrist to wrist in the chill glass and murmured,

> There is gold and here
> My bluest veins to kiss, a hand that kings
> Have lipped, and trembled kissing.

This produced a reluctant simper and a slow shudder which wriggled through from head to foot finishing with a sigh. After a minute she tried it again but this time it did not work.

Lifting her knees and pointing her toes like a cartoon of stealth, she fell back onto her *As You Like It* essay with an angry groan.

> It was a lover and his lass,
> With a hey, and a ho, and a hey nonino
> That o're the green corn field did pass
> In the spring time, the only pretty ring time
> When birds do sing, hey ding a ding ding.

'Anybody could write this sort of stuff,' she wrote. 'If Madonna put it in one of her lyrics, English teachers everywhere would say, how moronic.' Then she dashed off an inspired demolition job on Touchstone before losing her drift.

Flicking through the rice-paper leaves, she came to another juicy bit.

> Des: O, banish me, my lord, but kill me not!
> Oth: Down, strumpet!
> Des: Kill me tomorrow; let me live tonight!
> Oth: Nay, if you strive—

There was George, big George, looming like a tower in the half-dark, and herself in a white nightdress with pintucks from shoulder seam to waist, quite plain, no lace, his hot hands round her neck . . . She inhaled slowly and closed her eyes; leaned forward and pressed a bit against her windpipe with her thumbs; blushingly smirked; then felt a chill tinge of shame, a prickling under her arms like cactus hairs, and busily started to biro a blue swallow on the inside of her elbow.

Tattoos only lasted when the ink got into your bloodstream.

Maybe she would get her ears pierced this afternoon at Shangri La, she thought, though that was supposed to hurt a lot too, there was no anaesthetic, they just shot a spike through the lobe with a little gun like a paper-punch.

She sniggered as she remembered something rude. According to Valerie Mitchell from 6B, who was a Saturday girl at Shangri La and who was doing Louis XIV for a special project, the Sun King's bed was heaped with pillows stuffed with his mistresses' hair. 'And not with the hair from their *heads*,' Valerie had leered.

Now she described this conversation to George in her make-believe letter, and even enclosed a clipping to launch his collection. When it came to signing off this time, she added fifty smacking Xs. She then spat on the paper before smearing it with her fist. Across the envelope's seal she wrote SWALK in lipstick and from the Queen's mouth on the stamp she drew a balloon saying, 'Who's a pretty boy then.'

'*Please* come and play,' whined her sister from the other side of the door. 'You've been up here for ages now and I don't believe you're just doing revision.'

'Go away,' she said.

'We could go roller skating,' said her sister.

'Mum won't let me go out till I've done the washing up,' she said, 'and I'm refusing on moral grounds since it's not my turn, so I *can't* go out.'

Once her sister had gone stump-stump-stumping off down stairs, she crept along the landing, pausing to stare and bite her thumb at the rumpled bedroom shared by her mother and step-father. Then, when she was safely locked in the bath-room, she transferred all the plastic ducklings, sailors, mechanically spouting whales and dinghies from the bath to the lavatory and closed the lid on them.

During the chin-high soak which followed, she lay poach-ing in water so hot that a clear Plimsoll line appeared on her skin, all fiery lobster-coloured flesh below the water's surface while above stayed white and sweat-pearled. The little bathroom was dense with steam, the wallpaper's paisley invisible and the gloss-painted ceiling lustrous with moisture. She closed her eyes and saw George opening her letter, his crooked smile, his reaching for the telephone. They talked with sophisticated ease, and soon they were sharing a fondue down at the Mousetrap.

There was silence except for the rustle from the boa of weightless scented bubbles sitting on her shoulders. It came into her mind that it would be much more natural to give him a ring straight off, and she decided not to send the letter after all.

When at last she tottered back, lurid and wrinkled and dizzy, her sister was sitting on the bed.

'You've *got* to play with me now,' said her sister. 'I've done all your washing up and mum says you're horrible but you can go out on condition you take me roller skating.'

'Shift up,' she croaked, collapsing onto the bed, clutching at disappearing shreds of George as the towels came adrift all round her.

'So you *will* come when you're dry,' said her sister, gnatlike. 'I've got your skates out. I've tidied your room, see, so mum won't go on about that either. There's no excuse. I even went down the road to post your letters.'

'Letters,' she said stupidly, still stunned by the equatorial bath, before it dawned on her.

My Father's War

KEN SMITH

WHAT I'M AFTER is moments long: the cobbles of a farmyard in the north of England, somewhere on the Plain of York, the latter part of 1943, September perhaps. It is a large swept square, sheltered on all four sides by a farmhouse, the tied cottage where we lived, barns, sheds, a gateway from the road at one corner, at its diagonal another into the paddock, wherein cows, old bathtub water-trough, pond with hollow willow tree, more trees, and with increasing vagueness: village, school, fields, more farms, woods, towns, the world, which is at war with itself. The weather intermittent, balmy, the square sunlit, still, to one side a few sacks, a ladder, a rake, a roller, long afternoon shadows of eaves and chimneys across all, an overhanging apple tree. The buildings are brick and ivy covered, the farmhouse yellow painted with a lurid green trim, cheap government stock, black market or plain pinched. The air is hot, dusty, still, the farm inactive now the harvest's in, and this perhaps the first day's rest for everyone around the yard. Perhaps it is Sunday. Perhaps it is a holiday, though there is no sense of celebration. People gather in small groups, some aloof from each other, the farmhands smoking or dozing in the late sunlight, the Italian POWs lurking in the barn's shadow, playing cards for matchsticks. Most of the sounds are birds: crows in the high woods above the house, pigeons, swifts. In the square's centre, more or less, a hand pump above a well, a stone horse-trough and to one side three or four stone steps leading nowhere forming a mounting block. It is a farm worked by men and horses, its layout around the foldyard the old style of a Roman villa, a Danes' enclosure. From its ambience it is not yet milking time in a late summer season: the shadows lengthening, the guests departing. Perhaps it is around five.

With hindsight I can date the scene; from my memory of the season and from the evidence of history it is sometime after September 8th, when the Allies had announced their armistice with Marshal Badoglio at Cassibile, in Sicily, concluded seven days earlier. Thereafter the Italians were no longer prisoners, and slept in the barn. With hindsight it is an updated Brueghel, but that has nothing to do with the moment as it was, is. What I'm after was then, before memory and the outcome of history: a long hot summer with wind in the trees, and the war going on, and memory fading backwards into images of battle, black and white newsreels beginning with patriotic music and a cock's crow and a brisk voice describing the war in the deserts and on land and at sea and in the air.

The farmyard is in full colour: the grey cobbles and dust of the yard, the paintwork, green of grass and ivy and moss, old red and mauve of brick and tile, clear blue of the sky, with clouds. What I want is the quality of the light around events that day of rare rural idleness, but I am already beginning to supplement memory with invention; what was is one thing, and all but irrecoverable; what I remember is another scenario, and both are separate from each other as each is from what I want, now, to make of this memory, that can only turn into the sad falsehood of a story. In reality the mounting block stands further from the pump. In truth there may have been no apple tree, no rake, no roller, yet though the ladder is an imaginary ladder it is leaning on a real barn, and casts a real shadow. I'd like to think a radio played music through an open window, though I suspect the interlude passed without accompaniment. There is, perhaps, the dog sleeping in the shadow of the porch, there are perhaps chickens and farm cats.

So much that we recall is touched by what has happened since, and already, by calling it a moment, I have opened the space in which to make a fiction, when all I wanted was to remember it as I saw it, then.

In any case the impression of stillness is false, for there are people moving, lazily as befits the hour and the season. In my mind's eye I guess there are some twenty or so around the square, in various postures between talking and silence: about a dozen of them are Italians along the length of the barn's side, the English round their doorways. Out in the centre of the yard, the focus of all our attentions, is my father. By the horse-trough with his homemade bomb he is lighting matches that go out in the slightest breeze, and he is beginning to mutter to himself, knowing everyone is watching. And my mother is beginning to run towards him across the cobble-stones, bearing before her a white enamel bowl.

And that's as close as I can get to the moment I am hunting: a brief sharp sudden explosion, together with the moments leading to it and the long moments of time frozen that followed it. For the sake of that moment I must fix it with the continuity of all other moments, and I am obliged therefore to account for it, to fix it with time before and time since, to account for those present in the square. I am obliged at last to tell a story.

My father's war it will be called, wherein I'll circle the event, threading through the central instant of his bomb's going off, the sundry tales having little else to do with each other, these people who are variously together and variously apart. In their own small corner the farm manager and his wife and baby stand grouped to one side, aloof, superior, there to keep an eye on things. Away from them along the back porch of our next door house lean and sit several neighbours, visitors and farm hands, lads too young yet for the army, my friend Jake and Jake's mother and Jake's mother's friend and me, and the Italians. And in the middle of the square my father crouched by the pump cursing the matches and my mother who is calling him *a bloody fool*. Perhaps no one believes my father can make anything that works let alone a bomb, so no one seems inclined to take shelter though everyone, in various degrees, cringes. The Italians who have been in war are wary and make no effort at courage, and the English who have not seen action except on the newsreels are superficially brave. All eyes are on my father.

My father, who has made a bomb, hates the manager, who is what my father calls *a suckhole*. The manager has sacked him. That's how I know the season: the harvest's in, and we can leave, again. Therefore he has made a bomb, an act of defiance, a gesture of the powerless, I realise, with hindsight. All morning he has been in the outhouse dismantling shotgun cartridges, assembling powder and shot and fuse in a heavy glass ink bottle, packing and wadding. He wore a black determined look about his face, of anger; my father's anger was manic, famous, sometimes suicidal, always bleak and unpredictable, rendering him unstoppable. He was making a bomb. As ever he did not say why or how, or seek assistance or encourage anyone to join him as he worked, and I fancy that through the morning several attempts had been made to discover what he intended, and to deter him. If so, they had all failed.

For my father has fallen out with the farm manager, the suckhole, and has been sacked again, and will have to move on again, and the real reason again is because the harvest is over again, and with all these Italians living in the barn indefinitely the manager figures he can do without help he has to hire. It's very simple. The Italians, though no longer enemy prisoners, can't go home yet, as Italy itself is in dispute and at war, and so they must stay here, and work, cheap. *They don't work, they lark about*, I hear the manager say to his wife, off to one side. He'd prefer Germans, who have not yet been set to work: more disciplined, hard working, less trouble. As to the manager he has a wife and a young baby, and in my memory their house stinks of baby shit and milk, the mother is big and floppy, and throws the dirty nappies into the corner, behind the couch, I think anywhere, until he gets someone, usually my mother the hired hand's missus, to wash them. I think the wife was always eating cakes and sweets. With hindsight, I think she was having a breakdown, post-partum blues. Naturally I stayed away from her. And babies. I was five, almost six, and knew nothing of what frightened me in her. I had my friend Jake.

Jake was my mate, and lived with us as an evacuee, his parents away in the war. With Jake there was the farm with all its attics and rafters to explore, the orchard to raid, eggs to pinch, expeditions to the river and outward into the district, and the mysteries of the Italians. Though their status had changed little else had changed for them, but they now stayed on the farm instead of going back each night to a camp. They were trusted, which is to say they weren't. They dressed still in brown uniforms from which the distinguishing patches had been removed, leaving circles of a darker shade to distinguish them. They were still farm hands, longing to go home, and always hungry. That they sometimes sang we knew, that they quarrelled and sometimes laughed, and certainly they wept, for we had seen Paolo weep bitter angry tears one day as we watched him in the washhouse with the pliers crack and eat his way through the kernels of a great pile of plum stones, the leavings of my mother's jam making. We had laughed at him. We didn't know why, but he wept for his hunger and poverty and our contempt for it; he wept for the plums of his own country, and for its grapes and olives and cherries, and he wept for the scraps he was afforded in ours. As unthinkingly Jake and I set the great willow in the back field alight one late afternoon, coming home at twilight to find the whole village scrambling to put the fire out before the last of the Luftwaffe came over, everyone forming a chain of bucket passers from the pump to the burning tree. We hid for a long time, Jake and I, advertising our guilt by our absence.

We betrayed every secret of our parents, I repeating all mine said of his. His mother visited him most weekends. She was in the Land Army, working elsewhere on the plain, *Driffield way*. His dad was in the Army, overseas, for a long time, *in the desert*. His mother would turn up on a Sunday in the company of a flash fellow, her 'friend' – it was as if this was always said in quotation marks – who drove her over in his motoring car, and smoked little cigars, clutching his little trilby hat on his knee, impatient to be off. He'd drop her off and go elsewhere for the day while she visited. Later Flash would come to drive her back, sitting to take a cup of tea, not taking off his raincoat, conveying he was better than the rest of us. He was a businessman, who hired out the threshing machines that came at harvest, and was not described as anybody's uncle or anyone's brother and had, I suspect, no name.

So there he stands in the yard in his raincoat and his brown hat, ready for off, to one side fiddling with his car keys. And there's Jake and his mum getting ready to say goodbye, and waiting just to see. There's the Italians along the shady side, and some giggling among the onlookers, the manager and his wife and their baby, and there's my father lighting his fuse, and there's my mother, beginning her charge with the enamel bowl. Because everyone is looking at him, she burst on the scene from nowhere.

And then the fuse takes, and everyone tenses. In this moment that stops and resumes the flow of all moments everything happens at once, and everyone ducks. The fuse flares into rapid life, he begins turning to run as at the same moment she reaches him with the bowl. In one motion she scoops water from the trough to douse the fuse, yelling at him for a lunatic, only – scrunching up her face against the explosion – she misses it and catches him with the bowl across the head, and soaks him with the water. Colliding, they collapse into a tangle of arms and legs and fury. I think she cut him, and I think he bled. Then he's yelling at her, moving as if to hit her but the bomb goes off with a great crack and a roar of flame skyward, the bowl skidding over the stones, and everyone down on their knees.

And then silence: the taken for granted cawing of crows and pigeons and all the other birds suddenly hushed. Here the world stops for a long moment, wherein I now suppose everyone checks themselves for injuries, and my parents cease yelling at each other. And then, after what seems a very long time down from the blue Sunday sky a pigeon, pierced through the gizzard by the old man's shot, dead on the farmyard cobbles, its chest stained by fresh blood. Everyone agreed it was difficult to account for the long slur in time between the shot and the bird's fall, as if for the longest duration we all and the falling bird were suspended in aftershock.

And then the world resumes its flow, the dogs their barking, my parents their quarrel, the Italians move rapidly to the cool of the barn, the manager and his wife to their parlour, Jake's mum with Flash in his car, other visitors leaving as the row between my parents gets into its stride, and Jack and I clear off. Someone is no doubt already plucking the pigeon. The square is deserted. On the stones by the pump a patch of fresh blood marks where the bird fell.

Waltz Time

JONATHAN TREITEL

OH, THE *Donaudampfschiffahrtsgesellschaftsball*! What a glittering whirl that had been – a whole steamship erected in the ballroom, complete with real water, hanky-panky in the lifeboats, and a waltz orchestra rotating on the giant paddles – according to Mitzi, anyway, whose kind husband hadn't thought twice about escorting her, not to mention forking out for the ticket, unlike her own who had said, 'Pfuh! That kind of claptrap isn't fit for a bunch of boulevardiers,' and had gone out drinking and eating sausages with his tiresome cronies, leaving her at home in her boudoir reading Heine: a funny poem about a man giving pea soup to his darling and a sad one ending 'When we love we die.' Or the Bakers' Ball: quite a spree, too (said Mitzi) – real countesses dressed as croissants and seeded rye, mingling with sweaty bakery assistants. Or the Undertakers' Ball, with actual coffins. But now the pre-Lent season was almost over, and the only ball she'd managed to persuade her husband to attend was the one for members of the Lars Porsena Club, the exclusive thingummy he'd joined at his military college – a much staider affair.

Which they are at now. She is leaning against an anteroom wall, by the small square window that casts such an interesting light on her face – she presumes – next to the neoclassical urn filled with gladioli (? daffodils? asters? she was never much good at telling flowers apart), which will quite possibly induce her hay fever again. She sniffs, relishing the self-pity. And as for her husband (whom she still thinks of by his surname, Bedl, for all that they've been married five years) and Mitzi's husband, Dratfisch, and their little chum, Glibli . . . The three grown men are shuffling in a clump on the Persian carpet, swapping schoolboy jokes, addressing each other by the secret Club names (her husband is Brutus, Dratfisch is Hannibal, Glibli Caligula), simply refusing to dance, and, what's more, completely upstaging her own subtle lavender-and-mauve silk creation, which is actually quite fetching – though she did have to get the seamstress to add a little hip padding; it's shocking how thin she's getting these days, practically gaunt, not at all the chubby girl she was on her wedding day – in comparison to their sky-blue Hussar's uniforms and jangling spurs. She eyes them malevolently: willing Glibli to choke on his vast moustache and Dratfisch to trip over his big boots and her own husband to turn and look at her and sense her desires. When Bedl had first courted her, he'd been – well, not exactly dashing but at least an interesting sort of captain, and now he's turned into a colonel, as they do; they all do. What's the collective noun for colonels? A weariness of colonels. A boredom of colonels. An irrelevance of colonels.

Sometimes she thinks she should get a lover. Mitzi recommends this course: all the classier ladies have one, she maintains, and husbands are really quite pleased not to have to bother with that side of things, though they may posture for a while, claiming otherwise, and go red in the face. Mitzi's own husband, Dratfisch, is by now reconciled to her unfaithfulness, says Mitzi. It's funny, mind you: Mitzi had gone on and on about the handsomeness and virility of her lover, and then he'd turned out to be this quite sweet but very timid medical student with a brown moustache. No, if she herself were ever going to take a lover – and she said *if* – he would have to be some fabulous epitome of manhood who would literally sweep her off her feet.

Now the conversation of the colonels is drifting across to

her. (Either they're talking louder or the music is quieter.) They're discussing – wouldn't you just believe it? . . . during a ball . . . *men!* – politics. 'Macedonia,' says Bedl. 'Mark my words, Macedonia will be the flash point.' 'Bulgaria has designs on it,' says Glibli. 'If Serbia invades Macedonia, Caligula,' says Dratfisch. 'And Greece will be drawn into the conflict, Hannibal,' says Bedl. 'And the Turks won't stand idly by, Brutus,' says Dratfisch. Then Glibli shouts, 'Don't forget Bulgaria!' He yells, 'Bulgaria!' a few more times, guffawing as if it were the best joke in the world.

Then they tell real jokes – the usual ones. For example, they refer to the Emperor – who is officially designated as Royal and Imperial, which is abbreviated to *Ka & Ka*, which is reduced to a childish swearword. Which is shrieked by Glibli: the colonels smack their thighs and wobble with laughter till their spurs shake like tambourines, though they must have heard this pun a thousand times before. Then Dratfisch tells an anecdote about a lady – a duchess – suffering from syphilis, whose treatment consists of swallowing liquid mercury. 'So there she is at the ball, waltzing to the music, tra la la, la la, la la, la la, when her partner, the Emperor, he says to her, he says – ' Dratfisch bursts into choking belly laughs, unable to speak. Bedl bangs him on the back until he continues. '. . . He says, "I say, Madam, you've just dropped your – "' See, what happens, the mercury goes right through the system and comes out at the other end – "I say, Madam, your pearls are on the floor!" And the Emperor bends down on hands and knees and tries to scoop them up!'

Then the colonels almost topple with laughter and lean on each other for mutual support, blurting the secret names. 'Brutus!' 'Hannibal!' 'Caligula!'

She shuts her eyes. The smell seems to intensify: the flowers, and her own perfume, Nuit de Marienbad, and the floor polish, and the odour of champagne. And the music, too: a desperate, driving waltz rhythm; even her breath, even her heartbeat, is coming in six-eight time. How can anyone resist the desire to dance?

And she is being tapped on the shoulder. Her husband's voice is saying, 'Want to dance, eh?'

She opens her eyes. Her husband, her Bedl: a colonel in an absurd dress uniform like something out of an operetta, with his fluffy, greying side-whiskers and his damp lips. No, she can't bear to dance with him. She pats her hip, her belly, her pearl necklace, her forehead. 'Not tonight dear. I have a . . . you know, "headache".'

He grunts. 'Ah, yes. Woman's problem. Yes.'

He backs away cautiously, in the direction of his chums, scared by the mystery of female physiology. He seems relieved to have been excused from his obligation to dance with her, after all.

And her explanation is not altogether untrue, she realises. Her curse will start any day now. She can practically feel the thick blood battering its way out.

And, oh look, there's Mitzi, waving her fan at her. She doesn't really want to chatter with Mitzi – there's only so much one can say concerning the charms of Mitzi's real lover and her own hypothetical ones – but there's no getting out of it. Mitzi is approaching with a big man on her arm.

Mitzi kisses her effusively on both cheeks and introduces the new man, a Prussian major with a sabre scar on his cheek, who tightens his gloved hands into fists and doesn't say anything. He clicks his heels and bows.

Mitzi says, 'Oh, I know you two will have so much in common.'

Well, what is she to say to him? She tries 'Are you fond of balls?' He grunts, 'Hmf.' She says, 'Are there many grand balls in Prussia?' 'Hmf.' 'They say Bismarck is very light on his feet?' 'Hmf.' Meanwhile, they have been walking into the ballroom proper. The polished floorboards and the chandelier and the medals on the gentlemen and the orchestral instruments blaze.

And there he is!

He is a man, a civilian, in immaculate black dress clothes. His hair is rather long and swept back. His huge eyes shine. He is at the far side of the dance floor, striding directly towards them.

Suddenly Mitzi becomes flustered. The Prussian

disappears. All around this fabulous gentleman, dancers are sidling away, creating a vacuum about him, as if his very presence produced an unearthly radiation that pushes away mere mortals.

Without saying a word, he walks straight up to her and takes her by the arm.

Mitzi fiddles nervously with her fan. 'Er, this is my cousin.' For a second, she wonders if 'cousin' is a euphemism, and Mitzi has been saving up this glory for herself – but surely not, for Mitzi would hardly have kept it a secret. 'Your cousin,' she says. 'But why haven't you introduced him before?' Mitzi backs away. 'I'll, er, leave you two together. I, er, must . . .'

This is not the first time in her life she has encountered the perfect man. Once, in high summer, boating along the Danube, she glimpsed, in passing, a back view of a man on the bank. She had to bite her tongue to stop herself crying out. Then the boat drifted downstream, and the man passed from her vision. Another time, midwinter, stepping down from her carriage near the cathedral, she saw footprints on the snow – the even marks of high-quality summer shoes. She had followed the tracks for half a kilometre . . . and then the footprints had vanished: the man had climbed into a carriage, perhaps, or ascended into the heavens. But now the perfect man stands before her, in the flesh.

He gazes directly into her eyes. And she into his. His irises are a bright green, flecked with amber – beautiful! 'I know what you are thinking,' he says in a clear, breathy voice. 'I can see inside your mind.' She says, 'Yes. You are right.' 'My name is Rudolf,' he says. 'What is your name?' Imagine addressing a man by his forename on the first meeting! Imagine him addressing you by yours! She tells him all her names. He says, 'Do you like waltz music?' 'Yes! I adore it.' 'I have a Pianola in my head, so I can play any tune you want. What is your favourite?' She laughs; then he, looking slightly puzzled, laughs. 'The "Blue Danube", please, Rudolf.' He sings the melody quite badly, clashing with the music being played by the orchestra. Then he laughs more, and she laughs. He says, 'My teeth are black and white, and they go up and down when I play.' 'Yes, yes, how droll.' 'Sometimes my Pianola plays voices too – the anarchists did it.' 'I don't understand, Rudolf.' She has a sense of vertigo, as if the polished dance floor were slipping away from underneath her. She hangs on to his arm tighter. She tries to clear things up. 'What anarchists? Is this a private joke?' He whispers, 'The anarchists put a bomb in my head and I may blow up at any time!' He cackles with laughter. And then he pats her cheek gently, like a father soothing a crying child. 'But don't worry, my darling, I won't let it explode you; I will make sure nothing harms you, ever. . . . Shall we dance?'

Now she realises that this perfect man is mad – nothing more or less. He must have been let out of some asylum for a few hours, to take part in the ball. Everybody else must have realised this instantly, everybody except her. How she hates her own delusions; she wants the dance floor to open wide and swallow her up. And yet . . . Certainly she is a fool, a dreamer, but damn it if she is going to miss the chance to dance, once in her life, with the perfect man.

The two of them step out onto the floor. Now the orchestra plays the 'Blue Danube'. They glide to and fro in an easy waltz. He is indeed a splendid dancer: she feels she is stepping over clouds. All around them other couples swerve aside. She notices the shocked faces of soldiers and ladies; a duchess twists her head to avoid viewing the spectacle. Her husband and his chums are in the doorway, staring. Then the man begins to slip and slide, as if on board a ship in the middle of a storm – a sinking ship. He stamps nearer to the orchestra, then farther. He pushes her against other couples, he clutches her tightly against himself. He has her rampage with him in a huge swirling motion – she glimpses other couples panicking and dashing aside. Still the music plays on. Everybody else leaves the dance floor. She couldn't escape even if she wanted to: his grip is iron. She realises she is laughing and sobbing in a kind of absurd joy as the two of them – she and the perfect man – waltz their mad waltz across the polished floor of a ballroom on the first floor of a palace in the middle of a city at the heart of an empire in the spring of that year.

Old Flame

WILLIAM TREVOR

'GRACE DIED.'

As Zoë replaces the lid of the electric kettle – having steamed the envelope open – her eye is caught by that stark statement. As she unfolds the plain white writing paper, another random remark registers before she begins to read from the beginning: 'We never quarrelled not once that I remember.'

The spidery scrawl, that economy with punctuation, were once drooled over by her husband, and to this day are not received in any ordinary manner, as a newspaper bill is, or a rates demand. Because of the sexual passion once there, the scrawl connects with Charles' own neat script – two parts of a conjunction in which letters have played an emotional role. Being given to promptness in such matters, Charles will at once compose a reply, considerate of an old flame's due. Zoë feared this correspondence once, and hated it. 'As ever my love, Audrey': in all the years of the relationship the final words have been the same.

As always, she'll have to reseal the envelope, because the adhesive on the flap has lost its efficacy. Much easier all that is nowadays, with convenient sticks of Pritt or Uhu. Once, at the height of the affair, she'd got glue all over the letter itself.

Zoë, now seventy-one, is a small, slender woman, only a little bent. Her straight hair, once jet black, is almost white. What she herself thinks of as a letter-box mouth caused her, earlier in her life, to be designated attractive rather than beautiful. 'Wild', she was called as a girl, and 'unpredictable', both terms relating to her temperament. No one has ever called her pretty, and no one would call her wild or unpredictable now.

Because it's early in the day, she is still in her dressing gown – a pattern of dragons in blue-and-scarlet silk. It hugs her slight body, crossed over on itself in front, tied with a matching sash. When her husband appears he, too, will still be in his dressing gown – comfortably woollen, Teddy-bear brown stitched with braid. 'Dearest, dearest Charles,' the letter begins. Zoë reads all of it again.

This letter is special, of course, because of Grace's death. Others have been different. 'Grace and I wondered how you are getting along these days. . .' 'Grace and I have finally taken retirement. . .' 'I'm to give you this address Grace says. Just in case you ever want to write. . . .' 'A seaside house. Grace always wanted that. . .' In 1985, in 1978 and '73 and '69, Grace always had a kind of say. 'A quick lunch sometime?' each letter – this one, too – suggests before the 'As ever my love' and the single cross that's a reminder of their kissing. Somehow, Zoë has always believed, the quick-lunch suggestion came from Grace. Did she, Zoë wonders, make it again on her deathbed?

The affair had developed an extra sense in Zoë. Without making an effort, she can visualise a tall woman she has never met, now the lone occupant of a house she has never entered. She sees her smartly dressed in shades of maroon, her iron-grey hair fashionably arranged, the clarity of her eyes a little clouded. Creases have multiplied on the skin of her face and have become a map of wrinkles now. Zoë imagines her entering her kitchen and turning on the radio, to hear the same news she herself heard earlier: football fans on the rampage in a German city, shop-windows smashed, a bus turned on its side. She imagines her standing with a cup of Nescafé in the bow window of her sitting room: seen through drizzle on a pane, the sea is a pattern of undulations, greyish green, scuffed with white. The sky that meets it on the far horizon is too dull to contemplate. A single mackerel trawler slips into view.

'If it's inconvenient or if you'd rather not well of course I understand. . . .'

The Alp Horn is where they lunch, have done so since 1951. Her inquisitiveness getting the better of her, Zoë went there once. She actually went inside, giving a name she had made up, of someone she was to meet there. A musical instrument, presumably an alp-horn, stretched the length of a wall; Tyrolean landscapes decorated two others. There were checked tablecloths, blue and red; recorded music played; the place was modest. 'I'm awfully sorry,' Zoë said to a waiter – half a lifetime ago, it seems like, because in fact it is. 'Clearly there's been a muddle.'

She finds the Pritt where Charles keeps it – in the middle drawer of the dresser, with his writing things and sealing wax, Sellotape, and scissors. She boils the water in the kettle again, for coffee. She hears his footstep above her, crossing the landing from their bedroom to the lavatory, crossing it again to the bathroom. Pipes rattle when he turns on the hot water, because he has never learned not to turn the tap all the way in order to prevent its gushing so. All the years she has known him he has been impatient about things like that.

'It's time you saw Charles again,' Zoë knows Grace used to say in that house, and guesses Audrey's reply: that Charles has his own life now, that Charles made his choice. Grace always pressed, gently, because she loved Charles too, but had to keep it to herself. 'My dear, I'm certain Charles would welcome a sign.' Anything could have happened; they'd never know.

Forty years have passed since the year of the great passion: 1951. Charles and Audrey and Grace had met in that colourless time of disaffected lives and utility clothes, when nobody was having much fun except the remaining spivs. Audrey and Grace had been in the A.T.S. during the war, together all the time. When Charles arrived on the scene they were back in office life, both of them determined to use their secretarial posts as stepping stones to something better. The day Charles appeared – the first time they laid eyes on him – he was being led around by the snooty, half-drunk Miss Maybury, both of them with glasses of *vin rosé*, which was what La Maybury – her office title – drank every afternoon, sometimes in the mornings also. 'Hullo,' Charles said, a lanky young man with floppy fair hair. It wasn't difficult for Zoë to imagine the shy smile he'd darted at Audrey and then at Grace. Afterwards he'd told her about La Maybury and the wine and the tour round the office.

'Poor Charles' he would have become in after years. Poor Charles alone with his unloved, unloving wife. What was the point of any of it, now that his children were grown up? In their seaside house Audrey and Grace would have lived in hope – that one day he would sound less whispery on the telephone, passing on details of death by misadventure or disease. 'Given six months, a merciful release.' Or: 'Just slipped. A wretched plastic bag. In the rain, near the dustbins.'

Zoë places two slices of bread in the toaster but does not press the lever down, because it isn't time to yet. Before the affair got going it had been a subject of fascination to him that two such apparently close friends should, in appearance at least, be so vastly different. 'Oh, that's often so,' Zoë said, citing examples from her school-days, but he had never shown much interest in her school-days and he didn't then. 'Grace, the lumpy one's called,' he said. 'Back of a bus. Audrey's the stunner.' Old-fashioned names, she had thought, and imagined old-fashioned girls, frumpish in spite of Audrey's looks. Later, he'd always included Grace in his references to Audrey, clouding the surface because of the depths beneath.

Zoë measures coffee into the blue Denby pot, the last piece of a set. There was a photograph she found once: Audrey as handsome as he'd claimed, a goddesslike creature with a cigarette. Grace blurred, as if she'd moved. They were sprawled on a rug beside the tablecloth from which a picnic had been eaten. You could see part of the back wheel of a car, and it wasn't difficult to sharpen into focus Grace's frizzy hair, two pink-rimmed eyes behind her spectacles. Where on earth had that picnic been? What opportunity had been seized – a slack afternoon in the office?

Zoë props the letter against his cup, doing so with deliberation. It will vex him that she has arranged it so, the gesture attaching a comment of her own; but then she has been vexed herself. She tore that photograph into little pieces and watched them burn. He never mentioned its loss, as naturally he wouldn't.

'Ah, good,' she greets him, and watches while he picks up the letter. She depresses the lever of the toaster. The milk saucepan rattles on the gas, a glass disk bouncing about in it to prevent the milk from boiling over. She pours their coffee. He returns the letter to its envelope. She halves each piece of toast diagonally, the way he likes it.

She hadn't guessed. It was a frightening, numbing shock when he said, 'Look, I have to tell you. Audrey and I have fallen in love.' Just for a moment she couldn't think who Audrey was. 'Audrey and I,' he repeated, thinking she hadn't properly heard. 'Audrey and I love one another.' For what remained of that year and for several years following it, Zoë felt physically sick every time that statement echoed, coming back to her from its own Sunday morning: 9th September, 1951, eleven o'clock. He had chosen the time because they'd have all day to go into things, yet apart from practicalities there was nothing to go into. You couldn't much go into the fact that he wanted someone else more than he wanted her. After five years of marriage he was tired of her. He had spoken in order to be rid of her.

Finishing with the marmalade, she moves it closer to him. His face, less expert at disguise than once it was, hides nothing. She watches him thinking about the woman who has been left on her own, his sympathy reaching into a seaside house that's now too spacious for one. But Charles is not an imaginative man. He doesn't penetrate far. He doesn't see in the old flame's fridge a chicken joint for one, and fish for one tomorrow. Winter's a melancholy time to be bereaved, a mood reflected in the cold and wet, winds rattling and whining. Audrey'll miss her friend particularly when it comes to watching television, no one beside her to share a comment with.

'Oh, yes, the Alp Horn's still there,' Zoë hears, a little later that morning, having eased open a door he has carefully closed. 'Twelve-forty-five, should we say? If your train's a little late, anything like that, please don't worry. I'll simply wait, my dear.'

Before that, he'd been saying something she hadn't managed to hear, his voice unnaturally low, a hand cupped round the mouthpiece. Then there'd been the hint of a reprimand because the old flame hadn't written sooner. Had he known he'd have gone to the funeral.

'I'm sorry to have hurt you so,' he said later that Sunday, but words, by then, made no sense whatsoever. Five years of a mistake, she thought, two children mistakenly born. Her tears dripped onto her clothes while he stood there crestfallen, his good looks distorted by distress. She did not blow her nose; she wanted to look as she felt. 'You would like me dead,' she sobbed, willing him to raise his fist in fury at her, to crash it down on her, obliterating in mercy all that remained of her. But he only stood there, seeming suddenly ill-fed. Had she not cooked properly for him? her thoughts half-crazily ran on. Had she not given him what was nourishing? 'I thought we were happy,' she whispered. 'I thought we didn't need to question anything.'

'Nice to see the old Alp Horn again,' his murmur comes from the hall, and Zoë can tell that he's endeavouring to be cheerful. 'Tell you what, I'll bring a packet of Three Castles.'

There is the click of the receiver, the brief sounding of the bell. He says something to himself, something like 'Poor thing!' Zoë softly closes the door. Grace and Audrey had probably been friends for fifty years, might even have been school friends. Was Audrey the one whom other girls had pashes on? Was Grace a little bullied? Zoë imagines her hunched sulkily into a desk, and Audrey standing up for her. In letters and telephone conversations there have been references to friends, to holidays in Normandy and Brittany, to bridge, to Grace's colonic irrigation, to Audrey's wisdom teeth being removed in hospital. Zoë knows – she doesn't often call it guessing – that after Audrey's return from every visit to the Alp Horn, Grace was greedy for the morsels passed on to her. Not by the blink of an eye could Grace reveal her secret; the only expression of her passion was her constancy in urging another letter. 'We think of you with her in that coldness. . . .' 'Quite frail he looked,' Audrey no doubt reported in recent years.

He did not stay with Zoë in 1951 because of love. He stayed because – quite suddenly and unexpectedly – the emotions all around him seemed to have become too much: it was weariness that caused him to back off. Had he sensed, Zoë wondered years later, the shadow of Grace without entirely knowing that that was what it was? He stayed, he said, because Zoë and the children – the two who had then been born – meant more than he had estimated. Beneath this statement there was the implication that it wasn't fair to impose hardship on the innocent for the sake of his own happiness. That, though unspoken, had a bitter ring for Zoë. 'Oh, go away!' she cried. 'Go to that unpleasant woman.' But she did not insist; she did not say that there was nothing left, that the damage had been done forever. To the woman, he quoted his economic circumstances as the reason for thinking again. Supporting two households – which in those days was what the prospect looked like – was more than daunting. 'Grace says you wouldn't have to leave them penniless. What she and I earn can easily make up for that, Grace would love to help us out. . . .' Had he gone, Grace would somehow have been there, too.

Zoë knows when the day arrives. Glancing across their breakfast coffee at her, his eyes have a dull sparkle that's caused by an attempt to rekindle an obsolete excitement: he was always one to make an effort. In a letter once Audrey referred to his 'loose-limbed charm,' stating that she doubted she could live without it and be herself. He still has that lanky look, which perhaps was what she meant. What remains of his floppy fair hair, mainly at the back and sides of his head, is ash-coloured now; his hands – which Zoë can well imagine either Grace or Audrey designating his most elegant feature – have a shrivelled look, the bones more pronounced than once they were, and splotches of freckles on skin like old paper. His face is beakier than it was, the teeth for the most part false, his eyes given to watering when a room is warm. Two spots of pink come and go, high up on his narrow cheeks, where the structure of the cheekbones tautens the skin. Otherwise, his face is pale.

'I have to go in today,' he casually announces.

'Not here for lunch?'

'I'll pick up a sandwich somewhere.'

She would like to be able to suggest he'd be wiser to go to a more expensive restaurant than the Alp Horn. Cheap food and house wine are a deadly combination at his time of life. A dreadful nuisance it is when his stomach goes wrong.

'Bit of shopping to do,' he says.

Once there was old So-and-So to meet, but that doesn't work anymore, because, with age, such figures can't be counted upon not to give the game away. There was 'the man at Lloyds' to see, or Hanson and Phillips, who were arranging an annuity. All that has been tapped too often; what's left now is the feebleness of shopping. Before his retirement there was no need to mention anything at all.

'Shopping,' she says, without an interrogative note. 'Shopping.'

'One or two things.'

Three Castles cigarettes are difficult to find. Audrey will smoke nothing else, and it's half a joke that he goes in search of them, a fragment of affection in the kaleidoscope of the love affair. Another such fragment is their shared delight in sweetbreads, a food Zoë finds repellent. They share unpunctuality also. 'Grace can't understand how we ever manage to meet!'

'Should keep fine,' he predicts.

'Take your umbrella all the same.'

'Yes, I'll take my umbrella.'

He asks about a particular shirt, his blue-striped one. He wonders if it has been ironed. She tells him where it is. Their three children – the boys, and Cecilia, born later, all married now – know nothing about Audrey. Sometimes it seems odd to Zoë that this should be so, that a person who has featured so profoundly in their father's life should be unknown to them. If that person had had her way Cecilia would not have been born at all.

'Anything you need?' he offers. 'Anything I can get you?'

She shakes her head. She wishes she could say, 'I open her letters. I listen when there's a phone conversation.' She wishes he could tell her that Grace has died, that her friend is now alone.

'Back about four, I expect?'

'Something like that.'

Had he gone off, she wouldn't still be in this house. She wouldn't be sitting in this kitchen in her scarlet-dragon dressing gown, eyeing him in his woolly brown one. She'd be living with one of the children or in a flat somewhere. Years ago the house would have been sold; she'd not have grown old with a companion. It was most unlikely there would ever have been another man; she doubted she'd have wanted one.

'I dreamed we were on a ferry going to Denmark,' he unexpectedly says. 'There was a woman you got talking to, all in brown.'

'Prettily in brown?'

'Oh, yes. A pretty woman, too. She used an odd expression. She said she was determined to have what she called "a corking child".'

'Ah.'

'You sat me down in front of her and made me comment on her dress. You made me make suggestions.'

'And did you, Charles?'

'I did. I suggested shades of green. Deep greens – not olive like my trousers. And rounded collar ends on her shirt, not pointed like mine. I made her look at mine. She was a nice woman except that she said something a little rude about my shoes.'

'Scuffed?'

'Something like that.'

'Your shoes are never scuffed.'

'No.'

'Well, there you are.'

He nods. 'Yes, there you are.'

Soon after that he rises and goes upstairs again. Why did that conversation about a dream take place? It's true that just occasionally they tell one another their dreams; not just occasionally – they have always done so. But significance appears to attach to the fact that he shared his with her this morning; that is a feeling she has.

'Why did you bother with me if I didn't matter?' Long after he'd decided to stay with her she asked him that. Long afterwards she questioned everything; she tore at the love that had united them in the first place. It was her right that he should listen to her. Five years went by before their daughter was born.

'Well, I'm off.'

Like a tall, thin child he looks, his eyes deep in their sockets, his dark, conventional suit well pressed, a paisley tie, in swirls of blue, that matches the striped blue shirt. His brown shoes, the pair he keeps for special occasions, gleam as they did not in his eccentric dream.

'If I'd known I'd have come with you.' Zoë can't help saying that; she doesn't intend to, the words come out. But they don't alarm him, as once they would have. Once, a shadow of terror would have passed through his features, apprehension spreading lest she rush upstairs to put her coat on.

'We'll go in together next time,' he promises.

'Yes, that'll be nice.'

They kiss, as they always do when they part. The hall door bangs behind him. She'll open a tin of salmon for lunch and have it with tomatoes and a packet of crisps. A whole tin will be too much, of course, but between them they'll probably be ample for whatever's left this evening.

In the sitting room she turns the television on. Celeste Holm, lavishly fur-coated, is in a car, cross about something.

Zoë doesn't want to watch and turns it off again. She imagines the old flame excited as the train approaches London. An hour ago the old flame made her face up, but now she does it all over again – difficult with the movement of the train. Audrey doesn't know that love came back into the marriage, that skin grew over the wound. She doesn't know, because no one told her, because he cannot bring himself to say that the brief occasion was an aberration. He honours – because he's made like that – whatever it is the affair still means to the woman whose life it has disrupted. He doesn't know that Audrey – in receipt of all that was on offer – would have recovered from the drama in a natural way if Grace – in receipt of nothing at all – hadn't been an influence. He doesn't wonder what will happen now, since death has altered the pattern of loose ends.

Opening the salmon tin, Zoë travels again to the Alp Horn rendezvous. She wonders if it has changed and considers it unlikely. The long horn still stretches over a single wall. The same Tyrolean landscape decorates two others. There are the blue-and-red tablecloths. He waits with a glass of sherry, and then she's there.

'My dear!'

She is the first to issue their familiar greeting, catching him unawares, the way things sometimes do these days.

'My dear!' he says in turn.

Sherry is ordered for her, too, and when it comes the rims of their glasses touch for a moment, a toast to the past.

'Grace,' he says. 'I'm sorry.'

'Yes.'

'Is it awful?'

'I manage.'

The waiter briskly notes their order and inquires about the wine.

'Oh, the good old house red.'

Zoë's fingers, gripping and slicing a tomato, are arthritic, painful sometimes, though not at present. In bed at night he's gentle when he reaches out for one hand or the other, cautious with affection, not tightening his grasp as once he did. Her fingers are ugly; she sometimes thinks she looks quite like a monkey now. She arranges the fish and tomato on a plate and sprinkles pepper over both. Neither she nor Charles ever has salt.

'And you, Charles?'

'I'm all right.'

'I worry about you sometimes.'

'No, I'm all right.'

It was accordion music that was playing in the Alp Horn the day Zoë's inquisitiveness drove her into it. Young office people occupied the tables. Business was quite brisk.

'I do appreciate this,' Audrey says. 'When something's over, all these years . . . I do appreciate it, Charles.'

He passes the packet of Three Castles cigarettes across the table, and she smiles, placing it beside her because it's too soon yet to open it.

'You're fun, Charles.'

'I think La Maybury married, you know. I think someone told me that.'

'Grace could never stand her.'

'No.'

Is this the end? Zoë wonders. Is this the final fling, the final call on his integrity and honour? Can his guilt slip back into whatever recesses there are, safe at last from Grace's second-hand desire? No one told him that keeping faith could be as cruel as confessing faithlessness; only Grace might have appropriately done that, falsely playing a best friend's role. But it wasn't in Grace's interest to do so.

'Perhaps I'll sell the house.'

'I rather think you should.'

'Grace did suggest it once.'

Leaving them to it, Zoë eats her salmon and tomato. She watches the end of the television film. Years ago they saw it together, before 1951, long before Grace and Audrey. They've seen it together since; as a boy he'd been in love with Bette Davis. Picking at the food she has prepared, Zoë is again amused by what has amused her before. But only part of her attention is absorbed. Conversations take place; she does not hear: what she sees are fingers undistorted by arthritis loosening the cellophane on the cigarette packet and twisting it into a butterfly. He orders coffee. The scent that came back on his clothes was lemony with a trace of lilac. In a letter there was a mention of the cellophane twisted into a butterfly.

'Well, there we are,' he says. 'It's been lovely to see you, Audrey.'

'Lovely for me, too.'

When he has paid the bill they sit for just a moment longer. Then, in the ladies', she powders away the shine that heat and wine have induced, and tidies her tidy grey hair. The lemony scent refreshes, for a moment, the stale air of the cloakroom.

'Well, there we are, my dear,' he says again on the street. Has there ever, Zoë wonders, been snappishness between them? Is she the kind not to lose her temper, long-suffering and patient as well as being a favourite girl at school? After all, she never quarrelled with her friend.

'Yes, there we are, Charles.' She takes his arm. 'All this means the world to me, you know.'

They walk to the corner, looking for a taxi. Marriage is full of quarrels, Zoë reflects.

'Being upright never helps. You just lie there. Drink lots of water, Charles.'

The jug of water, filled before she'd slipped in beside him last night, is on his bedside table, one glass poured out. Once, though quite a while ago now, he not only insisted on getting up when he had a stomach upset but actually worked in the garden. All day, she'd watched him filling his incinerator with leaves and weeding the rockery. Several times she'd rapped on the kitchen window, but he'd taken no notice. As a result he was laid up for a fortnight.

'I'm sorry to be a nuisance,' he says.

She smooths the bedclothes on her side of the bed, giving the bed up to him, making it pleasant for him in the hope that he'll remain in it. The newspaper is there for him when he feels like it. So is *Little Dorrit*, which he always reads when he's unwell.

'Perhaps consommé later on,' she says. 'And a cream cracker.'

'You're very good to me.'

'Oh, now.'

Downstairs Zoë lights the gas fire in the sitting room and looks to see if there's a morning film. 'Barefoot in the Park' it is, about to begin. Quite suddenly then, without warning, she sees how the loose ends are. Everything is different, but nothing, of course, will ever be said. 'So good the little restaurant's still there,' the old flame writes. 'Just a line to thank you.' So good it was to talk. So good to see him. So good of him to remember the Three Castles. Yet none of it is any good at all, because Grace is not there to say, 'Now tell me every single thing.' Not there to say when there's a nagging doubt, 'My dear, what perfect nonsense!' On her own in the seaside house she'll not find an excuse again to suggest a quick lunch if he'd like to. He'll not do so himself, since he never has. He'll gladly feel his duty done at last.

The old flame bores him now, with her scent and her cigarettes and her cellophane butterflies. In her seaside house she knows her thank-you letter is the last, and the sea is grey, and again it rains. One day, on her own, she'll guess her friend was false. One day she'll guess a sense of honour kept pretence alive.

Grace died. That's all that happened, Zoë tells herself, so why should she forgive? 'Why should I?' she murmurs. 'Why should I?' Yet for a moment, before she turns on 'Barefoot in the Park', tears sting her eyelids. A trick of old age, she tells herself, and orders them away.

Love Among the Artists

FAY WELDON

'HAPPY CHRISTMAS, MY own true love,' said Lucy to Pierre, on the morning of December 25th, 1899. She woke among a flurry of white sheets and feather pillows and this was the nearest she would get to seasonal and romantic snow, for the day was mild and they were in the South of France, not Connecticut, which was Lucy's home, or Paris which was Pierre's.

Pierre stirred but did not wake. Lucy whispered in his ear again.

'Happy Christmas, my own true love,' and this time he murmured a reply.

'If you and I are to be free souls, Lucy,' said Pierre with a clarity apparently quite undiminished by slumber, 'we must put all such religious cant behind us,' and closed his eyes again and slept on. His arms lay brown and young among the sheets and his dark hair was wild and curly on the pillow and she loved him. But she loved Christmas too, and always had.

Morning sun shone in through the little square window and bounced back from the whitewashed walls. She smoothed down her white cambric nightgown and wound her hair back around her head and pinned it up, and climbed down from the high bed, and crossed the bare wooden floor and looked out of the undraped window. She could see across a river valley to vineyards which marched across hills like soldiers going to their death. She put the image from her mind. And if there was a smell of rottenness in the air, as if all the grapes which should have been gathered in the autumn to make wine had been allowed to fall and fester on the ground instead, that was nothing worse than French plumbing. Some things had to be bad, Pierre said, so bad there was nothing left for them to do but get better.

'Religion is the opiate of the people,' said Pierre from his pillow. 'God is a drug fed by the masters to the poor and hungry, so they are content with poverty and hunger. Jesus was never born: heaven does not exist. Blind relief is a thorn in the side of mankind and we will pluck it out.'

In one more week it would be 1900, the dawn of the twentieth century, and into that dawn would strike through the light of new hope and new liberty, and all the energy of free thought and free love, untrammelled by convention, and Lucy's soul soared at the thought that Pierre and she were part of it: that he and she were one step ahead of that new dawn. They would be in Paris by New Year's Eve to be among the anarchists; they would gather there together to drink to the future: the passionate brotherhood of the enlightened, and their sisters in that passion.

What a different stroke of midnight it would be to the one she would have envisaged just a few months back: a single glass of wine raised solemnly at the first stroke, in the parlour, in the company of Edwin her husband and Joseph her brother, and then to bed. And each stroke sounding its annual dirge to lost hope and failing passion: its welcome to the triumph of boredom and the death of the soul.

Pierre left the bed and stood beside her. He was naked. Lucy could not become accustomed to it. She had been married to Edwin for 14 years and had never caught more than a flash of white limb in the bathroom, a movement of bare flesh above her in the bed. Now Pierre unpinned her hair so it flowed around her shoulders.

'So never name that day again,' said Pierre, 'or it will drag you back to the Lord of the Dark Domain,' and they both laughed. Lord of the Dark Domain was their name for Edwin. Lucy's husband wrote novels for a living: once every five years or so, to the acclaim of serious critics, he would have published an extremely melancholy book, the text so closely printed that Lucy had no patience with it, but then she was not expected to. Edwin loved Lucy for her folly; she was his child bride, his pretty wife: now he would see how he had misjudged her! Now he would find out: now that another man understood her talent, her intelligence, her quality, her passion.

'All the same,' said Lucy, 'it comes as a shock! No mince pies, no gifts and ribbons and best dresses? Never more?'

'Never more,' said Pierre, 'or you will be dragged back into the Hell of Domesticity, which is the Death of Art.' Pierre was a composer of fine if difficult song cycles which so few people in the world could understand that when Pierre came to New York from Paris to perform, the concert hall was all but empty, the tour was cancelled and Pierre left penniless and stranded in a strange land. Edwin, as an act of kindness, had offered him work for the summer, teaching Bessie and Bertie the piano. Bessie was twelve and Bertie was ten. They would wake this Christmas morning to a house which lacked a mother. Lucy put that image from her too. Bessie had Edwin's beetling brows; Bertie aped Edwin's clipped, dry manner of speech. They were Edwin's children more than Lucy's. Pierre saw it. Edwin claimed it. The law acknowledged it: let the law have its way.

'An artist needs freedom, not a family,' said Pierre; he could so easily read her mind. She felt his warm breath on her cheek. 'The artist's duty is to all mankind; he must speak free of the chains of convention. And women can be artists too, as you are, Lucy, remember that!'

The first time Pierre had heard Lucy sing, in her sweet, clear, untrained voice, helping Bessie's fumbling notes along, he had claimed her as an artist; the one he had been waiting for, the one who could truly bring his music to life. Poor Bessie was forgotten: she could hardly get to the piano. Lucy and Pierre were always there: as she worked to catch the notes between notes he found so significant he could make them include the whole universe. Edwin was on the last chapter of a novel: a time he found particularly tense. There was to be piano-playing only between two and four o'clock of an afternoon. He said so with some force. The house trembled. People wept.

'He has you in prison,' said Pierre of Edwin then. 'For what is a home but a man's prison for a woman, and what is a wife but an unpaid whore? She lies on her back for her keep, bears children and cooks dinner likewise.' And when Lucy had recovered from her shock, the more she thought of it the more she perceived that what Pierre said was true. Lucy understood now that the sapphire necklace she wore round her neck was the symbol of her imprisonment: that her ruby earrings marked her as an instrument of lust, that the gold charms on her bracelet were for Edwin's benefit, not her own; for is not a willing slave more useful than one who is unwilling?

'You would not be my slave,' said Pierre, 'you would be my love.'

Lucy's eyes went to the suitcase, and she wondered whether she should check that they were still there, in the suitcase, tucked in tissue in a dancing shoe: the sapphire, the rubies and the gold. But of course they were. Why should they not be? And they were hers by right, every one, payment for years of servitude. In the new world women would have equal dignity with men. When the workers of the world rose up, they would lift up women with them.

'All the same,' said Lucy, 'on this day of all days, allow me to feel like a mother, not an artist, and cry just a little.'

'You should be ashamed to even consider such a betrayal,' said Pierre. 'Weeping is something which women of the *haute bourgeoisie* do the better to control men,' and Lucy was glad to understand that he was joking, for Edwin had scolded her and chided her and made her feel foolish from the day he had met her, and never ever joked about anything.

Pierre called down to the landlady to bring breakfast up to

the room. He stood naked at the top of the stairs and dodged behind the door when the woman arrived with the tray: she seemed to Lucy too small and old to carry such a weight. The servants at home were stout and strong.

'Don't upset her too much,' said Lucy when she had stopped laughing. 'We owe her too much rent for that. I don't know why you put off paying her.'

But Pierre said they would wait for dark and then slip away unnoticed and pick up the Paris coach before anyone realised, and he didn't want any silly nonsense from Lucy: the landlady was an old witch who took advantage of travellers and overcharged, and deserved what she got.

Lucy said nothing, but after she'd eaten the breakfast the landlady brought – hot coffee and fresh frothy milk, long crisp bread, and farm butter and apricot preserve – she said, 'I'd really rather pay her, Pierre.'

'What with?' asked Pierre. 'We have no francs left. The journey across France is costing more than I thought. An artist shouldn't be bothered by such sordid things as money: I don't want to talk about it any more. We'll send her some from Paris if you insist when we've sold your jewellery, but she doesn't deserve it. She is a lackey of the masters, that's all she is.'

Lucy felt her eyes mist with tears: she couldn't tell the difference between the frothy milk and the thick white china jug. They merged together. At home the milk jugs were of fine porcelain, and had little flowers upon them. One of them came from Limoges. She wondered where Limoges was, and if she'd ever go there. She could see such an event was more likely now that she was Pierre's lover, no longer Edwin's wife; on the other hand, any such journey would be accomplished in less comfort. She did not understand money: it seemed necessary for all kinds of things she had thought just happened – such as being warm, or welcomed, or treated with politeness by porters, and gendarmes, shop keepers and landladies. But money did not buy love, or freedom, or truth, or hope, or any of the important things in life.

'Don't cry,' said Pierre. 'You're homesick, that's all it is,' and he leaned towards her and removed a crumb from her lip,

311

and her heart melted; the act was so tender and true. Edwin would have mentioned the crumb, not removed it. Pierre put on his shirt and she was glad, though she knew she shouldn't be. 'I'm not homesick,' Lucy said, 'not one bit. You've no idea how dank and drear the woods around the house are at this time of year. How they drip and drizzle!'

'Worse than Bessie on a bad day,' murmured Pierre, nuzzling into her hair, and she thought why is he allowed to mention Bessie's name, and I am not, but Lucy laughed too, to keep Pierre company, to be of one accord in mind, as they were in body. Bessie was a plain girl and had not been blessed with a musical ear so Pierre could not take her seriously, and that made it hard for Lucy, now Bessie was at a distance, to do so either. Lucy could see that love unconfined, love outside convention, might well make a woman an unfit mother, you were one kind of woman or another: you were good or you were bad, as the world saw it, and no stations in between. They allowed you to choose; you could be the maternal or the erotic, but not a bit of both. The latter made you forget the former. Men married the maternal and then longed for the erotic. Or they married the erotic by mistake, and set about making it into the maternal, and then were just as disappointed. Edwin had married a child and tried to stop her choosing, but now thanks to Pierre she had grown up and made her own choice.

She hoped Edwin would keep Christmas without her. She hoped he would remember, when he brought in the Christmas tree, the little fir which had grown in its pot on the step since the first year of the marriage, that it had to be watered well. She hoped he knew the boxes in the attic where the decorations were. Lucy added a new one every year – would he remember that? Would he realise you had to balance the golden horses with their silver riders? And part of her hoped he'd get it all wrong. Part of her hoped that now she was not there, he would have no heart for any of it, he would be so sorry she had gone. She would find a letter from him in Paris, forgiving her, asking her to go home. Of course she would not go.

'A penny for your thoughts,' said Pierre, but he wouldn't have liked them if he heard them so Lucy said, 'I'm really glad I'm not at home, Pierre. This time of year. When the days are really short, and winter hasn't quite caught up with them and the skies just seem to sulk. Why, they sulk even worse than Bertie on a bad day,' and she laughed again, betraying her other child for the sake of love. 'And the rooms of the house are so crowded and sad,' said Lucy, 'and here everything is simple and graceful and plain. I promise you I don't miss a thing. You make up for it all, Pierre.'

Lucy's brother Joseph would have arrived on Christmas eve, as was his custom, bearing gifts. They would be the wrong gifts: an impossible doll, an unworkable cannon; a scarf she hated, the kind of pen Edwin never used. Joseph's talent for the wrong gifts was a marvel: it was a joke she and Edwin shared: a look between them every year, no more: that much they had at least – this equality of shared experience, which grew every year as the Christmas tree grew, so slowly you could never see it; but every Christmas an inch or so higher. This year it would have to go on its side to get through the front door, and could only stand in the window arch – would Edwin and Joseph talk about Lucy, or would her name not be mentioned? An impossible subject, an inexplicable situation: a woman lost to duty, lost to honour, lost to motherhood: a woman altogether vanished away, erased from the mind, nameless. A subdued source of sorrow, of better-never-born-dom.

'No children to tug at my skirts,' said Lucy, 'no brother at my sympathy, no husband at my conscience. A day like any other, dawning bright and fair on our new life together. Just you and I, the Art, and beauty, and love, and music. All the things that passed poor stuffy old Edwin by!'

'I pity Edwin,' said Pierre. 'He had no ear. A man who rations music to two hours a day has no ear and a man who locks a piano has no soul!'

The better to enforce his ruling, Edwin had kept the piano closed; unlocking it at two o'clock after lunch: emerging from his study at four o'clock to close it once again. In the mornings, thus freed from practice, Lucy and Pierre had walked in the woods, and talked about music, and presently love, and then more than talked, and Pierre had explained to Lucy how unhappy she was, and how her way of life stifled her, and how he could not be a great artist without her, and Bessie had seen them in the woods and Lucy had forged one of Edwin's cheques and paid both their passages over; and left Edwin a note and was gone, taking her jewellery because Pierre said she must, and the way not to think about any of it was to be in bed with Pierre. They had scarcely left the cabin on the way over: they had been the talk of the ship and she hadn't cared. To fly in the face of all things respectable intensified the pleasure she had with Pierre: what was forbidden was sweet: she hoped they would never reach Paris, where everyone felt as she and Pierre did, but of course that was silly of her: what was forbidden could not be kept up for long and in any case had to be sandwiched between the permitted in order to count – why had there been no one to stop her? If you were a child wasn't that what happened? That someone stopped you? She'd relied on Edwin for that all her grown life, but since she couldn't tell him about Pierre how could he have helped her? But she blamed him because he hadn't, because he'd been so busy with his book he hadn't even noticed the time she was spending with Pierre: it was Edwin's fault she had left.

She wondered what she and Pierre would do all day. When they were out of bed there seemed not very much to do, except wait for other days to arrive, or messages to come which didn't come from friends she had only heard of, never seen. If she was at home on this day she would be so busy – it would be all best clothes and mince pies and the gifts beneath the Christmas tree, and a formal kiss from Edwin before the unwrapping ceremony began.

Pierre said, 'We'll smuggle the suitcase out after lunch, when Madame takes her nap. She sleeps well: she doesn't care how the rest of the world toils for her profit! Then in the evening you dress as me and I'll dress as you, and that will be the best disguise in the world, and we'll escape. We'll be so clever!' Lucy thought it was probably better as an idea than it would be as an actuality – she could get into his coat but her jacket would never stretch over his shoulders – but didn't say so. It was the kind of prank Bertie would think of. Pierre had explained to her how Edwin was a father/husband – but what did she have now instead – a son/lover? Was such a thing possible?

'I could offer her a gold charm from my bracelet,' said Lucy. 'In fact I think I'll do that.'

And to her astonishment Pierre hit her, or she thought that was what had happened, since there was a sudden kind of stinging blackness around her head, but how could she know, no one had ever hit her before. For a second or so she couldn't see, and was perhaps suffering from amnesia, for she couldn't quite remember where she was; but yes, it wasn't home, it was indeed an inn somewhere in the South of France, and she was leaning against a whitewashed wall, while a strange man rather younger than herself apologised for something rather trivial, and she could hear a kind of knock, knock, knock, which she thought was Edwin chopping down the Christmas tree, the one that had started little and grown deep and strong. Edwin divided it root from branch, because it spoke of a celebration Lucy could no longer name, and anyway it spoke a lie. But of course the sound was only the knock, knock of the landlady at the door, demanding money she and Pierre didn't have, speaking in a language Lucy didn't understand, but who knew them better than they knew themselves. She could see that to look after yourself you would have to know yourself, but who was there in that land, in that time, to hear such a thing if it were said?

Biographical Notes
on the Authors

BRIAN ALDISS was born in Norfolk in 1925, and served in the army in the Far East during the Second World War. He lives in Oxford, has been both a bookseller and a literary editor, and published his first book in 1955. He is widely acknowledged as the *doyen* of science fiction and his most recent title in that genre is *Dracula Unbound*. He wrote *Trillion Year Spree: The History of Science Fiction* and has edited a number of anthologies. His next novel is entitled *Remembrance Day* and is set in 1985.

ANGELA CARTER was born in Sussex in 1940. She wrote nine novels, including *Wise Children* (1991) and *Nights at the Circus* (1984); three collections of short stories, was the editor of the *Virago Book of Fairy Tales* (1991) and she wrote three works of non-fiction, the most recent being a selection of essays and reviews, *Expletives Deleted*, published earlier this year by Chatto & Windus. She also co-wrote *The Company of Wolves*. She died in February 1992.

DAVID CONSTANTINE was born in 1944 in Salford, Lancashire. He read Modern Languages at Oxford and now teaches German at the Queen's College there. He is married with two children. He has published academic books on Friedrich

Hölderlin and on early travellers to Greece, translations of Hölderlin and four collections of poems, (all with Bloodaxe), the latest being *New and Selected Poems* (1991). He has also published a novel, *Davies* (1985), as well as short stories.

SEAMUS DEANE was born in Derry City, Northern Ireland in 1940. He was educated at Queen's University, Belfast, and at Cambridge University. He is now a professor of English at Univesity College, Dublin. He is a director of Field Day Theatre Company and a member of the Royal Irish Academy. His publications include *Celtic Revivals, A Short History of Irish Literature, Selected Poems* and *The Field Day Anthology of Irish Writing*.

HELEN DUNMORE was born in 1952, and writes both prose and poetry. She won the prestigious Cardiff International Poetry Award in 1990 and her most recent collection is *Short Days Long Nights – New and Selected Verse*, published by Bloodaxe. She lives in Bristol and has recently completed a first novel, *Zennor in Darkness*, which Viking Penguin will publish in Spring 1993.

STEPHEN GALLAGHER was born in Salford, Lancashire in October 1954. He first worked as a researcher in TV documentaries after graduating from Hull University, then moved to Granada TV's Presentation Department in 1975. He wrote for radio before breaking into print; novels include *October, Down River, Rain, The Boat House* and *Nightmare with Angel*. He adapted his own novel, *Chimera*, for television in 1991 and is currently working on the screenplay for *Rain*.

MAVIS GALLANT was born in Montreal and worked as a feature writer there before giving up journalism to devote herself to fiction. She left Canada in 1950 and after extensive travel settled in Paris. She is a regular contributor to the *New Yorker* and is currently working on a new novel and on an account of the Dreyfus case.

STEVEN HEIGHTON has had poetry, fiction and essays published in magazines and anthologies in Canada, the USA, Australia and the UK. He has published two collections of poetry, and a collection of stories set in Japan, *A Man Away From Home Has No Neighbours*, was published earlier this year in Canada. He lives in Kingston, Ontario, where he edits *Quarry Magazine*, and until recently worked nights in the city's only Japanese restaurant. *Flight Paths of the Emperor* will be published in Canada in 1992 by Porcupine's Quill.

JANETTE TURNER HOSPITAL was born in Melbourne, Australia in 1942, but grew up in Queensland. Her life has been unintentionally nomadic, and she has lived in India, USA, Canada and England. She teaches at La Trobe University, Melbourne, but was Visiting Professor at Boston University in 1991. She spends part of each year in Canada. Her first novel, *The Ivory Swing*, won Canada's Seal Award in 1982. Her fifth novel, *The Last Magician*, will be published by Virago in June 1992.

MATTHEW KRAMER was born in 1961 in North London, where he still lives. He read Law and Politics at Cambridge and now practises as a solicitor. He is currently working on a novel and a play for television. This is his first published work.

ISOBEL LUSTED was born and educated in New Zealand. She now lives in London with her husband. 'Meng's Pool' is her first published story. She has several short stories 'on the circuit' and has nearly completed a novel.

BRIAN MCCABE was born in 1951 in a small mining community near Edinburgh. His father was a coal miner, his mother a cook. He studied Philosophy and English Literature at Edinburgh University and was awarded a writer's bursary by the Scottish Arts Council in 1980, and has lived since as a freelance writer. Publications include *The Lipstick Circus* (1985), *One Atom to Another* (1987) and *The Other McCoy* (1991).

DAVID MACKENZIE was born in Easter Ross and was a social worker before teaching English abroad. He now works in London as a systems analyst. His first novel, *The Truth of*

Stone, was one of the four shortlisted for the Saltire Society's Scottish First Book Award.

BRIAN MACMAHON was born in 1909 in Listowel, Co. Kerry, where he is known as 'The Master' only partly because he has been a schoolteacher. He has published many collections of short stories and is also a poet, balladeer, novelist and playwright; the Abbey Theatre in Dublin has produced several of his plays, notably *The Honey Spike*. In 1992 Poolbeg will publish both his memoirs and *Mascot Patsy-O*, a collection of children's stories.

ADAM MARS-JONES was born in London in 1954. His first book of fiction, *Lantern Lecture*, won the Somerset Maugham Award in 1981. Since then he has edited *Mae West is Dead*, a collection of lesbian and gay fiction, and co-written (with Edmund White) *The Darker Proof: Stories from a Crisis*. His story, 'Bears in Mourning' will be included in the author's *Monopolies of Loss* (1992).

MARY MORRISSY was born in Dublin in 1957. She won the Hennessy Award for short stories in 1984 and has published in several magazines and newspapers. She reviews fiction for the *Irish Times* and is currently working on a novel; her first collection of short stories will be published by Jonathan Cape in spring 1993.

ALICE MUNRO is the author of a novel, *Lives of Girls and Women*, and seven collections of stories. Her stories are published in the *New Yorker* and the *Atlantic*. She and her husband live in Clinton, Ontario, near lake Huron.

WENDY PERRIAM was born in 1940 in an air-raid shelter, expelled from her convent boarding-school for heresy, and escaped to St Anne's College, Oxford, where she graduated in History Honours. She has written nine novels including *Cuckoo*, *Born of Woman* and *Sin City*. *Bird Inside* is her ninth novel and she now writes full time.

DON RODGERS was born in London, graduated from Oxford, and taught English for several years in Paris. He currently works for the West Glamorgan Archive Service in Swansea. His poems and stories have been published in *Critical Quarterly*, the *Spectator* and the *Literary Review*. He is a former prizewinner in the National Poetry Competition. A play, *Clown*, was broadcast on BBC Radio 4.

SALMAN RUSHDIE was born in Bombay in 1947. He is the author of seven books including *Grimus*, *Midnight's Children*, which won the Booker Prize, *Shame*, *Haroun and the Sea of Stories*, and *The Satanic Verses*.

HELEN SIMPSON read English at Oxford after which she worked as a staff writer for *Vogue* for five years before going freelance. She has published two cookery books. Her collection of short stories *Four Bare Legs in a Bed* won her the Sunday Times Young Writer of the Year award in 1991. Her stories have appeared in the *Listener*, the *Literary Review*, *Cosmopolitan*, *Vogue*, *Harpers & Queen* and *Company*.

KEN SMITH was born in 1938 in Rudston, East Yorkshire. He is the author of *Inside Time* (Mandarin) and *Berlin: Coming in from the Cold* (Penguin Books), and of sundry collections of poetry, the most recent of which, *The Heart, the Border*, is from Bloodaxe Books.

JONATHAN TREITEL was born in London in 1959. He has worked as a physicist in California, and has a doctorate in philosophy of science from Stanford University. He has published two novels.

WILLIAM TREVOR was born in Cork in 1928, was educated at Trinity College, Dublin and has spent a large part of his life in Ireland. Since *The Old Boys* was awarded the Hawthornden Prize in 1964 he has received many honours for his work including the Royal Society of Literature Award, the Allied

Irish Banks Prize for Literature and the Whitbread Award for Fiction. He is a member of the Irish Academy of Letters, and has been awarded an honorary CBE.

FAY WELDON was born in England, raised in a family of women in New Zealand, and took a degree in Psychology and Economics at the University of St Andrew's. Her eighteen novels and three collections of stories include *Praxis*, *Puffball*, *The Life and Loves of a She Devil*, *The Hearts and Lives of Men*, *The Cloning of Joanna May*, *Darcy's Utopia* and *Growing Rich*. She has four sons, and lives in London and Somerset.

Acknowledgements

'The Visitors' Book', copyright © Stephen Gallagher 1991, was first published in *Darklands* edited by Nicholas Royle (Egerton Press) and is reprinted by permission of the author.

'Forain', copyright © Mavis Gallant 1991, was first published in *New Yorker*, 24 June 1991 and is reprinted by permission of the author and Georges Borchardt, 136 E 57th Street, New York, 10022.

'Five Paintings of the New Japan', copyright © Steven Heighton 1991, was first published in *Stand Magazine* and is reprinted by permission of the author.

'The End-of-the-line End-of-the-world Disco', copyright © Janette Turner Hospital 1991. First published in *London Magazine*, June/July 1991; reprinted by permission of the author and Sheil Land Associates Ltd, 43 Doughty Street, London WC1N 2LF.

'The Sandcastle', copyright © Matthew Kramer 1991, was first published in *Panurge* 14, April 1991, and is reprinted by permission of the author.

'Meng's Pool', copyright © Isobel Lusted 1991, was first published in *Stand Magazine* volume 32, number 3, summer 1991, and is reprinted by permission of the author.

'Say Something', copyright © Brian McCabe 1991, is printed here for the first time by permission of the author and Curtis Brown & John Farquharson, 162–168 Regent Street, London W1R 5TB.

'Cybernetics', copyright © David Mackenzie 1991, was first published in *New Edinburgh Review* and is reprinted by permission of the author and John Johnson, Clerkenwell House, 45/47 Clerkenwell Green, London EC1R 0HT.

ACKNOWLEDGEMENTS

'Sing, Milo, Sing!', copyright © Dr Bryan MacMahon 1991. First published in *Ireland's Own*, 22 March 1991, reprinted by permission of the author and A P Watt Ltd, 20 John Street, London WC1N 2DR.

'Bears in Mourning', copyright © Adam Mars-Jones 1991, was first published in *Granta*, December 1991, and is reprinted by permission of the author and Peters Fraser & Dunlop, 503/4 The Chambers, Chelsea Harbour, London SW10 0XF.

'Possibilities', copyright © Mary Morrissy 1991, first published in *London Magazine*, October/November 1991, and is reprinted by kind permission of the author and Elaine Greene Ltd, 37 Goldhawk Road, London W12 8QQ.'

'Carried Away', copyright © Alice Munro 1991, was first printed in the *New Yorker*, 21 October 1991 and is reprinted by permission of the author, Virginia Barber Literary Agency, 353 West 21st Street, New York, 10011 and Abner Stein, 10 Roland Gardens, London SW7 3PH.

'Three Minute Egg', copyright © Wendy Perriam 1991, was first published in *Esquire* (UK), June 1991, and is reprinted by permision of the author and Sheil Land Associates Ltd, 43 Doughty Street, London WC1N 2LF.

'Queen Mahatonga Retires for the Night', copyright © Don Rodgers 1991, was first published in *Critical Quarterly*, volume 33, number 2, summer 1991, and is reprinted by permission of the author.

'Christopher Columbus and Queen Isabella of Spain Consummate Their Relationship, Santa Fe, January, 1492', copyright © Salman Rushdie 1991, was first published in the *New Yorker*, 17 June 1991, and is reprinted by permission of the author and Aitken & Stone, 29 Fernshaw Road, London SW10 0XF.

'Dear George', copyright © Helen Simpson 1991, was first published in *Woman*, December 1991, and is reprinted by permission of the author and Peters Fraser & Dunlop, 503/4 The Chambers, Chelsea Harbour, London SW10 0XF.

'My Father's War', copyright © Ken Smith 1992. First publication rights acquired by *Esquire* (UK) 1991 but published for the first time in *Best Short Stories 1992* by permission of the author and Sheil Land Associates Ltd., 43 Doughty Street, London WC1N 2LF.

'Waltz Time', copyright © Jonathan Treitel 1991, was first published in the *New Yorker,* 11 February 1991, and is reprinted by permission of the author and A P Watt Ltd, 20 John Street, London WC1N 2DR.

'Old Flame', copyright © William Trevor 1991, was first published in the *New Yorker*, 25 February 1991, and is reprinted by permission of the author and Peters Fraser & Dunlop, 503/4 The Chambers, Chelsea Harbour, London SW10 0XF.

'Love Among the Artists', copyright © Fay Weldon 1991, was first published in *The Times*, 24 December 1991, and is reprinted by permission of the author and Sheil Land Associates, 43 Doughty Street, London WC1N 2LF.

Further Short Story Collections Available from Minerva

While every effort is made to keep prices low, it is sometimes necessary to increase prices at short notice. Mandarin Paperbacks reserves the right to show new retail prices on covers which may differ from those previously advertised in the text or elsewhere.

The prices shown below were correct at the time of going to press.

☐	7493 9119 7	**Sixty Stories**	Donald Barthelme	£6.99
☐	7493 9136 7	**Complete Short Stories**	Noel Coward	£7.99
☐	7493 9051 4	**Minerva Book of Short Stories 1**	Giles Gordon & David Hughes	£4.99
☐	7493 9085 9	**Minerva Book of Short Stories 2**	Giles Gordon & David Hughes	£4.99
☐	7493 9144 8	**Minerva Book of Short Stories 3**	Giles Gordon & David Hughes	£5.99
☐	7493 9113 8	**Lust and Other Stories**	Susan Minot	£4.99
☐	7493 9063 8	**She Has No Place In Paradise**	Nawal El Saadawi	£3.99
☐	7493 9162 6	**Four Bare Legs in a Bed**	Helen Simpson	£4.99
☐	7493 9092 1	**Women's Decameron**	Julia Voznesenskaya	£5.99

All these books are available at your bookshop or newsagent, or can be ordered direct from the publisher. Just tick the titles you want and fill in the form below.

Mandarin Paperbacks, Cash Sales Department, PO Box 11, Falmouth, Cornwall TR10 9EN.

Please send cheque or postal order, no currency, for purchase price quoted and allow the following for postage and packing:

UK including BFPO
£1.00 for the first book, 50p for the second and 30p for each additional book ordered to a maximum charge of £3.00.

Overseas including Eire
£2 for the first book, £1.00 for the second and 50p for each additional book thereafter.

NAME (Block letters) ....

ADDRESS ....

....

☐ I enclose my remittance for ....

☐ I wish to pay by Access/Visa Card Number ☐☐☐☐☐☐☐☐☐☐☐☐☐☐☐☐

Expiry Date ☐☐☐☐